THE CAMBRIDGE CHRONICLES

LOVE EMBRACES DESTINY

THE CAMBRIDGE CHRONICLES

LOVE EMBRACES DESTINY

A Gentle Calling

Treasures of the Heart

TWO BESTSELLING NOVELS COMPLETE IN ONE VOLUME

DONNA FLETCHER CROW

Inspirational Press • New York

Previously published as two separate volumes:

THE CAMBRIDGE CHRONICLES

A Gentle Calling
Copyright © 1994 by Donna Fletcher Crow

Treasures of the Heart
Copyright © 1994 by Donna Fletcher Crow

First Inspirational Press edition published in 1999.

Inspirational Press
A division of BBS Publishing Corporation
386 Park Avenue South
New York, NY 10016

Inspirational Press is a registered trademark of BBS Publishing Corporation.

Published by arrangement with Crossway Books,
a division of Good News Publishers, 1300 Crescent Street,
Wheaton, Illinois 60187.

Library of Congress Catalog Card Number: 98-72455

ISBN: 0-88486-225-9

Printed in the United States of America.

Contents

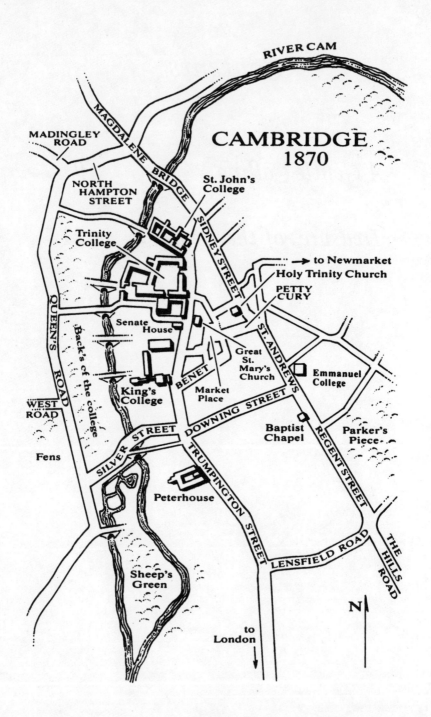

RIVER CAM

CAMBRIDGE
1870

MADINGLEY
ROAD

NORTH
HAMPTON
STREET

St. John's
College

Trinity
College

to Newmarket
Holy Trinity Church

PETTY
CURY

Senate
House

Back's of the college

Great
St.
Mary's
Church

Emmanuel
College

King's
College

BENET

Market
Place

Baptist
Chapel

Parker's
Piece

WEST
ROAD

SILVER STREET

DOWNING STREET

Fens

Peterhouse

LENSFIELD ROAD

N

Sheep's
Green

to
London

Newcastle

Miles 0 25 50 75
Kms 0 25 50 75

York

ENGLAND

Sandon Hall

King's Cliffe

Cambridge

Troy
House
Raglan   Badminton   LONDON
Bristol   Shoreham   Canterbury
Bath   Tunbridge
Wells   Wells

— — — — — the circuit ride

St. John's Wood
Regent's Park   EUSTON ROAD   LONDON

EDGWARE ROAD

MARYLEBONE   Tottenham
Mary-   Court
lebone   Chapel   The
Church   Foundry

CATO

Piccadilly   Lincoln's
Paddington   Circus   Inn

ALDERSGATE

MOORGATE

Bayswater   OXFORD   St. James FLEET   St. Paul's
                                                                 Cathedral
BAYSWATER ROAD   Mayfair   PICCADILLY
Hyde
Kensington   Park
Gardens   Grosvenor
Ken-   Square
sington   KENSINGTON

KNIGHTSBRIDGE

PALL MALL

South   Buckingham
Kensington   Palace   London
to   Brompton   Bridge
Osterley
Park   Westminster   Surrey
OLD BROMPTON   Abbey   Lane
                                              Parliament   Chapel
Chelsea   Thames River

GROSVENOR ROAD

The Cambridge Chronicles

A Gentle Calling
(1749–1750)
John and Charles Wesley
George Whitefield
William Law
Countess of Huntingdon

Treasures of the Heart
(1772–1773)
Charles Wesley
John Berridge
Rowland Hill
Countess of Huntingdon

"There are so few people now who want to have any intimate spiritual association with the eighteenth and nineteenth centuries . . .

"Who bothers at all now about the work and achievement of our grandfathers, and how much of what they knew have we already forgotten?"

—DIETRICH BONHOEFFER,
Letters and Papers from Prison

A GENTLE
CALLING

To Betty Waller
librarian, teacher, friend
who inspires all who cross her path
with a love of books.
I'm thankful our paths crossed.

$\mathcal{N}$ed, you're bleeding!" Catherine Perronet rushed across the room to her brother. "What happened?" She took his arm to lead him to a chair, but he drew back sharply.

"Don't touch it, Cath. It may be broken."

"Broken!" This was too much even for Catherine's usually unruffled calm. "Were you attacked by a mob again?"

Edward Perronet smiled weakly. "I attempted to sow the seeds of truth to a crowd at Brixton. Shall we just say they were stony soil?"

"Apparently they found plenty of stones to hurl at you." Catherine started after a bowl of water and some rags. "We must call a doctor for your arm, but I'll wash your wounds first. If Durial sees you like this, I wouldn't vouch for the safety of your future child."

"Pray, do clean me up, Sister, though I would guess that Durial will be more distressed for her chair cover and carpet than for our child." He looked at his boots caked with fresh mud from the April rains.

Catherine directed a servant girl to bring a roll of bandages and sent the stable boy into Greenwich for the doctor. When she had staunched the flow of blood from her brother's head wounds and had cleansed all the caked blood and mud from his hair and face, she paused. "I must say, Ned, this is a fine way to make your homecoming after three weeks' absence. I suppose the family of an itinerant preacher should become accustomed to such behavior, but still you could have sent us some word of your progress in Wales. Were you beaten there too?"

Ned raised his tall, lanky body straighter in the chair, moving carefully to protect his damaged arm. His expression became suddenly serious, far graver than it had been over his physical injuries. "Sit down, Catherine. I have news I didn't want to put in a message. I fear it may distress you."

Catherine sat with quiet dignity. "In that case, let us have it quickly."

"My stay in Wales was extended because I attended the marriage of Charles Wesley to Miss Sally Gwynne."

Catherine stared at her brother. She heard the words, but her mind refused to make sense out of them. "Charles is married? Charles Wesley?" *My Charles?* "But I thought . . . I hoped . . . I was almost sure . . ." She forced a little hiccup to cover what wanted to come out as a sob.

"Forgive me, Ned. I fear I have been indulging in foolish fantasies. But after you told me I was on the list of women John Wesley thought would make eligible wives for his brother—"

"That was most unwise of me. I should never have told you."

"On the contrary, the information provided me many happy fancies with which to while away dull hours. You made it quite clear that there were three names on the list and that Sally Gwynne's was among them. I fear that I simply relied too much on the fact that Catherine Perronet was first on the list."

"And lest you hear from another and think me a traitor, I must also tell you that the letter I carried to Mrs. Gwynne from our father was instrumental in winning that reluctant lady's approval to the match."

"You and Father both? And what of our own Charl? Surely you knew he had spoken of a fondness for Miss Gwynne too."

Ned nodded. "Yes, I am fully aware that many hopes will be disappointed."

"If you carried a letter to Mrs. Gwynne, you must have known what was to take place. Why didn't you tell me?"

"I had an idea it was likely. I knew Charles hoped most fervently. But I also knew her parents had not consented and might not, so I wished to spare you pain in case nothing came of the matter."

He rose and crossed the room to take his sister's hand. "I'm sorry to be the bearer of news that wounds you so deeply, Catherine. But I thought it best to come from one who loves you. I wish I could say something to ease your pain."

She shook her lace-capped head of rich, dark curls and forced a trembly smile. "It's nice to know someone loves me, Ned." She withdrew her hand and resumed her composed posture. "Now I think you had best finish what you've begun and tell me about the lady . . . at least that she is worthy of so great a prize."

"I can assure you that Sally Gwynne is a fine musician and a beautiful young woman. And she is from one of the first families in that part of Wales."

"Fah, that is not what I wish to hear. Will she make . . . the Reverend Mr. Wesley a good wife? Will she keep him comfortable? Support his work? Make him happy?"

"Yes. As far as it's possible to predict such things, I believe she will do all that. She's much younger than he, by twenty years I should think, but she has the heart of one much more mature. When Mrs. Gwynne tried to make Charles promise never to return to Ireland where he was nearly stoned last month, Sally jumped to her feet and said, "'Indeed, I shall go with him!'" Ned paused before driving the final nail. "And Charles is much in love with her."

Catherine nodded, then turned slightly away so that her brother could not see the tears that brimmed in her eyes no matter how staunchly she ordered them not to. "Thank you, Ned. I am content. At least, I shall be soon." She stood, shook out the panniers under her wide blue skirt, and checked to see that the fine lawn fichu at her neck was in place. "I believe I hear the wheels of the doctor's carriage on the gravel. I shall prepare my sister-in-law for the shock of receiving her battered husband. But don't forget to put on a clean jacket before you present yourself to her."

Durial Perronet was resting in her room upstairs, her curtains drawn against the midmorning sun and a cloth of lavender water folded on her brow. It was indeed fortunate that the Perronets received a good income from their family estates in France, for no mere itinerant Methodist preacher could afford to keep such a wife as Durial.

"Am I disturbing you, Sister?" Catherine asked.

Durial sat up, carefully laid the lavender-water cloth on the marble stand by her bed, and arranged the neckline of her sprigged cotton dressing gown. "I am happy for a visitor. What is all the coming and going I hear below?"

"Ned is returned from Wales."

Durial pulled back her sheets without care for wrinkling them. "My husband home and I not told? Oh, where are my slippers?"

Catherine produced the slippers from under the four-poster bed.

"He will join you in a few minutes. But I must tell you first—there was an altercation—"

"Oh, no." Durial sank back on her pillows. "Was he stoned again?"

"I'm afraid so. But he was not injured badly—except for his arm. The doctor is with him now."

"Doctor! Oh, why won't he give up this dangerous enthusiasm and take a settled parish? I don't ask him to stop preaching, although I could wish he gave more time to his hymn-writing; but why can't he be a respectable vicar like his father? Your father has been settled at Shoreham for thirty years, and your mother didn't have to bear any of her twelve children while in fear for her husband's life."

Catherine was still doing her best to reassure Durial when Ned entered, his arm in a sling. "Edward," Durial said, "if I weren't so glad to see you, I should give you the thorough scolding you deserve. If you don't take any thought for your wife's nerves, at least you might think of your son." She put her hand to her waist where evidence of new life was just beginning to show.

"If you will excuse me, I shall leave you two to sort this out. I must get to work. The children should find their teacher in her place." Catherine crossed to the door.

"Cath, you aren't going to the Foundery today? Not after— everything?" Ned turned away from Durial. "I'll send a message that I am unable to drive you. The wrist is not broken, but still—"

"Fah! Our father taught me to drive when I was twelve years old. One of the stable boys can accompany me." Ned started to protest, but she stopped him. "Please. I would much rather be alone."

She tied a broad-brimmed hat of leghorn straw firmly under her chin, drew a bottle-green wool cape around her shoulders, and proceeded to the stables.

Catherine had never been more thankful for her work with the Methodist Society or of the long drive from Greenwich to Moorfields. She needed solitude. Catherine had always felt deeply, but in spite of her intense feelings, or perhaps because of them, she needed to examine the true state of her mind. She did not want sympathy or company; she wanted uninterrupted time. Whatever was to come to her, she could find the strength in God to face it; but she must understand her feelings first.

"You will sit up in back, Joseph, and be very quiet."

"Yes, Miss." The lad scrambled up on the box, and those were the only two words Catherine heard from him.

Old Biggin knew the way to the Foundery as well as Catherine, so she could give her full mind to Ned's devastating

15

news. The fact that her dear Charles would be happy was a consoling thought; but all her dreams of being the one to make him happy, of sharing his work in close companionship, of singing his hymns with him . . . Well, she would simply have to amend her dreams. After all, it wasn't as if Charles had ever offered any concrete encouragement for such fancies. But the dreams had been so real to her.

No, they had been more than dreams—or at least she had believed them to be. Certain this was God's will for her life, she had often claimed Psalm 32:8: "I will instruct thee and teach thee in the way which thou shalt go: I will guide thee with mine eye." But how could she believe the Lord was guiding her when a beautiful young girl from Wales could shatter everything?

Catherine picked up a book from the bag at her feet—*Pilgrim's Progress.* It was her favorite, next to the Bible. She held the reins in one hand and left Biggin to plod down the country lane toward the Thames. With less than half an eye on the road, Catherine let the book fall open to its most-read passage:

> . . . just as Christian came up with the Cross, his burden loosed from off his shoulders, and fell from off his back, and began to tumble, and so continued to do, till it came to the mouth of the Sepulchre, where it fell in . . .
>
> Then was Christian glad and lightsome, and said, with a merry heart, "He hath given me rest by His sorrows, and life by His death." Then he stood still awhile to look and wonder, for it was very surprising to him that the sight of the Cross should thus ease him of his burden. He looked, therefore, and looked again, even till the springs that were in his head sent the waters down his cheeks . . .

She laid the book down. Today that joyful scene brought cold comfort, for it reminded her of her own conversion; and although the joy and exultation of that moment were still alive in her soul, her heart couldn't disconnect the spiritual experience from the earthly. Her mind mocked her heart with the fact that it had been Charles Wesley's preaching that had brought her to that sublime experience—doubly sublime because she had met her Savior and Charles at the same time.

Of course, no child of the godly Vincent Perronet could be far from a knowledge of God or a desire to do right. Catherine, always grave and thoughtful, had from her earliest days tried to keep the commandments and to please God and man. But the trouble was, she had never been *sure*, never completely satisfied that she had done enough to please God. Her parents and numerous brothers and sisters were quick to tell her in no uncertain terms if she failed to please them: "Cath, you forgot to lock the gate, and the cow could have gotten out." "Catherine, you tore your skirt again." "Your sums are all wrong." Not that these things happened often or that her family was hard on her, but her sensitive nature took each reproach far more seriously than the childish offense deserved.

But God was not so direct. How could she be *sure* she would someday hear, "Well done, My child; enter into My rest"? And so for twenty-one years Catherine had prayed and read her Bible and toiled to do good to those around her, hoping to find salvation—until that glorious summer day when Ned took her to hear Charles Wesley preach in the fields near Oxford. Charles had prayed with Edward when he had received the faith a few days earlier, and Ned was anxious for his sister to find the same assurance.

Catherine could still see the daisies bending on their slender stems in the long grass, feel the gentle sun on her head, and smell the freshness of God's earth whenever she thought of that meeting. They had sung Charles Wesley's hymn: "Jesus, Thine all-victorious love / Shed in my heart abroad; / Then shall my feet no longer rove, / Rooted and fixed in God." Catherine was certain she had heard an angel sing along with Charles's sweet voice as he led the singing.

And the words of his sermon had brought joy to her soul. Now she *knew* she was God's child. The warmth of the sun on her head and the warmth of the Son in her heart had fused in an ecstatic moment of light to drive all darkness of doubt from her mind and soul. From that moment she had never doubted God or her acceptance by Him. And from that moment also, she had never doubted her love for Charles Wesley.

Now her attention came back to her driving as she guided the gentle horse across London Bridge, lined with shops and bustling with traffic. Back in a more quiet street, she returned to her reminiscing. There had been three wonderful years of growth in her assured relationship with God and in her friendship with Charles—working with him and the others of the Methodist band at the Foundery, attending his meetings when he was preaching in London or when she could get Ned to take her to a nearby area, singing with him when he visited in their home.

Since her conversion, she had made her home with Ned and his wife so she could work regularly with the Methodist Society. And last year she began teaching in the day school with twelve students in her charge. She had not made the move just to be closer to Charles. Her supreme reason had been to express more fully her joy and her thanksgiving to God for His perfect salvation and for loving her; she wished to "labor more usefully in the vineyard," as so many Society members were fond of saying. She wanted to fulfill the purpose God had for her life. For with the assurance of her salvation came also the assurance of His guidance, and she had never wavered in this assurance . . . until now.

How could she be sure of God's leading when something so important—so fundamental to the foundation of her life—could go so devastatingly wrong?

But she still had her Savior. God was in His heaven, and He was here to share her day—all her days. And she had work to do. She clucked to Old Biggin, urging him to a faster pace along City Road. Soon she pulled up before the large white building that had been an abandoned foundery in ruinous condition before John Wesley purchased and reconditioned it. Now the galleried chapel could hold seventeen hundred people, with a smaller chapel to the back, a day school, private apartments, and rooms for many other Society activities.

Catherine left the carriage to Joseph's care, crossed the cobbled courtyard, and entered the deserted schoolroom, making sure each bench was straight and the floor spotless. The Foundery school educated sixty poor children under Headmaster Silas Told and two other masters, with the help of two female teachers. The children began their day at five o'clock by listening to preaching and then attended classes from six until twelve. After a midday meal, they returned to their studies from one until five in the afternoon. Catherine instructed the younger students in reading, and Miss Owen supervised the girls' needlework, which was sold to benefit the school. A frilled shirt brought two shillings, a plain shirt one shilling. The remaining instruction, primarily of writing, casting accounts, and studying Holy Scripture, was in the hands of the masters.

"Good morning, Miss Perronet." Her first pupil had arrived. Red-headed Isaiah Smithson took his seat on the front form. The others filed in behind him.

Teaching reading was usually Catherine's greatest joy— opening young minds to the wonder of language, giving them the ability to read God's Word. Of the sixty children attending the Foundery school, fewer than ten paid their own tuition; the others were so poor that they were taught, and even clothed, gratuitously. Catherine looked at the small heads bent over their books. What chance would any of them have to know the Savior or have a better life if it weren't for the Society? But today the job seemed unendingly tedious.

After a review from their abecedarian, Catherine asked her pupils to take out their primers. "Isaiah, will you please read the first lesson aloud."

Isaiah stood and rubbed his freckled nose with the back of a grubby hand. "Christ is the t-t-tr . . ."

"Truth," Catherine supplied.

"Truth. Christ is the l-l-light. Christ is the way. Christ is my life. Christ is my—" He came to a complete stop.

"Savior." Catherine suppressed a sigh of impatience.

"Christ is my hope of gl-gl-glory," Isaiah finished. Catherine reminded herself of John Wesley's admonition to his teachers: "We must instill true religion into the minds of children as early as possible. Laying line upon line, precept upon precept, as soon as they are able to bear it.

"Scripture, reason, and experience jointly testify that inasmuch as the corruption of nature is earlier than our instructions can be, we should take all pains and care to counteract this corruption as early as possible. The bias of nature is set the wrong way; education is designed to set it right."

Catherine looked at Isaiah's bruised jaw and scabbed knuckles, undoubtedly won from scrapping with ruffians in the street. She breathed a prayer of thanks that he and his brother and sisters were all in the school, no matter how tedious it was to listen to his halting reading.

She moved on to the lesson in moral precepts. The students read silently and then responded to the printed dialogue following the brief table. "What is the usefulest thing in the world?" she asked.

"Wisdom," they responded.

"What is the pleasantest thing in the world?"

"Wisdom."

At last when Catherine pulled out the watch tucked in her waistband, she saw it was time to release her students for the midday meal and prayers. Each child placed an abecedarian and primer on the table and filed from the room in orderly fashion. Clearly, the school had succeeded in instilling that meekness which John Wesley prescribed for young minds.

All except Isaiah Smithson. He shuffled his feet at the end of the line, hands behind him, eyes on the floor. "You shall miss your bread and pease porridge if you don't hurry along, Isaiah." Catherine tried not to sound impatient.

"Yes 'um, Miss Perronet. I jest wanted to say good-bye."

"Well, good-bye, Isaiah. I shall see you tomorrow."

"No, Miss. That's not what I mean. I'll not be comin' back."

"Isaiah, what are you talking about?" She saw a tear glisten at the corner of his eye.

"Me da' lost his job at the docks. Me and Esther and Samuel got to sweep."

Catherine's mind drew a sordid picture of what those few words meant. The two older children would spend their days and most of their nights sweeping horse droppings from the dusty street crossings in hopes that fine ladies who wanted to cross without soiling their skirts would reward them with a farthing. Isaiah was smaller, too small to defend his place at a crossing against bigger boys and small enough to be sent up a chimney to sweep. Altogether the children might earn a penny or two a day to supplement what their mother could make taking in washing. Catherine could only hope that the little bit wouldn't be spent on gin by an idle father.

"Isaiah, we shall see what can be done about this. Perhaps the Methodist Lending Society—I shall look into it."

Isaiah's blank look told Catherine he had no idea what she was talking about.

"Well, I shall tell you good-bye for the moment only. Isaiah, if I give you a primer, will you promise to take very good care of it and have Esther help you read in it every night?"

"Oh, yes, Miss. I will."

Catherine wished she could feel as sure as he sounded, but she must do something to keep the flicker of knowledge burning in this young mind. She placed the small brown book in his hands. "Isaiah, if you persist in your reading, you will find all that's necessary in here—the Creed, the Lord's Prayer, the Ten Commandments, even a chapter on manners."

"Miss Perronet . . ."

"Yes?"

"You sure are pretty." And he ran out the door, leaving the echo of a sniff behind.

In the empty room Catherine suppressed a desire to cry out, "Why, God?" Instead she straightened the already tidy tables before crossing the courtyard to the small chapel at the back of the Foundery. Even at midday the room with its small windows and dark wood was cool and dim. She knelt at the altar and thought again of Charles, of Isaiah . . . She groped her way through her own darkness.

Her one solace was her teaching, and now she was to lose her favorite pupil. She had been so happy to feel she was helping bring about the will of God for Isaiah and his family. But now that was to be taken away from her too.

If God was leading at all, was He leading in another direction? Maybe she was to leave the Foundery. Maybe she should not make her home with Ned and Durial. Nothing seemed to be working right for anyone in her life. Maybe, maybe . . . She didn't know, couldn't even guess. She felt as if she had nothing to care about. Her hands on the altar clenched with tension as she sought something to hold to.

She must care about something, if not Charles, if not her teaching, at least something, someone. And as soon as her mind formed the question, her heart answered, "God." She must care about Him, believe that He cared about her. That was the still, fixed point in her universe. If God dissolved into the maybe, she would be truly lost.

Perhaps she had misunderstood what she thought was God's way for her. But wouldn't the Shepherd be capable of making the sheep understand? Maybe . . . maybe . . . Her thoughts slowed, groping for the idea. . . . Maybe this was all part of the process. Maybe the Shepherd was lovingly leading her through a dark valley where she couldn't see the path. . . .

As she unclenched her fingers and relaxed, she became aware that she was not alone in the chapel. A tall, gaunt form was kneeling at the far end of the altar. His black suit and hose told her he must be a preacher; his pale blond hair was not powdered, but tied back neatly with a black ribbon. It was Philip Ferrar whom Ned had introduced to her just before his trip to Wales.

Catherine supposed she should leave Philip to pray in solitude, but she was caught by the earnestness of his posture and face. Ned had told her that he had held a curacy somewhere in Sussex and was now seeking another living. Strange. Ned hadn't explained why he left his position and was now doing itinerant preaching. The normal thing would have been to stay in Sussex until he found something else. She couldn't help thinking that the position he left couldn't have paid very well—he didn't look as if he'd ever eaten a really full meal. Even in the dimness, Catherine could see the patch on the elbow of his coat and the holes in his shoes.

As if suddenly aware of her observation, he ended his prayer and looked her way before she had time to bow her head discreetly. They regarded one another for a moment, and then both walked silently from the chapel. In the courtyard he paused. "Miss Perronet, may I hope you recall our introduction some weeks ago? I must ask you to forgive my intrusion on your prayers."

"Indeed, I remember, Mr. Ferrar. But I'm afraid it was I who intruded on you."

"No." He put on the tricorn hat he carried under his arm. "I had nothing more to say."

The forlornness of the words struck her because that was just how she felt. She looked at the hollows under his deep blue eyes. "Mr. Ferrar, my brother has just returned from Wales, and I believe you were about to make a journey to Hereford when we met. Won't you come to dinner tomorrow night? I am sure you and Ned will have much to talk about."

He accepted her invitation with a formal bow and with such seriousness that she abandoned her usual reserve. "Mr. Ferrar, you appear troubled. Mr. Wesley admonishes us to bear one another's burdens. Do you wish to speak of anything? I should be happy to pray for you."

Again he bowed slightly. "I appreciate your care, Miss Perronet. But the problem is not a new one. I went into Hereford in hopes of securing a living I had been told was open, but was turned down without an interview because of my Methodist enthusiasm. I shall, of course, continue my itinerant preaching if that is the way God chooses, but I do yearn to shepherd a settled flock." He paused. Her silence encouraged him to continue.

"It is always the same. There were many converts after my meetings in Hereford, but then I was forced to leave them. Lambs who had just set their feet on the path I had to abandon to all the wolves the devil can send. God knows my desire is to stay among them, nurture them, watch them grow. But it seems that it is not to be.

"Forgive me, Miss Perronet, I did not mean to weary you with my troubles. It was most kind of you to concern yourself with me."

"I assure you, I am not at all wearied, sir." Indeed, she felt she would like to know more of this strange, stiff man with the kind, troubled eyes. "My brother will be happy to receive you tomorrow evening."

Philip watched Catherine cross the courtyard to the stables, her wide blue skirts just brushing the cobbles. He turned and walked slowly through Bunhill Fields toward his furnished room upstairs in Mrs. Watson's rooming house. He climbed the dark stairs to his room. The "furnished" part of the arrangement was an iron bed with sadly sagging springs guaranteed to produce a backache, a washstand with a cracked bowl and miniscule blackened mirror, a creaking straight chair, and a chest. There was a window for fresh air if one could pry it open and a fireplace for warmth if one could endure the smoke.

In the months he had lived in the room, Philip had done nothing to relieve the starkness, perhaps because it was comforting in its likeness to the orphan asylum he had grown up in.

Yet, compared to the orphanage, Mrs. Watson's boarding house bespoke opulence. A small shelf of books was his only effort to make the room his own. Other than those few volumes, the space between the four whitewashed walls was as cold and impersonal as if Mrs. Watson still had the To Let sign in the window.

Only once in his thirty years had he really taken possession of a place by putting something of himself in it, and that had brought disaster. He had put everything he had, heart and soul, into his curacy in Midhurst, his enthusiasm carrying over even into furnishing his cottage. He had polished a Jacobean table he found in the attic under the thatched roof and then had so praised the pot of flowers the housekeeper set on it that she prided herself in always keeping it full, if only of holly sprigs in the winter. She saw that the rag rug on the hearth was shaken every day. And she kept the teacup on the little drop-leaf table freshly washed for the young curate to use when he sat by the fire at night to complete his day's reading.

That so much contentment and peace should have ended in such bitterness and hurt left a scar that Philip no longer expected to heal. But at least he had learned to live without leaving anything of himself about—without putting down any roots that could suffer such an emotional amputation. As he had just been refused for yet another vacancy, it appeared he might never be faced with the temptation to put down roots.

If the longing in his heart for a settled parish was from God, as he believed it to be, was he wrong to cling to the Methodist tenets that barred him from such a life? But what would be the good of having a congregation if he couldn't really share the gospel with them and lead them in the way of salvation to knowledge of a personal God? No, as long as he had breath in him, he must proclaim God's truth as he knew it. And that meant another preaching tour next week. With such a schedule there was no danger of his putting down roots even if he tried.

2

After an unusually violent bout of morning sickness, Durial was more than happy to leave the ordering of dinner for her husband's guest in the hands of her sister-in-law. So the next day Catherine could fulfill her wish of setting a really full meal before the painfully thin Mr. Ferrar.

But Durial joined the party to do her duty as hostess and serve from the top of the table. The Perronet household had readily taken to the new "French ease" method of table service whereby the master and mistress carved and served the dishes before them at each end of the polished mahogany table, before the guests helped themselves to the other dishes. "May I cut you another slice of beef roast, Mr. Ferrar?" the hostess asked.

Philip declined the sirloin, but accepted another serving of oyster loaf, and Edward served Catherine a slice of boiled turkey with prune sauce. "You are doing very well with your injured wrist, Ned."

"Yes, thank God it wasn't broken. What a nuisance that would have been. Afraid it will take awhile for some of these bruises to heal though." Ned gingerly touched a swollen spot on his forehead.

"Pray, don't let's talk of such unpleasant things." Durial

averted her eyes from her husband's wounds. "Tell us of the more pleasant aspects of your trip, Ned. What of the wedding?"

Edward hesitated, not wanting to distress his sister. "Yes, Ned. Tell us." Catherine's voice was composed.

"Charles had kept it so quiet we were all rather surprised to learn that he had been courting Miss Gwynne almost since he first met her four years ago when he was holding service with Howell Harris near her home in Garth. She attended that day with her father, Marmaduke Gwynne, who, as magistrate of the county, came with a warrant in his pocket to arrest the irregular preacher. But Gwynne was a fair man and wouldn't arrest a man without hearing him preach first. As it turned out, he was converted."

"And his daughter?" The lace lappets of Catherine's ruffled cap fell across her shoulders as she leaned forward.

"Oh, the whole family was soon converted and, it seems, all quite smitten with the younger Wesley brother. All except Mrs. Gwynne, who holds the accounts in the family and had some-one of a higher station in mind for her eldest daughter."

Durial swallowed a delicate bite of fish. "La, is that why it took Mr. Wesley four years to bring it about?"

"There were many hindrances, his lack of a settled home, her age—she's twenty years younger, you know—the fear of causing trouble in the Society."

"Trouble?" Durial asked. The conversation had now become a dialogue between the host and hostess with Catherine and Philip giving their full attention to the stewed venison.

"Yes, John especially feared that the many disappointed hopefuls for both Sally's and Charles's affection might cause dis-sension in the Society." Edward showed his discomfort at stating that in front of his sister and rushed on. "But Charles provided an acceptable marriage settlement from his book sales, and our father's letter seemed to soothe away some last-minute problems."

"How enchanting to hear such a charming story, my love."

Durial smiled across the candle-lit table. "And now everyone is blissfully happy."

Edward gave his wife an uneasy smile and turned to his plate.

Catherine, relieved that the painful talk seemed to be dropped, looked at their guest across the table and realized that he had spoken hardly a word during the entire first course. Indeed, instead of the good effect she expected her excellent meal to produce, he seemed more tense and drawn than before. This made his nose seem even larger and his dark blue eyes darker yet in startling contrast to his pale hair. She would have dearly loved to say something to put him at ease, but her own reserved nature could find no light words. At Durial's direction, the servant removed the first course and replaced it with another pattern of dishes bearing anchovy toasts, potato pudding, strawberry fritters, and jam tarts.

Edward turned to their guest. "And what of your work, Ferrar? Is the life of an itinerant suiting you?"

"If it suits our Master, I shan't complain."

Ned smiled and shook his head. "You're a man of few words. I should like to hear you preach. I think you might easily avoid the trap of tediousness, as John Wesley admonishes us."

"Would you truly, Edward?" Philip raised his fine, dark eyebrows in question. "I should be most happy of your companionship on my next tour. Someone to lead the singing would be more than useful, as my abilities in that area are woeful."

Ned opened his mouth to reply, but Durial spoke first. "Indeed not, sir. My husband is not yet recovered from the treatment he received at the hands of the last mob he sought to evangelize. If the rabble insists on going to the devil, I cannot see why you shouldn't leave them to it."

"My treatment was nothing compared to that received by our Lord and His disciples, and that was not His attitude, my love." Edward's reproof to his wife was gently delivered.

"You are right, of course. Forgive my temperamental state."

Her apology included Philip as well. "But I must ask you not to tempt my husband into danger before his wounds are healed."

"I would do nothing to distress you, Madam, but there should be very little danger in Canterbury. I have received many letters from Society members throughout Kent requesting a preacher."

"But, Ned . . . ," Durial began and then laid aside her fork with a sigh. "I know I waste my breath. You must excuse me if I withdraw now. I find I cannot keep late hours."

"I shall come with you, Sister." Catherine began to rise.

"No, Cath, please don't trouble yourself on my account. Audrey will help me. You stay and serve our guest."

Catherine settled back. She served pink pancakes to Philip and her brother as the men continued to discuss Philip's upcoming preaching trip. "My father has a farm at Canterbury I should be happy to see to. And from Tunbridge Wells we could come up through Shoreham," Ned said. "I should much like to visit our parents."

"But what of your injuries and—the other objections? I fear I shouldn't have spoken so rashly."

Ned smiled. "My wife is overly careful for my safety. She will get on much better without me here to mess up the house with my books and sheets of music."

Her serving finished, Catherine felt it was time for her to withdraw, but again her attempt to exit was thwarted. "Don't leave us, Cath. If I'm to serve as musician to Mr. Ferrar's evangelistic efforts, I should give him a demonstration of what he's in for. Let's have a bit of music."

That was a request Catherine always granted with eagerness, although she hoped Ned would not choose to sing one of Charles Wesley's hymns. She led the way into the parlor and seated herself at the harpsichord while Ned lit the tapers with a stick from the fireplace. The candlelight shimmered on the holly leaf pattern of her blue damask skirt; the three tiers of Valenciennes ruffles fell gracefully from her elbows as she fingered the keys. The lace was the finest French bobbin work, and Catherine spared a thought for her aunt in France who kept her well supplied in fashionable finery.

"What shall I play, Ned?" She ran a scale up and down the keys, the bright silvery tones of the harpsichord responding to her quick touch.

"Here." He set a piece of music before her. "Let's begin with this by our friend Count Zinzendorf. 'Jesus, Thy blood and righteousness . . . '" His rich tenor filled the room. "'Thou hast for all a ransom paid, for all a full atonement made.'"

"Come, come, Philip. You must join us." Edward placed another sheet of music on the rack. "You sing too, Cath. This old Welsh hymn melody is best with a group of voices."

Catherine hesitated at the words her brother had put before her. Was it a random selection, or did he guess at her spiritual struggles? She forced her fingers to play and hoped her light soprano voice could stay on tune without wavering. "Guide me, O Thou great Jehovah, / Pilgrim through this barren land; / I am weak, but Thou art mighty, / Hold me with Thy powerful hand. . . ."

The words sank into her heart as vocalizing the prayer brought its own pledge of faith. Her voice grew stronger on the second verse. ". . . Let the fiery, cloudy pillar / Lead me all my journey through; / Strong Deliverer, be Thou still my strength and shield. . . ."

She had been caught up in the song as the Lord assured her through its words that He would lead her. It wasn't until the repeated refrain that her ear caught the discordant note behind her. The voice didn't lack strength, just correctness of pitch.

She was caught off guard and gave a gurgle of laughter before she realized what she had done. The dissonance stopped at once. She turned to their guest, afraid she had wounded him by her thoughtlessness.

But instead of seeing pain on his countenance, she met the merriest twinkle she had seen in his blue eyes and a smile so broad it balanced the size of his nose. It was the first open emotion she had seen from him. "Please forgive me; I—," she stammered.

"There is nothing to forgive in your quite natural reaction." The smile continued. "You see now why I hoped your brother would accompany my tour? I take great pleasure in hymn-singing, but it must be indulged in only under the harmony from a large congregation." Then the smile broke into a deep chuckle considerably more melodious than his singing, and Ned and Catherine joined in the laughter.

At last Ned spoke. "Catherine, I see I've taken on a much greater challenge than I realized. I fear I shall need help. I doubt the ability of even a great congregation to drown out this fellow's caterwauling. Won't you come with me on his tour? It would be a shame if all the potential hearers of the Word in Kent were to be scared off by the hymn-singing."

"Oh, Ned, I'd love to!" Her reaction was instinctive before common sense took over. "But, alas, I fear it's impossible. I mustn't leave my school duties, and we can't both abandon Durial." And then fear replaced common sense. "No, I really couldn't. So far on horseback . . ."

Ned put an understanding hand on her shoulder. "We could take the carriage, my dear. As to the school, couldn't Miss Owen oversee your students for just two weeks? And I've been thinking that our sister Elizabeth would be happy of an excuse to be closer to the London Society. She could stay with Durial."

Catherine laughed in spite of her concerns. "My, how efficient you are. But perhaps Mr. Ferrar does not want his tour so invaded."

Philip gave one of his small, stiff bows, which made the white Geneva bands at his neck fall forward from his black coat. "On the contrary, I would be very honored to have your company, Miss Perronet." And in spite of his stiffness, his eyes twinkled. "Besides, your brother is sure to need all the help he can get."

"We shall consider the matter further," Catherine said. She turned again to the keyboard where she played a brief melody before stopping to ask, "And have you a new hymn for us to try out, Ned?"

"Not yet ready to show even to so select a company, I fear. I have an image that seems stuck in my head every time I try to write, but I haven't succeeded in putting it in words. I see Christ on a great white throne with angels kneeling around Him, each one offering a crown and praising the power of His name. But the wording eludes me. I want to write a hymn of regal power and dignity that will bring honor to His majesty. I pray I will be worthy of the task."

"That is the prayer of each of us, is it not? To be worthy of our task." Catherine rose from the harpsichord bench and joined her brother in bidding their guest good night.

Later, alone in her room, the side curtains of her bed drawing her into her own little world, Catherine pondered Ned's parting remarks to her: "Do come with us, Cath. You need a change of scenery. It will take your mind off more painful things. And you can do some real good."

Catherine doubted just how much actual good she could accomplish. It seemed to her that the female members of the Society accompanied the preachers more for their own enlightenment or amusement—or for more subtle purposes, as she suspected of Grace Murray who often traveled with John Wesley. But then she scolded herself for being unfair. Women Society members counseled the women seekers in matters about which men would have no knowledge.

She had almost decided in favor of going when the vision of a large bay horse loomed, snorting, before her. She cowered into her pillows. *What utter nonsense... I should be ashamed...* Unthinkingly, she rubbed her fingers over her left collarbone and felt the sharp dip there. The imaginary horse snorted again, and the remembered pain in her shoulder was lost in the cries of her little brother who had toddled too close to the stamping feet.

But that was years ago. The crazed horse had been put down, her shoulder rarely ached anymore, and a rambling rose grew over the grave of little David in the Shoreham churchyard. She had overcome her fear sufficiently to ride when the occasion absolutely demanded it, but her greatest victory had been in becoming an expert driver.

So if they could take the carriage, and Elizabeth could stay with Durial, and Silas Told would allow Miss Owen to take her classes . . . She must admit there was something that appealed to her in the idea of helping Ned's strangely aloof colleague. As Ned had said after Philip left that evening, "We're not exactly friends. I certainly like him well enough. He's a fine fellow—don't know that I ever met better—but one can't get close enough to him to feel free to use the word *friend*." Yes, it might be worth knowing what was on the other side of that wall Philip Ferrar had erected around himself.

Three days later as the carriage rolled eastward along the old Roman road through the green countryside below the Thames, Catherine was glad of her decision. Whatever else might come of the journey, Ned's promise of a change of scene had been gloriously fulfilled. Hedgerows in new leaf sprouted buds that promised busy jam-making in cottage kitchens this summer; and rich, brown earth, yielding to the farmer's plow, would in a month or two show equal promise for a joyous fall Harvest Home festival. The fact that few trees had advanced past the bud stage did not daunt the flocks of chirping birds building their nests.

"Oh, Ned, just listen to that chorus," Catherine said to her brother beside her on the carriage seat. "Surely that will inspire your hymn-writing."

"Pardon?" He looked up absently from his paper.

34

"What poor company you make. You are far too busy listening to the tunes in your head to attend either to your sister or to nature's choristers. I find you quite hopeless."

"Philip!" Edward called to the rider just ahead of the carriage. "You must help me. My sister complains of my company, and I find her incessant chattering an intolerable interruption. Give me your horse."

"Incessant chattering! Sir, I protest. It was the second line I spoke to you in the better part of an hour. And how, pray tell, do you think to go on with your work on horseback?"

"I shall go on very well. Charles Wesley composes nearly all his hymns on horseback; he says the pace of the horse aids his sense of stately rhythm."

"Yes." Catherine guided Old Biggin around a mudhole left by recent rains. "And John Wesley gives all his attention to reading while on horseback. And they are both famous for their continual riding disasters because they never attend to their mounts. This time you're sure to break your arm, and then what will Durial say?"

But soon Philip was sitting beside her on the carriage seat while Ned, his reins looped across the saddle, followed at a distance. Here was her chance to get acquainted with the enigmatic man beside her, but her reticence took over, and she could think of nothing to say that didn't seem prying. So despite her denouncement as a chatterbox, it was Philip who broke the silence. "I am pleased you chose to come, Miss Perronet."

"Yes, I am too. But you must call me Catherine. Being traveling companions is almost like being family members."

"I would be honored—to use your name and to be so considered. You have a large family, I believe?"

Well, if she couldn't ask him about himself, she could tell him about herself; then maybe he would feel comfortable to be more open. "There were an even dozen of us, Mr. Ferrar."

"No, no. That will never do. If I am to call you Catherine,

you must call me Philip. Would you call your brother Mr. Perronet?"

"No, I wouldn't—Philip."

"There. Now, tell me more of your family."

"I shall do so, but you must absolve me of all accusations of chattering."

He raised his hand in a gesture of absolution.

"Well, Ned was always my favorite brother. With twelve children in the family it would be easy to get lost, to be just one of a crowd, but I was never that to Ned. He taught me to climb trees, helped me with my sums—which were always so easy for him and so impossible for me. He took me on long walks in the woods and taught me the names of the birds and flowers. I still keep my scrapbook of pressed flowers and hope to gather some new specimens on this trip."

She paused to observe the clumps of violets growing along the road.

"Ned encouraged my music when I became disheartened. Later I was able to return the favor by sharing the excitement over his compositions, and usually I'm the first to play one of his new hymns." She felt Philip's urging to continue her story.

"Little Charl was always my special charge, like I was Ned's. I suppose that's the way it works in all big families—each one looking out for the next younger. At least, that's how we did it. Anyway, Charl needed all the attention I could give him. He was forever wandering off and getting lost, getting hung up on a blackberry bush, or losing a boot in the mud. And it was my job to rescue him. Most of the time I didn't mind even if it did interrupt my reading.

"I suppose I was bred for Methodist Society work even before there was such a thing, because from my earliest memories I accompanied Mother when she visited the sick and needy in Papa's parish every week. Tuesday, Thursday, and Saturday were her regular visiting days, and at least three of us children always went with her, carrying baskets of garden vegetables, a fresh cheese, or herbs from the woods—whatever we had at hand or something she knew was needed.

"Dudy and Ned and I, or whoever accompanied her on that day, would occupy the children in the home so Mother could minister to the adults. Then we all joined in prayer before we left—or sometimes in song, especially when Ned was with us. His beautiful voice always made people feel better. I suppose that was one of the reasons—" She stopped abruptly, thankful for the lurch of the carriage that made the interruption seem natural. She had felt so at ease talking to Philip she had almost said that one of the reasons she loved Charles Wesley was that his was the only other voice she'd ever heard that was as sweet as her brother's.

"Yes?"

"So working with children has been my life since I was old enough to walk and talk. I've always loved it, and I can't imagine doing anything else.

"Gracious, I've talked an alarming distance. You must tell me of yourself now, er, Philip. What of your family?"

His level gaze that had so encouraged her comfortable reminiscences withdrew, and she felt as if the tremulous April sunshine had gone behind a cloud. Throughout her narrative he had leaned toward her, focusing on every word; but now he sat stiffly upright and looked straight ahead. It was obvious she had put a foot wrong. "Forgive me if I trespass. I—"

For a moment she thought she saw a flicker of emotion on his stoic features. "No, you have a right to know. I see now my error in not telling your brother. He would not have wanted his sister exposed—"

Before she could press him to complete his muddled remarks, Edward rode alongside them.

"How is it progressing, Ned?" Catherine asked.

"I don't know. I'm working on the phrase, 'All praise the name of Jesus.' It's the right idea, but it doesn't quite sing. I came to ask if Philip thought we should put up at the next village. The sky seems to be darkening rapidly."

Philip looked at the sky. "I had hoped to reach Rochester tonight and preach there in the morning before going on, but perhaps we could stop at Cobham if the inn is suitable for your sister's comfort."

Both men looked questioningly at Catherine, but she made no response. "What do you think, Cath?" Edward asked.

"*Hail*, I think."

Ned looked at the dark sky. "Perhaps, but I think rain more likely."

"Have you taken leave of your senses? *Reign* wouldn't suit at all. No wonder you're having trouble with your song."

"Catherine—I'm not talking about my writing. Philip and I want to know if you wish to put up at the nearest inn. It looks like rain coming."

"Oh, I daresay. Do as you think best. But try 'All hail the name of Jesus' in your song."

By the time they reached Cobham, the hypothetical rain had become a drenching reality. Travelers and horses didn't question the advisability of stopping at the inn, disreputable though it looked.

"I do apologize, Miss Perronet. You should never have been brought to such a place." Philip stood just inside the door surveying the dingy interior.

"Catherine," she reminded him firmly. "And do not worry yourself over the accommodation. I chose to come, and I shall make do with what presents itself."

But her brave words met a severe test when, after a brief washing in her damp-smelling room, she joined the men in the inn's only parlor. The room was crowded with ill-clad, unwashed villagers all talking in voices clearly emboldened by ale. "This is intolerable," Edward declared and strode off in search of the innkeeper.

"Catherine—" Philip took a step toward her.

"Mind your head!" The sharp crack told her that the warning came too late as Philip struck the low, blackened ceiling beam.

He rubbed his forehead ruefully. "You'd think one of my height would learn."

Ned joined them. "I gave orders for our supper to be served in my room. Its cramped condition will be preferable to this."

Indeed, Ned's small room, even with the fireplace that refused to draw properly, was an improvement, but the food set before them by a slatternly serving wench couldn't have been worse. The pools of fat floating on the stew had congealed into a stiff, white crust by the time it reached them. Even after Catherine pushed the fat aside and found a piece of meat, it was too tough to chew.

Ned took a bite of the bread. After no more than three chews, he grabbed for his cider mug and choked down a swallow of the sour liquid. "I advise you to avoid the bread." He wiped his mouth with the back of his hand, as no napkins had been provided. "In this dismal light I failed to see the mold on it, but the taste was unmistakable."

Philip chewed stoically on the rubbery meat and soggy vegetables. Then, after a sip of cider, he remarked, "It's no worse than the orphan asylum. Quite like, if my memory holds."

"Orphanage?" Catherine's fork hit her wooden serving trencher with a clatter.

Philip nodded without expression. "I started to tell you this afternoon. But I think it best to present you both with the full details now. Then if you wish to turn back in the morning, I shall understand."

"Turn back?" Catherine began, but her question was ignored as Philip turned to her brother.

"Edward, please believe that on my honor as a Christian I

would not have embarked on this journey had I realized the harm it could do to your sister's reputation."

"Nonsense. I am sufficient chaperone for her good name. Such travels are common practice."

"But not in the company of one with my background. I wish you to know the plain facts. I am a foundling."

There was no reply.

"An abandoned foundling. Which can mean only that my mother was a servant girl, or worse, and my father a care-for-nothing nobleman or a rake. Whatever the case may have been, the fact remains that, except at the very highest and lowest extremes of society, foundling means bastard and therefore disgrace. I know you will not want to expose your sister to such company."

Catherine broke in before Ned could reply, "What contemptible rubbish! I'll hear no more of it, sir, and neither will my brother."

Ned was thoughtful for a moment as the rain washed against the windows in great unremitting waves and the weak flame fluttered on the grate. Finally he spoke. "God has accepted you. With Him as your Father, there can be no more to say on the matter."

"You are very kind, Edward. But your sister—"

"My sister has spoken for herself most adequately."

"Both now and at some length this afternoon when I related my childhood to you. I think you should reciprocate, unless to do so would cause you pain." Catherine truly wanted to hear more of his history and felt in no hurry to leave even so small a comfort as Ned's weak fire for the chill dreariness of her own room.

"The subject is not at all painful to me," Philip assured her. "I simply fear disgusting others."

"Then be at rest, Philip. Ned is quite right. We share the same Father, so we are of the same family. There is no offense possible."

Philip nodded and stared into the fire. "I always took some comfort in the fact that Mrs. Ortlund found a remarkably clean and well-cared-for infant on her doorstep in the rush basket. It was most unusual, for a foundling often had little more than a few rags to protect it from the chill fog."

"Mrs. Ortlund raised you?" Catherine asked.

Again Philip nodded without looking at her. "She named me for a brother who died young. She had been a nurse at the Royal Asylum of St. Anne for Children Whose Parents Had Seen Better Days. The institution was no longer operating by the time I made my unwanted appearance into the world. But she ran a small asylum from the goodness of her heart and her own small living."

The wind and rain that whipped at the old inn made the three occupants of the room draw closer together. "I have never ceased to give thanks for Mrs. Ortlund. Were it not for her, I should have been sent to the parish poorhouse where it is unlikely I would have seen my first year through, amidst the filth, disease, and starvation."

Catherine shuddered.

"I have visited such places as an adult. Pandemonium and vice rule jointly among the paupers, fallen women, neglected children, vagrants, lunatics, aged, and ill. Had the usual fate befallen me, I should have been put in such a place where the best I could have hoped for was that some feeble crone might choose to care for a mewling infant for the short time it could be expected to survive."

"Were there no parish nurses?"

"Yes, but many were as lethal as the parish workhouse. Some are even called 'killing nurses.' More than three-fourths of the infants cared for by parish nurses die every year. I have looked into the subject with some interest. It seems that parish nurses who continue to bury infants week after week, with no criticism and no lessening of the number of children given them, take the hint. Society considers it very fit and convenient that such a child should die. After all, it relieves society of the care of an object that at worst is loathed and at best ignored. I thank God that by the large part of such society I was ignored."

All was silent in the room save for the incessant pounding of the rain. Then a violent gust of wind rattled the window panes so sharply that the three started. Catherine rose and smoothed her muslin skirt over its quilted petticoat. "It's past time we were in bed. Do you plan to preach in the fields at five in the morning as Mr. Wesley does?"

"I often do. It's a good idea to give the workers the Word of God before they begin their labors. But I fear we would have few hearers in the morning, even if the storm has passed. Let us rise at five and go on to Rochester for our first meeting. There is a small but faithful Society there."

"I will light you to your room." Ned picked up a candlestick.

Philip's room was next to Edward's, and when he opened the door, Catherine could see that his fire had gone out. She started toward the stairs and then turned back to say good night. In the frame of the dark doorway Philip looked remote and lonely. For a moment she felt she couldn't leave him like that. She took a step toward him.

"Cath!" Ned called impatiently from the stairway. She gave Philip a last small smile and rushed to her brother.

Philip watched Catherine fly up the stairs with a detachment that persisted from his orphanage days. He had learned early that it didn't pay to get too attached to people or things. People moved—went on to school or work; things were lost or stolen. He remembered the one thing that had been truly his, the blanket Mrs. Ortlund found him in. He had always kept it carefully folded in the bottom of the chest under his bed in the orphanage. But one day he returned from chapel to find the contents of the trunk spilled on his bed and the blanket gone. He hadn't even reported the incident, as the knowledge that he attached any importance to a worn, faded baby blanket would have made him a laughingstock.

His most determined efforts at detachment had failed him in one tender matter, however—the matter of Sally Gwynne. It was his own fault. He had broken his rule.

It happened without any rational awareness on his part. Indeed, until word reached him and other workers that day at the Foundery that Charles Wesley and Sally Gwynne were wed, he had had no understanding of the depth of his feeling. The fact that every young Methodist who preached in Wales or met Sally when she visited the Foundery with her father was more than half in love with the beautiful Welsh girl was no comfort to Philip. Nor did the fact that he would never have made an attempt to win her affections—nor have stood a chance had he done so— lessen the intensity of his feelings.

The cut was much sharper, although less deep, than the severing from his curacy had been. But both had produced the same results—an increased determination to remain aloof.

He turned to see if he could fan the few sparks on his grate into life. Then he saw his bag open on the floor. While he was next door in Ned's room, a thief had been at work here. His two leather-bound books and a linen shirt would fetch a few shillings when resold. Fortunately he always kept his purse with him, and he had little else of value to steal.

Gathering up his scattered goods brought to mind the theft in the orphanage and reminded him yet again of the rightness of forming no affections for things or people. There must be nothing in his heart worth stealing either.

*P*reachin' in the cockpit! Preachin' in the cockpit!" Two urchins ran through Rochester the next morning publicizing the meeting. And in the amphitheater usually used for much rougher purposes, the hymn-singing of a curious crowd attracted newcomers willing to stand in the drizzling rain for a fresh entertainment.

Catherine walked among the women on the edges of the crowd, welcoming them, helping them with their children, urging them to join in the singing, and ignoring the rude suggestions of two young ruffians who made no attempt to hide the bottles in their coat pockets.

The faithful of the Rochester Methodist Society sang loudly so that those unfamiliar with the songs could follow them. One of the members had requested permission to share his testimony. He took his place in the center of the ring, standing staunchly in spite of the jeers of the crowd.

"Need a drink, Buddy?"

"Haven't seen you at the inn lately; religion got you down?"

"Hey, Barber Bolton, how about a shave and a haircut—for a swig of gin?"

Bolton's voice rang above his rowdy audience. "I praise

God. When Mr. Wesley were at Rochester last, I were one of the most eminent drunkards in all the town—"

Cries of "'S truth" and "Don't we know it!" and "Miss the old times, Charlie?" interrupted him, but they subsided, and Bolton continued.

"Mr. Wesley was a-preachin' at the church. I come to listen at the window, and God struck me to the 'eart. I prayed for power against drinking. And God gave me more than I asked; 'e took away the very desire of it."

An egg flew through the air and landed at the speaker's feet. "Run 'em all out of town! They'll ruin business."

Bolton held up his hand. "Yet I felt myself worse and worse, till on April 25 last I could 'old out no longer. I knew I must drop into 'ell that moment unless God appeared to save me. And 'e did appear. I knew 'e loved me, and I felt sweet peace. Yet I did not dare to say I had faith—till yesterday was twelvemonth. God gave me faith, and 'is love 'as ever since filled my 'eart."

A combination of "amens" and jeers followed the speech, but then the audience became unusually quiet as Philip rose to preach. Catherine breathed a prayer that the service might continue without disruption.

Philip opened his Bible and began to read, "For by grace are—"

A loud squawking came from the back of the crowd, and the way parted for two men, each carrying a flapping, screeching rooster toward the center of the cockpit ring. "Now, me fine lords 'n ladies, as so many of you are gathered 'ere a'ready, we'll give you some *real* entertainment. On this side, Chanticleer, my fine red Pyle, and on t'other, Acey Jones's Wednesbury Grey. Fine fightin' cocks both in prime form. Who'll lay odds as to which of these fair-feathered fighters will be first to draw blood?"

Many in the audience surged forward to place bets. Philip turned to Ned. "Sing loudly and follow me." Holding his Bible aloft like a banner, Philip led the way through the mob, Ned and

Catherine behind him singing the Isaac Watts hymn, "We're Marching to Zion."

A vast number of people followed in parade to the market cross in the center of town, and more joined them along the way. Catherine hoped that now the chaff had been separated from the wheat and Philip would have receptive hearers. But as soon as he mounted the steps of the cross, the crowd began thrusting to and fro, and Philip was knocked from his perch on the highest stone step. Catherine started to cry out for fear he had been seriously hurt, but she saw him rise quickly and remount the steps.

The audience continued to shove, but Philip held his back firm against the stone cross and continued his Bible-reading. "'For by grace are ye saved through faith; and . . . '" Seeing they could not dislodge the preacher by pushing, those who had come for sport—considering field preachers fair game—began throwing stones. At the same time, some got up on the cross behind Philip to push him down. One man began shouting in his ear, making it impossible to continue the Scripture reading. Suddenly the tone of the shout changed to one of pain, and the man fell at Philip's feet, his cheek bleeding profusely where a stone intended for Philip had struck.

Then a second troublemaker, far more burly than the first, forced his way toward Philip. Before he could reach the cross though, a misdirected stone hit him on the forehead and bounced off. Blood ran down his face, and he advanced no farther.

A third reached out to grab Philip from the left. But a sharp stone aimed at Philip struck the attacker's fingers. With a howl of pain, the man dropped his hand and then stood silent. As if following his cue, the others became silent. Philip continued, "'By grace are ye saved through faith.' These two little words, faith and salvation, include the substance of all the Bible, the marrow, as it were, of the whole Scripture."

Catherine couldn't believe the change that came over

Philip as he spoke to the vast audience before him. Even in the press of the crowd when she had feared for his life, she had detected no change in his face, no show of emotion. But now his features took on a glow—an intense shine of joy that she would not have thought possible. And his voice—always so controlled, so evenly modulated, so devoid of any betraying feeling—now rang with the passion for truth. She felt as if she could see the Savior whom he proclaimed.

"And what is this faith through which we are saved? The Scripture speaks of it as a light, as a power of discerning. So St. Paul says, 'For God, who commanded the light to shine out of darkness, hath shined in our hearts, to give the light of the knowledge of the glory of God in the face of Jesus Christ.'"

As he spoke, the rain, which had been lessening for some time, stopped altogether; the clouds parted, and a shaft of sunlight fell on the fair-haired speaker standing on the market cross. His black cassock fluttered in the breeze, and his white satin surplice, remarkably unmuddied from the treatment he had received, gleamed in the sun.

"Faith is a divine evidence and conviction, not only that God was in Christ, reconciling the world unto Himself, but also that the Christ loved me and gave Himself for me. It is by this faith that we receive Christ . . ."

Catherine was so caught up by the preacher and his ringing words that for a moment she lost awareness of the people around her. Then she felt a sharp tug on her sleeve and turned to the woman beside her. "Sister, will ye pray with me? I 'ave need of such a faith."

Catherine led the seeker to the side of the crowd where they both bowed their heads. Catherine prayed first, then the woman. When Catherine looked up, she saw tears running down the woman's wrinkled, weather-beaten face. "Bless you, Sister; I've often 'eard these Methodists at their 'ymn-singing and wanted to join them, but I didn't know how. Now I've got a 'ymn-sing a-goin' in my 'eart."

Catherine introduced the new convert to a local Society member and turned to another who appeared to be seeking. "Would you like me to pray with you?" Perhaps twenty hungry souls were seeking the Savior around the old stone market cross.

A rough voice interrupted Catherine's prayer. She looked up, expecting more rabble, and a surprising sight met her eyes. A man in ragged, dirty clothes with greasy, matted hair hanging beneath a disreputable hat was holding a crisp white linen shirt aloft in one hand and two leather-bound books in the other. "I knowed it was a preacher cove I burgled in the inn last night when I seed 'is Bible an' preacher's garb. But I took w'at I could anyway. I was on my way to sell it for w'at I could w'en 'is words struck me to 'eart. 'Ere's yer swag, Mister. I repent a' me wicked ways."

Philip placed a hand on the man's shoulder. "I'll take the books as I doubt you have use for reading material. But you keep the shirt; you need it worse than I. Let it remind you of the new heart Christ has given you."

A chorus of "amens" and "praise the Lords" rose from the believers, turning to calls of "farewell" and "God go wi' thee" as Philip and the Perronets continued their journey.

From the carriage, Philip looked back at what was left of the congregation with open longing in his eyes. "It is always the same—the wrench at leaving new babes in the faith. How I long to stay among them! I believe this preaching like an apostle, without joining together those that are awakened and training them up in the ways of God, is only begetting children for the devil to steal. How much preaching has there been for ten years all over England! But where there is no regular preacher, no discipline, no order or connection, the consequence is that nine in ten of the once-awakened are now faster asleep than ever."

"The Society members—," Catherine began.

"Will do what they can to encourage one another in the faith, of course. But these people need a shepherd. What hope is there for such as that thief to build a new life without firm guidance?"

"The parish vicar?" Catherine tried again.

"Undoubtedly the holder of at least six livings who visits here once yearly as required by law in order to keep his income. What counsel exists is in the hands of a curate who, without the supervision of his superior, may be as lazy or drunken as suits him."

"Surely you exaggerate. My father—"

"Is a rare example of a godly man. One whose work I would emulate if a place were open to me."

"I understand you were formerly a curate . . ." Her sentence went unfinished as Old Biggin slipped in the deep mud. Ned drew alongside his sister. "We are nearly to the Medway. I think I should drive across. The waters are sure to be full and swift after the downpour."

The men changed places, and in a few minutes they approached the raised earthen causeway of ancient Roman construction. At least, that was where the crossing should have been. It was invisible under the rushing waters. "Can we ride the causeway?" Ned asked the ferryman.

"Yes, sir, if you keep in the middle."

Ahead of them, Philip urged his mount to cross the swollen stream. Obedient to her master's voice, Jezreel led the way into the water. Catherine held her breath, determined to remain calm.

Crossing with the carriage was more difficult. The water rose above the horses' knees and came to the bottom of the carriage. Catherine could feel the current pushing and sucking at the wheels to pull the vehicle sideways. She gripped the seat as Ned urged Biggin forward. "Easy, old boy. One step at a time. 'Atta boy. Keep going."

Just past the middle a swirl of water rushed over the causeway with the swiftness of a sluice. Catherine gave a cry of alarm as she saw Jezreel ahead of them lose her footing. But the horse gave a spring and recovered the roadway. With two final lunges, she scrambled up the eastern bank.

Biggin, older, and less agile than Philip's mare, was not so lucky. A few feet from shore his right forefoot slipped off the ramp. The carriage jolted as the horse fought to regain his footing. He couldn't find a hold in the muddy swirl. He swam valiantly, his heavily muscled thighs straining against the downstream rush.

The carriage, already nearly afloat in the deep water, tilted dangerously, then righted itself, and rode the tide behind Old Biggin. Catherine, soaked to her knees in the icy flood, gripped the seat as Ned fought to guide his horse. She tried to pray, but holding on took all her concentration.

Philip shouted to a group of men on the bank waiting for the ferry. Forming two rows of human pulleys, they reached out with strong hands for each side of Biggin's harness as he neared shore. The first man missed his grab at the wet leather, but the second grasped it firmly. Straining, they pulled the heaving horse up the miry bank.

Catherine took in a great gulp of air and started to relax when a grating crunch of metal on stone rent the air. The carriage wheel on Ned's side had struck a boulder half-buried in the mud. For a moment the vehicle balanced on one wheel. Then it toppled on its side, spilling passengers and luggage into the mud and water.

The world blurred and darkened. Catherine felt her hands slide through the slimy brown ooze of the river bank. She smelled the heavy, wet earth. She slid toward the raging waters, her wet, heavy skirts pulling her downward. She screamed and clawed at the slimy bank.

Just as the cold grasp of the river tugged at her feet, a strong hand encircled her flailing arm. Philip, supported by two burly river men, pulled her from the clutches of the water. In a few moments she was on top of the bank.

The men unhitched Biggin and retrieved the suitcases

from the muck. Ned, Catherine, and Philip sat down on tree stumps above the river to survey the wreckage.

"Compared to what I feared when I saw your carriage go into the water, I cannot regard the broken axle as a disaster," Philip said. He turned toward Catherine, but he said nothing more.

Trembling, she reached out to him, disregarding the mud covering them both. "You saved my life."

Ned put his arm around his shivering sister. "We are much indebted to you, Philip. We are indeed fortunate. Neither of us nor Biggin is hurt, and only one bag is lost in the river."

"It's easy for you to say 'only one,' considering it was my case." Catherine forced a lightness as she regarded her muddy gown and thought of her belongings swirling away down river.

"Chatham is just ahead. You can purchase some necessities there while Philip and I arrange to have the carriage repaired and hire a chaise for the rest of the journey."

"Hire a chaise?" Catherine wiped a sodden curl away from her cheek and tried to sound casual. "What nonsensical extravagance, Brother. You would be far better served to purchase a saddle for Biggin." She forced a smile that showed by its very brilliance how terrified she was. The other Methodist sisters rode pillion on circuit. She could do it too. It was high time she laid her fear to rest.

"But, Cath—" Ned tightened his arm encircling her shoulder. "That would mean you must ride pillion. I can afford to hire—"

"No. No chaise." The words were firm but were followed by a small gulp. "I'll be all right. There must be an inn up the road where we can dry out and get warm."

"Cath," Ned tried again.

"I'll be fine." Her insistence was more for her own benefit than for her companions'. To give action to her words she stood and began walking up the road. Without thinking about it, she put a hand on her left shoulder. The cold, wet weather had made the injury ache, as it often did, and brought the old experience vividly alive to her . . . The big bay horse lowering his head and lashing out with his hind feet, then rearing in front, and landing stiff-legged with a jolt that jarred her teeth. The helpless, sick feeling of slipping, at first slowly, then faster and faster, and plunging to the hard earth. The blowing snort from the horse, the cry from her baby brother, and then silence as the pain in her shoulder brought the blessed oblivion of unconsciousness. When she woke, they told her about David.

She never saw the horse again nor her brother. She had probably ridden only ten or twelve times in her life since then, and never pillion. Could she do it now? The answer was there as soon as the question formed: "I can do all things through Christ which strengtheneth me." She gave her shoulder a final rub as she pulled a foot from the mud and set it on the path before her.

The inn they found was a considerable improvement on the one they had stayed in the night before. As the hour was late by the time Ned completed arrangements for the carriage and they were wet and cold, they decided to stay the night.

The next morning the travelers continued their journey to the accompaniment of the dawn chorus. Since Old Biggin, for all his gentleness, was not really a saddle horse, they decided it would be better to tie their cases on behind Ned and have Catherine ride pillion on Jezreel. Catherine accused her brother of caring more for his privacy than her comfort, and he replied that she had already informed him of her opinion of his companionship, thank you. In this spirit of raillery, Catherine covered her fears as Ned made a stirrup of his hands and tossed her onto the blanket behind Philip.

Sitting sidesaddle, she smoothed her round skirt over her petticoat and placed her left arm loosely around Philip's waist. "Are you all right?" he asked. "Ned told me of your accident. If I can do anything to make you more comfortable—"

"I thank you for your thoughtfulness, but I assure you I am quite all right."

"Very well. But if at any time you wish me to stop or ease the pace, please say so at once."

Catherine appreciated his concern, but she was determined to conquer her fear. Besides, with this stalwart man in the saddle and the birds singing them on their way in the fresh spring air, riding didn't seem so frightful. Even so, she had an idea that it might be well to occupy her mind with conversation.

So a few minutes later when a gentle mist fell on them through the lightly-leaved trees that arched over the road toward Canterbury, Catherine was reminded of a line from Chaucer. She began quoting, "'When the sweet rains of April fall, they of England to Canterbury wend.' If the rains in Chaucer's time were anything like yesterday, that is surely one of the greatest understatements in the language. Might as well call Noah's forty days and nights of deluge 'sweet rains.'"

"We are not far north of the Pilgrim's Way. The road Chaucer's pilgrims took is still in use," Philip said.

"As well as the road the murderers from Henry's court would have taken to slay Thomas à Becket?"

They talked for a while of the Archbishop whose martyrdom had turned Canterbury Cathedral into the most popular pilgrimage shrine of the Middle Ages and of Chaucer who had immortalized the journey. Then the topic seemed to pall, and Catherine sought another to occupy her mind. "Before our misadventures yesterday, I believe you were about to tell me of your curacy."

The back before her stiffened slightly, and she wondered how she could have given offense. Then the wide shoulders squared. "I don't know what I was about to tell you, but my brief curacy in Midhurst was a poor living. Yet it gave me the feeling of having come home. I thought it was the place God had prepared for me and that I would be there forever, serving Him and those people—belonging to them.

"Forever lasted almost two years. Until the second time the vicar, on his yearly round of visits to his several livings, heard that his curate was an enthusiast who preached a personal salvation from the pulpit, read the prayers with fervor, and had the effrontery to suggest that good Englishmen ask forgiveness for their sins.

"I was given the briefest of hearings and promptly replaced with a young Oxford graduate whom the vicar knew from his card parties."

His words were astringent, but Catherine, her sensitivities enhanced by the days of being so close to Philip and by having lost something dearly longed for herself, could hear between the lines. She knew that for the young man who had never truly belonged anywhere, those brief months had shown him that belonging was what he wanted most in life. She knew that they had provided an identity he lacked. And in the months since leaving Sussex, riding circuit, preaching with the band of Methodist ministers in fields or meetinghouses or wherever people would listen to him had satisfied his desire to share God's Word, but had in no way fulfilled his need to belong.

Indeed, she realized the desire had grown stronger, as she had witnessed at Rochester. Each time he would meet new people, new converts would come into the fold, and a new Society would be established; then Philip would have to ride away, leaving the people. He longed to be a part of their lives. He wished to marry them, to christen their children, to bury their dead, to attend to all the daily needs of a flock—not just come into their lives for a day or a week and then ride out again.

He told her of the day he had left Midhurst, how little Jennie Franks came early in the morning with a drooping bunch of bluebells crushed in her childish hand. Catherine could see him accepting them gravely as the tribute they were intended to be. She could even see the corn-silk pigtails shining in the sun as he patted Jennie's head and the single tear that slipped from the corner of her eye just before she ran for home.

Jennie had been the first of a long string that morning—old Mrs. Machin with a loaf of fresh bread for his journey, Mrs.

Patching with a crock of pickled peaches, the Timmon sisters with a hand-worked altar cloth—which he had never had a place to use.

As Philip's crisp sentences matched Jezreel's gait, Catherine could see that string of loyal, taciturn people, each expressing their love in a tangible way, but without words. Her arm tightened ever so slightly around his thin waist as they rode in silence for several minutes. Then Catherine reached back and patted the shiny chestnut rump of their mount. "Jezreel's a good horse. It won't tire her too much carrying us both?"

Sitting behind Philip, she heard rather than saw his rare smile. "It would take a great deal more than your extra weight at this sedate pace to tire Jezreel. She is an excellent animal. I fear you've uncovered my one extravagance, but I'll admit to a great fondness for horses. I can't remember a time when I wasn't hoarding a small pile of farthings for 'my horse.' At least my curacy lasted long enough that I was able to add a few more shillings to my cache and accept farmer Brock's generous offer of sale. I've no doubt the animal could have fetched twice his price at market. Even then she is an extravagance for me. But I salve my conscience with the argument that nothing can be more important to a circuit-riding preacher than a good mount."

Again Catherine stroked the satiny horsehair. Somehow the information that Philip was fond of horses increased her determination to conquer her fear. Each mile she rode became a small victory.

They reached Sittingbourne in time for a late afternoon meeting in a green, tree-encircled meadow near the town. Their timing was perfect as the meeting attracted the laborers leaving the fields for their evening meal. Soon a crowd of several hundred had gathered. The rain ceased, and a gentle setting sun shone on the field. Catherine hoped the service would not be disrupted.

But Philip had no more than read his text when a raucous

shout began on the far side of the field. Several men were driving an ox into the congregation. It was impossible to preach, so Ned jumped up beside Philip on the low stone wall and started a hymn. The efforts of the disorderly were in vain, for the great white ox ran round and round the field, one way and the other, eluding the men's sticks. At length he broke through the midst of his drivers and loped off toward the woods, leaving the worshipers rejoicing and praising God.

The next day the service at Faversham met worse resistance. The Society there had arranged for the preaching to take place at a little meetinghouse, but the vast numbers who thronged to the service quickly overflowed the room. They moved a small wooden table into a nearby field, and Philip mounted it to preach. He had no more than begun when a young man rushed in, cursing and swearing vehemently. The people near him tried to make him leave.

"No, Brothers. Let him stay if he will agree to be quiet," Philip said. The curses subsided to a mutter, and Philip resumed preaching.

"Repentance means an inward change, a change of mind from sin to holiness, but first we must know ourselves sinners, yea, guilty, helpless sinners."

"That's no way to talk to respectable folk, Parson!" The shout came from a young man dressed as a gentleman but with oddly bulging pockets.

Another young man nearby cried, "Why, if it isn't my old mate, Bradford White!" He threw out his arms and embraced his friend, bulging pockets and all. Even from where Catherine stood some distance away, the cracking sound was audible. And then the air reeked of rotten eggs.

The crowd drew back from the pungent sulphur odor; women put handkerchiefs over their noses, and the young man, dripping a sticky yellow trail, beat a hasty retreat.

Philip had only begun again on his topic when a mob of ruffians rushed upon the crowd with a bull they had been baiting. They tried to drive him in among the people, but the beast continually dodged to one side and then the other.

The drivers saw that their sticks and goads were not going to succeed with the beast, so they tied ropes around his neck and dragged him through the people. By this time the poor animal was tired and bloody from having been beaten and torn by dogs and men. When its tormenters thrust it in front of Philip, the greatest danger was that the bull might bloody the preacher's cassock. More than once Philip put his hand out to thrust the poor creature's head away so the blood would not drip on his clothes.

But in the end, the rabble almost won the day. They so pressed the bull against the small table Philip was standing on that it began to rock dangerously. The bull moved away, but it was driven again against the table. This time there was the sound of splintering wood, and Philip, going down with his table, fell toward the horns of the bull.

Strong arms of those nearby grabbed Philip just in time. Defeated, the rabble trudged off, leading their bewildered bull behind them.

Philip found a small rise of ground where he could stand to finish his sermon. Ned again led in singing, and groups began praying all around the field that still bore spatters of rancid egg yolk and red drops of bull blood. Then yet another shout interrupted the prayers. This came from the man who had interrupted the service with shouts and curses early on, but now his tone was far different. He declared that he had been a smuggler and had his swag bag with him to prove his claim. "But I'll never do that no more. I'm resolved to 'ave the Lord for my God."

Even the exhilaration of a victorious service overcoming such obstacles, however, wasn't enough to sustain Catherine's spirits when she saw the night's lodging that had been provided for them by the poverty-stricken Society members. Her room was little better than a cellar. She had to go down three steps and duck her head through the doorway to enter. The initial sensation in the room was one of chill dampness. After some time of restless tossing, however, she realized the major obstacle to comfort and sleep was the stuffiness of the cramped quarters. Throwing off her covers, she groped her way across the room to where she could see the dim light of the moon shining against the waxed paper covering the window. She tore the paper from one of the panes and took a deep gulp of the fresh, sweet air now blowing through the opening.

Back in her bed, huddled under her covers, a strange new thought came over Catherine. If the near drownings, stonings, and bull-tramplings, followed by fatigue, starvation, and discomfort of the past days were typical of itinerant preaching, she certainly did not envy the former Miss Sally Gwynne. With a flash of humor and amazement, Catherine found herself pitying the young woman who was newly wed to one of the most active circuit-riding preachers in the Methodist Society. As she drifted off to sleep in her cryptlike room, Catherine wondered if her bitter disappointment had, in truth, been a blessed deliverance.

It rained during the night, so on a washed and shining morning their little party set out on its last lap to Canterbury. Having accomplished one day of pillion riding without disaster, Catherine was now a little more at ease and still smiling over the Society member's parting admonition, "Don't get carried off by no Frenchies!" She sat in silence behind Philip as they rode through the bright green and gold morning.

She thought about her companion's silence—so still, so reticent—and yet she felt at peace in his company even without knowing him well. Perhaps it was because he was at peace with himself, if not with his circumstances.

After more time passed, she asked, "Have you always wanted to preach?" Her soft words matched the rhythm of Jezreel's hoofbeats.

"I had not thought to preach until I came really to understand the basis of my faith while at Cambridge. But from earliest memories I loved the church. Other boys at the foundling school complained about having to attend services, and at Cambridge my fellow gownsmen universally sneered at and slept through the twice-daily chapel. But I felt differently."

The taciturn Philip obviously found it difficult to speak of his feelings, and Catherine could only guess at all the words encompassed. Philip had loved the church for more reasons than the spiritual—the peace and beauty there satisfied an aesthetic need deep within him, which certainly nothing in the orphanage or his daily school life could fulfill. And something else, perhaps the sense of being near God—of belonging to Him—met his undefined need.

"The orphanage school was a good one?"

"An excellent school—strict and proper. Then I attended Cambridge as a Sizar." And again it was necessary for his listener to embroider between the spoken words to picture the training in cleanliness and manners far beyond what most boys of his class would have received at home and the well-grounded, if coldly formal, religious training to which his soul had responded with unaccustomed warmth. And at the university, this training supplied the discipline and humility required to fulfill his role as a servant to other students.

"At Cambridge you found assurance of your faith?"

He nodded. "Through reading the works of William Law. Long before that time, Law had been forced to leave Cambridge for refusing to take the oath of allegiance to George I. After I read his *Serious Call to a Devout and Holy Life*, I called on him for counsel."

"As did the Wesley brothers, I believe."

"Yes. Like so many others who read his excellent book and sought out its author, I found the assurance of my salvation." He had found there a place of belonging for his soul. But having his heart set on a heavenly home only increased his feelings of not belonging here. And grasping the warmth and comfort of that hitherto foreign word *home* only increased his undefined longing for an earthly home.

Suddenly the sound of pealing bells rang on the bright air, calling all who would to worship. Through the tree branches, past a field of new-sprouted grain, beyond the medieval stone wall and town buildings rose the triumphant square towers of Canterbury Cathedral.

As they rode along St. Peter's Place and then turned up High Street, the church grew before Catherine's fascinated gaze. She felt her excitement mounting. Here Christian worship had flourished since Roman times; here the Christian Queen Bertha and her ladies had faithfully prayed for the conversion of this island every day for forty years; here stood the Saxon font where Bertha's husband, the newly converted King Ethelbert of Kent, was baptized by St. Augustine on Whitsunday in 597, an act symbolizing the first official acceptance of Christianity in the Anglo-Saxon realms; here St. Augustine himself became the first Archbishop. Here was the mother church of English Christendom, the cradle of English Christianity.

And now Catherine would attend Sunday morning worship on the spot where Christian worship had been offered continuously for 1,150 years. They tethered the horses by the southwest porch and entered the magnificent perpendicular nave where Catherine's gaze was drawn up, up, up to the very heavens along with the prayers offered there daily to the glory of God. They took the seats the verger led them to in the choir, and Catherine thought of the Old Testament account of how the people under Solomon's direction had built the Temple of God. Here too at Canterbury the workmen had labored, as generation after generation of stone masons, glass-blowers, and wood-carvers plied their humble trades to express their faith.

Throughout the singing of the anthem, the praying of the collect, the reading of the Epistle and Gospel, the preaching of the sermon, the ministry of the sacrament, and the singing of the Gloria, Catherine kept thinking of how God had helped Solomon and all those in the Old and New Testaments to build and spread the faith, of how He had helped the Christians in England down through the ages. Surely He would help His people now who were doing His work. As she looked up the nave to the high altar and above to the ceiling with its pillars and arches spreading like a vast forest of trees with their branches entwined in prayer, she prayed that Philip would not be forced to leave his historic faith in order to minister. *Find him a place, Lord.* She breathed it over and over.

"Glory be to the Father and to the Son and to the Holy Ghost; as it was in the beginning, is now and ever shall be: world without end, amen." Catherine sang with the congregation and then knelt for the singing of the blessing.

After the service, Ned and Philip decided to climb the tower to the belfry to view Canterbury and the surrounding countryside. But Catherine preferred to make her own pilgrimage. She climbed a series of stairs to the highest level in the cathedral where for hundreds of years the shrine of St. Thomas had drawn the faithful. As she ascended each worn stone step, she took care to place her feet in the deepest of the hollows, stepping where centuries of devout travelers had worn the solid stone away with steps of devotion and penitence.

She was thankful for a faith that didn't rely for its assurance on such outward works, but she was also thankful for those faithful ones who were willing to do what they thought right. At the shrine she walked around the wide barren floor that had once supported Thomas à Becket's tomb. She remembered that the golden, gem-encrusted casket had been destroyed during the Reformation. Surely, Thomas himself would have preferred this powerful symbolism of the empty space left by a man's death. The thought moved her deeply. In a great cathedral of carved marble and jeweled stained-glass, what could better express the vacancy left by the death of a man who gave his life for his faith?

Thomas à Becket had built the cathedral with his death. His martyrdom had brought pilgrims from all over the world, and much of the splendor of architecture and decoration had come from the wealth brought by these pilgrims.

Suddenly overwhelmed, she whispered, "Thank You, Lord, that no matter how difficult it is for Philip and other Methodist ministers, they won't have to die as martyrs." They might be forced to preach in the fields, to live a life of itinerant hardship, even to sign the Act of Toleration and declare themselves dissenters, but at least there *was* an Act of Toleration. No longer were men put to death in England for their faith as St. Thomas was, or the Lollards, or any whose faith happened to disagree with the king's. King George II might have his faults, but he didn't behead those who disagreed with him.

Along the wall Catherine saw statues of great men of history kneeling in prayer—priests and bishops, as one would expect in a cathedral; but even more impressive, Catherine felt, were the generals, dukes, and ministers, the lords temporal who acknowledged their reliance on God as they made decisions and led armies that determined England's destiny.

She descended the stairs on the other side of the chapel, again feeling the swale in the stone made by both the great and the humble, in whose footsteps she walked. And she remembered a couplet John Wesley wrote after visiting a famous castle purported to be the most ancient building in England:

> A little pomp, a little sway,
> A sunbeam in a winter's day,
> Is all the great and mighty have
> Between the cradle and the grave.

Catherine, Edward, and Philip had just time to eat a light lunch before the service they were to hold for the Society John Wesley had founded and nurtured on his many visits to Canterbury. They left the city through the ancient Quenin Gate, and outside the wall they met a large number of Society members who had gathered to accompany them up the hill to St. Martin's Church.

Before they could reach the church, however, a crowd of rabble gathered, like flies to a honey sandwich. The troublemakers followed them up the hill through the grounds of St.

Augustine's ruined abbey, showering cups of water over the marchers. When that failed to dampen any spirits, they tossed lighted fireworks into the crowd. Fortunately, the water had wetted the ladies' skirts and caps and the men's coats so that no serious fires started. The procession speeded up, to the accompaniment of explosions and shrieks.

By the time they reached St. Martin's Church, the rabble had run out of weapons and lost interest. Undoubtedly the sight of several hundred soldiers in the congregation helped curb their enthusiasm. Canterbury hosted a major army garrison, situated as it was in a strategic position to guard the English Channel from invasion by England's ancient enemy, France. Indeed, since the recent French attempt to capture Minorca which, along with Gibraltar, gave England naval supremacy in the Mediterranean, Pitt's government was almost neurotic about a French attack. So of late the garrison numbers had been greatly increased. Wesley's services had always been well attended by red-coated soldiers, and many had been converted by his preaching.

The lusty male voices rang out as Edward led them in one of the hymns newly penned by Charles Wesley, "Oh, for a Heart to Praise My God." St. Martin's was far too small to hold all their hearers, but the square Saxon tower of stone and Roman brick made a backdrop like a high altar canopy, and the grave-covered hillside formed a natural amphitheater, with the fir trees spreading their branches overhead like the finest Gothic arches. Birdsong accompanied the singing, as more worshipers and curiosity-seekers made their way up the hill from town.

The crowd now settled down and entered wholeheartedly into the singing. Then they gave rapt attention to Philip's preaching. "If any of you lacks wisdom, let him ask God, who gives to all men generously . . ." Catherine thought of her own lack of wisdom and her own doubts. But instead of concentrating on the preacher's words, she found herself focusing on the preacher. The long nose with skin drawn tight over the cheekbones, the deep-set solemn eyes, the strong jaw line and squared-off chin—his features spoke of might and durability as clearly as the ancient stones around him. The preacher stretched out an arm, and a long, thin wrist bone extended beyond the white cuff of the shirt sleeve beneath his black cassock. Catherine found the gesture so appealing that she had to force her mind back to the words of Scripture Philip was quoting: "'I will instruct thee and teach thee in the way which thou shalt go; I will guide thee with mine eye . . .'"

Catherine prayed silently, *Father, please show me the way you want me to*—The rustle started so slowly she first thought it was the wind rising in the fir trees. Then it grew. Suddenly the disturbance moved through the whole congregation like wildfire. "Landed at Dover?" "Less than an hour's march from Canterbury?" "Burning the fields!" A woman shrieked, "Lord, have mercy on us!"

The soldiers came to attention as a sergeant barked out orders. Civilians milled in the way, but in the best order possible, soldiers assembled for command. And everywhere rose the cry, "The French have landed!" "The French!" "It's the French—they're coming!"

Imperturbable, Philip shouted, "Don't panic. Keep calm. Just move toward your homes quickly and in order. And look to God." But pandemonium reigned. Catherine watched the fleeing backs of people who moments ago had worshiped beside her.

"Do you think it's true?" she asked Ned. Her voice was calm, but her eyes were wide with apprehension.

"It's doubtful. Such alarms go around regularly, I'm told. More than likely the rumor was started by one of the rabble, since no army messenger arrived with a dispatch. In this part of Kent small children are taught obedience with the warning, 'And if you don't, the French will get you.'"

"But there *is* war on the continent these seven years past . . ." She hesitated, for to her "the French" meant Aunt

Nicola and a noisy family of cousins living on the Perronet family estate in Nyon; but France was also England's rival, and it was just possible . . .

Philip joined them. "All the more reason to suppose the French well occupied on the continent. But the fox is with the hens now—the story of an invasion will spread through the town, and tumult will reign for at least twenty-four hours. We may as well go on. There'll be no chance of holding another service for some time."

Back at the Chaucer Inn, Philip removed his cassock and replaced it with a black frock coat, close-fitting to the waist, with a flared skirt to knee level, its back and side vents making it comfortable for riding.

Each day's travel made Catherine miss her lost luggage more. She had purchased an ivory comb and a boar bristle brush and a few other items of absolute necessity, but chose to hold out until she reached Shoreham and her mother's dressmaker before replacing her wardrobe. She tied a full-length cotton apron over her gown to cover the worst of the spots and could only be thankful that the day of the accident she had been wearing the warmer of her two dresses and her long hooded mantle. Even if the rain returned, she would have some shelter. But that was her only comforting thought as they set out again on their journey. She had never traveled the road to Tunbridge Wells, the next town where a Society was awaiting them, but she knew it was a long ride and that the reception at the meetings along the way was unlikely to be friendly.

As they left Canterbury and rode into the lush green countryside of Kent, Catherine thought that surely this had to be the sweetest, greenest land God had ever smiled on. Fields of hops and wheat and vegetable gardens were beginning to green as April passed into May; fruit orchards showed promise of bloom; and the hawthorn tree, called the May tree by the poets, graced the landscape with its sweet spring blossoms. The sheep on the hillsides made Catherine think of the psalmist's words, "We are the sheep of His pasture." And here and there the pastoral scene was dotted with red brick tile-roofed farmhouses and round cone-roofed oast houses where the locally grown hops were dried for brewing.

They made one detour to spend the night at the farm owned by Vincent Perronet. The stone house was surrounded by rich, black soil and green pastures that fed the red-brown Guernsey cows. The land agent greeted the travelers warmly, and his wife served tea and parkin while Ned went over the account books. Catherine savored the heavy oatmeal spice cake sweetened with honey as she listened to Mrs. Adisham's gossip about the tenants and her own brood.

"Our Mary was the last to go. She married a ship's chandler over to Dover way. I'd like it right fine to go visit her when her first is born, but Adisham says he can't take me until after the harvest. And I says the child will like to be walking by then, and isn't it time he thought about taking it a little easier? His rheumatiz troubles him something fierce when the rains come on. But your father is the fairest of landlords, Miss Perronet, a right finer man to work for, there isn't."

When the refreshments were finished, Farmer Adisham conducted his guests on a tour around the farm. "They's good, hard-working tenants," he said pointing to a small cottage nestled in a clump of trees. "But you won't see much labor about today, not with the Maying." He indicated a group of milkmaids walking beside the road, boughs of pink-tinged hawthorn blossoms in their arms.

After taking leave of their guide, they rode through the village of Chartham. Suddenly the merry music of a fiddle and the sound of laughter came to their ears. Rounding the corner of a tavern, they saw the village green stretching before them. A maypole, fifty feet high, rose from the grass. Ribbons and garlands of flowers and greenery wound around the pole, the work of village young people shortly after sun-up that morning. And circling the pole danced a cluster of country revelers.

To one side sat the floral-crowned May Queen, the most beautiful girl in the village, chosen to represent summer and to preside over all the May celebrations. Near her the Jack-in-the-Green cavorted with a band of small children carrying flower-entwined hoops. He wore a heavy wicker cage completely covered with greenery so that only his eyes and feet were visible. On yet another part of the common, a band of Morris men in their white flower-and-ribbon-bedecked suits danced gaily to the rhythm of the bells attached to their ankles and the tune of the piper who led them.

Catherine's heart soared with delight at the beauty and carefree joy. How wonderful that England could celebrate May Day again. It was nearly a hundred years since the festival had been sternly outlawed by Cromwell's Puritans. Now it was again in full flower. She would have loved to spend the day there, but she knew they must go on.

With such happy scenes and the agreeable weather, the miles at first seemed to pass more quickly beneath their horses' plodding feet. But as mile after mile wore on, Catherine began to weary. The countryside was no less green and pleasant, but her capacity to appreciate it faded faster than the afternoon sun.

In all, it took five more days of wearisome pillion riding before they reached Tunbridge Wells. Catherine felt as if she had grown to Jezreel and wondered: if a mythological male with four horse's legs was a centaur, what was a female creature?

The hardest day was at Goudhurst. Catherine rose at four o'clock for private devotions; Philip held the first preaching service at five o'clock in a field. Wet with morning dew, Catherine was sure she and all the congregation would catch pneumonia. Then followed three more services throughout the day at neighboring villages, each with some share of rowdyism and of spiritual victory as well.

By that evening as they rode the last few miles to an inn, Catherine's head, shoulders, and back ached. She wondered if she'd ever feel good again. She did the only thing she could—

hang on and pray, "Help me to travel in Thy strength, O Lord. Thy strength which is made perfect in our weakness . . . and, O Lord, I am so weak."

Catherine was determined not to utter one word of complaint. And when Catherine Perronet was determined, she was very determined indeed.

She thought of Jesus sitting at the well of Samaria—"Jesus, therefore, being wearied with His journey . . ." And she prayed, "Yes, Lord, You do know how I feel. You were weary too." Some of the tenseness left her body, and before she knew it, she began singing Martin Luther's words: "Did we in our own strength confide, / Our striving would be losing, / Were not the right Man on our side, / The Man of God's own choosing. . . . Christ Jesus, it is He, . . . And He must win the battle."

Philip joined her on the last line. They were drawing near to an inn that promised nothing but poor food and a lumpy bed, but Catherine's spirits were revived.

As Philip followed Ned and Catherine into the inn, he suddenly realized that he was so tired he could hardly stand up. This had been one of the most demanding and draining days of his life. He was not unused to hard riding after little sleep, nor was he unaccustomed to facing large and hostile crowds; but he had never before had the additional burden—no, challenge—of responsibility for another. And although Edward was always nearby on Old Biggin, it was Philip who worried about Catherine's physical comfort and mental ease as she rode behind him.

In meetings he had always been concerned for the souls he spoke to and conscious of his responsibility to God. But over the past days, he had felt a new self-consciousness as he thought about Catherine being in the congregation. It disturbed him that it should be so, and the additional strain fatigued him.

In spite of the meanness of the inn, the landlord Crimpton

was able to provide a private parlor where the travelers could eat their brown bread, cabbage, and collops with eggs. As they sat near the fire that evening, Edward, as usual, bent over a book at a small table with a branched candelabra, leaving Catherine and Philip in a world of their own, talking softly by the fire. Perhaps because of their brief burst of duet that day, the conversation turned to hymns and hymn writers. Without giving any thought to her words, Catherine said, "Yes, I'm sure the beauty of Charles Wesley's hymns was the cause of much of my attraction—" She gave a small gasp as her hand flew to her mouth.

Philip leaned forward, his elbows on his knees, his level, solemn gaze focused on her. "That day we met at the Foundery, you had been praying in much agony of spirit."

She gave a tiny nod. "I had just heard of the marriage."

He nodded. "And I too."

"You too? . . . You mean, Sally?"

"She was very special. Of course I had no expectations . . ." He tried to keep his eyes free of any flicker of pain that might show how deep the wound had gone.

"So the refused curacy was not your only disappointment that day." Catherine put out her hand in a tentative gesture as if she would touch the creases at the corner of his sad eyes, then hesitated, and lowered her arm, her fingers just brushing the back of his hand.

But that brief touch, as light as a butterfly wing, was the most warming human contact he had known in a long time. The gentle friendliness of it went all through him.

They continued to sit for some time, the occasional crackling of a log the only sound in the room. Neither one moved, and yet it was as if they had drawn closer together.

At last Ned closed his book, blew out a guttering candle, stood, and stretched with noises that seemed raucous in the quiet of the room. "We must go to bed; we have a full day of riding to reach the Wells tomorrow."

As if to cover the telling intimacy of the quiet, Catherine

crossed to her brother with unaccustomed vivacity and gave him a good-night kiss upon the cheek. Ned, his arms still spread out in a stretch, enfolded her in a huge embrace. "Sleep well, Cath." He released her with a brotherly pat on the shoulder.

She turned in a flurry from Ned to Philip and became suddenly shy. She held out her hand. "Good night then." She fled from the room.

Philip was left alone in the suddenly empty parlor, trying to understand the strange emotion he felt. He hesitated to put a name on it since it seemed ludicrous, but . . . why should he feel jealousy at the closeness of brother and sister? What did such a scene have to do with him? Or was that the reason? He had never been part of such a scene.

5

*L*ate the next afternoon they arrived at Tunbridge Wells nestled in a valley of steep sandstone hills. The road into town led down the hill known as Mount Ephraim, the most fashionable residential section of the elegant city. Since the discovery of its mineral water wells in 1606, Tunbridge Wells had grown to be the chief resort of London intellectuals and was second only to Bath as the most popular watering place in England.

Sitting on their mounts, the three travelers watched elegantly clad strollers promenading beneath the grove of trees. The men were outfitted in coats of rich velvet and brocade, heavily embroidered on the wide cuffs turned up to the elbow. Their waistcoats displayed equally intricate needlework in silver and colored silks, with froths of lace at the neck and wrists. Most men wore braid or feather-trimmed tricorns atop their tie-back wigs or carefully powdered hair, but some coiffures were sufficiently complicated to make the wearing of a hat uncomfortable, so those gentlemen carried their hats under their arms.

And the powdered and pomaded ladies strolling on the arms of the gentlemen were dressed in sackback gowns of exquisite fabric fastened at the waist to reveal heavily embroidered stomachers, their V-shape meeting the embroidered petticoat flaring at the hips over an oblong hoop to emphasize the wearer's tiny waist. Triple flounces of lace finished the sleeves which ended at the elbow; lace caps showed beneath the wide-brimmed Bergere hats.

Catherine thought it one of the prettiest scenes she'd ever seen, and she felt a slight tinge of envy when she looked down at her own soiled clothes. She had acquired a strong fashion sense from her French grandmother, and although life in a vicarage had taught Catherine the vanity of worldliness, she didn't believe it honored God to look like a dowd. But after almost two weeks in her travel-worn gown, *dowd* was the only word to express how she felt in proximity to these exquisite creatures. After one elegant lady in a yellow ribbed-silk gown trimmed with metal lace and artificial flowers eyed her with raised brows, Catherine urged her companions to ride on. Ned and Philip, who always looked proper in their black cleric's coats with white Geneva bands at the neck and their neatly tied hair, could have little notion of how she felt.

The ride down the steep hill into town increased her discomfort as she tried to keep from leaning against Philip and at the same time craned her neck to see the unusual outcroppings of sandstone separating the fashionable houses built along the road.

At the foot of the hill they met, not a promenade of the fashionable, but a cluster of small boys and dogs chasing wildly after a runaway hoop. At first the scene amused Catherine, reminding her of similar scenes at Shoreham vicarage. But suddenly the speeding hoop veered into the roadway in front of them, and shouting boys and yapping dogs turned almost directly at Jezreel.

The startled horse skittered sharply sideways, rearing with a jerk. Catherine clutched for Philip's back, but already she had slipped beyond its grasp. With a cry, she fell to the ground.

Philip and Ned were beside her in a moment. Ned turned with a sharp command to send the boys on their way, and Philip knelt beside her. "Catherine, I'm so sorry. Are you hurt? I couldn't hold her steady. Catherine . . ."

Catherine looked at his distressed face, and a small trill of laughter broke from her. "It is a good thing you didn't hold her. By sidestepping, Jezreel managed to unload me in the only patch of long grass anywhere near this stony road. Very thoughtful of her!" And she drew one of his rare smiles which she had learned to cherish for their scarcity.

"Are you truly all right, Cath?" Ned asked.

"Truly. I wasn't the least terrified, beyond the quite natural fear of falling." She paused to consider. "I realize now that I haven't been afraid for days." With a wide smile she clasped her hands in gladness. "I am entirely recovered." And then she flung her arms out to express a relief beyond words.

Catherine had been a person of few fears. She knew a brief fear of the dark as a child, and she could still remember her father coming into her room, not hers alone, of course—one was never alone in a family of twelve—after the others were asleep. And if Father were gone, Ned would come with a simple good night, to let her know he was there and cared. Therefore, the fear hadn't lasted long.

And then there had been her one fearful experience in the woods, when at the age of twelve she had wandered too far in search of a blue jay and gotten lost. It was long after dark when she heard Ned calling, and the fear fell away as if the woods were lighted.

But her fear of horses had found no such happy ending, until today. She smiled at Philip, thinking how a fine horse was the one thing that invariably made his cool eyes glow dark and warm. And now she was free of the fear that prevented her from sharing this interest with her new friend. Just as with the help of others the small Catherine had conquered her fear of the dark and of being lost in the woods, so she had conquered her fear of horses—with the help of Philip and of God. The God, who at least in this instance, did indeed seem to be still guiding her way.

Philip remounted, and Ned gave her a leg up to her pillion seat. Then, in spite of the increased dowdiness the dark grass stains added to her dress, Catherine Perronet rode in triumph through Tunbridge Wells.

The accommodations here were unlike any others they had experienced on the journey, or were likely to on any itinerant preaching tour. The town had changed remarkably since the time of Charles I when his queen, Henrietta Maria, arrived with her court to take the spa waters and had to camp in tents on the common because so few houses or public inns had yet been built.

"Ned, are you quite sure we can afford this?" Catherine was looking at the brocade and gilt of the Louis XV furniture in the parlor, but her mind was on Philip's slim purse.

"Perhaps—," Ned began, but was interrupted by a flurry of activity as they were caught between a party arriving at the door and the landlord with the entire staff of the inn rushing to greet the new arrivals alighting from their elegant coroneted coach. At the center of the maelstrom was a tiny, sharp-featured woman, her graying brown hair tucked firmly inside a cap of the finest white linen, the severe plainness of her Spitalfields silk gown in no way hiding the excellent quality of the fabric or workmanship.

"Welcome, My Lady. My humble establishment is yours, and I your most devoted servant." The innkeeper bowed so deeply it seemed for a moment he would overbalance and fall on his nose.

The lady began giving orders for the dispatching of her entourage and possessions, all of which were carried out with the greatest alacrity. When the room had been fairly cleared of servants, trunks, and portmanteaux, the noble lady sighted the three travelers who watched from a corner of the room. "Edward Perronet. You may present yourself."

Edward stepped forward and made his bow. "Lady

Huntingdon, may I beg leave to present my sister and our companion?"

The lady inclined her head.

"Lady Huntingdon, my sister, Miss Catherine Perronet, and our friend, the Reverend Philip Ferrar."

"Ah. I recall now, Mr. Ferrar. John Wesley told me you were preaching in this area. I shall hear more of your work. You will join me for dinner." Her gaze included the three of them; then she turned to the hovering innkeeper. "You will provide accommodations for my friends on my account also." She turned back to Ned. "I dine at seven o'clock." Her exit from the room was as straightforward as a military march, the small train on her dress following in obedient folds.

The second assistant to the landlord approached the three still standing in the center of the floor. "May I show you to your rooms?"

In her room a dismayed Catherine surveyed her dress. Her only comfort was that she had washed and pressed her lawn fichu, so she would have a fresh covering around the neckline of her bodice. But what the countess would say to her soiled skirt, Catherine quailed to consider. She heated her curling iron over a candle and framed her face with small round curls, then drew the remainder of her hair into a bun on the top of her head, to be covered by her ruffled lawn cap.

It was also fortunate that when she entered the countess's private parlor with Ned and Philip at the commanded hour, the shadows in the candle-lit room concealed the most disreputable of her travel stains. And, as always, Catherine's dignified carriage overshadowed anything she wore.

The countess introduced her traveling companion, her aunt, Lady Fanny Shirley, and directed her servants to set the first course. The roast pork with turnips suited milady's taste, but the butter pond pudding would not do. "My constitution cannot abide this. Remove it at once." A servant hurried forward. "There is enough butter in that to have drowned the pig, had it been alive. I have come to the Wells to have my health restored, not further endangered by rich puddings."

The offending dish was hastily removed and replaced by jugged pigeons with pease and onions. "I more frequently take the waters at Bath," Lady Huntingdon explained to her guests, "but my condition did not respond well to my last visit there, so my physician recommended the chalybeate spring here. You must accompany me in the morning, Miss Perronet. You look entirely too peaked. You want fortifying. You know, after Dudley Lord North discovered these springs early last century, he was miraculously cured from a lingering consumptive disorder."

The other diners made appropriate responses to her monologue. Then she focused on Philip sitting on her left. "Young man, you are entirely too thin. You must eat more." She carved a thick slice of pork and placed it on his plate. "Preaching the Word of God requires stamina. You must fortify yourself physically as well as spiritually for the slings and arrows of the enemy. Have your services met with success?"

Philip responded that there had been many victories in spite of the resistance of the rabble. He was about to elaborate when the countess went on. "This is a benighted area. The season is just beginning, but already you shall see the luminaries of society on the promenade. Dr. Johnson, David Garrick, Mr. Pitt—they come here regularly now that that self-appointed potentate from Bath has undertaken to establish his routines of vice here. I speak, of course, of Beau Nash. Coffee houses, balls, concerts, gambling rooms—that is what Tunbridge Wells offers to kill the souls of those who would drink her waters for the health of their bodies."

The countess placed a pigeon and another turnip on Philip's plate. "I thank God that you have come to do battle with the evil one in his very stronghold. But it will not be easy. Not that we are ever to expect the way of our Lord to be easy, of course. But the only established church in the district is the

Chapel-of-Ease, dedicated to King Charles the Martyr, and it is little attended and is closed altogether between the seasons.

"When I was here with my chaplain, Mr. Madan, he was not allowed to preach in the Chapel-of-Ease because of his evangelical beliefs, even though, of course, he is fully ordained and a most godly man. Mount Sion, the Presbyterian place of worship, was put at his disposal; but such a man is not a dissenter and must not be forced from his own church."

All eating at the table had stopped as the countess's guests gave attention to her monologue. She paused to regard Philip. "Eat, sir. Did I not tell you to?" Philip obediently picked up his fork as the countess continued.

"Mr. Wesley also attended me here once. The Presbyterian place was freely lent for his use, but it was insufficient to contain the numbers who wished to hear. He addressed the assembled multitudes in the open air. This was a new and extraordinary occurrence at Tunbridge Wells, and it created no small stir.

"I have been forced to travel without a chaplain this time, Mr. Madan having fallen ill with an ague and Mr. Whitefield not yet recovered from his latest journey to America. But God, in His never-failing graciousness, has provided. You shall preach for me, sir."

Philip inclined his head in obedient compliance.

"Tomorrow after we take the waters, I shall inspect the subscription list at the assembly rooms to learn who is in town and draw my list. Fanny," and she turned to her aunt, "you shall send invitations to a drawing room."

"Yes, indeed, Selina," Lady Shirley replied.

"Sir Thomas I'Anson shall open his home for me again as he did when last Mr. Madan preached here."

"Yes, indeed, Selina."

The servants entered to remove the dishes. "Nothing sweet," the countess directed. "You may set a cheddar cheese and some nuts, and perhaps dried apricots if they're nice."

"Yes, Milady, very nice indeed."

She looked at Philip. "And a dish of sweet whey for this young man and the other young people. But no nutmeg. My physician warns me it is most harmful to the constitution."

Catherine quickly raised her napkin to her mouth to cover a smile. They obediently ate the milk junket with sugar and cream, flavored with rosewater but no nutmeg.

Later when the party was sitting at ease around the room sipping cups of finest Hyson tea, taken with milk to lessen its stimulating effect, Catherine confided to Lady Fanny Shirley, "My portmanteau was lost in a flood. I fear I have nothing appropriate even for drinking the waters in polite company, let alone attending a drawing room in the home of Sir Thomas I'Anson."

"The waters are drunk in dishabille. Have you no morning robe?" Lady Shirley asked in her soft voice.

Catherine wanted to laugh, but she was afraid the countess would frown on such levity in her parlor where she now engaged Ned and Philip in theological conversation on her strictly-held Calvinist tenets. "Alas, no closer than Greenwich," Catherine said. "One's needs are quite simple on a preaching circuit."

"Yes, I can guess they might be. You are to be commended for your courage in making such a journey. Although I am aware many women do so, I know I should never attempt it. Why, I've heard that Mrs. Murray even attended Mr. Wesley into Ireland." Lady Shirley emphasized her words with a small shudder. "But as to your wardrobe, I fancy we can contrive something. You are much taller than I, but perhaps we could let down a petticoat and gather up the overskirt into puffs in the shepherdess style. It was quite the rage when last we were in London and would look very charming on you—if Selina approves," she added hastily.

Selina approved. So the next day Catherine appeared on the Pantiles in a charming sprigged muslin dress worn shepherdess-style over a fashionably short petticoat. Lady Fanny Shirley had even been able to produce new blue ribbons for Catherine's wide straw hat. Fanny had at first suggested pink, but

Catherine did not feel that was the most flattering color for her dark complexion, and so was delighted with the light blue.

Catherine and her escorts entered the colonnaded row of shops shaded by lime trees along one side of the promenade— the heart of Tunbridge Wells. There a large crowd of the fashionable gathered every morning around the chalybeate spring at the entrance to the square. And, indeed, they were in dishabille, as Lady Fanny had predicted. The men wore long damask dressing gowns which swept the paving tiles, or the shorter banyon, cut similar to a dress coat with flared skirts, but with the hem ending well below the knees. All the men were wigless, covering their shaved heads either with caps of fabric matching their dressing gowns or with the more fashionable turbans. The women wore simple muslin saques, most of them with long, elegantly embroidered white muslin aprons.

A small group of musicians entertained the visitors as they waited for the dipper to ladle their glass of water from her sunken stall beneath the colonnade. The dipper's appointment, by legal act, was the gift of the Lord of Rusthall Manor, owner of the area. The small sum Edward paid her for their glasses was not for the water but for her service.

Catherine took the glass from her brother and sipped the slightly yellow liquid. "Fah, it tastes like rust."

"Iron water," Ned agreed. "From the forge of St. Dunstan."

Catherine returned her glass to the dipper. "What are you talking about, Ned?" She placed her hand lightly on her brother's arm and smiled at Philip on the other side of her as they strolled up the shaded promenade.

"It's the source of the amazing properties of the water," Ned replied. "In the tenth century, St. Dunstan had a forge nearby. He was visited there one day by a most seductive young lady whom the saint immediately recognized as the devil. The holy man seized a pair of tongs from the fire and gripped the devil by the nose. Whereupon the devil plunged his face into the cooling waters of the spring, thereby imparting to them forever their distinctive metallic tang."

Catherine smiled at her brother's story and then looked up at Philip, catching one of his brief smiles—which sometimes made her want to cry.

They went up the steps onto the Upper Walk and strolled past houses and shops fronted by rows of Italianate columns, past a general store, the Musick Gallery, the Assembly Rooms where later in the day Beau Nash would preside over the gaming tables, coffee houses filled with patrons bearing the latest gossip, and booksellers, where already a few who had taken their water early were gathering to pen letters or the "water poetry" so popular in the town.

At the end of the walk they turned and left the colonnade for the more open promenade under the lime trees, walking on the flat paving tiles that gave the area its name. They had almost returned the length of the Pantiles to the dipper's stall when a short rotund man in a full-bottomed wig and embroidered red damask coat puffed up the avenue toward them.

"Sirs and Madam," he punctuated each word by tapping on the tiles with his walking stick, "I have the honor of being Squire Penshurst."

Apparently their polite replies to this information did not fulfill his expectations. "Of Penshurst Hall," he added with an additional tap. "I am the local magistrate."

As Catherine wondered if they were to congratulate him upon this achievement, he drew from his pocket a large piece of parchment with an official seal attached to it. "It has come to my attention that you have held irregular preaching services in this vicinity, and as the duly sworn representative of His Majesty's law, it is my duty to inform you that we shall permit no such activities in Tunbridge Wells."

"Sir, it is–" Ned began, but got no further as a small figure in a large white cap took command.

"Good morning, Squire Penshurst. I see you have met my

friends Mr. and Miss Perronet and Mr. Ferrar. I shall present them at a drawing room I am holding at Sir Thomas I'Anson's home tomorrow night." The round figure in the cherry coat put the warrant back into his pocket and bobbed a bow of assent to Her Ladyship. "I shall expect to see you there, Squire."

And, indeed, Squire Penshurst was among the elegant assembly that filled the drawing room in Sir I'Anson's Palladian home atop fashionable Mount Ephraim. The Countess of Huntingdon presided as hostess and made the introductions. "Lady Lincoln and Baroness Banks, may I present our speaker for the evening, the Reverend Philip Ferrar."

The baroness extended her hand. "How do you do? Are you connected to the Yorkshire Ferrars, sir?"

Philip bowed over the white hand. "I am from London, My Lady."

Observing from across the room, Catherine gave a grateful thought to the orphanage matron's careful drilling in manners that could teach a foundling to be at ease in this exalted company.

"... the Duchess of Richmond ..." The countess continued her tour of introduction around the room and then took a seat in the center as Sir Thomas's liveried servants handed round refreshments.

"Mr. Loggan." She signaled a powdered gentleman in a suit of Genoa velvet with a gold-tissue brocaded waistcoat to take the seat beside her. "I viewed your paintings in London."

"Indeed, I am honored, My Lady."

"Charming. Quite charming. You have an excellent eye. But you must avoid an overuse of too bold colors. You will get nowhere by shocking refined tastes."

"I thank you for your condescension in noticing me, My Lady."

"It is well that you came tonight. You did not attend when Mr. Madan spoke."

"Indeed, My Lady, I was not in Tunbridge Wells at the time."

"Very careless of you, Loggan. You must take more care for your soul. Mr. Madan exhorted all to seek the Lord while He may be found. Whilst Mr. Madan was offering that gracious invitation of our Lord, 'Come unto Me, all ye that are labor and are heavy laden,' a man in the congregation dropped down and instantly expired."

Mr. Loggan shook out the lace frill at his wrist. "Egad, that must have caused a sensation."

"Indeed, so strong and general an influence on a congregation I seldom remember seeing. Many were melted to tears and seemed resolved to fly from the wrath to come."

"Very understandable."

The company having finished their refreshments, the countess called for the general attention of her guests and introduced Edward and Catherine who were to present a number by the greatest hymn-writer of their day, Mr. Charles Wesley. With her usual grave solemnity Catherine took her seat at the harpsichord and after a few sharp, clear chords, blended her voice with her brother's: "Love divine, all loves excelling, / Joy of heav'n to earth come down; . . . Jesus, Thou art all compassion, / Pure, unbounded love Thou art; / Visit us with Thy salvation, / Enter ev'ry trembling heart."

At the conclusion of the song the countess introduced Philip, and Catherine sent him a small smile of encouragement, knowing this audience could be far more daunting than any fireworks-throwing or bull-baiting rabble. Philip stood at the end of the room, his silver-blond hair and white bands glowing like lights at the top of his tall, black-clad figure. With perfect self-possession he spoke to the distinguished assemblage on the text, "The fear of the Lord is the beginning of wisdom." And every word rang absolutely true because spoken by a man whose relationship with Christ was more than head knowledge. He had true fear of the Lord based on reverential awe of His love and greatness.

Catherine watched as Philip spoke in the elegant drawing

room, and she admired how he was carrying everything off. Whatever inward struggles he experienced, he was neither awkward nor exuberant. He brought to the situation the same quiet detachment he had shown in all other occasions; and now, with the full glare of the most elegant nobility turned upon him, his solemn grace was as perfect as any to the manor born. Amazing in one who had been essentially on his own since childhood. God had given this man a natural excellence that needed no other guidance than His grace.

At the end of the sermon many appeared genuinely moved. It seemed truly that "Those who came to scoff, remained to pray," as Wesley had reported of a similar meeting. "I am moved to consider what you say." The artist Loggan shook Philip's hand. "I would hear more of this."

The countess was delighted. When the last guest had departed, she turned to her speaker and musicians. "A remarkable service. Many were cut to the heart. Truly God was in our midst to wound and to heal. Such happy indications of God's approval induce me to hope that He will smile on my humble efforts. I mean to take up the sword for the glory of His great name and the good of the people of this place. Today has given me assurance that He will ultimately crown my efforts with distinguished and lasting success."

She walked the length of the room with her rapid steps and then sat on a straight chair, her back ramrod, her small, pointed chin forward. "Perhaps I shall build a residence here on Mount Ephraim that I might work more among these people. But I am forever conscious that every effort is impotent without God's almighty aid. I cry continually to Him for wisdom and strength. What am I, that He should condescend to make me instrumental in communicating any good to others? Is it not a sobering thought? I am humbled in the dust before Him. It is the Lord, *the Lord Himself* that has done the work. The treasure is in an earthen vessel, but the excellency of the power is of God *only.*"

She sat for a moment with her head bowed. Then suddenly

the head jerked up, and the dark, bright eyes snapped. "Miss Perronet, I do not like you riding pillion across the countryside. It isn't ladylike. I understand the gentlemen must go on tomorrow, but you will remain here with me, and I shall return you to London at the end of the month."

"Your Ladyship, I thank you for your concern. But my father expects me. I cannot disappoint him."

The countess blinked as if she could not take in disagreement with her plans. Her thin cheeks became even thinner, and for a moment Catherine feared her response. Then the countess spoke. "Fine man, your father. Perhaps the most heavenly minded man I know. Give him my regards."

*T*he next morning Catherine hoped that her bold behavior had not placed her in the countess's bad graces, but the ride through the glorious May morning assured her she had made the right decision. The road led between ferns carpeting the incline on both sides of the path and across little streams meandering through spinneys of white-barked birches. Birds sang from hedgerows laced with blossoms. Masses of purple and yellow wildflowers colored the fields, and wild daisies smaller than farthings grew from the shortest of stems.

"Philip, pray stop a moment. I should like to collect some samples for my wildflower book."

He pulled Jezreel to a halt and helped Catherine dismount. "You don't have this variety in your collection?"

"Not this particular shade of lavender." Her long fingers spread the leaves aside and pinched the stems to gather a small nosegay. "One of the things I most look forward to in being at Shoreham again is walking in my dear woods."

As they rode further into Catherine's native corner of Kent, she recognized a growing tranquility and felt a new contentment in being with Philip. They could ride for miles with only the briefest of comments on the scenery. Then quite suddenly one of them would begin a conversation, and they would talk without pause for an equal number of miles. Either way, Catherine found a repose she had never known in the companionship of another. And one of the chief gratifications was her certainty that Philip, who had such need of fellowship, found equal tranquility in her company.

And whether they were discussing a deep spiritual truth, the meaning of a poem she had read lately, or merely a commonplace observation, Catherine felt she had never been listened to so totally. Philip's capacity for giving his absolute attention was one of his most endearing charms. Even though she sat behind him, obliged to talk to the back of his head, there would come the little nod that told her he was listening. And for all his customary silence, his mind was extraordinarily active. Whenever he made a comment, it was incisive and to the point but always spoken with a characteristic gentleness.

With the hours passing so pleasantly, it seemed impossible that evening shadows should already be lengthening, but then the pathway through thick woods curved sharply, and Catherine knew they were nearly home. "Whenever I'm away, this is how I think of Shoreham—buried under the trees, so green and protected." Another curve in the path, and she saw ahead of her the dearly loved golden stone vicarage with its high curving wall around the large garden where Charity Perronet managed to keep flowers blooming from spring to autumn.

The many wings and gables of the house showed where it had been built onto through the centuries—first the low, gray rock two-room structure; then a red brick wing added at the same time the square Norman tower was put on the church; and now the lovely golden Georgian wing with the curving fanlight over the door. A symphony of familiar sounds sang Catherine's welcome home—birds twittering in the lime trees, chickens clucking from the henhouse, laughter from the inn around the corner, and the voices of children in the vicarage yard.

Then sixteen-year-old John saw the travelers approach. He

gave a shout that brought family and servants running to meet them. It was Catherine's first visit home since she had left to work for the Society in London, and now she wondered how she had managed to stay away so long. Her mother, wisps of graying hair escaping from her cap, engulfed them each in her comfortable embrace and warm smile. Vincent, his full-bottomed wig slightly askew, greeted them more quietly but no less warmly, his pleasure shining from his kindly eyes. And Damaris, Henry, William, Philothea, Thomas, and John all gathered around to welcome them.

"Betsy, we shall be three more at dinner. Come in, my dears. You know your rooms. Philip, Ned will show you. I'm sure you'll want to wash. Philly, you and Tom take cans of hot water up for them." Charity Perronet managed to direct the entire household without ever raising her voice.

All was orderly bustle when they gathered again in the dining room a short time later. Catherine noted Philip's pause at the door; he hung back as if not sure of his place. Only the slightest tightening of his straight mouth showed his nervousness; but as he stood aloof, Catherine could see him as he must have been at the orphanage, watching the others, but never fully part of them. Such a contrast to her own family, with a dozen noisy siblings all belonging to each other. Their eyes met, and Catherine smiled to let him know she welcomed him as part of the family.

When they had all found a place at the table, Vincent stood and offered grace, remembering the needs of the parish, mentioning each one of his children by name, and including Philip as well. By the time he concluded with a doxology the roast joint in front of him had cooled considerably, but not the diners' appetites.

Vincent carved the roast while Charity served the potted venison. Dishes of currant suet pudding and boiled parsnips with carrots were passed.

"Well, Damaris, are you still the mainstay of the Shoreham

Methodists?" Edward asked his maiden sister, who had elected to live at home and take charge of the Society work there.

"It continues to grow remarkably, Ned. We hold preaching in Father's kitchen every Friday night, but we shall soon outgrow even that room."

"One of Damaris's special tasks is seeing to the care of itinerant preachers when they are in the area; so if you find any lack in the hospitality, Philip, you must apply to her." The gentle Vincent spoke in a teasing manner, but his pride in his daughter's work showed in his eyes.

"Quite right for the daughter of the man who is often called the Archbishop of Methodism, Father," Ned said.

"And what of your preaching tour, Son? Have you met much resistance?"

Edward recounted some of their hardships at the hands of the rabble. Vincent shook his head. "So much of that could be avoided if only our preachers were allowed to use the church buildings."

Edward suddenly struck the table as if he had just come to a hard decision. "As we are all family here, I shall speak my mind boldly on a matter to which I have given considerable thought." An unusual cutting edge to his voice made Catherine hold her breath. She had noted his sometimes brooding quiet on the trip and knew that, although he was the kindest of brothers to her, he was capable of being hotheaded and sharp-tongued.

"We must give thought to separation."

"Edward!" Charity's voice was the first to break the shocked silence. "And your father a vicar of the Church of England these past thirty years, twenty-one of them right here in this very church. And you and your brother Charl ordained priests! How can you say such a thing?"

"I am sorry, Mother. But I believe we will come to it. Our brother Charl means to bring it up at the next conference. We should grant license to our own ministers to serve the sacraments."

"You are thinking of becoming a nonjuror, Son?" Vincent asked in his quiet voice.

"I don't know, Father. I can see that I spoke in haste, especially in front of my younger brothers and sister, but the problem is serious, indeed. Philip here is one of the finest men I've ever heard preach; must he spend his life in a cow pasture? He was dismissed from his curacy for enthusiasm and has been without a post these two years, although he has made frequent application. Something must be done. A dissenting chapel must be better than no place at all!" In spite of himself, his voice rose to an impassioned pitch.

"I would remind you, Son, that our Lord had nowhere to lay His sacred head. And His Sermon on the Mount was a pretty remarkable precedent of field preaching. When John Wesley was last here, he told me of the huge multitude he preached to in Moorfields. For usefulness, there is none comparable to field preaching, he said. What building except St. Paul's Church could contain such a large congregation as a field? One can command thrice the number in the open air. And do you not feel the convicting, convincing power of God at work among the people in the fields?"

Edward agreed that was true.

"Then, my Son, do not despise the means which our Lord hath put at your hand. I believe one hindrance of the work of God in York has been the neglect of field preaching; and I am apt to think that many of the hearers at your meetings have scarcely ever heard a Methodist before, or perhaps any other preacher. What but field preaching could reach these poor sinners? Are not their souls also precious in the sight of God?"

"Your reasoned words are a help to me. I shall attempt to control my impatience, Father. But I confess to feeling a shadow of bitterness over the situation at times."

"Oh, no, no, my Son. Pray earnestly for the grubbing out of all roots of bitterness. You must replace them with love. Love is all."

There was a knock at the door, and Betsy hurried from the kitchen to answer it. "It's Mr. Claygate, sir. Come for the Bible reading. I 'ad 'im sit in the parlor."

"You still hold your nightly Bible readings, Father?" Catherine asked.

"Indeed, Daughter. But I have put the hour back to seven. And a good thing too, or we should have missed this stimulating conversation tonight. Never fear to speak to your family of what concerns your heart, my children." Vincent rose. "Now, let us go to prayers."

The large vicarage parlor was crowded as family, servants, and parishioners gathered for nightly Bible reading and prayers. And Catherine was sure that, in spite of all that had been said in favor of field preaching, one of the prayers Philip would offer would still be for the Lord to open the way to a parish of his own. She too prayed that that petition would be granted.

The next morning being Sunday, the village bell-ringers put to full use the eight bells in the Shoreham parish church of St. Peter and St. Paul. Catherine entered with the other villagers through the porch, which had been built in the fifteenth century from the root of a huge upended oak. She took her seat on the second pew where she had worshiped since she was three years old.

As she sang the familiar hymns, listened to the lessons, and knelt for prayers with these people she had grown up among, the conflicts and struggles of the past weeks seemed to slip away. It seemed impossible that there could be such disturbances in God's world. The collect for that fifth Sunday after Easter seemed to hold the key to all problems:

O Lord, from whom all good things do come; Grant to us thy humble servants, that by Thy holy inspiration, we may think those things that be good, and by Thy merciful guiding may perform the same; through our Lord Jesus Christ, amen.

While her father preached, she let her eyes wander over the dear church. She had always loved the dark wood-vaulted ceiling. One of her earliest memories was of peeking up at it when her eyes should have been closed in prayer, counting the golden stars embedded in the wood. One time Ned caught her at her game and reprimanded her later—the stars weren't there to be counted; they were to serve as reminders of the infinity of God, and counting them would spoil everything.

She disagreed, however. One warm Saturday afternoon when the church was empty, she slipped into its lovely, cool stone interior, lay right down on the flagged floor, and began counting. But she kept getting confused and having to start all over again. In the end she fell asleep and received a dreadful scolding for not helping Elizabeth peel the potatoes for supper.

Later that afternoon she recounted the memory to Philip. "I am surprised to hear of the scolding. It seems to me that your family never raises their voices to one another."

"Well, perhaps we only do so in a very restrained way. And then we always say we are sorry as soon as the moment has passed."

They crossed the vicarage garden back to the church. Catherine had volunteered to take the children's service for her father if Philip would help her, which he readily agreed to do. She turned to him now against the backdrop of the rambling vicarage and its riotous garden, with their talk of her happy, loving family hanging in the air. She saw him standing there, tall and thin in his dark suit, and thought how austere his life had been.

When she looked at him a short time later as he explained the story of the Good Samaritan to the village children, she saw his face aglow as it was only when he preached. A great wave of feeling washed over her; it was a feeling she couldn't identify but that she wanted to clasp to her, in spite of the ache it brought with it.

It was to be a day of strange feelings for Catherine. When her family gathered around the parlor fireplace after Evensong,

Philip was the last to enter. Again he paused just outside the doorway, and she saw him alone, as she was accustomed to thinking of him. Then he entered and sat down and was suddenly part of the family when young Thomas climbed on his lap and Philothea sat so close as to be leaning on him. It was as if in this rural vicarage Philip Ferrar had dropped into place.

When they had their fill of visiting and cold meats, the family slowly straggled off to bed. Vincent and Charity were the last to leave them. "Thank you for giving us that fine sermon at Evensong. You can come preach for me anytime," Vincent said to Philip. Then he kissed his daughter good night.

Charity also kissed Catherine. "We shall begin our parish visits at nine o'clock in the morning. Old Mrs. Claygate is very poorly, and the Ightham children weren't at the children's service today, and—oh, well, there are so many. My dear, it will be so good to have you visiting with me."

Then Philip and Catherine had the fireside all to themselves. For the moment it seemed as if this parish where they were preaching, teaching, and visiting the sick and needy was their own, as Midhurst must have been for Philip. Catherine poured out a final cup of tea for her companion who sat with his feet up on the hob. The very "everydayness" of it made her feel as if she were a little girl playing house. But she longed for the reality.

It seemed to Catherine that this return to her home brought constant revelations and understandings as she accompanied her mother the next morning. She watched as Charity dealt with the needs of the people of the parish. Gradually, it was as if she were watching a new person—or perhaps, for the first time, a real person in the place of the generalized, comfortable image of "mother." She had always seen her mother as an extension of her father, a woman who found her being in her many children as she directed the household to revolve around

Vincent. Father's meals were always on time, composed of his favorite foods, prepared the way he liked them; Father's study hours were always to be undisturbed by children, parishioners, or other clergymen; Father's work must receive her help—visiting the sick, distributing charity from the poor box, arranging flowers on the altar; and Father's children must always be orderly, clean, well-behaved, respectful. Not that Vincent Perronet was a demanding tyrant—a kinder, softer-spoken soul couldn't be imagined. But this was the natural order of things.

It had given Catherine's childhood a focus, a pattern, a security. Father was the center of the household and the parish, just as John Wesley was the center of the Methodist Society, the King was the center of England, and God was the center of the universe. But now Catherine realized how important a focus her mother was for her own sake—the love and warmth and comfort she shared unstintingly with her twelve children and the three hundred souls in their parish.

Charity Perronet was far more than an extension of her husband; she was a person who chose to be a helpmeet and to fulfill Christ's call to servanthood. And for the first time in her life, Catherine truly saw her mother—an insight a bit like the first time an infant sees the world outside. And with it came a new love and appreciation for her mother.

But most important, she felt a desire to carry on in her mother's tradition of love and service. She would be the person God created her to be, serving out of love—if only God would show her how and where. "O God," she prayed, "surely You would not have given me this desire if You did not have a place for me to use it."

The final stop for mother and daughter was in the center of the village where the Misses Simpson plied their expert needles in the little Tudor shop that was also their home. With her mother's help and the fluttery attendance of the elder Miss Simpson, Catherine looked through the pattern cards and fabrics and chose an open gown to be made from dimity of simple texture but lively pattern, with little bouquets of scattered flowers. The flowers, stomacher, and petticoat reflected Catherine's love of nature as she selected a clear blue like the sky and the bluebells that grew in the woods around Shoreham in the spring.

"You have chosen well, my dear," Charity told her. "Buying good fabric is never extravagant because it lasts so much longer. Sometimes I buy French fabric, but only from established shops—one must be careful not to support the runners by buying smuggled products. This lace will make a lovely trimming for the neckline and sleeve flounces."

Catherine hesitated. The lace her mother held was lovely, but many Society members avoided such worldliness. She had never considered removing it from the dresses she already owned, but wondered about the propriety of ordering it on a new gown.

"There can be nothing displeasing to God in a bit of lace, my dear. Even your father's best surplice has a trim of lace on it." Charity handed the lace to the dressmaker at Catherine's nod. "And now we must hurry home for tea. I told Betsy to make a special treat."

But even the veiled hint from her mother and the broad smiles from her siblings did nothing to prod Catherine's suspicions—not until she had been served a thick slice of seed cake with a dish of sweet tea. Philothea burst out between giggles, "She's forgotten, hasn't she? Cath, don't you truly know what day this is?"

Catherine looked puzzled. "No, I've given it no thought. I lost all account of the days on our travels. It must be May . . . oh, is it truly the twelfth of May? My birthday?"

She had to set her tea dish aside very quickly before she was engulfed in congratulatory hugs and birthday kisses.

"And you too, Philip, you must wish Cath happiness." Philly led their guest forward.

"Felicitations, Catherine."

"Oh, fah! It won't do if you don't kiss her. Don't be so shy, Philip." Philothea gave him a sisterly shove that almost landed his lanky form in Catherine's lap.

He bent over gravely, picked up her hand, and brushed it with his lips. "Many happy returns." And suddenly Catherine felt they would be.

Ten-year-old Philothea applauded the performance of the guest she had adopted wholeheartedly as her personal property. "Well done! And when is your birthday, Philip?"

He withdrew to the back of the company. "I fear I have no idea. I have never given the subject any thought."

Catherine chilled with fear for his feelings. She knew how sensitive he was about his foundling status. But she could think of nothing to distract her little sister as Philly insisted, "Oh, but you must know how old you are."

"Yes, I know that. I've had the good fortune to accomplish thirty years."

"How odd not to know your birthday." Philothea frowned at the problem. "Perhaps you could celebrate your saint's day. May first is Saint Philip and Saint James's Day—pity Philip didn't get one of his own; the other apostles did. I suppose it was because he was so quiet. If he'd talked more, he'd have more stories in the Bible, and then they'd have given him his own day." She thought for a moment. "But don't feel bad. I'm sure he was really a very important apostle. The collect says, 'Following the steps of Thy holy apostles, Saint Philip and Saint James, we may steadfastly walk in the way that leadeth to eternal life.' Pity it's just past. Will you mind dreadfully waiting a whole year for your birthday?"

Philip started to say that he wouldn't mind in the least, but Damaris joined in with another suggestion. "Perhaps you could celebrate your spiritual birthday."

"Oh, yes! A splendid idea," exclaimed Philly. "The day you were born again. That *would* be a birthday. Do you remember when it was, Philip?"

"Yes, it was the second Sunday in Trinity. I remember because Trinity term had just begun when I had the opportunity of calling on William Law."

Catherine steered the conversation away from the uncomfortable subject of birthdays. "How fortunate you were—to be able to counsel with a man who has influenced so many."

"Yes, I was perhaps the one man in all Cambridge who prayed in a formal way every day; but Law made me see that saying the right words with the mouth while the heart is far from God is worthless in God's sight."

"And you found assurance of salvation then?" Vincent asked.

"Truly. As soon as I saw that my hope and trust must be fixed solely in my Creator and Redeemer. Law showed me that attempting to appease or please God by an outward system of good works was totally erroneous. When I saw that all I needed to do was open my heart and receive from Christ His righteousness, I knew a great peace."

"Eight Sundays after Easter," announced Philothea who had been looking up Trinity Sunday in the "Table of Lessons" in the Prayer Book. "So the second Sunday in Trinity is nine weeks after Easter, which will be—," she paused to count on her fingers, "the second Sunday in June. You must remember to celebrate."

He nodded solemnly at the child's earnest instruction.

"Might I have another piece of cake, Mother?" John held out an empty plate.

"Here, have mine." Philip's response was so natural, and he placed the cake on the younger boy's plate so quickly that it was a moment before Catherine realized what had happened. Back in a group, Philip had reacted as he undoubtedly had at the orphanage to the needs of another. She wondered how often his unselfishness had led him to give his food away?

"And now in honor of this day, dear Sister," Edward bowed to Catherine, "I have the pleasure of announcing that I have completed my new hymn."

"Oh, Ned, how splendid! Is it the one you were working on during our trip?"

"Yes, I have seldom had a composition cost me so much effort, but I flatter myself that I have captured some of the stateliness I sought." He began to read.

> All hail the power of Jesus' name!
> Let angels prostrate fall;
> Bring forth the royal diadem,
> And crown Him Lord of all!

Catherine felt a thrill as her mind's eye glimpsed the splendor of that heavenly throne where her King and Lord ruled the universe. Each of the four verses brought smiles and nods from the appreciative audience until at last Edward concluded with:

> O that with yonder sacred throng
> We at His feet may fall!
> We'll join the everlasting song,
> And crown Him Lord of all!

"Oh, Ned!" Catherine was the first to respond. "It's wonderful! So worshipful and majestic! I can feel the greatness of God. It makes me want to shout glory to Him."

"Catherine, I couldn't imagine you so demonstrative." Edward laughed.

"Well, my spirit shouts even if I don't," she amended.

Charity dabbed at her eyes with a linen handkerchief, but whatever she was about to say was interrupted by a knock at the door.

Vincent moved to answer it before any of the servants could respond. "Why, Charl, what an unexpected pleasure!"

He stepped back to admit his newly arrived son, but his smile faded as he looked at the messenger's face.

"Ned, I am sent for you. Your wife is dangerously ill."

*T*hey set out at first light, and by continually pressing their horses and themselves, the riders covered the eighteen miles from Shoreham to Greenwich in just five hours. Edward rode always at the front, urging his horse and his companions to greater speed, showing by the sharpness of his voice how near to distraction he was. At Kidbrooke, a mile from Greenwich, he kicked his horse and galloped ahead.

"Go with him, Charl," Catherine told her brother. "I shall be there soon, and he may need your support."

When she and Philip arrived half an hour later, the stable-boy was still cooling the two horses. Joseph helped Catherine dismount, but Philip stayed in the saddle. "Shall I see you in, or would it be best that I not intrude?"

"Oh, please come in." The thought of his riding off was suddenly more than she could bear. She looked toward the doctor's black carriage waiting by the house. "I don't know what we may find inside. I should be grateful for your support."

And having him beside her did make walking into the unknown easier. The house was ominously quiet. Catherine paused at the foot of the stairs.

"Ned is upstairs." Charl's voice from the parlor startled her.

"Is—is she—"

"Alive. But very weak. She lost much blood."

"The babe?"

Charl shook his head, and Catherine nodded in reply; she had feared it would be so.

"Thank God, Durial's alive. I dreaded the worst." She turned to Philip. "I must go up to her."

He nodded.

Audrey, hovering outside her mistress's door in case she should be wanted, ushered Catherine into the dimly lit room. The physician, thoroughly in charge, was addressing Durial. "You've had a very narrow escape, and you are not to stir from that bed for a fortnight. Do I make myself clear? I shall instruct your cook in making a restorative elixir from the juice of red meat, to be taken morning and night without fail. And I shall call again in the morning."

"Is he just now come?" Catherine whispered to her sister Elizabeth.

"No, no. He sat with her all night and then came back this afternoon. We despaired of her life."

"What happened?"

"She fell. It was the spring cleaning, and she *would* take a hand in turning out the linen closets." Elizabeth moved to the door to see the doctor out, leaving Ned and Catherine alone with the patient.

"Durial, dear, we are so sorry." Catherine moved closer to the bed and received a weak smile from her sister-in-law. Even in the dim room, Durial's pallor was frightful. She was whiter than her linen sheets and seemed shrunken into her pillows. "My husband, I am so sorry. If only I hadn't been so headstrong and house-proud. Now I'll never have aught to give you but a clean house."

Ned moved to take her hand in both of his. "No, no, my dear. There shall be others."

Durial moved her head from side to side slowly, as if the

movement cost her great effort. "No, Dr. Eltham says there shall be no more."

Edward turned his head so that his wife couldn't see the pain, but Catherine saw. After a moment he turned back. "But I shall have your precious self, Durial. Now rest and fret not."

Durial relaxed at his words and closed her eyes. "I shall sit with her," Ned said. "You get some rest, Catherine."

Catherine was still wearing her mud-stained traveling cloak and half-boots. She went to her room and washed before returning downstairs. The parlor seemed unaccountably chill and empty. "Where's Philip?" she asked Charl.

"I tried to persuade him to sup with us, but he seemed to think his presence would be an intrusion."

The room no longer seemed merely empty to her—it was desolate.

The room Philip entered was equally desolate. For the first time, he saw it in its emptiness and shabbiness. Its bleakness brought to mind winter evenings when Matron would send her charges out to take the air after classes. The other children would join in rolling hoops or a noisy game of tutball. But Philip preferred to stay to himself, breaking up the ice from the puddles on the north side of the building with a stick. What began as a simple time-filler became something of a challenge, and he worked hard to keep ahead of the refreezing.

But he had never learned how to chip at the emotional ice inside. Keeping to himself had always seemed such a good answer to his fear of abandonment—if there was no one else in his life, if his relationship to God was the only one he relied on, there could be no one to leave him. But these past weeks with the Perronets—with Catherine especially—had produced a hairline crack in the ice. He now wondered whether the infraction should be encouraged.

In not letting others get to know the man inside, he had not gotten very well acquainted with himself—with that emotional, feeling part he had always kept so tightly controlled. Could he be more truly open to God if he were to be more open to those around him? He shivered at the thought of becoming transparent and vulnerable, of being hurt once more, as he had been at Midhurst and then over Sally Gwynne.

Philip encouraged the uncooperative flame in his fireplace, ate the soup and brown bread Mrs. Watson provided, and turned to his bed, just as he had turned to his iron cot at the orphan asylum. It had been the last in the row, and he had found that lying with his back to the room was as good as being alone. But now there was no need for that device to achieve solitude.

The next morning Philip went to the Foundery customhouse to inquire of William Briggs, John Wesley's secretary, if there was any mail for him or further itineracy assignments. He was surprised to find Elizabeth Perronet also in the office. "I have taken to helping Mr. Briggs with some of his correspondence when I can be spared at home," she explained with a hint of a blush.

"And how is Mrs. Edward Perronet this morning?"

"Her sleep was much disturbed. Dr. Eltham was there when I left. But Ned insisted I should come assist here while Catherine teaches her class. Ned won't leave Durial. I fear he blames himself much for being away when the accident occurred."

"It is said by many that itinerant preachers should not be wed." Philip nodded.

"Here is a letter come for you last week." Briggs handed the wax-sealed paper to Philip. "And you will preach the evening service tonight?"

"I'll be happy to. Thank you, William. I hope to hear of your sister-in-law's speedy recovery, Miss Perronet." Philip took his leave.

In the courtyard he perused his letter. It was from his old friend George Whitefield.

The 9 of 4, Glous.

My dear Philip,

As I wish to inform my friends at the Foundery of my recent return from America and report on my work there, but am not assured of my welcome in the Society, nor of my desire to be so, I shall communicate with one whom I have always known to be unfailing in his generosity and fair in his judgment, that he might advise me. I have heard the most disturbing reports while abroad. Can it be that John Wesley preaches universal redemption? That cannot be consistent with the scriptural doctrine of election. Can Wesley have strayed so far?

Although my heart aches at hearing that the work may have fallen astray (although I am assured that that most excellent lady, the Countess of Huntingdon, continues faithful in the doctrines of Calvin), the work in America progresses apace. I had great success in Philadelphia in raising money for my school and orphanage in Georgia, which I feel is the heart of my work. I employed that most excellent American, Benjamin Franklin, as a printer, who after my sermon confessed he had been determined to give nothing, since I refused to locate the orphan house at Philadelphia. But upon hearing me preach, he said he began to soften and concluded to give copper. "Another stroke decided me to give silver," he said. And at the finish he emptied his pocket into the collector's dish, gold and all. I should most heartily like to build a school for negroes in Philadelphia.

Dr. Franklin said it was wonderful to see the change soon made in the manners of their inhabitants after my revival services. I met only one case of rudeness—and that from a non-Episcopal divine. "I am sorry to see you here," he said.

"So is the devil," I replied.

And the Lord continues faithful in that part of the country which they call New England, where my friend Jonathan Edwards is one of the few truly awakened preachers. I am persuaded that there, as in England, the generality of preachers talk of an unknown and unfelt Christ. The reason why congregations have been dead is because they have dead men preaching to them. How can dead men beget living children?

And I thank God, the Harvard Awakening continues, where, to the consternation of much of its faculty, I preached against the liberalism making its way into that formerly excellent institution for ordinands. I was told subsequently that the students now are full of God.

Advise me how I shall go on, as regards our friends, and I shall remain,

Yr ever affect,
George Whitefield

His mind on how he might advise his friend and try to heal the rift between these strong leaders of the Methodist movement, Philip went on into the Foundery and back to the book room where the newly arrived printing of Charles Wesley's hymns was causing much interest. Then he realized, to his consternation, he was simply wandering around without purpose, and he took himself to his room to prepare for the evening service.

Several hundred ardent voices sang at the leading of a Society worker who opened the service that evening. Philip sang the words of the song with his mouth, but his heart missed his musical companions of the circuit trip.

In his sermon he spoke of the great, loving heart of Christ, so open to all who would come, so ready to receive sinful men. No sins were too great to be forgiven, no person too lost to be found by Him. And at the close of the service, it was apparent that Christ was ready also to receive sinful women, as a wretched-looking female waited at the back of the chapel to speak to Philip.

"You would have words with me, Sister?" He hoped to make his voice kind to calm the fear in her eyes.

She pushed a scraggle of red hair into her cap with a roughened hand. "Ah, sir. I was accidentally passing the door, and 'ear-ing the voice of someone preaching, I did what I 'ave never been in the 'abit of doing. I come in."

"You were right to do so. You are most welcome."

"I 'eard you say that Jesus Christ was so willing to receive sinners that 'e made no objection to receiving the devil's castaways. Now, sir, I am cast down so low that I was returning from seeking work in a bagnio when I passed your door."

"You had gone to sell yourself?"

"That was my attempt. I cannot keep food in my children's mouths. I thought this a way to provide for them, but they wouldn't 'ave me. To be turned away from a brothel is in truth to be one of the devil's castaways. Do you think, sir, that Jesus Christ would receive me?"

"There isn't the least doubt of it," Philip assured her, and he called two of the Society women to join him in praying for her.

When her radiant face gave assurance of new life inside, Philip asked where she lived, so Society members might call on her and her children. Here was a convert he could continue to disciple. It wasn't quite the same as having his own parish, but at least he wasn't required to ride away the next morning.

He felt ashamed that even in the rejoicing over the recovery of a lost lamb, his joy was less than complete. He wondered why God would have given him this desire for a people to shepherd if it was to remain unfulfilled.

And then the unaccustomed amount of self-analysis he had been undergoing lately led him to turn again to the Great Shepherd for guidance. In the empty chapel he knelt. "Lord, make me more useful for Thy service. I have prayed long for a place of service, but first do what You will to the server."

He went home still fearful of the vulnerability he had opened himself to, but he was sure he was on the right course.

The next morning, Catherine, back in the schoolroom, looked at the eleven eager faces in front of her. Well—seven eager, two cautious, and two bored. What did she most want to teach them in the short time she had with them? How could she best prepare them for life? How could she most clearly impart the love of God to them?

Three could barely form their letters; six read stumblingly; two were good readers for their age, but might be forced to leave school at any time as Isaiah Smithson had been. Then they would have very little exposure to books or to the Scriptures.

As she looked at them, longing to reach their minds and souls, she was filled with a new awareness of her love for them. And then she knew—she must reach them just as God had reached her—in the only way that one personality could reach another—with love.

She smiled at them. Eleven chubby, grubby faces smiled back. Well, nine smiled back; two were making faces at each other.

"Good morning, children. I am most anxious to hear what you have learned in my absence. Hettie, will you please read for us first."

Hettie stood, smoothed her apron, sniffled, and began reading, "'The eye of God is on them that do ill. Go not from me, O God, my God. The Lord will help them that cry to Him. My Son, if thy way is bad, see that you mend it.'"

"Thank you, Hettie." She called on three more to read aloud; then the scraping of little feet on the wooden floor told her it was time to vary the routine. "All right, class. You may turn to the syllabarium and copy out your letters." Primer pages rustled until all the children had before them a page of five columns of two-letter syllables that formed the basis of reading instruction. "And mind that you make your lines straight."

For a few minutes the heads bent over their slates, until a scraping sound told her someone was not applying his slate for its proper function. "William, you will stand in the corner for ten minutes, after which time I expect your writing instrument to work more smoothly." She had no more than dealt with that than a squeal from Kitty, the smallest girl, told her that Joshua had pulled her long braids again. "Joshua, please present yourself."

Discipline was not her favorite part of the job, but she struggled to put to rest her earlier visions of directing the children with nothing but the power of love as she held the birch rod before her. "Hold out your hands."

At such times she had to rely on the wisdom of John Wesley's instructions to his teachers:

> We must, by the grace of God, turn the bias from self-will, pride, anger, revenge, and love for the world, to lowliness, meekness, and the love of God. From the moment we perceive any of those evil roots springing up, it is our business immediately to check their growth, if we cannot root them out. As far as this can be done by mildness, softness, gentleness, certainly it should be done. But sometimes, these methods will not avail, and then we must correct with kind severity. For where tenderness will not remove the fault, he that spareth the rod, spoileth the child. To deny this is to give the lie to the God of truth and to suppose we can govern better than He.

Wesley's words gave her the courage to administer the full number of lashes. "You may take your seat and resume your work, Joshua." The students worked quietly, and Catherine prayed for the balance Wesley wanted them to achieve. He warned that some teachers may habitually lean to an extreme of being overly remiss or severe. If they gave children too much of their own will or needlessly and churlishly restrained them; if they used no punishment at all or more than was necessary, all their endeavors could be frustrated.

She pulled the watch from her waistband. The hands had barely moved since last she looked. "William, you may take your seat. And now, class, we shall read together. On the next page of your primer, please listen carefully and pronounce each word as I do."

Durial continued weak, mourning the loss of their child, and Ned stayed close to her side. Philip departed for a tour of Gloucestershire, and Catherine's students droned on. Duty and routine took over. Each morning brought the splash of cold water in her basin, the rumble of carriages on dry rocks, the scratch of styluses on slates. The Foundery looked as grim to her as when it was used only for metal forging.

Where were the birds' songs? Where were the roses? The scent of new-mown hay and the freshness after rain?

"Are You there, my God? Do You care? Are You still the loving Person who touched my heart and changed my life? Or have You too become only duty and routine?"

And in the stillness of her aching heart the answer came, "As I have been, so shall I be." God had promised help for the dry, dull times too, and so she must claim it and simply go on. She looked at her students.

"You may read, Joshua."

"Yes, Miss Perronet. 'Christ is the truth. Christ is the light. Christ is the way. Christ is my life . . .'"

At the end of two weeks, a feeble Durial was allowed to arise from her bed for a short time. Ned carried her to a lounge chair in the garden and tucked robes securely around her. Catherine was reading aloud to her sister-in-law from the *Meditations* of John Donne when they heard the clatter of horses' hooves on the driveway. For an instant Catherine's heart leaped—could it be their friend returning early from Gloucester? She had refused to dwell on the thought, even to admit it to her mind; but in the furthest recess of her heart she knew that much of the dryness of the past weeks could be laid to Philip's absence.

But the newcomer, although clad in the familiar black, was not her Philip but their brother Charl, just returned from a circuit to the north with Charles Wesley.

"Did you meet with success, Brother?" Catherine asked.

Charl removed his tricorn and ran his fingers through his hair. "I have never met with greater discord."

"Oh, Charl, were you treated rudely by the mob?" Durial asked with quick concern.

"No, no. We met little rowdyism. I speak of the Societies—of the preachers to be exact."

"Discord among the preachers?" Catherine couldn't believe her ears.

"First, there was the matter of James Wheatley—who was accused of embracing the doctrine of polygamy and, we were told, scandalized the Society by practicing it openly."

"Charl, was there any truth to such an accusation?"

"At the direction of John Wesley, his brother and I immediately set up an inquiry into the matter." Charl shook his head. "There was no polygamy, but that would perhaps have been easier to deal with. I heard Wheatley preach with my own ears. I cannot say whether he preached false doctrine or true, or any doctrine at all, but pure unmixed nonsense. Not one sentence did he utter that could do the least good to any soul.

"And there lies the weakest point of our Methodist system of preaching. The majority of those who fill the pulpits are working men who have abandoned their trade to follow what they believe to be their vocation, but without education or preparation or support, except from family or Society."

"What is to be done?" Catherine asked.

"Charles Wesley has declared that every preacher must work at his own trade or business during the week, preparing his sermons as he finds time and delivering them on Sundays in the neighboring chapels. This way they will at least not lose touch with the common man."

"Well, then, it seems the matter has been taken in hand."

"Yes, but that was not all. We encountered amongst the more prominent of the preachers a spirit of disloyalty to the Church of England that horrified Charles, whose allegiance to the Anglican faith knows no bounds."

"Oh, Charl, not more separatism talk?"

"Of a truth, the remedy is simple, and more and more of our harassed preachers are availing themselves of it. For the sum of sixpence they are furnished with a license which puts them under the protection of the law. Once they are recognized as 'protestant dissenters,' they are no longer at the mercy of the mob. And a similar license will protect their meetinghouses from wreckers and incendiaries. We are beating our heads against the wall in refusing this way."

"But to leave the church . . . ," Catherine said in horror.

Charl laughed. "Cath, you sound like Charles Wesley. He said he should rather see his brother in his grave than a dissenter. But it will come to it in time."

Catherine went alone into the garden—alone to consider this further unhappy news. Dissension and faulty standards among the Society preachers, widespread agitation for separatism. What were the answers? On every hand trouble was invading the world of the Methodist Society—what had seemed to her the best of all possible worlds. And Catherine felt afraid. She had conquered her fear of horses. But this new fear was much worse—fear of the future was like walking down a long, dark tunnel without a candle. Without assurance of God's guidance, she could feel no assurance of His caring. If no caring, did He then truly provide salvation?

No! She put the question aside as one that came directly from the enemy. She would not doubt that. She would choose to believe, no matter how little she felt the closeness of the Savior at times.

With that determination she suddenly knew what she would do. There was one place where she had always felt closer to God than any other. She would go for a walk in the woods.

She ran to her room for her half-boots and a shawl. Telling Audrey where she was going, she hurried out again into the day, which now seemed brighter. Once in the woods the beauty began to seep into her soul—a greenness of trees, a trill of birdsong. And her spirits rose higher, as if the trees that shut the world from view behind her shut out the problems too. Here were no rowdy crowds, no dissenting preachers, no disobedient schoolchildren, no poverty-stricken families, no disappointed loves. Here there was a coloring of flowers, a sparkle of water, a warmth of sun. One could not possibly doubt the personal love of a God who created such a world.

Catherine felt her inner doubts, fears, and anxieties slip away. She knew they would come back later when she returned to the real world, but for now she could laugh, thank God, and shout hosanna.

Had anyone been watching her, however, they would have had no idea all this was going on inside the outwardly composed young woman who walked down the wooded path, stopping occasionally to pick a specimen for her wildflower press. An especially lovely hawthorn tree brought back to mind the Maying she and her companions had watched on the Kentish village green. She decided to collect a sprig for her book.

The hawthorn branch was just beyond her reach. She stretched her hand to the delicate cluster of berries that would soon turn red, but even when she stood on her tiptoes, they eluded her grasp. Then a gentle breeze, just a small stirring of the air, brought the branch into her hands.

She picked it gladly, freely, as it had been given to her, and savored its beauty in joy. At that moment she understood. She had thought she must reach God's will and had strained her arms and stood on tiptoe to grasp it. But the truth was that He reached down to her. Just as the heaven-sent breeze had placed the hawthorn berries in her hand, so God, in His reaching down to her, had placed and would place all good things in her life according to His perfect way.

The shadows were falling long across the path. It was time to return. With only the slightest reluctance, she turned her steps back to the world with its challenges and opportunities. "Help me to view them as such, my God, rather than as threats or burdens. Help me, I ask, to serve You more gladly. As gladly as You gave me the hawthorn blossom."

At first the faint calling of her name sounded as a rustling in the trees, coming so immediately after her prayer that it seemed as if the voice of God were calling her. And then she thought she had imagined it, recalling her childhood experience when her brother's voice had come to the little girl lost in the woods. But on the fourth call, she knew it was not the wind, not her Creator, not her imagination. It was a very human male voice. And on the fifth call, she identified the caller. With a cry of gladness, she turned and ran up the path to Philip.

8

*P*hillip stood on the path in a shaft of late afternoon sunlight. For a moment Catherine felt as if she were seeing him for the first time—his striking height, his endearing thinness, his fleeting smile. During the past two weeks she had thought of him with confused emotions because she hadn't the slightest idea of whether he was thinking of her at all. Indeed, it was impossible ever to guess what he thought, much less what he felt. And now, except for a light in his blue eyes that she hoped she wasn't imagining, his chiseled features were a perfect mask—a barrier between the man inside and the world outside.

Catherine had become part of his outside world; would she ever get inside behind the mask? She would like to have thrown her arms around him in welcome, but instead offered him a composed smile. "How pleased I am that you are returned. Tell me about your journey."

They walked up the path toward the house together. "I met with my friend George Whitefield," he told her. "He was desperately ill on his voyage from America, but he is recovering. He hopes to accompany Lady Huntingdon to London in a few days."

"And what of your services? Had you success?"

"Yes, but the most remarkable victory over Satan was scored before I left the Foundery." Now, as he talked about his work, the stiffness gave way to animation. "Have you heard of the conversion of Mrs. Smithson? The night before I left, she wandered in off the street while I was preaching—"

"Smithson?"

"Yes. I instructed the sisters to call on her. Do you know if any have? Her tale was absolutely remarkable. She was returning from a bagnio where she had sought to sell herself for the sake of buying bread for her children—"

"Had she red hair?"

"It seems so, if I recall—"

"Oh, Philip!" Catherine so forgot herself as to take his arm. "It must be the same. Isaiah Smithson was my pupil, but he had to quit and go to sweeping when his father lost his job. And you say she found the Lord?"

"Indeed, it was a remarkable conversion. She seemed truly a new person."

"Philip, we must help that family. Do you think the Society might—"

"Lend to an unemployed man whose children sweep? I believe the Society lending policies to be sounder than that. The Society will lend up to twenty shillings, but the sum must be repaid within three months. It seems most unlikely Smithson could meet those terms."

"But we must do something."

"Indeed we must. Will you call on her with me?"

Catherine readily agreed, and they continued on up the path. She saw no reason to let go of the arm she held.

And the following day Catherine clung to the same arm as protection from the squalor around her. Chitty Lane off Tottenham Court Road ran past a row of dilapidated houses that had been turned into one-room dwellings. Children with pock-marked faces and emaciated limbs played in the gutters, which obviously were disposal systems for all manner of waste.

"Catherine, I should not have asked you to accompany me. I had no idea—," Philip began.

"I believe we had this conversation once before, sir. Surely this is what our Lord had in mind when He reminded us, 'As ye have done it unto the least of these.'"

It seemed impossible to Catherine that such a pocket of misery could exist in the very center of London, almost equidistant between the purity of the Foundery and Aldersgate Street to the east, and the elegance of Mayfair and Park Lane to the west. She turned her eyes away from the sight of a scraggly dog shaking a rat to death and resisted the impulse to put her hand over her nose.

An urchin directed them down a mud path to an unpainted door hanging crooked on its hinges, and then he held out his filthy hand for a farthing. It wasn't the dirt on the hand that shocked Catherine. He had a running sore on his inflamed palm. "Philip, if that isn't treated, he'll lose his hand."

The stench from the street followed them into the Smithson home where at least there was some semblance of order, some attempt to keep the filth at bay with sweeping and scrubbing. With a toddler clinging to her skirt, Elmira Smithson was at work over a stack of linen, ironing with alternating flatirons kept hot on the hearth.

Elmira's greeting seemed cheerful beyond all possibility in her circumstances. "The good Jesus you told us about 'asn't left me for one minute," she assured Philip. "And the Methody sisters bring two loads o' wash. More'n I've 'ad in as many weeks afore."

But her accounting of her blessings was interrupted by a fretful cry from a pallet in a dark corner of the room.

"Are you awake, Isey? We've visitors."

"Miss Perronet!" The fussy voice changed to a whoop of joy.

"Isaiah! I didn't see you there. Are you ill?"

"'S me feet. I got stuck an' the sweep built a fire under me. I wasn't a'feared—t'weren't that. I were stuck."

The sight of Isaiah's badly blistered feet brought tears to

Catherine's eyes. His mother had attempted to soothe the fever in her son's feet with cool rags. "Have you no salve?" Catherine asked.

Elmira shook her head.

"I shall bring you some first thing in the morning," Catherine promised. "Now, young man, where is the primer I loaned you? Let us see if you have remembered what I labored so hard to teach you."

Isaiah produced the book, in much better condition than Catherine had dared hope for, from under his pallet. They spent half an hour reviewing the answers to the picture catechism while Philip instructed Mrs. Smithson from the Bible.

"And what of your husband? Has he found work?" Philip asked as they prepared to take their leave.

"Da's in the Fleet," Isaiah said, before his mother could answer.

"The Fleet?" Catherine couldn't have kept the horror out of her voice if she'd tried. The Fleet was the largest of London's debtors' prisons, notorious for its dirt, debauchery, and harsh treatment of prisoners—and for the hopelessness of gaining release.

"'E owed Mr. Pinchbeck two quid. When 'e couldn't pay, ol' Pinchy swore out a complaint, swore 'e owed 'im twenty. 'Course they would a taken 'im for the two just the same. Tha's why I went to the bagnio; it's the only place I could think of to earn that kinda money. But they didn't even want laundry done by the loiks of me—let alone any other service."

"For twenty pounds he could be freed?" Philip asked.

Mrs. Smithson shook her head. "There's the garnish for the jailer and the warden and the guard. Upwards of fifty quid, I should think."

"Fifty pounds!" Catherine was thunderstruck. She knew the graft and corruption in the prison system was unconscionable, but fifty pounds amounted to the yearly salary of a well-to-do man. It was far beyond anything Smithson or any of his family could ever hope to raise. Even Catherine, who would gladly have paid his release, couldn't imagine where such a sum could be found.

The toddler began to whimper for some of the thin gruel heating on the hearth beside the flatirons. Catherine was glad she had brought a basket of bread. Before she and Philip left, they prayed with the family in a small circle around Isaiah's mat. "I will return with medicine for your feet, Isaiah," Catherine promised from the doorway.

"You must not come here alone," Philip told her sternly when they were back on their way to the Foundery. "It's not safe. I shall accompany you tomorrow."

And he did, as soon as her class was dismissed the next day. And the next as well. Catherine was pleased that Isaiah's blisters were responding to the calves' jelly salve, but she feared having him fully recovered and going back to sweeping chimneys again. "Philip, I've been thinking about Isaiah. I can't supply the money to get his father out of prison, but I can spare enough to keep him in the charity school."

"What do you have in mind?"

"I'm not sure yet—maybe supplying the family with the amount of food he could have bought with his earnings as a sweep. If it's done through the Society, surely they would accept it."

"That is most generous of you, Catherine. I should like to share the responsibility with you."

"Oh, but, Philip—forgive me, but you have so little."

"On the contrary, I have so much. A visit such as this makes me conscious of it. Please pardon me if I seem presumptuous when I say that it is my observation that children reared by well-to-do parents accept what comes to them as a right—demand it even. One who has received everything from another's open-handedness learns appreciation quickly. And since there is nothing I can do to repay those who gave to me, I must give to others."

Catherine nodded. "The theological implications seem boundless."

"God's grace to us all—unmerited favor, you mean?"

"Yes, and adoption—we are all adopted into God's family and made heirs by His love."

For a moment it seemed to Catherine that Philip was considering his next movement very carefully. Then, decidedly, for the first time in their acquaintanceship, he offered his arm without her making the first move.

That small linking action stayed with Catherine throughout the evening. Later that night, when reading in her green vellum volume of John Donne by the light of a branched candelabra, she came upon his "Meditation 17." But she found it impossible to think of mankind in general, as the grave image of Philip Ferrar fixed itself in her mind's eye.

"No man is an island entire of itself." Ah, here was the part she looked for. Philip was such a remote island, and she had no barque to reach him. With a sigh she returned to her reading. "If a clod be washed away by the sea, Europe is the less, as well as if a promontory were, as well as if a manor of thy friend's or of thine own were. Any man's death diminishes me. . . ."

"And any child's pain," she added. She wished she could take all the urchins in London under her wing, put salve on their sores, teach them to read. But at least she could minister to the one God had placed directly in her path. Tomorrow she would approach Elmira Smithson about Isaiah's returning to school.

But the next morning Catherine's day presented a full schedule of duties before she could visit the Smithsons. John Wesley was now returned to London, living in his rooms over the Foundery, and he would be preaching at five o'clock in the morning, which meant that Catherine must arrive early to be assured of a good seat.

It had been many weeks since John Wesley had filled his

pulpit, and yet when he stood before them, it was as if he had never been away. In spite of his forty-six years, he appeared fresh, his eyes bright and piercing and his long hair still a rich auburn. But most compelling was the intelligence, energy, and love he radiated to all around him.

He launched quickly into his sermon on Matthew 25:43: "I was . . . sick, and in prison, and ye visited me not." And he spoke eloquently of love for one's neighbors, love that endures everything, that feeds an enemy and gives him drink, "thus continually heaping coals of fire—of melting love—upon his head."

Wesley continued, speaking more specifically about prison visitation, and gradually Catherine became sensible of her own negligence. Never had she visited a prisoner. She didn't even know how to go about it.

Then Wesley concluded the service by introducing Sarah Peters who had come to the Foundery looking for volunteers to visit prisons. "This very week in the Fleet," Miss Peters told the congregation, "there are ten malefactors under sentence of death who would be glad of any friends who could go and pray with them."

Quailing inwardly, Catherine joined the band of workers around Sarah Peters at the side of the altar after the service. "I shall go with you," Catherine pledged.

She was still shaking inwardly when she turned to leave and saw Philip among the volunteers. Then she knew she could do it.

But that afternoon when they met Sarah Peters outside the Fleet, Catherine had second thoughts, even with the support of Philip, her headmaster Silas Told, and two other Society members.

"There are three large wards on the common side," Miss Peters explained. "Here the prisoners are obliged to lie on the floor if they cannot furnish themselves with bedding—this is hired out at a cost of a shilling per week. There are also two smaller wards, including an exceedingly noisome one for women. A number of rooms on the master's side are let out at indefinite charges to occupants who can pay the warden. In some rooms persons who are sick of different distempers are obliged to lie together or on the floor and must pay two shillings, ten pence per week for such lodging. But," she hastened to add, "you may be assured we shall in no wise go near cases of small-pox or similar contagion."

As Miss Peters turned to lead the way to the prison gate, Silas Told asked, "I have been given to understand that even prisoners for debt must pay garnish to the jailers."

"Yes, that is true. James Oglethorpe who heads a reform committee has made two reports to Parliament on these abuses. We still hope for amelioration. But at present, when taken into custody and sent to the Fleet, every prisoner is expected to pay a total of five pounds, sixteen shillings, and four pence in fees. This is divided between the warden, the tipstaff, and the clerk of the judge who ordered the committal."

"But what if they can't pay?" Catherine could think only of Mrs. Smithson's happiness over being given a pitiful pile of laundry whereby to earn a few shillings.

"When the miserable wretch has worn out the charity of his friends and used up the money raised from the sale of his clothes and bedding and has eaten his last allowance of provisions, he soon grows weak for want of food, with the symptoms of a hectic fever. When he is no longer able to stand, if he can raise three pence to pay the fee of the common nurse of the prison, he obtains the liberty of being carried into the sick ward and lingers on for a month or two on charity rations, and then dies."

"But can nothing be done about it?"

"Oglethorpe's committee is sending petitions to Parliament, and there is hope of Parliament passing ameliorating legislation. But in the meantime, it seems most fit that we should strive for the souls of these unhappy prisoners. There is little we can do for them here but prepare them for a better world to come. Let us proceed."

Sarah Peters, a seasoned warrior in this arena of graft and corruption, approached the Ordinary, a Mr. Taylor who, but for the fact that he stood outside the walls, looked far meaner and more disreputable than any of his prisoners. "You shall not obstruct our entrance today, Mr. Taylor. The God of all compassion shall make an entrance for us so that our acts of compassion and mercy may continue." When she accompanied her bold words with the clink of bribe money, the group was allowed to pass.

Catherine thought she was prepared for the fetid air and squalid, verminous surroundings. But as the great iron bar clanked into place across the heavy oak door behind them, and she knew herself locked inside with desperate murderers and felons as well as with the malignant diseases that ravaged the rag-covered bodies she saw on every side of her, she felt panic.

"You needn't do this, Catherine. Shall I take you home?" With the sound of Philip's voice, the terror subsided.

"I can do it, Philip. But stay by me."

He ducked his head in a nod of assurance, and she was almost sure she saw a flicker of an encouraging smile cross his face. It was for Catherine as if a brilliant light filled the murky room.

But she had no leisure to consider her own feelings, as the determined Miss Peters shepherded their small party forward to the cell of a prisoner named Lancaster. The turnkey opened the barred door and then closed it behind them.

Sarah encouraged Lancaster to tell his story. He was very young, just above twenty, Catherine judged, yet he told of having lived a life of great wickedness, including having robbed the Foundery of all its brass and candlesticks. "But shortly I shall be with Jesus in paradise. This morning, about five o'clock, the Son of Righteousness arose in my dark cell, and I am now so full of God and Heaven that I am like a barrel of new wine ready to burst for vent."

The visitors joined him in praising God, and Lancaster

gave praise for Miss Peters and her workers who had shown him the way to God.

They visited another cell where six prisoners, all under sentence of death, seemed assured of their acceptance by the Savior. The workers were about to leave when another prisoner, having bribed the turnkey, entered the cell. His sullen face showed he had not come to praise God with them. "Come to scoff at us, are ye? Come to turn us into milksops 'afore we face the hangman? I'll none of your pap!"

Philip stepped forward and said softly, "My friend, let us tell you what we have come to tell any who will hear."

The prisoner muttered, but seemed less violent, so Philip continued, "We have come to invite you to the Lord Jesus. To invite you to come as a lost and undone sinner because Jesus is the sinner's only friend. Jesus, the King of Heaven, laid down His life for you."

As Philip spoke, the man's countenance softened. But there was time for no more. The iron door clanked open, and the warden stood before them, filling the passage with his straddle-legged stance, a fearsome sight in his heavy boots and leather jerkin, with black, greasy hair falling to his shoulders. He grasped his sword hilt with a broad hand. "The report has been made, and the dead warrant just come down. Four of you are ordered for execution. Look to your souls."

As the visitors were ushered from the cell, Sarah Peters assured the condemned men she would come again before their execution.

They were almost to the outer door, passing the largest and, therefore, dirtiest and noisiest of the common cells, when Catherine recognized a woman in the corridor. "Elmira, I didn't think to see you here." She hurried to Mrs. Smithson.

"I must come to bring Dick 'is loaf." She held up a small hunk of bread. "Some weeks 'tis all 'e 'as to eat if the rations is withheld."

Catherine dug in the pocket she wore tied under her skirt

for a coin with which to bribe the turnkey. "Allow me a few minutes longer with my friend."

He jerked his head in assent.

Philip joined her as they stood beside the cell bars with Mrs. Smithson. As unobtrusively as possible she slipped the loaf through to her husband and introduced Catherine and Philip.

Their reception was less than gracious. "What the devil possesses you, Elmiry? Bringin' canters to see me. I 'ope you've not been among the Methodists! I'd sacrifice what's left of my soul rather than you shall go among those miscreants." He shook his fist through the bars. "You're the ones wot filled Isey's 'ead so full of larnin' 'e ain't no good t' sweep."

Elmira moved the visitors to the other side of the passage. "It's th' gin talkin'. 'E didn't use to drink bad, but there's naught else to do 'ere."

"Gin? But where do they get it?" Catherine asked.

Philip answered. "What isn't smuggled in under the skirts of female visitors is sold right here."

"What? In the gaol?"

"I have read some of the accounts of Oglethorpe's committee. Upwards of thirty gin shops operate inside the Fleet alone."

Back in her carriage in the fresh air, it seemed to Catherine that the sun had never shown more golden, the flowers bloomed more brightly, nor the trees waved greener in the breeze. She took in great gulps of air, as if she had been holding her breath the entire time she was behind the high stone walls of the Fleet. "Oh, I don't think I've ever truly appreciated freedom before!"

The men agreed with her. Each determined to work harder in his own field—Philip the preacher, who sought to free people from the prison of sin, and Silas Told the schoolmaster, who fought the prison of ignorance. But the metaphor Catherine was living in was the sunshine and the light that had dawned in her world in the darkness of the prison. And that light was Philip

Ferrar. For weeks now he had been central in her thinking—as a dear friend, a special person in the Society work. But now, from the blackness of the Fleet had dawned the light of love.

He had said nothing any gentleman of casual acquaintance might not have said, but the simple fact of his presence had been all. As she tried to make sense of this, to understand what it would mean in the days ahead, the darkness of the prison experience offered another metaphor. She recognized the inability to see into the future as a kind of blindness. "We see through a glass darkly," as the Scripture said. But now she realized that God had so ordained this in order to develop faith— that one must rely on the Heavenly Guide as a blind man relies on an earthly guide. But someday it would all be known, and all knowledge would be as clear as knowledge of the past now was. Clearer, really, because His perfect light would illumine the whole.

She shuddered at the thought of what life without God would be like—like one physically blind walking without a guide. She had experienced a little of that in the days after her crushing disappointment, when she had lost faith in God's guidance. She had been blind, and in a way, she still was. She had no more ability to see the future than before, but she did have faith in her Guide.

*C*atherine hoped that the tall, quiet man on the carriage seat beside her would have a place in that future. The thought of his being taken from her as Charles Wesley had been was more than she could bear.

"Shall you mind that very much?"

Philip's words so nearly echoing those in her head made Catherine jump. "I beg your pardon. What did you say?"

"I said I have been commanded to bring you and Edward to Lady Huntingdon's drawing room to hear Whitefield preach tomorrow afternoon." He turned his head away from Silas Told, who was now reading beside him, and spoke quietly. "Charles and Sally Wesley shall be there. I thought you would want to know."

"You are thoughtful to warn me, but I shall be fine. And you?"

For a moment he looked puzzled. Then the level blue eyes so close to hers cleared. "Absolutely fine."

The next day gathering storm clouds darkened patches of London's sky as Catherine and Edward Perronet and Philip Ferrar set out from the Foundery for Park Lane. It was the first time the three of them had traveled together since their circuit ride and almost the first time Edward had been abroad since Durial's desperate illness. So whatever the clouds might do to the sky, the renewal of old times and the strong sense of companionship in the carriage could not be dimmed.

The crush of coaches with armorial bearings outside number 14 Park Lane facing on Hyde Park told the new arrivals that they were hardly alone in their obedience to the countess's summons. A select circle of aristocratic acquaintances had frequently accompanied the countess to Whitefield's sermons in London churches years before; but Lady Huntingdon's long retirement from society after her husband's death and her own bouts of illness had ended these excursions—until now. Whitefield's return and the renewal of her energies coincided in perfect timing.

At the top of the pillared portico the door was opened by a liveried butler who announced their arrival, but once into the high-ceilinged, marble-floored reception room, they made no more progress. The aged widow of the Duke of Marlborough stood in front of them, clasping the hand of her hostess. "My dear Lady Huntingdon, I really do feel so sensibly all your kindness and attention that I must accept your obliging invitation to hear Mr. Whitefield, though I am still suffering from the effects of a severe ague." She waved a white lace handkerchief as supporting evidence.

"My dear Duchess."

The duchess not only outranked Lady Huntingdon—she was also the only woman Catherine knew of who could out-talk her. "Your concern for my improvement in religious knowledge is very obliging. God knows we all need mending, and none more than myself."

"Won't you come into the drawing room, Your Grace?"

The duchess took two steps at her hostess's bidding and then paused again. "The Duchess of Ancaster, Lady Townshend, and Lady Cobham were exceedingly pleased with many observations in Mr. Whitefield's sermon at St. Sepulchre's Church, which made me lament ever since that I did not hear it, as it might have been the means of doing me some good—for *good*, alas! I do want."

"As we all do, Your Grace. And there is the ill-used Lady Anne Frankland." The countess pointed her fan in the direction of a wan-looking woman. "The poor thing is so unhappy in her new marriage. To think that a great-grandson of Oliver Cromwell could abuse his wife so. Do see if you can comfort her." With that, Lady Huntingdon dispatched her garrulous guest and turned to Catherine. "So you are come. I have been in town these three days. You must call on me more often."

"I should be happy to, My Lady. Of late I have been much engaged in calling on the sick and imprisoned."

"Yes, indeed. Very worthy work. You must tell me more of it. But we must also carry our message to the wealthy and aristocratic, if the work is to be a lasting one. The influence of money and society is too much overlooked by John Wesley."

The arrival at that moment of two women sumptuously clad in ribbed silk embroidered with silver thread, their skirts spread wide over flattened hoops, proved the success of the countess's campaign.

"The Dowager Duchess of Buckingham," the butler announced. "And the Duchess of Queensberry."

"Well, Selina, I have brought Eleanor with me to hear your favorite preacher," the Dowager Duchess announced with a flip of her ivory fan.

The Duchess of Queensberry managed to nod at her introduction while still keeping her nose in the air. "La, I am exceedingly fatigued. I trust he will not tire me beyond endurance."

Catherine and her escorts started to follow the newcomers up the stairs to the drawing room, but at the entrance of another party the countess halted them and made her own announcement even before the butler could. "Catherine, this is Sally Wesley; Charles you already know." She dismissed the husband.

"You young ladies are to become great friends." And with that decree she waved them up the stairs.

But Catherine could not so easily dispense with the arrival of Charles Wesley. Her first glimpse of the glowing brown eyes and fair features most frequently described as "angelic," which had so long held preeminence in Catherine's heart and mind, made her catch her breath. But a second, more-considered look told her that the far-from-classic features of the gaunt man beside Charles had become much dearer to her.

"I am most happy to meet you, Miss Perronet," Sally Wesley acknowledged the introduction, as the ladies led the way up the stairs. "Your brother was so kind in supporting our cause in Garth."

"Yes, Ned has told me of your wedding. I am happy to meet you too." And as she spoke the words, Catherine realized how very much she meant them. Sally was short and vivacious, with dark curls bouncing beneath her lace cap and snapping dark eyes that made her appear even younger than her twenty-one years. And every time those black eyes fell on her husband of three months, they bespoke how much she loved him.

They barely had time to find seats in the green and rose room when the countess called on Mr. and Mrs. Charles Wesley to provide music for her guests. Sally, in a flowered dimity dress over a pink petticoat, looked the perfect part of the happy new bride as she seated herself at the harpsichord and filled the room with its delicate music. And then her husband stood by her side as together they sang: "Rejoice, the Lord is King; Your Lord and king adore! / Rejoice, give thanks, and sing and triumph evermore: / Lift up your heart, lift up your voice! Rejoice, again I say, rejoice!"

It was obvious that the musicians were rejoicing in their life together and in the grace of which they sang. The hearts of their hearers were lifted with them. Sunshine streamed through the tall windows of the room as they sang. Catherine's heart could sing along with the musicians—Charles and Sally were so right for each other! After all her struggles over God's guidance, it was still impossible to know where He was leading her; but that these two were right for each other was indisputable. She must simply trust that God had an equally right answer in store for her life. And seeing that God had led so graciously in the lives of others could help her believe that He would make His way plain to her.

Then George Whitefield stood at the end of the room beside the east windows. He was of middle height, slender, fair, and good-looking except for a squint in one eye. Nothing about his appearance would predispose his audience to pick out this young man as the one who had brought thousands to Christ on both sides of the Atlantic.

But when he began to speak, they understood. Remarkably, he could speak rapidly and yet have every word distinctly heard. "We are all dead in sin and cannot save ourselves. We are saved by the free grace of God, without the assistance of good works which have no share in the matter, though it is impossible for us to have this free grace applied to us without its being followed by good works.

"Good works are, however, the sure tokens of our being born again.... Everybody that pleases may obtain this free grace by simply praying for it. It is therefore by faith in Christ alone that we are saved, not by our good works."

Clouds alternated with sunshine as Whitefield continued to build the solid doctrinal foundation on which he based every sermon. In a moment when a shadow crossed the room, he stretched out his arm. "See that emblem of human life! It passed for a moment and concealed the brightness of heaven from our view. But it is gone! And where will you be, my hearers, when your lives are passed away like that dark cloud?

"O my dear friends, I see you sitting attentive, with your eyes fixed on this poor, unworthy preacher. In a few days we shall all meet at the Judgment Seat of Christ, and every eye shall behold the Judge! With a voice whose call you must abide and answer, He will inquire whether on earth you strove to enter in at the strait gate. Whether you were supremely devoted to God. Whether your hearts were absorbed in Him."

Now the sun was gone, the room dark, and thunder rumbled in the distance. "My blood runs cold when I think how many of you will seek to enter in and shall not be able. What plea can you make before the Judge of the whole earth?"

The storm was almost overhead. In the eerie light of the thunderclouds, George Whitefield held his arms aloft and cried, "O sinner! By all your hopes of happiness I beseech you to repent. Let not the wrath of God be awakened! Let not the fires of eternity be kindled against you."

Forked lightning streaked past the windows. "See there! It is a glance from the angry eye of Jehovah. Hark—" He lifted his finger and paused. A tremendous crash of thunder shook the room. As it died away, the preacher's deep voice spoke from the semidarkness. "It was the voice of the Almighty as He passed by in anger!"

Whitefield covered his face with his hands and fell to his knees in silent prayer until the storm subsided. When the sun shone again in a few minutes, the windows reflected a magnificent rainbow. The preacher rose and pointed at it. "Look upon the rainbow and praise Him who made it. Very beautiful it is in the brightness thereof. It compasseth the heavens about with glory, and the hands of the Most High have bended it."

It was several moments before anyone moved in the room. At last Lord Bolingbroke rose, shook out the lace ruffles beneath the wide cuffs of his green velvet coat, and crossed the room to the speaker. "Sir, I am much moved by your address. Will you call upon me tomorrow morning?"

"I would be much honored, My Lord."

It seemed that Bolingbroke's stamp of approval was what all were waiting for, as now all the guests surged around the speaker. Lord Chesterfield, godfather to the young Earl of

Huntingdon, the countess's son, shook Whitefield's hand. "Sir, I will not tell you what I shall tell others—how I approve of you." He stayed for some time, affably conversing with the preacher.

But the outspoken Dowager Duchess of Buckingham was less enthusiastic as she took leave of her hostess. "I thank Your Ladyship for the information concerning the Methodist preacher. But I find his doctrine most repulsive. It is strongly tinctured with impertinence and disrespect for his superiors."

She turned toward all the room and tapped her walking stick on the parquet floor. "It is monstrous to be told that you have a heart as sinful as the common wretches that crawl upon the earth. I find this highly offensive and insulting. I cannot but wonder that Your Ladyship should relish any sentiments so much at variance with high rank and good breeding." With a toss of her head, she exited, the still-fatigued Duchess of Queensberry following in her wake.

As the noble guests made their departure and the room became easier to move about in, Catherine gravitated to Sally Wesley's side, wishing to compliment her on her excellent musicianship. But they had exchanged only a few words before the guest of honor joined them. "And how is the excellent Mrs. Wesley?" Whitefield asked.

"Very well, sir. I thank you."

"And how are you getting along in the book I gave you?"

"Exceeding well." She turned to Catherine. "Mr. Whitefield made me a wedding present of William Law's *A Serious Call to a Devout and Holy Life.*"

"It is a gift I never tire of giving to others, for I never forget the great longing I had to possess a copy." Catherine was especially interested in Whitefield's words, as she recalled Philip having told her that the book and its author had a great influence on his life. "I was just leaving for my first term at Oxford," Whitefield continued, "when I called on a friend who kept Gloucester's best bookshop. He showed me the brand-new book which had just arrived that day from London, but allowed me to hold it for a few minutes only, lest my grubby fingers spoil the calf. In those brief moments, though, I read enough to fire me. I still recall the passage: 'He therefore is the devout man who lives no longer to his own will, or to the sway and spirit of the world, but to the sole will of God; who considers God in everything, who serves God in everything, who makes all the parts of his common life, parts of piety, by doing everything in the name of God. . . . .'"

"That precise passage provided the recipe I followed for salvation," Charles Wesley said, as he joined them. "Law was counselor-in-chief to both my brother and myself during the years of our legal night. We often walked from Oxford to London to talk to him. His book convinced me of the exceeding height and breadth and depth of the love of God. The light flowed in so mightily upon my soul that everything appeared in a new view, and I cried to God for help."

The artist Loggan, who at Tunbridge Wells had declared his desire to hear more of the countess's doctrine, and the poet Lord Lyttelton had joined them in time to hear the last statement. "And reading that dissenting fellow's book changed your life? Remarkable!" said Loggan.

"The book and its author. They convinced me of the absolute impossibility of being half a Christian. I determined, through His grace, to be all devoted to God, to give Him my soul, my body, and my substance."

"But what did the fellow say to bring on such a determination?" Loggan asked.

Wesley returned Loggan's bow. "With respect to an inward means of atonement, or reconciliation to God, Mr. Law declared his unequivocal belief that through the body and blood of our Lord Jesus Christ alone, and by means of His suffering on the cross solely, mankind can be delivered from a state of sin and misery. That was the good news I had sought for years."

Lord Lyttelton made a deep bow accompanied by a flourish of his green velvet coat skirts. "That's William Law, you say? I once took up his book at a friend's house. I was so fascinated I could not go to rest until I had finished it. You can well imagine I was not a little astonished to find that one of the finest books ever written had been penned by a crack-brained enthusiast. Oh," Lord Lyttelton surveyed the circle to whom he spoke, "I daresay, that wasn't very tactful of me, was it?"

Wesley laughed. "Don't give it another thought; if crack-brained were the worst we were ever called, we should be remarkably complimented. But I believe much of Law's greatness lies in the fact that his sensitivity to logic is as marked as his sensitivity to conscience. Many of our number may be crack-brained, but I don't believe the term applicable to Mr. Law."

The poet bowed, and the silver thread on his coat shone in the light now streaming in the windows. "Perhaps that is why the book had such a powerful effect upon Dr. Johnson. I recall he told me he had become a sort of lax *talker* against religion, for he did not much *think* against it. He said this lasted till he went to Oxford and there took up Law's *Serious Call*, expecting to find it a dull book as such books generally are. 'But I found Law quite an overmatch for me; and this was the first occasion of my thinking in earnest of religion after I became capable of rational inquiry.' I believe I have his words exactly, as they made a profound impression upon my mind."

The conversation then became general and the Perronet party left a few minutes later, with Sally expressing her warm desire that she and Catherine should meet and visit more during the Wesleys' stay in London.

The very next afternoon, just after Catherine had dismissed her students to their noon meal, Sally saw her in the courtyard and called, "Do come up to John's rooms; he has begged that Charles and I make free of them while we're here." Sally led the way to Wesley's apartment and prepared tea for them in the large ivory and blue teapot made especially for John Wesley by Josiah Wedgewood. Catherine read the inscription on the pot:

Be present at our table, Lord,
Be here and everywhere ador'd;
These creatures bless and grant that we
May feast in paradise with Thee.

Sally poured the tea into little handleless dishes. "Oh, how good it is to be in a well-appointed house. I so long to set up housekeeping."

"Have you and Charles no place of your own?" Catherine tried to keep the surprise out of her voice.

"Alas, no. We have been riding circuit."

"On your honeymoon?" And this time Catherine made no attempt to hide her shock.

"Do not misunderstand. I'm not complaining. I'm most eager to share in my husband's work. And always we have the most sweet fellowship in the sacrament and in prayer. I could ask for nothing more, truly." She paused. "It is just that sometimes the circumstances have been rather, er—uncomfortable."

Such gentle understatement aroused Catherine's sense of humor, and soon the tea was cooling in the dishes while they exchanged stories of their circuit-riding experiences. ". . . and then my mare dropped a shoe, which occasioned so much loss of time that we could not ride across the sands, but were obliged to go round through a miserable road. And then our guide lost his way, so that we arrived at the ferry too late for the last crossing . . ." Sally paused for a sip of tea while Catherine told of their near-disastrous crossing of the flooded river.

Then Sally took up the conversation. "The next day Charles was preaching to nearly three thousand when the press-gang came and seized one of the hearers. They even tried to take Charles, but he told them that as a duly ordained minister he was acting under protection of the king's law, and they left him alone."

Catherine then contributed her experience with the military in Canterbury.

"I do not believe Satan likes our work," Sally said. "But a higher One protects us. We were in a Society meeting in a home in Camborne when a member cried out, 'We will not stay here; we will go to Lefroy's house.' That house was in quite a different part of the town, but we all rose up and went, though none of us knew why. Soon after we were gone, a spark fell into a barrel of gunpowder, which was in the next room to the one we had vacated, and blew up the house."

"Such a story builds my faith. I have wrestled long with the matter of God's guidance in our lives."

"And have you reached a conclusion?"

"I am certain He guides . . . if we but have the faith to follow. I think it is now a matter of understanding His perfect timing. Perhaps it is just that I am too impatient." Catherine spread her hands in a helpless gesture.

Sally laughed and took Catherine's hand. "Oh, how good it is to talk to one who shares my feelings! I have no answers either, but so many questions. And I do know that holding on to the good times—all the times God has answered and fulfilled His promises—has gotten me through the bad times.

"Like the evening Charles was preaching in a barn when he began to sink out of sight before my very eyes. I never knew worse fear. I thought he was to be taken away from me right there. It turned out that the barn had been built on a marsh, and the weight of the crowd made the floor sink. No one was hurt, and we continued with a glorious service in the field. That night many even fainted under the sense of God's love."

Then Sally laughed again and finished her story in a hushed voice. "And that night in the inn, the mattress collapsed right through the bedstead, and we were obliged to sleep on the floor."

Catherine had promised Durial she would not be late, so the women parted, promising to have many more such visits.

But that was not to be; for when Catherine reached Greenwich, she found Durial headachy and fretful and still struggling to carry on with the housework. For many days Catherine's time was fully consumed and allowed no leisure for anything but duties at school and home. Even her resolution to visit Elmira Smithson had to be postponed.

Philip, however, was carrying forth his program of prison visitation with success. He had gone back every day since that initial visit to pray with the little band of condemned men. There were now fifteen who regularly crowded into the murky, fetid room to sit on dirty straw that covered the cold stone floor and listen to Philip's words of comfort. Lancaster continued to be his strongest support, every day bringing a new prisoner to the group.

But most remarkable of all was Doyle, who had entered spewing curses on that first visit. Following Lancaster's continued witnessing, Doyle had asked forgiveness for his sins and was now a most enthusiastic worker among his fellow prisoners, going from cell to cell, sharing his own clear sense of forgiveness and striving to bring the same to his fellow sufferers.

Today Philip sat on the straw with the condemned men and listened to Doyle preach. "I say to you, it matters not which side of the walls we be on. It is absolutely impossible to be happy, either in time or eternity, without knowing your sins are forgiven . . ."

Philip couldn't help thinking what a shame this man was due to be hanged in two days. If he could have received an education, he would have made a fine preacher. His voice, which reverberated so well off the stone walls, could have carried as well in a parish church.

But then as Philip rose and his own voice filled the stone room with prayer, he reflected that the same could be said of himself. He too was preaching in prison when he would sooner be ministering in a church. At the end of his prayer, he looked at the faces around him and had to ask forgiveness that he had complained. For the moment this was his place of ministry, and he would do it to his utmost, with thankfulness to the God who allowed him a place.

He turned to Atkins, a youth of about nineteen. "Are you afraid to die?"

"No, sir. Really, I am not."

"Wherefore are you not afraid?" Philip continued the catechism.

"I have laid my soul at the feet of Jesus; therefore, I am not afraid to die."

Philip continued around the room. Next was Gardner, a journeyman carpenter, about fifty, who gave a strong report of what the Lord had done for his soul. And on down the row, to one Thompason, an illiterate young man who, in spite of a severe speech defect, gave assurance that he too was saved from the fear of death and was perfectly happy in his Savior.

That evening Philip went home knowing that the next night would be his last with those men. Although hardly a humorous situation, he couldn't suppress a small smile at the irony. He had prayed fervently for a congregation he wouldn't have to leave. So he was supplied with a congregation that would be leaving him.

He lit his fireplace, but did not take off his coat. It would be some time yet before the room was comfortably warm, even on a June night. But the flame would be enough to fry a rasher of bacon to accompany his evening tea. Stepping to his cupboard, he saw the letter his landlady had laid on his bed.

At first the name Perronet made his breath come in a strange way; but on second look, he saw that the post was from Vincent, not from his daughter. He lit a candle to supplement the dim light from the window and read. The words brought such a surge of hope to his heart that he jumped to his feet and circled his small room in five strides before making himself read the letter through a second time.

. . . As the Bishop of Ely is an old friend of mine, I have

taken the liberty of writing to him myself to recommend you for this post. I was able to tell him I have personally heard you preach in my own pulpit. Further, with Cambridge in his diocese, he should be well-disposed to your academic credentials.

I wish you well, my Son. May His blessings go with you.

Vincent Perronet

The living at Grantchester was open, and it was in the gift of the Bishop of Ely. That lovely village on the banks of the Cam, just outside Cambridge, was without a vicar. A vicarage—not just a curacy. It was far more than he had dared pray for.

Philip's first impulse was to pack clean linen in his bag and set out at once. He smiled for the second time that evening. Such impulsive behavior was unlike him; besides, he could not leave yet. He had a commitment at the Fleet to fulfill first. He cut two slices of bacon from a slab and placed it in a wire rack to cook over the fire. In spite of the excitement in his heart, this night would be spent the same as every other—alone in his room.

The next night, however, was unlike any other he had experienced. Armed with adequate money for garnishment, Philip convinced the keeper to allow the condemned men to assemble together in one cell so that they might pass their last hours together in prayer. The men came in quietly and sat on the straw and stone. Nothing in their outward appearance showed that they had but a few hours to live. Philip began the gathering by reading from the Prayer Book, first the Commination: "'Now seeing that all are accursed who do err and go astray from the commandments of God, let us (remembering the dreadful judgment hanging over our heads) return unto our Lord God with all contrition and meekness of heart, bewailing and lamenting our sinful life . . .'"

Lancaster led the others with a loud, "Amen."

Then Philip turned to the Psalm: "'Have mercy upon me, O God, after Thy great goodness; according to the multitude of Thy mercies do away mine offenses. Wash me thoroughly from my wickedness; and cleanse me from my sin, for I acknowledge my faults; and my sin is ever before me.'"

And finally the prayer, as those who were sitting shifted to their knees: "'O Lord, we beseech Thee, mercifully hear our prayers, and spare all those who confess their sins unto Thee; that they, whose consciences by sin are accused, by Thy merciful pardon may be absolved; through Christ our Lord. Amen.'"

The men then continued in prayer, some extemporaneously, for it seemed that the Lord had opened their mouths and their hearts. Philip was sure he had never before so truly sensed the reality of God's mercy. Tonight this mercy was ennobling these illiterate, condemned prisoners who so wholeheartedly sought it and so fully accepted it.

All too soon the clanking of the iron door brought with it an announcement of the time. The turnkey barked his orders and led the prisoners into the press yard. But even in the gray of predawn in the stone-walled yard, with the carts that were to transport them to Tyburn parked by the gate, a solemn joy and peace shone on each countenance. Philip took Doyle's hand. "My dear man, how do you find yourself?"

"Find myself! Why truly, sir, my soul is so filled with light, love, and peace that I am the same as if I had naught else within me!" He then turned to the jailers in the yard and began telling them of the love of God to him and his assurance of knowing that God for Christ's sake had forgiven all his sins.

But this was cut short, as the jailers began pushing their charges into the carts. Philip, who had received permission from the warden to accompany the men, was shoved into the first cart with Doyle and Lancaster as roughly as all the rest. Lancaster sat on his own coffin. Doyle, who could not afford one and so would share a pauper's grave, sat on the rough floor of the tumbril.

The horses started off with a jerk, bouncing the heavy wooden cart on its iron wheels over the rough stone pavement. The procession went down Ludgate Hill and turned into Holborn. Already a crowd had gathered along the street. This was a hanging day, and the populace was prepared to enjoy it to the full. Hanging day held the status of a holiday. Throughout the city master coachmakers, tailors, shoemakers—any who must deliver orders within a given time—always bore in mind to observe to their customers, "That will be a hanging day, and my men will not be at work."

Holborn became Oxford Street, and as the carts approached Tyburn Road, the crowds became denser and rowdier.

"Hey, wanta rubber neck, Mate?"

"Swing 'em up 'igh, Charlie, so's they can 'ave a better view!"

"Cooee, they got a parson too! I always knowed they was a thievin' lot!" A tomato squashed through the bars of the cart, and red streaks ran down Philip's sleeve. He suddenly realized that to the observers, he was no different from the prisoners. He felt shame wash over him as he understood that the crowd thought him condemned too.

And then he was ashamed of his shame. Was this not exactly what Christ had suffered for him—to be numbered among the transgressors? And was it not appropriate that he, who but for the mercy of Christ would be condemned eternally for his own sins, should taste just a small portion of what Christ suffered in taking on the sin of others, in identifying with the damned?

The tumbril lurched to a stop. Two carts from Newgate were there ahead of them. A great cheer went up from the crowd as the pealing of church bells, led by those from St. Sepulchre's, announced that the proceedings were to begin. Holidayers passed gin bottles from hand to hand; children clambered atop their parents' shoulders; and the lucky ones with front-row spaces spread picnic baskets on rugs.

And then a louder cheer rose as the first cart opened, and the most popular of the condemned, a well-known highwayman called Daring Dirk, stepped out. Highwaymen held the ancient privilege of heading the procession of malefactors, and he was immediately mobbed by spectators trying to snatch a memorial such as a lock of his hair or a piece of his clothing. With an air of *noblesse oblige* Dirk pulled bits of lace from his sleeve and buttons from his coat and bestowed them upon the throng.

Jack Ketch, as all public executioners were called after a well-known hangman from the previous century, stepped forward as if to greet the highwayman. But in truth, his hand was not held out to shake, rather to receive his agreed payment from his victim. The larger the bribe, the easier the hangman could make the death, even to pulling on the legs of the victim or to sitting across his shoulders to accelerate strangulation. Dangerous Dirk produced a fat wad; he had no intention of suffering long. Then with a jaunty wave he mounted the scaffold. At the top he turned again and tossed his feathered hat into the crowd with a flourish. The story of his gallant death would be told and retold, and his fame as a folk hero was assured.

But in the third tumbril, the mood was not one of such reckless bravado, nor of grim resignation, but rather of quiet rejoicing as Philip led the men in a hymn.

The door of the cart opened. Doyle was the first to stand up. Lifting his eyes to heaven, he said with a loud voice so all around could hear, "Lord, didst not Thou die for sinners? Thou didst die for me!" Turning around to the multitude, he prayed out loud. When he was finished, Philip could not see a dry eye anywhere around him. Then all from the cart went forward together.

Philip paid Jack Ketch. At the top of the stairs Doyle, Lancaster, Gardner, and Thompason turned as one man and cried, "Lord Jesus, receive our spirits!"

*C*atherine was sitting with Durial going over the linen cupboard lists and checking the mending needs when Audrey interrupted with a soft knock. "Mr. Ferrar's below askin' for the mistress and Miss Perronet. I told 'im Mr. Ned was still on circuit."

"Will you see him, Catherine? I simply must get this chore finished this afternoon." Durial sighed at the mountain of folded linen beside her.

"Gladly." Catherine was out the door before her word was finished.

But at the bottom of the stairs she halted sharply. "Philip! Are you ill? You look ghastly." She was accustomed to the thinness of his frame and the sharpness of his cheekbones, but the hollowness around his normally bright eyes was alarming. "Audrey, bring a tray of coffee and cold meats to the parlor." She led the way into the sitting room.

"Thank you." Philip folded his long body into a wing-back chair. "I am not ill, but I have had such an experience. . . . I have just watched four dear friends die." And he told her of the execution.

Catherine poured coffee from the silver pot Audrey set

147

before her on a small table and considered his account. "Do you not rejoice that their souls are now in Heaven?"

"Assuredly I do. I think my grief is more for myself. For them it is a glorious release. I feel bereft. Is that selfish in me?"

If his question had not been so earnest and at such a sad time, she would have laughed. He was the most unselfish creature she had ever met. "On the contrary, Philip. It is your great desire to give of yourself in service that causes you grief. Like a mother when her last child marries, you now have no one left to minister to." And with a flash of insight she understood that he was again, but in a different way, suffering the kind of trauma he had known in the loss of his curacy. Again he had put down roots. Even as shallow as the stone floor of the prison had required those roots to be, the pulling up was painful.

"Philip," she spoke rapidly in her rush to comfort him, "the Lord will provide a new place of service. He has promised. 'He that walketh in a perfect way, he shall serve Me.' I do believe that, Philip. He knows your desire. You shall serve Him."

"Thank you, Catherine. I believe it too. And your hopeful words put me in mind of something I had quite forgotten. I didn't come to mourn with you, but to tell you of the letter I received from your father and to take my leave."

"Leave?"

"Yes, your father has recommended me to the Bishop of Ely for a living that has come open. I shall leave in the morning for an interview. It is just possible—"

"Oh, Philip! It's more than just possible. It's quite certain!" She jumped to her feet. "Philip! What a wonderful answer to prayer! Bishop Gooch is an old friend of Father's. I'm certain he will give you a warm interview."

Philip held up his hand in protest and tried to argue that the matter was by no means certain, but Catherine would not hear of it. She had prayed too long for a place of service for Philip and had reaffirmed her faith in God's guidance too fully to allow any doubt now. They talked at length of the vicarage and of Philip's travel plans.

"And when will you return?" Catherine asked.

"If the weather's fine, Cambridge is only three days' ride, then half a day on to Ely. I should be able to accomplish it in just over a week."

"And will you preach on the way?"

"Oh, of course. I haven't thought this through well. Yes, the Cambridge Society has requested a preacher. I shall hold services in Cambridge, Newmarket, Burwell . . . two weeks at least. Will Ned be back by then?"

"I think not. He and Charl have gone clear to Newcastle. But, Philip, if you are not back by Sunday, you will miss your birthday. I had thought to make you a poppy-seed cake."

"My birthday?"

"Yes, don't you remember at Shoreham when Philothea decreed the second Sunday in Trinity to be your birthday?"

"No, I had entirely forgotten. I shall be sorry to miss the cake."

And that was as personal as his leave-taking was to be—he would miss the cake. The conversation turned briefly back to his prison ministry, with Catherine renewing her vow to aid the Smithson family and Philip telling more of Doyle's conversion. In spite of her serene exterior, however, Catherine was troubled inside. She didn't want to talk only of Philip's work. Did he care for nothing else? No one else? Was his every thought only for those to whom he could minister? As important as his work was, couldn't there be more?

She looked into those steady eyes of his, so revealing and yet so shuttered at the same time. Warm, kind, intelligent eyes that told nothing about the man behind them and made no revelation of his emotions.

The fact that she at least partially understood his isolation didn't always make it easy to accept. There were times, like right now, when she wanted to smash the wall he had erected around himself so that she could get to the real Philip inside.

At times she wondered if, indeed, he had emotions behind that unrevealing face. But she never wondered for long because, attuned to him as she was, she had learned to read the tiny looks and gestures that gave him away. And she never, not even in her most depressed moments, doubted that, once she reached him, the real Philip would be worth finding.

Now the tightness around his mouth and the jerky motion with which he placed his black shallow-brimmed hat on his head told her of the importance he placed on this journey.

"God go with you," she called from the doorway as he mounted Jezreel.

The thought that he was going to interview for a living should have raised Catherine's spirits; but as she turned away from the closed door and crossed the darkened hall, she felt heavyhearted. She searched her mind for a comforting thought and was horrified at the verse that came to her mind: "And Stephen went out and preached the word of God boldly." No! She would not think about that—about the stones, the mad bulls, the drunken threats Philip would face. Nor would she think about what preaching in similar circumstances had cost Stephen. That was in God's hands.

There was only one thing she could do, and that was what she would concentrate on. Right there in the hall she closed her eyes; and forcing frightening images away, she deliberately thought about Philip preaching calmly to the throng, Philip proclaiming God's love and God's Word, Philip placing all his faith in the power of God's protection.

She would pray and continue with her own work. Doing whatever her hand found to do could be a great comfort in times of difficulty. And in Durial's home, there was never any lack of work. Catherine returned to the drawing room to find her sister-in-law hard at work polishing the furniture. "Durial,"

Catherine protested, "Audrey rubbed the tables with lemon oil not a fortnight ago. Can't you rest?"

Durial ran an impatient hand across her forehead. "With Ned forever away on his preaching trips, someone must keep our home from falling to bits around our ears. The furniture should long ago have been revarnished with alkanet root, rose pink, and linseed oil, but when do you think Ned could have time to see to such as that?"

With a sigh Catherine picked up a rag and the bottle of lemon oil. Monday she would return to her class and would be certain to call on Elmira Smithson.

A few days later when Catherine kept her resolve, the worsening of the Smithsons' situation made her almost wish she hadn't called on them. "I ast Dick about lettin' Isey go back to yer school like you said—" Elmira's speech was interrupted by a racking cough that made Catherine put her hands to her own chest in sympathy. "Dick won't 'ear none o' it. Knew 'e wouldn't—but was good o' you to offer."

Isaiah had returned to sweeping, and Elmira was doing a careful job of all the laundry she could take in, even if bending over the tubs of water made her cough worse. Catherine spoke what words of comfort she could, placed two wheaten loaves on the bare table, and gave a boiled sweet to little Susanna before she left.

The days dragged slowly, and Catherine was more thankful than ever that she had her faith in God's guidance to cling to. No matter how gray the day or how dismal the prospects around her appeared, Catherine could say with the psalmist, "As for God, His way is perfect. . . . He is a buckler to all those that trust in Him." And then Sally's letter came in the next post.

My Dear Catherine,

How precious my memories of our friendship are to me. What joy to know that one other creature has shared my difficulties and understands my feelings. You will note this letter is sent from Ludlow. I fell ill on the way to Bristol from London, so my dear Charles brought me home to my mother for her excellent nursing while he set about his next preaching tour. My sister Betsy is also a most excellent nurse. Perhaps if I am recovered when Charles returns, he might think me strong enough to set up our own home. Write to me of our friends in London. It is beautiful here in Wales, but I miss news of the Society.

> Yr ever-faithful friend,
> Sally Wesley

The words that fell between the lines of Sally's careful script were the ones that tore at Catherine's heart. Here she was in good health and had only a brother and dear friend to worry about facing the dangers of a circuit. Sally was ill, longing for her own home, missing and fearing for her new husband. Catherine breathed a prayer for her friend and then determined to avoid going the same road herself. No matter how fond her feelings for Philip, she had no desire to spend her life traveling from one decrepit inn to the next so that a new crowd of ruffians might pitch stones at her husband. Not that Philip had ever given her the least indication he would make such an offer; but if he did, she knew she must refuse him. Of course, if he found success with the Bishop of Ely . . .

Philip's great haste to reach the Bishop caused him to plan only one night for revisiting the familiar sights of Cambridge. He tethered Jezreel in St. Andrew's Street and, for the first time since his graduation five years before, entered the gates of Emmanuel College. Here he had worked and studied for three years as a sizar, acting as servant first to young Lord Leatham and then to Percy Chalmers, noblemen who came to the university to acquire a smattering of classics and mathematics between rounds of parties. Since men of independent means who were not destined for the Church or the Bar weren't hindered by any requirement to take examinations or attend classes, Philip's life had been a constant struggle to please his cavalier masters while maintaining his own academic standards. Examinations were required of one like Philip who came of the servant class and who would take Holy Orders.

Philip recalled the nights of study constantly interrupted by demands that he serve liquor, polish boots, and carry notes to ladies. At first he had had only his own determination to carry him through. But then, after acquaintance with William Law's book led him to understand the basis for a devout and holy life, the service ceased to be a yoke and became instead a challenge which he met gladly.

Now he walked across the wide green court toward the colonnade built by Sir Christopher Wren and entered the chapel behind. Emmanuel College, founded in the sixteenth century by Queen Elizabeth's chancellor of the exchequer, had been built on the site of a Dominican friary which was abandoned during the dissolution of church properties by Henry VIII. From the first the college had had a Puritan bias, ties which were strengthened during Cromwell's reign and which even now Philip could sense in the austere white walls, stone floor, and plain glass windows of the chapel. The only contrast came from the well-proportioned carving in the dark wood furnishings.

Philip left the chapel and walked on beside the herb and rose gardens lining the Elizabethan walls of the court, built largely from the stones of long-crumbled Cambridge Castle. He paused at the doorway of the elegant, unpuritanical Hall and recalled serving his superiors at high table. But for all the nobility who had passed through these doors, the two most famous students had been commoners—William Law and the Puritan cabinet minister, John Harvard, who went to America and founded a college to train clergymen in the colony of Massachusetts.

Philip smiled as he turned away from Hall. His university years, as his orphanage years, had been marked by his detachment from his fellow men. He had not minded wearing his coarse gown, signifying the lowest rank of undergraduate in the scale topped by the elegantly robed noblemen. They had been years of vast mental and spiritual growth, in the sum, not unhappy to look back upon.

Philip had intended only a brief walkabout before he settled into a room at The Sun, but when he reemerged onto St. Andrew's Street, he ran almost bodily into a figure from his past. "Thomas Thornton!" Philip clasped the man's arm as much to steady him from their near collision as in greeting. "Are you still in Cambridge?"

Thornton had been a close friend of Percy Chalmers whom Philip served at Emmanuel. "Went into the family firm of solicitors in Newmarket. See by your garb you took orders. Seems I recall you had Methody tendencies—didn't become a Jacobite or anything crack-brained, did you?" Thornton looked over his shoulder as if he didn't want to be seen in suspect company should the answer be wrong.

"Oh, I assure you I'm anything but a political rebel. Long live King George. I am with the Methodist Society, however."

"Meeting tonight, but I suppose that's what you're here for."

Philip assured him he had no idea what he was talking about.

"Big Methody meeting on Christ's Pieces. Some Welch fellow, Harris, preaching. Thought I'd look in on the doings. Care to come along?"

Philip started to refuse. He'd planned on an early evening and riding on at dawn the next morning. But his conscience smote him. In his intense desire to reach Ely, he had forgotten his stated intentions of holding meetings in the area. Certainly he should go and lend his support to the preacher.

They arrived at the open green field at the end of Emmanuel Street just as the crowd began singing. It was a new experience for Philip to stand at the back of such a gathering. He found the perspective most interesting as he surveyed the farmers and housewives still carrying their baskets of vegetables from the Cambridge market. In spite of a few catcalls, they seemed an unusually peaceable group—until the leader began the third song and complaints began.

"What's a' matter—preacher afraid to speak?"

"Yeah, Parson—cat got yer tongue?"

"What is this 'ere? Some 'oity-toity musical society?"

"We want preachin'!"

And then the rumor spread through the crowd—Howell Harris had not arrived as scheduled. It was certain the local vicar would not under any circumstances preach in an open field. Philip knew what he must do.

"Seems I'll have to take leave of your company." He bowed to Thornton. "They need a preacher, and that's my calling."

He didn't wait for the startled expression to leave his companion's face. "I daresay, field preaching—"

As Philip pushed his way through the throng, he breathed a prayer, "O Lord, show me what to say to these people."

The crowd made way for him, and he met no obstacle until he reached the wooden platform that the Society had dragged onto the grass to make a speaker's platform. In the very front stood a surly young clergyman who would not give way. "My brother, I have come to offer my services as a preacher, but I see you precede me. Perhaps you would like to address this congregation. I should be happy to be numbered among your hearers." Philip made him a bow.

The cleric gave Philip a haughty look and stepped aside just enough to allow him to pass. Relief flooded the distressed song leader's face, and he introduced the preacher newly arrived from London. Philip gave only the briefest thought to the tomatoes and peaches he saw in many market baskets before he announced his topic. He had only his Bible with him, but that was enough to carry him through his favorite sermon on 1 John 5:12, "He that hath the Son hath life; and he that hath not the Son of God hath not life."

The crowd was remarkably well-behaved, and the few tomatoes and dirt clods thrown were poorly aimed. One juicy peach, however, landed squarely on the head of the surly clergyman who was standing so as to block as much of Philip's access to his audience as possible.

Next morning Philip put Cambridge and its memories behind him as he set out for Ely. By midday the path across the flat fenland brought him in sight of the cathedral standing on its island like a lighthouse on a hill. Even at this time of day mists from the surrounding waters rose around the building, emphasizing the fact that it was bordered on all sides by wild and treacherous marsh. A hundred years before, Cromwell had completed the plans begun by Charles I to drain the fens and thereby brought hundreds of square miles of land under the plow. So now Philip rode through fields of flax, wheat, and hay.

For much of the sixteen miles, Philip meditated on his forthcoming interview and prayed that this would be the answer to his waiting. But then Jezreel's hooves clattered over one of the many wooden bridges spanning the drains that crisscrossed the fens, and he saw the eels swimming in the water. His thoughts turned to his surroundings, and he gave a smile for the legend which lent the town its name. These eels and all those populating the streams of East Anglia were believed to be the descendants of the monks of the tenth century who had taken wives and were punished by the reformer St. Dunstan by being turned into eels.

Philip sat even taller than usual in the saddle as he rode past the great cathedral and on to the Bishop's Palace. The bishop's chaplain answered Philip's knock. For a moment Philip couldn't believe what he saw. Just in time he checked his impulse to groan and bestowed an uncertain smile on the man before him. It was the surly cleric from last night's meeting.

"Philip Ferrar. I believe My Lord Bishop is expecting me." Philip offered his letter of introduction from Vincent Perronet.

"Please wait here." The chaplain turned, and Philip noted

that his hair and clothes were scrubbed clean of any traces of the peach. He ushered Philip into a richly appointed gallery presided over by the portrait of a dour-looking bishop in a black velvet cape. In contrast to the luxuriousness of the furnishings, the severe austerity of the attitudes around him chilled Philip. He dared not think what his future held if he met yet another refusal.

The sound of the chaplain's quick step on the polished wooden floor told Philip he wouldn't have long to wait. "His Lordship will see you now." The chaplain's lips curled in a cross between a smirk and a smile, but his eyes were hard.

The bishop sat at his desk, light from the leaded window beside him falling on his white hair. A wave of his ringed hand told Philip to take a seat. The bishop looked at the papers on his desk and went straight to the heart of the matter.

"You seek appointment to the vicarage of Grantchester. Mr. Perronet is most warm in his support. Why did you leave your curacy in Midhurst?"

The unpleasant must be brought into the open sooner or later. Philip was glad to have it be sooner. "I was dismissed for teaching Jesus Christ and Him crucified, My Lord."

The ringed hand waved the statement aside. "And what have you been doing since that time?"

"I have been doing itinerant preaching."

"Ah, yes. I have heard of your unseemly enterprise last night. Grantchester is a quiet, well-behaved parish. I do not believe an enthusiastic vicar would best suit their needs."

The thrust came so rapidly and so quietly that at first Philip was not aware of the pain from its cut.

"I thank you for the courtesy of your call. But do not let me detain you any longer." Dr. Gooch rose and rang a bell. When the chaplain appeared in the doorway, the bishop added, "Mr. Flagg will give you a glass of Madeira on your way out."

Philip rose, made a mechanical bow to the bishop, and left the palace without the support of the offered glass of wine. The complete interview, upon which his entire future hung, had lasted less than five minutes.

As if of their own volition, his feet carried him across the grass to the cathedral. He continued his sleepwalk down the great nave until he stood beneath the glory of the cathedral—one of the wonders of medieval engineering and carpentry—Ely's lantern. Arching his head back, he looked up into the glorious aureola formed from the light shafting downward through the high traceried windows of the octagonal tower. As he looked at the display of pure light that spread from the lantern over the wooden ceiling and throughout the whole church, it seemed that some of that same light touched his soul. Its warmth thawed just a drop of all that was frozen within him. But it was enough to allow the Word of God to speak through his numbness, "Cause me to hear Thy lovingkindness . . . for in Thee do I trust; cause me to know the way wherein I should walk; for I lift up my soul unto Thee."

It seemed he had come to the end of the path. But then he looked up into the light, and his Guide was there to lead him through the uncharted way. In the great cathedral, Philip knelt with the light from the magnificent lantern of the tower shining on him like a benediction. And in his pain, he thought of another who had been denied all he had worked for and hoped for because he did what he believed to be right. Perhaps it was his recent visit to Emmanuel College that brought William Law so strongly to his mind as he prayed. Soon Philip realized he was no longer praying, but instead meditating on Law's life and feeling a great kinship with this man. After achieving the goal for which he had worked and studied—after becoming a Fellow of Emmanuel—Law had it taken from him just five years later when he refused to swear the oath of allegiance to the new line of German kings.

Though a priest of the Church of England, though a man with the highest sense of the responsibilities of the clerical office and the duties of his order, Law gave up all right to conduct a service, to celebrate the Holy Communion, or to preach a sermon. He chose instead to live in seclusion—studying, praying, and guiding souls through his writing and his charities.

As the light from the lantern spread throughout the cathedral along the vaulted arches, so the light of God's leading spread through Philip's heart and mind. He knew what he would do. He rose to his feet with a much lighter spirit. He would go to King's Cliffe. William Law would be his counselor.

It was a long ride the next day on across the fenland and finally through the edge of Rockingham Forest to the tiny village where Law lived. Not until the three symmetrical chimney stacks of the Hall Yard House came into view did Philip doubt his inspiration to make the trip. What if Law weren't at home? What if he were home, but had no inclination to receive an intruder? What if . . .

Jezreel drew up before the comfortable house built of the local freestone, roofed with greenish slates, and announced their arrival with a whinny. The noise attracted the attention of a black-suited, stout man with broad shoulders and round face who was escorting a bent, ragged man carrying a clean shirt and basket of fresh vegetables across the courtyard. "I shall see you again, my dear friend. Meditate on the words of our Lord." The merry-countenanced man held the gate for the beggar and then turned to Philip, who dismounted with some chagrin at coming so abruptly into the presence of the esteemed William Law.

Philip introduced himself, but found it impossible to explain the purpose of his visit, since he didn't understand it himself. Law, however, seemed to find nothing in the least unusual about having a caller he had not seen for more than five years arrive at his gate in search of counsel and comfort.

"Come in, come in. You have had a long ride? I believe our distribution of food and raiment is done for the day. If any other comes, one of my house can see to it. You have come from London? You must stop here for a time. We get so little word from the great city."

He led the way through the courtyard and into an old wainscotted hall. "My study is upstairs." He waved his hand at an ascending staircase. "But let us go through here first; I should like you to meet my companions." The parlor was unoccupied, so Law went through the back door and into the garden. "Ah, we've found you at last," he called to two women sitting on a garden bench. "Mr. Ferrar, Mrs. Hutcheson and Miss Gibbon, my companions and spiritual pupils."

The ladies put aside their books and came forward to welcome Philip, and in a moment he was being given as complete a tour of Law's property as if he were expected to take up residence there. ". . . and on the other side of the paddock," pretty, lace-capped Miss Gibbon said, "is the footbridge over Willow Brook. Beyond that are the schools and almshouses which Mr. Law and Mrs. Hutcheson erected and endowed."

"We now have fourteen girls receiving instruction and clothing in our school," the small, plump Mrs. Hutcheson added.

"And there is my oak tree." Miss Gibbon pointed to a small green sprout. "I planted that when I came to reside here—1744 that was, so it's just an infant yet, but someday it will shade the paddock."

Law's gray eyes and ruddy complexion glowed as he looked at the field washed in the golden light of evening. "It is my habit to take an hour's walk in my fields before supper. Would you care to join me?"

Philip begged time to stable Jezreel and then joined his host with pleasure. They walked along a footpath bordered on one side with a field of waist-high dark green grain and on the other with a brambled hedgerow, lush with ripe berries and vibrant with birdsong. "My favorite form of vesper," Law said, after they had walked for some time with the birds' arias as the only accompaniment to the rustle of their footsteps in the long grass. "You have sought me out for counsel?"

And suddenly Philip found it so easy, so natural to talk to

this man. He told briefly of his curacy and rejection and now of his work with the Methodist Society. But through all his words rang clearly his desire for a call from God to a place of ministry— a settled, peaceful place to shepherd a flock. And he told of his latest refusal by the bishop.

"And would you have acted differently in Cambridge had you foreseen the results?" Law asked.

"Fifteen souls sought the Savior that night. I could do no other, so help me God."

Law nodded, and his open, agreeable countenance took on an expression of nostalgia. "Relinquishing my college Fellowship for conscience' sake was a melancholy affair, but had I done what was required of me to avoid it, I should have thought my condition much worse. The benefits of my education seemed at an end, but yet the same education had been more miserably lost, had I not learned to fear something more than misfortunes.

"If I were not happier now for that earlier trial, I am persuaded it would be my own fault. Had I brought myself into troubles by my own folly, they would have been very trying; but, I thank God, I can think of them without dejection."

A smile broke across his face. "I recall writing something of the like to my brother George shortly after the occurrence. I remember that my most pressing concern was for my mother. I feared she would be overcome in her concern for me. But the Lord was faithful to sustain those dear to me also."

The bell ringers of King's Cliffe Church began their ancient custom of pealing the hours of the day as the two men turned their steps back toward Law's house.

"It has always been so. I have found the Lord ever faithful. As we are faithful in our devotion to Him, He supplies our need for others to minister to. That is the key to happiness, meeting the needs of others."

When they returned to the house, Law ushered Philip into a long, low-ceilinged dining room where the table stood by a bow window looking onto the garden. Supper was the simplest meal imaginable, consisting of a few biscuits, cheese, and wine. The household servants then joined Law, his guest, and the women for evening prayer and Law's reading of Scripture before everyone retired at nine o'clock.

Alone in his room with only the light of the moon shining through his window, Philip thought of the light that had shined on him at Ely and led him to this house, to this counselor. He was reminded of the Scripture that spoke of coming out of darkness into God's marvelous light. He felt assured that William Law would be instrumental in shedding God's light in his life. Perhaps the first spark had been struck. He thought back over their evening stroll in the fields and recalled Law's words of the importance of filling others' needs with oneself. Thinking on this, Philip felt light and warmth and comfort sink into his soul. He had been so very much alone all his life—isolated in a crowded orphanage. He saw in his own mind the child he had been—the repressed, quiet, good little boy. And he saw the man that little boy had become—quiet, withdrawn, alone, not opening himself to anyone nor allowing anyone close enough to reach his needs.

Catherine was the nearest he had admitted anyone. But the thought of allowing her to come closer and then abandon him was too painful to be borne. However, here in the Hall Yard House he had found sanctuary.

And the peace of King's Cliffe, the peace William Law practiced with his fellow men and before his God, permeated Philip's soul in the following days. Philip had long known peace in solitude, in the ability to withdraw and be comfortable with himself and with God. But this was a new kind of peace Law practiced, as he lived his devout and holy life in a complete giving of himself.

Law rose early and breakfasted in his room on a cup of chocolate before appearing in the drawing room to lead family prayers at nine o'clock. He would then invite Philip to join him in his bedroom upstairs where the morning light fell through the stone-mullioned windows of the bedroom and adjoining study. And throughout the day, William Law put aside his studying and writing to interview each applicant for relief who came to the garden door.

On his third morning there, Philip sat before the fireplace in Law's oak-beamed bedroom while Law interviewed the fourth suppliant of the day in the tiny study that he called his "closet." Philip looked at the hearthstone of the fireplace and noted the hollows Law had worn in places by rubbing his cold feet upon the warm stones. Then he turned to gaze out the windows; through the trees he could just glimpse the school's library and also the almshouses endowed by his host. From the next room he heard Law's counsel to the beggar. "My good man, I shall be happy to meet your needs for half a crown, but see that you spend it wisely. And be assured that I shall do the same. Just as I would not give a poor man money to go see a puppet show, neither would I allow myself to spend it in the same manner. It is a folly and a crime in a poor man to waste what is given him in foolish trifles whilst he wants meat, drink, and clothes. And it would be no less folly or a less crime in me to spend that money in silly diversions which might be so much better spent in imitation of the divine goodness and works of kindness and charity."

Law rose and took the pauper's hand. "And so, my brother, let us both go forth to serve God and man in the doing of good. And remember the words of the Holy Scriptures, 'Blessed be the man that provideth for the sick and needy: the Lord shall deliver him in the time of trouble.' Go now and give as it has been given unto you.

"Miss Gibbon will supply you with a loaf fresh from her oven on your way out." Law stepped to the clothespress in his bedroom and drew out a coarse linen shirt that looked little-worn. "And take this in remembrance of Him who said, 'When one asks for your cloak, give him your coat also.'" Law rang a bell, and a servant appeared to show the man out. Then Law sat in the chair across from Philip.

"You interview every petitioner personally?" Philip asked.

"Certainly. It is only by making our labor a gift and service to the poor that our ordinary work is changed into a holy service and made acceptable to God as our devotion. As charity is the greatest of all virtues, so nothing can make it more amiable in the sight of God than adding one's own labor to it."

Philip shook his head. "And for such as this they call you an enthusiast?"

Law gave his familiar guffaw of laughter. "I believe the term is 'a celebrated enthusiast,' the very worst kind—one who not only teaches the way of salvation, but lives it as well."

In an uncharacteristic show of emotion, Philip hit the arm of his chair. "But that's monstrous. To call a man an enthusiast is to call him a leper—a man to be carefully shunned." A note of bitterness attended his words.

"My two housemates and I strive to live our lives based on a literal application of the principles of the Sermon on the Mount, so I guess it is appropriate that some should say all manner of evil against us for righteousness' sake. We attempt to rejoice and be glad in it. But I do not live like a nonjuror. I delight in attending every service of my parish church." Just then the bells pealed the hour from their Norman tower across the field. "And at my special request the rector always has the Psalms sung. I have always been a high churchman. Through my study and writing, I wish to dispel the prevalent notion that piety is generally accompanied by intellectual weakness."

"*A Serious Call* has done much to dispel that notion."

"The Lord's leading is a great and marvelous thing. I often wonder if I would have written it if I had retained my Fellowship. I left Emmanuel and went as tutor to Mr. Edward Gibbon, brother of my excellent companion. By the by, my old student now has a son of his own who is showing a precocious interest in Roman history. Shouldn't be surprised if the young scamp might make a name for himself someday. At any rate, the following year I accompanied young Edward to Emmanuel as his governor and wrote the book while there. The Lord has seen fit to bless it in His work."

"Its detractors have said it sets impossibly high standards—that it is not practicable. But I see that you indeed practice it thoroughly."

"Indeed, the standard is high. But we shall do well to aim at the highest degree of perfection if we may thereby at least attain to mediocrity."

A knock at the door interrupted their discussion. A shabbily dressed woman stood there seeking charity. After a short interview, Law gave her a pail of milk from the four cows he kept and sent a large kettle of soup to her hungry children. But the soup was not ladled from the pot over the kitchen fire until Law tasted it first himself. After a careful sip of the steaming liquid, he went to the garden door and called, "Miss Gibbon, are there any more leeks in the garden? The broth is a bit weak today."

The additional vegetables strengthened the soup, and the woman went home to feed her children.

"Do you ever turn any away?" Philip asked.

Law gave his ready, cheerful laugh. "If a rogue came for money, even if I knew him to be a rogue, I would give him money, hoping for the best and believing it my duty to give to all who might be in need. It may be that I often give to those who do not deserve it or who will make ill use of my alms, but what then? Is this not the very method of divine goodness? Does not God make His sun to rise on the evil and on the good? Shall I withhold a little money or food from my fellow creature for fear he should not be good enough to receive it of me? Don't I beg of God to deal with me not according to my merit, but according to His own great goodness? And shall I be so absurd to withhold my charity from a poor brother because he may perhaps not deserve it? Shall I use a mirror toward him, which I pray God never to use toward me?"

It was now tea time, but Law, as was his custom, did not join his companions at the tea table. He chose rather to eat a few raisins, standing while they sat. As at all meals, the food was served on wooden platters. Not, Law explained, from any notion about unnecessary luxury, but because it appeared to him that a china plate spoiled the knives.

The days at King's Cliffe would forever remain in Philip's mind as a foretaste of Heaven, with William Law coming the closest he had ever known to an earthly father. But at last the time came when he must leave. On Philip's last night in Hall Yard House, Law hosted a musical gathering. This was Law's most pleasurable recreation, and he had constructed a handsome wainscotted room with a high-coved ceiling, elegantly decorated with festoons of plasterwork, where Miss Gibbon played works of Bach on the organ.

The next day, beginning his long ride back to London, Philip looped Jezreel's reins over the saddle, drew Law's book from his saddlebag, and read again a favorite passage.

> All worldly attainments, whether of greatness, wisdom, or bravery, are but empty sounds; and there is nothing wise, or great, or noble, in any human spirit, but rightly to know and heartily worship and adore the great God. That is the support and life of all spirits, whether in Heaven or on earth.

He put the book away and thought of the way ahead. Now, after this time of spiritual refreshment, he must return to the real world, to live these principles in the place God had for him. As he guided Jezreel down the road, he thought of the map he sought for his life—looked at his past and thought of the future.

And he could not think of the future without thinking of Catherine. His time with Law had taught him the importance of giving of himself. For the first time in his carefully detached existence, Philip was aware of the possibility, perhaps even the necessity, of filling another person's need with himself—his presence and his personality. It was a totally new concept for him. As he had long ago determined that he didn't need anyone, it had never occurred to him that the reverse might be true—that someone could need him, and not just his preaching.

He was trained and experienced in meeting others' needs with Jesus Christ—with introducing them to Jesus as a person— but the idea of filling a need by presenting himself left him shaken.

But, of course, that was ridiculous. Catherine had turned to him as a friend in her disappointment over Charles Wesley, had leaned on him for support in the darkness of the Fleet, had shared her concerns with him for the safety of her brother, but Catherine didn't really *need* him. She had a large family she could turn to; the Society had the deepest respect for her and all the Perronets . . . anyone would help Catherine. Why would she need him? But then why had she turned to him?

And what could he offer her? All the new spiritual insights he had gained from William Law did not change the realities one jot. He was still a foundling receiving only a meager stipend from the Society for his preaching, and he had no prospects of ever securing a settled living.

And Catherine would be the first person he must tell of his rejection when he reached London in five days' time. When he thought of the disappointment he would see in her eyes, he shrank from the task.

He couldn't go back; he couldn't tell Catherine. He had failed, had been rejected again. Even the recommendation of Vincent Perronet hadn't been enough. He had hoped so to have this to offer her. Now he would never be able to speak what was in his heart. He would be forever alone.

*I*n spite of her outward composure, Catherine was experiencing inner panic. Ned had returned from his circuit ride with Charl, bringing reports of unrest and division among the Methodist preachers in the north. . . . Sally Wesley was expecting a baby, and she and Charles had taken a house in Bristol—good news except that this would mean he would be severely reducing his itinerant ministry, a move causing concern for the work and back-biting gossip among Society members divided in their support of the Wesley brothers. People now openly talked of the rift between John Wesley and George Whitefield, and there were rumors of a split between Charles and John. . . . Elmira Smithson's cough sounded worse each time Catherine visited, and there seemed no possibility of freeing her husband from debtors' prison. . . . Durial's sharp tongue was more caustic than ever as she hectored her husband for a settled lifestyle, to give up circuit-riding and spend more time at home with her.

The list went on, but the fact that almost overwhelmed Catherine was Philip's continued absence. He was never out of her mind, and she hated to admit how much she missed him.

When she looked in her own mirror, she hardly recognized the strained, white face and the round, dark eyes with their hollow look of bereavement. She prayed silently, *I do believe You will take care of all this, Lord. But when?*

On Thursday she returned from the Foundery feeling more wilted than usual. Her students had shown more propensity to wiggle and giggle than to read, and the late summer combination of high heat and higher humidity made the mere thought of labor exhausting. Yet Durial persisted with her housekeeping schedule. With a sigh, Catherine donned a large white apron and joined the entire household staff in the kitchen to help with the preserving.

"There is a peck of plums in the garden that needs pitting," Durial said. "We shall be glad of my special damson jelly this winter."

Catherine pulled a bentwood chair into the shade and began her sticky task. But the peck was less than a quarter done when she heard a horse's hooves on the gravel. The pale blond head she saw above the hedge made her forget the heat and the plum stains on her hands and apron.

"Philip! You've been gone so long." As on that spring day in the woods, she ran toward him, and even more fiercely than then she longed for him to open his arms to receive her.

But his bleak face stopped her. "Philip . . ." It was as if she had run into a wall. Tears threatened to brim in her eyes, but she looked quickly away. If only he would open up to her—could open up. "You've had a long ride. Would you care to walk in the garden?"

They walked where they had before, but the glory was gone. Even his long-awaited presence beside her brought no comfort. The set of his shoulders and the jerky motion of his hands told her his news was bad.

He hesitated, and she knew he wanted to break the news to her gently. But there was no gentle way. "I was refused."

The thin line of his sensitive mouth told her how much he hated saying those words; no matter how calmly he spoke, they had come at great cost. The very briefness of the statement was as final as a locked gate. And it cost her to respond in a likewise unemotional manner, to honor his reticence. For a moment she could not speak. Then, "I shall tell Audrey to prepare some lemonade."

They sat in the shade and sipped cool drinks, but inside, Catherine was seething. Her world had crumbled. This was far worse than the news of Charles Wesley's marriage had been because she cared far more deeply for Philip. And now even if her inklings that Philip returned her regard had any foundation in truth, she had no hope for a future with him. A few nights ago in a dream, she had viewed herself through the eyes of another. She had been at Shoreham, kneeling in the garden, wearing a blue dress, and holding an infant in her arms. She rose and walked toward the person watching her, cuddling the precious bundle to her breast. When she woke, she knew that she had been walking to Philip, carrying their child. But now it could not be.

"Would you care for more lemonade?" The words were a mockery, but she must say something.

Before Philip could answer, a clatter of hooves and flying gravel called them to the front drive. They arrived just as Ned rushed out the front door and Charles Wesley flung off his sweating horse. "My brother intends to ruin himself!" Wesley began his story even as Ned led the way into the parlor.

"You must help me. This insanity must be stopped." Charles drew a crumpled letter from his pocket and handed it to Ned. "He didn't even write to me personally—just sent a copy of a letter to a third person. He intends to marry Grace Murray."

Catherine had never seen the soft-spoken Charles so agitated. He strode around the room spouting disconnected sentences. "The scandal will be unthinkable. It will bring to an end everything we have labored for. She has been promised to John Bennett for months. And now she accepts my brother too! In the past she has suffered serious mental illness, and I have grave concerns for her balance now." He threw his hands into the air.

"It is unthinkable. You must help me. There's no one else I can turn to. This calamity must be stopped."

"Of course, we will help you." Ned clasped his friend's shoulders. "What would you have us do?"

"Ride with me. We must go to Newcastle now."

Catherine's heart sank, thinking of the three-hundred-mile ride. "Philip, you've just returned from a journey and have not even had a good meal yet." As always, his thinness caught at her heart.

"Durial will set a table for us, and I can supply you with clean linen." Ned flung her objections aside. Within a short time the three men departed. In spite of the lateness of the hour, they were determined not to delay. Catherine felt more alone than ever. She was left with the drudgery of her duty and the difficulty of the situations around her; but worse, the one shining hope she had held to for the future had been extinguished. No light shone at the end of the tunnel.

In the month that Ned and Philip were gone, one island of brightness arose. Catherine's sister Elizabeth, who had been laboring so diligently at the Foundery that Catherine had hardly seen her all summer, announced her engagement to William Briggs, John Wesley's secretary.

"Oh, Elizabeth, I am so happy for you." Catherine hugged her sister and then embraced the smiling bridegroom-to-be. "What a perfect couple you will make. I can't fathom why I hadn't thought of the match myself. You'll go to Shoreham to be married by Papa?"

The couple planned to be off the next day so the banns could be published that very Sunday. And then, though happy for her sister, Catherine felt her desolation even more sharply. "When will it be my turn, Lord? In Your perfect timing, do You have a time for me?" As in answer, she thought of words from Ecclesiastes: "To everything there is a season, and a time to every purpose under the heaven. . . . A time to weep, and a time to laugh; a time to mourn, and a time to dance; . . . a time to embrace, and a time to refrain from embracing; . . . He hath made every thing beautiful in His time: also He hath set the world in their heart, so that no man can find out the work that God maketh from the beginning to the end."

No one can find out the work that God maketh? Then she would have to continue groping her way one step at a time, but with continued faith in her Guide and in His timing.

One thing Catherine refused to give up on was her determination to help the Smithson family. So next Monday when school was dismissed, she took her courage in hand, made sure she had adequate bribe money in her pocket, and hired a carriage to take her to the Fleet. She alighted on the walk outside the huge gray walls that concealed the horror, brutality, disease, and death she knew to be inside. The last time she had stormed these walls, Philip was beside her. Now he was on his way to the north of England, and she was alone. No, she reminded herself, never truly alone. "For Thou art with me, Thy rod and Thy staff, they comfort me."

Just as Sarah Peters had taught her to do, Catherine ignored the stares of sightseers who gathered daily outside the massive entrance gates to watch and wait and steep themselves in the malevolent atmosphere of the gaol. And she ignored as well the jeers of those who thought she was the wife or sister of a prisoner.

"Got a file under your skirts, 'ave ye?" a watcher called.

"Another Edgeworth Bess a' goin' out the window down bed sheets with yer Jack Sheppard, 'eh?"

The rabble roared in delight at this reference to Newgate's most notorious escapee who had made daring breaks to freedom on three occasions with the aid of female friends.

The clanking of the heavy doors cut Catherine off from further taunts. The turnkey took her to Dick Smithson's cell, which seemed to Catherine to be even darker and more crowded than before. Smithson sat in almost exactly the same spot, undoubtedly on the same patch of filthy straw where she had seen him months before. He looked at her with hollow eyes. "What're you doin' 'ere?"

"I'm Catherine Perronet. I was here with Elmira last summer. I used to be Isaiah's teacher."

He nodded slowly, and Catherine felt a surge of hope as she realized that he was not drunk. He had probably run out of money to purchase gin. "I 'member. You was with the tall towheaded feller that kept comin' back to sing 'ymns with those fellas they 'anged."

"Yes." She sorely wished for Philip's company today.

"Must be somethin' to a religion that makes men sing the night afore they go to Tyburn. And that would bring a fella like that one 'ere just to sing with 'em. I 'eard tell 'e rode in the death cart to the gallows with Lancaster and Doyle."

"News travels in here."

"Ain't nothin' else to do." He shrugged.

"And do you know that Elmira is sick? Her cough is worse every time I see her."

Even in the gloom of the cell Smithson's eyes showed his fear at the hopelessness of his situation. "I know. Don't know what'll become of the young'uns if she takes poorly."

"Mr. Smithson, would you reconsider my proposal to allow Isaiah to return to school?"

"Might do."

"Would you like me to pray with you, like Mr. Ferrar did with Lancaster and the others?"

But the curl of his lip and the set of his jaw told her she had gone too far. The turnkey returned to escort her out. "Mr. Smithson, think about Isaiah. If he could read and write, he could get a good job as a clerk. I'll return in a few days for your answer."

Before leaving she arranged with the warden to rent a pillow and blanket for Dick Smithson and to have a loaf of bread delivered to him from the jail's bakehouse. And she left an equal amount of garnish for the jailer as well to be certain her instructions were carried out.

At first Catherine felt considerable hope as she looked forward to Smithson's decision. But when, on her promised return a few days later, she found him far gone with gin and unwilling to hear more of her proposal, her heart sank.

And at home Durial's news was no better. A letter from Ned told them that the men had arrived at Grace Murray's orphan house and hostel in Newcastle where Charles had burst in at eleven o'clock in the morning and cried, "Grace Murray, you have broken my heart!" The letter followed with a tangled account of Charles rushing Grace off to Leeds where she was to meet both men she had promised to marry—John Wesley and John Bennett—then of their return to Newcastle where Bennett awaited without having seen Wesley.

But the part of the account that worried Catherine most was Ned's report that the affair had produced mass unrest and dissension among the Society in Newcastle. "All in the house were filled with anger and confusion; some threatened to leave the house and preach no more with Mr. Wesley." Catherine foresaw dark days ahead for the Methodists who faced enough opposition from outside, without dissension in their own ranks.

That night she went to her room in a cloud of despair. A quick glance at the books on her shelf told her what she wanted to read. Taking her well-worn copy of *Pilgrim's Progress* to a lighted candle by her bed, she turned to the scene of Christian and Hopeful's imprisonment in Doubting Castle, for certainly she felt as much a prisoner of the Giant Despair as Dick Smithson was of his jailer in the Fleet. She read through the scene of Despair exhibiting the bones of doubting pilgrims he had torn limb from limb and thrown into the courtyard, threatening to do the same to his captives in a few days. But later, after Christian and Hopeful prayed, Christian said:

> "What a fool am I to lie in a stinking dungeon, when I may as well walk at liberty! I have a key in my bosom called

Promise, that will, I am persuaded, open any lock in Doubting
Castle. . . ."

Then Christian pulled it out of his bosom and began to
try at the dungeon door, whose bolt, as he turned the key, gave
back, and the door flew open with ease, and Christian and
Hopeful both came out.

And Catherine knew that she too held the answer to the
despair that threatened to imprison her—a key called Promise.
She turned the pages of her Bible. "As for God, his way is perfect
. . . He is a buckler to all those that trust in him. . . . It is God that
girdeth me with strength, and maketh my way perfect. Commit
thy way unto the Lord: Trust also in him, and he shall bring it to
pass. . . . Wait on the Lord, and keep his way, and he shall exalt
thee to inherit the land."

Catherine snuffed her candle and slept better than she had
for weeks.

The next week when she drew up before the Foundery and
found a freshly combed and scrubbed Isaiah Smithson awaiting
her, she knew just how Christian felt when he was back again on
the King's Highway.

"Isaiah! Your father said you could come to school again?"

"Yup. Da' said you cared enough to sit on the dirty straw
with 'im and then rent 'im a blanket, so 'e figured you was a right
'un."

Catherine shuddered at the degeneration in her pupil's
speech. "Isaiah, the class is now several months ahead of you.
You shall have to work very hard."

"I brung m' book." He held out the primer she had given
him. It was dog-eared and dirty, but it would serve.

A fortnight later when Ned and Philip returned, however,
Catherine found that the key of Promise had not yet unlocked
the door to solving the Society's problems. The marriage that
Charles Wesley felt would be so disastrous for his brother had
been averted, but at what cost?

Ned, Durial, Catherine, and Philip sat before the parlor fire on an early October evening as Ned recounted the events of their trip. He spoke slowly and dramatically, relaying the tension of the events that had resulted in the marriage of Grace Murray to John Bennett. The incident had caused a grievous rift between the Wesley brothers and a tidal wave of dissension throughout the Society.

"We pushed straight through to Yorkshire. Charles found George Whitefield preaching to the Societies there and enlisted his help. Whitefield at first counseled that Grace's betrothal to Wesley superseded her promise to Bennett. But in the end Charles's arguments prevailed, and Whitefield acted as Charles's assistant at the wedding of Grace to Bennett."

"Oh, no," Catherine said. "That is sure to drive the wedge between Whitefield and John Wesley deeper yet."

"No." Ned shook his head. "That is the one bright note to this affair. John Wesley joined them in Yorkshire two days after the wedding. He had ridden under great strain for almost forty-eight hours and was too exhausted even to take a room of his own. He lay down beside Whitefield on his bed. It was Whitefield's lot to inform John of the marriage of his intended. In Whitefield's anxiety to console his old friend, he actually wept. Wesley remained dry-eyed, but he was so touched with Whitefield's concern for him that he reestablished fellowship with Whitefield. The rift between them came from a misunderstanding due to being separated by such a great distance. When they were together again, the bond reformed."

"So even though John Wesley lost a wife, he regained a friend," Catherine mused. "And how does Charles view his handiwork in preventing his brother's marriage?"

"Charles is certain he has saved his brother from a great mistake and their life work from shipwreck."

"And John?"

"Reportedly he has not spoken to Charles since the incident."

"Oh, Ned, what will happen to the Societies if there is a rift between the brothers? I continue to hear whispers at the Foundery about disagreements over standards for preachers and of movements to separate—as Charl told us. It frightens me. Where will it end?"

Ned made no reply, so Philip spoke. "It's hard to say. I have always stood firm against separation, and yet it is a possibility I've considered lately. If I were to sign the Acts of Toleration, I could fill a pulpit in a dissenting chapel."

"But, Philip, to leave the Church of England—" Memories of her visit to Canterbury Cathedral and all it meant to her rose in Catherine's mind. To leave the Church of England seemed as unthinkable as to leave England itself.

Philip nodded. "I know. I feel the same way. And any time I consider it, I think of William Law. Even though forced into the position, he refuses to live like a nonjuror; though not allowed to minister in his parish church, he never misses a service. Miss Gibbon told me the rector has preached against Law in his presence; and yet Law continues to sit in the midst of the congregation, saying his prayers and listening to the Bible readings. With his example before me, could I voluntarily dissent?"

The question hung in the air, unanswered. But a few days later something unexpected happened. First, Ned received a letter from Charles Wesley with good news.

> I snatch a few moments before the people come to tell you what you will rejoice to know—that the Lord is reviving His Church; and that George Whitefield and my brother and I are one, a threefold cord which shall no more be broken. My dear friends, you shall have the full account not many days hence, if the Lord bless my coming in, as He has blessed my going out.

The news that the crisis had passed brought great rejoicing at the Foundery; the next week George Whitefield came to

London to give a firsthand account. After the Wednesday preaching service, Whitefield, Ned, Catherine, and Philip gathered in the apartments the Society maintained for visiting evangelists.

"Edward, let me hear this new hymn of yours that seems to be on everybody's lips since I've returned from America. I should like to hear it sung by the man who wrote it."

An organist friend had composed a majestic melody that suited the words perfectly. Ned stood and sang the first three verses of his hymn, and Catherine and Philip joined him on the last verse: "Oh, that with yonder sacred throng / We at His feet may fall! / We'll join the everlasting song, / And crown Him Lord of all."

"Well, Edward, your place in history is secure. I look forward to our singing that around the throne together in Heaven." In spite of his constant squint, which gave his face the impression of a frown, Whitefield's eyes sparkled with pleasure.

"I look forward to singing with you anytime," Ned replied. "And now tell us of the reconciliation you effected between the brothers Wesley."

"I did nothing; the Spirit of our Lord and the love the brothers hold for each other did all. John was with me when Charles arrived at the inn outside Newcastle. At first, he refused to see one he considered to be a Judas. Charles, on his side, declared he would renounce all conversations with his brother except what he would have with a heathen or publican. I simply ignored such inflated stubbornness and constrained the brothers to meet each other."

Whitefield's narrative was interrupted by a servant bringing in dishes of tea. Catherine poured for the company and then urged Whitefield to continue.

"Both brothers were wound up to the highest pitch of emotion and were almost beyond speech, but when they faced each other, the tension snapped and they fell on each other's neck."

"And so the Society is safe?" Catherine asked.

"I pray it will be. But the hardest task still remains—to prove to the Methodists that the work of God is not to be interrupted by any private dissension. And also that though the companionship and love of Grace Murray has been transferred from leader to disciple, the bereavement has left no lasting bitterness behind."

"Can that be done, do you think?"

Whitefield took a deep drink of tea before answering. "In time, pray God." After another pause, made to seem longer by the flickering of candle flame caught in a draught, Whitefield spoke again. "There is much concern of a 'general deadness' in the Society. I have felt it in London in a few persons who are eager to make mischief. Charles says the same is true in Bristol where he feels almost universal coldness, heaviness, and deadness among the people. They have lost near to a hundred members there alone."

"What the people need," Ned suggested, "is something to shake them up."

Whitefield's next words did exactly that to the company in the room. "I am concerned about the work here, but my heart is most truly with my work in America. I must return there soon. I dare to believe that my preaching might help create one nation from those thirteen scattered colonies—unite them under God with each other and with the mother country. I envision the mighty Atlantic Ocean becoming a highway of exchange for gospel preachers.

"Philip," he asked, turning to their silent companion, "will you go with me to help in this work?"

$\mathcal{A}$s winter closed in, bringing with it shorter, darker days and cold winds blowing off the frozen Thames, Philip wrestled with Whitefield's offer. Could he go on without a parish, without his country, without family? Must he forever be alone?

He spent Christmas Eve alone in his room in spite of repeated invitations to come to supper at the Perronets after service at the Foundery. He must reach a decision soon. If he was to go, he must prepare; and if not, Whitefield must be told so he could seek another companion. And whatever he decided, Catherine must be told.

The thought seemed so counter to the new determination he had brought back from King's Cliffe. In the turmoil over Grace Murray, and now as he considered Whitefield's offer, he had made no move to embark on his brave resolve to open himself to Catherine. Indeed, she too seemed more withdrawn than before. For a moment he longed for the days of easy companionship they had shared on their circuit ride.

But before he could decide anything about Catherine, he must know what God desired of him. He picked up his Bible and turned to the Psalms, his heart praying, as David had, for God's guidance: "Show me Thy ways, O Lord; teach me Thy paths . . .

lead me in Thy truth, and teach me; for Thou art the God of my salvation, on Thee do I wait all the day . . . teach me Thy way, O Lord, and lead me in a plain path . . . for Thou art my rock and my fortress; therefore, for Thy name's sake lead me and guide me."

And then he turned to the New Testament where Paul addressed the believers: "For this cause we also, since the day we heard it, do not cease to pray for you, and to desire that ye might be filled with the knowledge of His will in all wisdom and spiritual understanding."

Philip desired with all his heart to know God's will. But as he meditated, a fear gripped him. Had he somehow, somewhere, missed God's will for his life? Could that be the source of his conflict now? "My God, please don't let me be out of Your will." His heart's cry was desperate.

As he continued in God's presence, he felt his prayer answered with a sense of peace and release; and he remembered that the Christian's first responsibility in knowing God's will is being willing to do it. With that thought came the confidence that because he was willing, God would not allow him to miss His divine will. When William Law had told him this, he had not realized its immense implications. If he believed God capable of guiding, he must also believe Him capable of making His will known. The key was seeking God in prayer. And then waiting for the answer to be revealed in His perfect time.

A heavy snow fell on London, choking the streets and making travel from Greenwich to Moorfields slow and hazardous, so Philip did not see any of the Perronets for several days. But on New Year's Eve when the Society held its traditional watch night service at the Foundery, the entire Greenwich household attended. And Philip made no attempt to deny his joy in seeing Catherine standing tall and serene and lovely.

Perhaps because so many had been isolated by the recent storms, there seemed to be a special unity among those who filled the chapel to sing, pray, and worship God as the year 1750 began. At midnight John Wesley served them Communion. Kneeling at the altar with the others, Philip felt a special awareness of God's presence. It was certain to be a momentous year for the Societies and perhaps for himself also. Knowing that he must soon make a decision, he found great comfort in the words of the closing prayer:

> Almighty God, who hast promised to hear the petitions of them that ask in Thy Son's Name, we beseech Thee mercifully to incline Thine ears to us that have made now our prayers and supplications unto Thee; And grant that those things which we have faithfully asked according to Thy will may effectually be obtained . . . to the setting forth of Thy glory, through Jesus Christ our Lord, amen.

And then they stood and sang the song with which all Methodist watch nights concluded: "Hearken to the solemn voice, / The awful midnight cry! / Waiting souls, rejoice, rejoice, / And feel the Bridegroom nigh."

With only a parting bow to his friends, Philip went out into the night of the new year, his confidence in God newly reaffirmed. Whatever the year held, Philip had courage to face it.

Catherine's patience in awaiting God's timing was tested as the January snows drifted into February, and still there were no answers. She sensed Philip's difficulty in responding to George Whitefield's offer. And she knew her hopes for a future with Philip could bear no fruit until that question was settled.

Only once had her brother broached the subject to her. "Cath, I was thinking of the offer Mr. Whitefield extended to Philip. If he should decide to go—that is—I understand the orphan house in Georgia is in need of teachers. Had you ever thought—"

"A teacher of red Indians? Are you weary of my company?" Though she sought to make her answer light, his question continued to plague her. Her head told her that the discomforts and trials of a circuit ride would be as nothing compared to what must be faced by a missionary to the new world. But no matter how sternly her head lectured her heart, her heart would not listen.

And so she lived from day to day, anxious to hear from Philip, and yet reluctant to know his answer.

That Thursday she awoke uncommonly early and lay for a moment, wondering what had disturbed her. Then she realized that the sparrows in the garden bushes below her window were making an unaccountable racket. A cat must have gotten in among them. She pulled the quilt over her head in an attempt to go back to sleep. But when she heard other noises from the stable yard, she pulled a shawl over her shoulders and went to her window. When she opened the sash, she saw nothing amiss. It was unusually mild for the eighth of February.

But later that morning the placid Old Biggin was almost uncontrollable as she drove to the Foundry. And her students were no better. If the sky hadn't been such a clear blue, she would have been certain a storm was about to strike. She had never been more relieved to see the hands of her watch approach twelve. "Your behavior has been most unacceptable this morning. Tomorrow you must be prepared to work harder, or I shall be obliged to have Mr. Told in." The rascals looked duly smitten at her words, but still they failed to leave the room in proper order.

Suddenly a great rumbling thunder shook the building and drowned out the noise of the departing children. Catherine turned to place an armful of books on her desk. But the desk was gone. As if the earth had suddenly spun off its axis, all the furniture in Catherine's room slid to the north wall.

The roaring and shaking continued for minutes that seemed like hours. As the earth heaved, the doors and windows in her room burst open. Bricks from the crumbling chimney fell past her window.

Leaning against the undulating wall for support, Catherine felt a kind of terror she had never known. As her knees gave way and she slid to the floor, she relived her childhood experience of falling off a horse, but now not even the earth was solid. All the fears she thought conquered swamped her again. Where was Philip?

When at last the rolling earth subsided, Catherine didn't move. She suddenly realized how much she had come to rely on Philip in the past months. He was the person she could always turn to, even when the foundations of the earth shook. She had sensed this, but she had never experienced so deeply her need of his calm stability.

And then as if in answer to the cry of her heart, Philip rushed into the room. "Catherine, are you all right? I was so afraid I wouldn't find you—that you might be hurt or . . ." He made a muffled choking sound.

She blinked in unbelief at his sudden appearance. She had not even known he was at the Foundary that day. Now here was a solid core of stability in a world with no underpinnings. "I— I'm . . ." She wanted to say she was fine, but found she was so shaken she couldn't speak. And her stomach was rolling so she was afraid she might be sick. All she could do was hold her hand out to him.

When his hand closed over hers, warm and strong, enough of her tension eased to allow the tears to spill from her eyes. Her whole body began to tremble. Philip slipped to the floor beside her and held her in his arms while she shook as hard as if the earthquake were repeating itself.

At last she relaxed enough to be able to rest her head on his shoulder. The comfort was indescribable. She could have continued so for hours, but the sound of running feet and excited voices in the courtyard intruded.

"We must help." Philip got to his feet and extended a hand to Catherine.

"Do you think there's much damage?" She surveyed the chaos of her room.

"There's sure to be a great deal in the poorer parts of town. Pray that there won't be a fire."

They had just moved into the courtyard when the second shock struck, this even harder than the first. Catherine was certain the earth would split apart beneath her feet. But Philip held her. And even in the midst of the terrified shrieks, the crash of falling bricks, and the roar of the jolting earth, Catherine knew she could not live without this man's support. Even if it meant going to the ends of the earth—even to America. Life without Philip was unthinkable.

That decision filled Catherine with peace. In the midst of the turmoil around her, her heart was calm. And she knew she had made the right decision. "My peace I give unto you: not as the world giveth . . ." Peace was the one emotion Satan could not counterfeit. It was the complete assurance of being in God's will.

And Catherine sorely needed that peace in the days to come because internal peace was the only quiet available. A throng of frightened people crowded into the damaged Foundery in last-minute hope of turning aside the wrath of God by repenting. Affluent, smug London had needed this reminder of the wrath of God and the judgment to come, and Ned had been unwittingly prophetic in saying that squabbling Society members needed shaking up. Now a frenzied earthquake theology spelled the end of optimism. Londoners' nerves became raw, incited by such predictions as Sir Isaac Newton's: "Jupiter is going to approach so close to the earth as possibly to brush it."

Whitefield and Wesley conducted all-night services for those too wrought-up to sleep and those who no longer had a bed to go home to. Philip held open-air services in Hyde Park. As on their circuit ride, Catherine frequently accompanied him and led the singing. The favorite song was Isaac Watts's: "O God, our help in ages past, / Our hope for years to come, / Our shelter from the stormy blast, / And our eternal Home!"

The crowd sang with a lustiness brought on by desperation, and then listened to the preacher as drowning men cling to a lifeline. Philip chose Isaiah 2 as his theme: "The haughtiness of men shall be made low; and the Lord alone shall be exalted in that day . . . for the glory of his majesty, when he ariseth to shake terribly the earth."

At the mention of shaking earth, cries of fear rose from the women and shouts of "amen" and "'s truth" from the men. Then Philip read to them the reassuring words from Psalm 46—that God was their refuge and strength, their help in trouble. They need not fear, though the earth be removed and the mountains fall into the sea. The preacher went on to explain the way to find refuge in such a God.

Catherine saw what a pillar of strength Philip was, as he led these frightened people to an understanding of the comfort and security God had for them. And she renewed her vow to stay by his side—that is, if he should want her to do so.

A few days later, when Catherine and Philip went to Chitty Lane to call on Elmira Smithson, they were appalled at the desolation the earthquake had wrought in the slum areas of the city. Although an ancient building code required the use of brick in order to prevent fire, no one could afford to pay any attention to the code, and the flimsy lath and plaster buildings had crumbled like sand castles.

Elmira was attempting to shelter her family in a room that now had only three walls. "You must come with us," Catherine said, as she picked up little Susanna and started toward the carriage.

"But where'll we go?" Elmira cried, her voice showing how torn she was between hope and despair.

Catherine stopped. She could think of nothing. She couldn't take them home with her. Durial would never hear of it. The spare rooms at the Foundery were already bursting with now-homeless Society members. There was not an extra inch in Philip's room.

Then Catherine thought of a place where there was space aplenty. "To Park Lane," she said.

The Countess of Huntingdon's butler did not so much as raise an eyebrow at the sight of the dirty, ill-clothed persons with Miss Perronet and Mr. Ferrar. "Please come in. I will see if Her Ladyship is at home."

Her Ladyship was. "This is most convenient." She bustled into the reception hall wearing a black cloak and a dark straw bonnet over her lace cap. "Lady Fanny and I were just setting out to deliver baskets of food to the needy. It is much better that they should come to me. Rettkin!" The butler materialized out of nowhere. "See that these children are fed and properly clothed. Their mother shall accompany me and direct my charities to the most deserving. I do abhor the thought of bestowing gifts upon the undeserving. You shall be a great help to me in my work, Mrs.—ah, I don't believe we've been introduced."

Her head spinning as always from encounters with the countess, Catherine accompanied an open-mouthed Isaiah and his brother and sisters to the housemaid's quarters and saw that they were settled before she left. "And now you shall have no excuse for coming to school with dirty hands, Isaiah," she said with a smile.

The winter evening was closing in fast when Catherine and Philip left Park Lane. "I must return you to your brother," Philip said. "The quake has turned many Londoners' minds to the judgment of God; but an equal number have adopted the philosophy of 'eat, drink, and be merry, for tomorrow ye die.' The streets are not safe for a woman."

Catherine sighed. "I expect you are right. But I had hoped we might call on Mr. Smithson and inform him of his family's good fortune."

"Tomorrow," Philip promised.

Catherine had had no time alone with Philip since the cataclysm. She could not speak to him of her new resolve unless he gave her an opening, some encouragement, just the slightest chink in the wall he kept around himself. But Philip's wall of isolation was perhaps the only one in London not cracked by the earthquake.

The next day Catherine saw that the walls of the Fleet were likewise intact. Outside, the mob listened to a thundering street preacher: "Earthquakes, by their majesty and dreadful horror, show God's hand stretched out in anger. This is why they are specially frightful. They are sudden, unavoidable, and threaten us with a peculiarly dreadful form of death."

A high shriek rose above the wailing of the crowd, and several women sank to the ground.

"The preservation of London was a miracle. God deliberately refrained from destroying the city, but damnation will have its numbers, come when it will . . ."

As the lamentation of the mob rose to a higher pitch, Catherine was for once grateful for the doors of the Fleet which cut her off from the sound.

To her relief, Smithson was sober today and eager for news. "I've 'eard tell such tales about London—tell me what it's like."

Catherine told him what had happened to Elmira and his children, holding her breath after mentioning the Countess of Huntingdon. She remembered Smithson's earlier resistance to "evangelical toffs mucking about in his affairs." But today his gratitude was wholehearted.

He even allowed Philip to read the Bible to him and the others in his cell. Philip chose Acts 16, explaining, "This is the story of others unfairly imprisoned at the time of an earthquake." He read of Paul and Silas being beaten and cast into prison where they prayed and sang praise to God. When he reached the part about the earthquake that shook the foundations of the prison and broke the prisoners' chains, the inmates gasped in amazement.

"Lor', I wisht the quake 'ad broken the Fleet down," a prisoner said.

"That's th' only way you'll see th' light o' day, Uriah."

Philip went on reading above the comments. The convicts erupted in jeers when Paul and Silas chose to remain in jail rather than escape, but Dick Smithson was silent. Indeed, he was so deep in thought when his visitors left that he did not even bid them farewell.

When Catherine arrived home, she walked into another crisis. Durial had been listening to a preacher at the Greenwich Village green that afternoon. Her high-strung nerves were now at the breaking point. She demanded the family leave London, and nothing Ned could say had any effect in calming her.

"Allow that I know what the preacher said, Husband. And allow me to judge the good sense his words made. Listen to his reasoning. This present earth, a very unsatisfactory second version of the first earth more or less destroyed by the flood, is going to end in a great conflagration that will burn it up. The fire will naturally begin at Rome, the headquarters of the Antichrist, but England is sure to be a particularly unpleasant spot because of our extensive coalfields."

"Durial!" Ned was never a patient man, and his wife's vapors drove him to distraction. "If the entire earth and especially all of England is to be burned up, what can it matter *where* we are living when it happens? My work is here."

"But you can take work elsewhere." Durial's voice rose another pitch. "I do not wish to compare London to Sodom, for London contains many good people, but because of its size it also contains a proportionately large number of evil people. And setting aside all other considerations, London, by reason of its crowded and insecure buildings, is of all places the most dangerous."

Ned turned away.

Durial flung herself across the room at him. "Do not turn your back on me. If our baby had lived, if I could have given you a child, you would not treat me so!" Racking sobs began to shake her body.

Ned turned and took his wife in his arms. "Durial, Durial. I will write to my father. Perhaps he will know of something."

Catherine, who had not intended to eavesdrop, fled to her room. It had been a full month since the earthquake; surely the hysteria would soon die down. People would rebuild their chimneys, replace their crockery, and reglaze their windows, and the great London earthquake would become nothing more than a memory.

Catherine gratefully accepted Audrey's offer to brush her hair for her. "Mmm, that feels good, Audrey. Thank you. Please snuff my candles on the way out. I feel as if I could sleep till the day of doom."

Those words were the first thing Catherine thought of early the next morning when an eruption of the earth broke forth with a thunderous roar and tumultuous shaking. Catherine jumped up with a cry, thinking the powder house on the green had exploded. But as her writing desk lurched, chairs shook, doors slammed, windows rattled, pewter and crockery clattered from their shelves, and the great elm tree outside her window crashed to the earth, sending shards of broken glass flying across her room, Catherine knew London was being visited by yet another earthquake.

13

A sharp cry, followed by a moaning wail, tore through the house. At first Catherine thought Durial was hurt. Then she realized the cry had come from the servants' quarters. She shook the bits of broken glass out of her slippers and off her shawl before donning them and running in the direction of the noise. When she arrived, along with the rest of the household, at Audrey's room, she found the maid sitting in a tangle of bedclothes, smashed crockery, and disordered furniture, cradling an oddly twisted arm and shrieking, "It threw me outta bed, it did. Just threw me out. My arm 'it the trunk, owww!"

"All right, Audrey, you will stop shrieking so that we can see to your injuries." Durial waded through the shambles. Her housekeeping instincts aroused by the disarray, she began giving orders for the care of Audrey and the righting of the room. Catherine smiled. All her sister-in-law needed to take her mind off her troubles was a house to clean. By the end of the day the house would not only be orderly, but also freshly scrubbed, and all the broken dishes replaced and on the shelf.

But not everywhere in London was the damage so quickly repaired. This quake was far more violent than the first, and buildings damaged by the first were leveled by the second.

People frightened by the first were terrified now. All over the city, church bells rang of their own accord, adding to the noise and confusion. People had run into the streets in their nightclothes and were still milling about hours later when Catherine arrived at the Foundery. The panic continued for days. In spite of the attempts of Wesley and other clergymen to calm their fears, the people flocked to the prophets of doom who shouted at the tops of their voices on every street corner, "The end of the world is at hand. Prepare to meet thy Maker."

In order to be of more help in the emergency, Catherine moved into London temporarily, staying with her sister, Elizabeth Briggs, in her newly established home. A small room that Elizabeth usually used for a private sitting room was at Catherine's disposal whenever she could snatch a few hours of sleep.

After a week of such a schedule, John Wesley fell ill, putting an even greater burden on Society members. In spite of the fact that they were working almost twenty-four hours a day in the same building, Catherine seldom saw Philip. But when she did, his calm self-containment and quiet efficiency reaffirmed her confidence that he was the one God had prepared for her.

After Catherine had spent a particularly tiring day of dispensing soup and changing dirty bandages for the charity school children, Philip came to her. She gave him a bowl of soup and bandaged a scrape on his hand, as if he were one of her charges.

When he had finished eating, she said, "I have heard rumors of damage and riots in the Fleet. Perhaps we should visit Dick Smithson?"

"I would not take you into that danger. There is no knowing what the rabble may be up to."

"Nonsense!" A flicker of a smile crossed Catherine's face; here was her chance to tell Philip a little of what she felt. "I am more than willing to go anywhere you go, to face anything you face." She said the words with confidence, ignoring the disquiet they caused in her heart.

He looked at her, a questioning wrinkle across his brow. "Catherine?"

The two of them were a small island of quiet in the tumult of post-earthquake London. She would have liked to remind him of the mad bulls, swollen rivers, and lighted fireworks she had already faced with him. She would have liked to tell him she was now willing to face an ocean voyage, wilderness living, and Indians with him. But she felt she had said quite enough, so she held out her arm. "Shall we go?"

The fact that the second shock had followed exactly four weeks to the day after the first gave rise to alarm in many quarters over what might follow on April 8.

The same preacher they had heard before still held forth from the corner near the Fleet. "What is God going to do next? Will He order winds to tear up our houses from their foundations and bury us in the ruins? Will He remove the raging distemper from the cattle and send the plague upon ourselves? Or—the Lord in His infinite mercy save us—He may command the earth to open her mouth and, the next time He ariseth to shake terribly the earth, command her to swallow us up alive, with our houses, our wives, our children, with all that appertains upon us."

A great weeping and moaning accompanied his words, much stronger in intensity than the first time Catherine heard him.

At first, the prison provost informed Philip that no amount of garnishment could buy his way in to visit a prisoner in the Fleet. But when Philip mentioned the name of the man they wished to visit, the response changed. "Oh, 'im. Guess that's all right then. Inside with yer." He pocketed the coins Philip offered.

Inside, a surprise met them. The jail seemed lighter, the air fresher, as if someone had opened all the windows. And then Catherine saw that was precisely what had happened. The dirty panes of glass from the small, barred windows had broken out, allowing fresh air and light into the prison. But more than that, at the end of the hall one section of the wall had broken away, forming a v-shaped passage to the street. The breech in the wall was well guarded, as a prisoner would need only to scramble up a small pile of fallen brick and leap through the hole to escape.

"Smithson!" the turnkey shouted.

To Catherine's surprise, one of the guards came forward. "Dick! You've been made a guard? What has happened?"

"It was like in that story you read us from the Bible," he addressed Philip. "Where the earthquake set the prisoners free. I gave a good piece o' thought to that and decided they was right to stay. Just 'a cause they was put there unfairly, didn't mean everybody was, and ya can't have murderers runnin' about the streets—wouldn't be safe for the women an' children. So when the quake shook that there 'ole in the wall, I stood in the gap, as ye might say."

"You prevented a jailbreak?" Catherine asked.

Dick's smile was sheepish behind his shaggy beard. "'Ad a might 'a trouble convincin' some it were a good idee. So I threw a few bricks 'ere and there to persuade 'em."

"And you've been promoted as a reward! Dick, that's wonderful! Will you get paid?"

He nodded. "Yep. Soon's my debt's paid off, I can go 'ome to Elmirey at night."

Catherine's heart sank. It would take more than a year for him to earn enough to pay his debt—unless he demanded bribes from the other prisoners. "Dick, that's wonderful, but you don't want to become like them." She pointed to the hardened jailers standing by the wall.

"No, I'd rather be more like 'im." He nodded toward Philip. "Thought I might try a piece o' prayin' or 'ymn singin'—course, I can't read the Bible none. Do you ever have any of these Methody Societies of yours in jails?"

Through the break in the wall, they could hear the street preacher still ranting, but Catherine could not feel alarmed by his words. She had just witnessed a miracle, and no fear for the future could diminish that glory. If only she and Philip could speak of the future—their future. Surely now, with London crumbled around them, they needed each other more than ever. She knew she needed Philip; if only he would say he needed her.

As they settled into the relative quiet of the carriage to drive back to the Foundery where Catherine would spend another night with Elizabeth, she thought, *Perhaps now he will speak. We are alone—perhaps now . . .*

And perhaps he did. But Catherine, worn out by the long days of work and emotion with only brief snatches of sleep, fell asleep to the swaying motion of the vehicle. And much to her surprise, she awoke late the next morning, not in the tiny closet off her sister's room where she had been staying, but in her room in Greenwich.

"How did I get here?" she asked Audrey, who was carrying on with her duties with one arm tied in a sling. Catherine recalled that just a year ago, Ned had been the one with a damaged arm. It seemed as if her life was ever to be punctuated with upheavals no matter how much she prayed for a more gentle calling.

"Mr. Ned brought you in sound asleep last night. The mistress sent him for you—said it wasn't right for you to be working day and night in London when you needed to be here making your earthquake gown."

"My what?" Catherine sat upright in her bed.

Audrey handed her a cup of coffee. "All the ladies is makin' 'em. Mistress 'as us all at it—but I'm not much good sewing with only one 'and."

"Audrey, what are you talking about?"

"Earthquake gowns. To wear for the all-night vigil when the final quake comes. Mistress says we'll all go out in the fields— since she can't convince Mr. Ned to take us clean out of London as some are doin'."

"That will be enough, Audrey. Thank you."

Catherine finished her coffee, dressed quickly, and hurried downstairs. Sure enough, Durial had assembled all the female servants in the south sitting room where each one was stitching intently on a garment of ivory muslin. While they stitched, Durial read to them from a printed earthquake sermon. She looked up as Catherine entered. "Hello, Sister. As you see, the next visitation of the Lord's hand shall not find us sleeping. I have ordered a length of muslin for you too."

The sound of an approaching horse eliminated the need for Catherine to reply. "Don't put down your sewing, any of you. I shall see to the door." She fled from the room, wondering what in the world she would do with such a garment. As if it would matter what one wore when being swallowed alive by the earth.

Her heart soared when she saw their visitor. She ran down the steps, and, as in all her dreams, Philip opened his arms and she went into them. For a moment they stood there in the morning sunshine, secure and belonging.

"I have come to speak to you," he said at last.

"Come into the front parlor. Everyone else is in back. You can't imagine what Durial has them doing."

"Making earthquake gowns?"

"How did you know?"

"It's all the rage in London. I called on the countess this morning, and even her household is set about it."

"Has the panic not subsided at all yet?" She led him to a small sofa.

"The countess said seven hundred coaches have been counted passing Hyde Park Corner with whole parties moving into the country. It is said lodging is unattainable in Windsor and nearby villages."

Catherine had no desire to continue a discussion of the earthquake now that she finally had Philip alone in a quiet room. She looked down at her hands, but she couldn't quite suppress the smile on her lips.

Still he hesitated, so she made an opening for him. "You

have determined to accept Mr. Whitefield's offer?" Why did those simple words make her think of walking into a dark night?

He gave her a deep, level look, but before he could reply, a carriage sounded on the drive. No servants appeared from the sewing circle, so Catherine went to the door. The sight of the beloved figure in a full-bottomed wig brought a joyous cry from her. "Father!" For the second time that morning, she flew into a caller's arms. "What a wonderful surprise! What brings you to London when everyone else is fleeing the city?"

"That is precisely what brought me, Child. Your mother could not rest until I could bring her my personal assurances that all her children in London are well. We have received the most alarming reports—"

A small figure bounded out of the carriage and threw herself into Catherine's arms as well. "Philothea!"

"Isn't it famous! I convinced Mother that Father shouldn't travel so far alone, and she could spare me much more easily than any of the boys." Then she saw Philip who had come into the hall to greet the arrivals, and she abandoned her sister for her idol. "I brought you a poppy-seed cake. We'll pretend it's your birthday."

Catherine ushered them all into the parlor and had turned to summon Durial when she saw that yet another coach had arrived. Perfect in its shiny fittings, with golden coronets on its doors, this coach carried the Countess of Huntingdon.

George Whitefield alighted first and offered his hand to assist Lady Huntingdon; then, as yet another surprise, Charles Wesley emerged behind her. The countess issued an order to her driver and then led the way into the house, past Catherine standing at the door.

"I have come to speak with you," she addressed Philip. "I do not know what is to be done with that man Smithson. Oh, hello, Vincent. What brings you to London? This is an insane time to be visiting the city—they say it will be level in a short time. But never mind. You're looking well." Without giving Vincent a chance to reply, she went on from her position in the center of the room.

"I paid Mr. Smithson's debts as you suggested, Philip, but he has declined my offer of a place on my estate at Donnington Park. What do you say to that?"

Whitefield answered for Philip, "My Lady, if he feels a calling to minister to those unfortunates in prison, are we to interfere with that?"

"Calling? What does one of his class know of a calling?"

"The disciples were simple men, My Lady. Our Lord called them," Whitefield said.

The countess tossed her head in the air with a sniff. Just then Ned and Durial entered, and the conversation became general. Not even the Countess of Huntingdon was able to upstage a reunion of the Perronet family.

Across the room Catherine sought to catch Philip's eye. He stood tall and alone in the corner, isolated from all the joyful family greetings. Catherine felt an overwhelming desire to reach him, to tell him she would be his family, that he never need be alone again. But Charles Wesley was beside her, and she must speak to him. "What has brought you to London?"

"I received word my brother was gravely ill—at death's door. I came to nurse him, but when I arrived, I found him in the quite capable hands of Mrs. Vazielle."

"Humph," the countess said. "Clutches is more like. It will not do, Charles. She must not ensnare him."

Charles nodded. "Indeed, I believe she is a woman of sorrowful spirit."

"She will not do." The countess issued her edict with another toss of her head and moved on around the room, instinctively playing hostess as if she were in her own London drawing room.

"And how is Sally? I haven't heard from her for months," Catherine asked.

Charles's face became somber. "My dearest is not well. The

babe miscarried. It may have been the shock of the first earth-quake . . ."

"Charles, I'm so sorry. Is there fear for her health?"

"No, no. The doctor says we may look forward to a full quiver. But this one is mourned."

And Catherine too ached for Sally's empty mother-arms, for the unheard baby laughter, for dreams unfulfilled—an ache of might-have-beens.

Again the question arose in her heart as she looked at Philip and wondered if her own dreams must also die before they could be born. *My God, where are You? You have promised a perfect way—but where? And when?*

Just then Vincent Perronet joined her and Charles. "Ah, Mr. Wesley, tell me of the work in your part of the country. Is there still a movement for separation?"

Catherine knew how strongly Charles opposed such ideas and listened carefully for his answer. "It seems the great shaking-up God gave us has not been without its consequence in the minds of the brethren. We had a conference of the northern and midlands Societies just a week ago. All agreed not to separate. So the wound is healed—slightly."

Catherine realized she had been holding her breath await-ing Charles's answer. Now it escaped in a great sigh. It seemed that suddenly in the very wake of destruction God was answer-ing her prayers. Was this His perfect time? The time she had so long awaited?

It seemed even more likely as Ned joined them and his father turned to him. "My Son, I have come not only as an emis-sary from your mother, but also as a petitioner in my own behalf."

"Sir?"

"I think you know from visiting my estate in Canterbury last year that Adisham has been looking for retirement. I can put him off no longer. He must be pensioned into a cottage and the burden of running the farm passed to younger, stronger hands. Would you consider being those hands, Ned?"

"Move to Canterbury? I must give it some thought. I believe Durial would like it above all things."

"And you, Ned? It should give you more uninterrupted time for hymn-writing, and the Societies in Kent are in need of a firm hand among them."

Catherine's head was reeling. This would solve Ned and Durial's problem. But what about hers? She looked across the room at the still-silent Philip. In the midst of the noisy room he was calm and detached. And yet he looked sad, as if instinctively missing the belonging he had never known.

She started toward him, but Philothea intervened. "Catherine, I'm longing to hear all about your earthquake adventures! Was it alarming? All we got in Shoreham was a gentle rolling—no more than a rocking chair."

And then Whitefield approached Philip, and Catherine heard him ask, "And what of my invitation? Have you decided to go to America with me?"

But Philip's voice was softer than Whitefield's, and she could not hear the answer.

*D*urial was at the height of her glory directing her well-trained servants and seeing to her guests' comfort. When Ned spoke briefly to her of Vincent's offer, she immediately declared that the entire company should stay to dinner in celebration. Her larders were up to any challenge—even to serving the Countess of Huntingdon on short notice. She dispatched Joseph from the stables to London to fetch Elizabeth and William Briggs so that all available family members might be there.

Ned and his father went into the study for further discussion of their plans, and Philothea requested Catherine to show her around the house and garden. As she left the parlor, Catherine heard Whitefield and Philip discussing the plans for sailing to America, but only one voice was distinct. "America? Nonsense!" And the countess snapped her fan to punctuate her words.

After giving Philothea a quick tour, Catherine took her sister to the guest room to wash and change for dinner and retired to her own room to do the same. Audrey brought her a brass can of hot water from the kitchen, and Catherine reveled in repeatedly splashing her face and arms as if she could wash away the fatigue and strain of the past weeks.

But when she turned to her mirror to arrange her curls, she was shocked at how clearly her recent fatigue and worry were written there. What was wrong? God had answered all her prayers—all but one. And surely it was only a matter of time— probably tomorrow Philip would call and their conversation would be uninterrupted. She had known for weeks what her answer would be. Then she stopped.

Suddenly she knew the cause of the weight around her heart and the hollow feeling in the center of her stomach. She had known peace the moment she acknowledged her love for Philip. But she had known nothing but internal turmoil, far greater than any caused by the earthquakes, over her decision to go to America. What of her criterion that if a step were directed of God, it would be accompanied by His peace?

Could the fact that she had been thwarted at every attempt to speak to Philip of her decision to go and the lack of peace over the decision mean she *wasn't* to go? It was true that she felt no real call to the work in America—no intense desire to minister in that field. But wasn't a desire to be with the minister himself enough? Had she mistaken her wish to be with Philip for a call to be a missionary? Must she choose between Philip and God's call? If that were the case, there could be no choice.

The arrival of yet another carriage told her the Briggses had arrived. She must go down and take her place in the family cir- cle. Inside, Catherine felt nothing but a gaping hole where her dreams had been, but outside she wore her usual air of calm serenity. Durial's excellent meal choked her, and when she attempted to reply to a remark directed to her, her tight, con- trolled voice sounded more awful to her ears than if she had shouted.

Across the table Philip responded to a question from Charles Wesley in his slow, thoughtful voice and then looked across the table at her. For an awful moment their eyes held. Then he gave that tiny half-smile of his, and she could sit there no longer.

Summoning all her natural dignity, Catherine asked her hostess to excuse her and walked slowly to her room. Mechanically she went through all the motions of her night-time ritual and then drew the heavy side curtains of her bed around her. She had no sense of God's presence with her in that small enclosure. She could only cling to her determination to believe that He was still there.

The next morning it seemed a miracle to her that she had slept, that the sun had risen again, that birds were singing. Such things were entirely alien to the desolation inside her. Durial was surprised by her announcement that she did not intend to go in to the Foundery that day.

"Regular lessons have not been resumed yet; I am certain they can get along very well without me."

"A very wise decision, Catherine. I am just surprised you would take so sensible a course. After all, your earthquake gown is yet unfinished. And now we must make one for Philothea too, as Father Perronet does not intend to return to Shoreham before the end of the week. And all the china must be packed. How fortunate that one packing will suffice for earthquake protection and for our removal to Canterbury. I can think of no more satisfactory solution for our needs. Will you live with Elizabeth when we are gone? That seems far the best plan—assuming there remains a London to be lived in, that is."

Durial thrust Catherine's half-sewn gown into her hands and began cutting her final length of muslin for Philothea. "How fortunate that I have just enough fabric left. Now we must decide whether to hold our vigil in the meadows by Hither Green or take to a boat in the Thames. Which do you think would be the best, Ned?"

Edward looked up from the manuscript of a poem he was composing. "Where do you think we'd find a boat? Besides, those gowns will show off to the best advantage in an open field."

Durial was completely unscathed by his sarcasm. "Yes, I suppose that is best. There's always the danger of a great wave swamping a boat. But I did think that in case of fire, the river might be a wise choice."

"Well, to the best of my knowledge, there are no coal fields under Hither Green Meadow, so you should be quite safe there from a conflagration."

The prophets had pinpointed the night of April 4 or early morning of April 5, so all day Wednesday Durial worked everyone around her to a frenzy, storing the last of the crockery and silver, securing the furniture with ropes, and packing huge hampers of food. "If the destruction is great, we may have to live in the open for some time. Audrey, you and Joseph fill the pony cart with blankets."

Catherine obeyed, as did all the others, including Vincent Perronet. Hysteria was in the air, and there was no sense in trying to fight it. "Ned," Vincent admonished his son about to depart for the Foundery, "could you bring an extra hymnal or two from the book room? We might keep the folks occupied with a candlelight hymn-sing."

Ned agreed and assured Durial for the seventh time that he would not return late from his visit to encourage John Wesley in his convalescence.

By the time Ned returned at five o'clock, Durial had household and carriages in perfect order and all the females of the family and staff properly clad in their earthquake gowns. "Yes, I suppose you must take your cloaks, but it does seem a pity to cover the gowns. Although I imagine by the time it's really cold it will be dark also. But then if great fires start, you won't need a wrap, will you?"

Catherine was pleased with Ned's news that the countess would join them at the meadow. She was bringing her household staff and the Smithson family as something of a celebration for the newly reunited family. But then she was alarmed at his next piece of information. "George Whitefield left yesterday for his parents' home in Gloucester, so she is bringing Philip in place of her private chaplain."

Catherine climbed into the carriage next to Philothea and was thankful for her sister's chatter all the way to the meadow. The exit route from London was choked with carriages, horseback riders, and pedestrians. A festival air accompanied the evacuees as they called and waved to their friends. But Catherine sat motionless. Philip would be there tonight. She was certain he would speak to her, and she would much rather encounter an earthquake than to tell him she couldn't go to America with him.

The sun was setting when they reached Hither Green. Durial selected a pleasant spot near a spinney of trees and directed the servants to spread out rugs on the grass. Catherine remained inside the carriage as long as possible; but when the countess's party arrived and chose to park not far from them, she could no longer remain hidden. "Come, Cath! Let's go listen to the preachers!" Philothea tugged at her hand.

They walked across the meadow grass, their gowns devoid of familiar hoops and panniers and swishing around their ankles. They stood behind a crowd listening to a doomsaying preacher. "It says it right here in the Book of Matthew, 'There shall be earthquakes in divers places. All these are the beginning of sorrows.'" A moan went up from the overwrought audience. "'Then shall they deliver you up to be afflicted, and shall kill you . . .'"

A warm hand touched Catherine's shoulder, and Philip's deep voice said, "He seems to be overlooking the exhortation to avoid the false prophets that come at that time."

It was now dark, and as Catherine turned, the glow of the lantern Philip carried fell on his hair and gentle eyes. She had never guessed that her determination to follow God could teeter so precariously.

"Durial sent me to fetch you. She is serving supper from the hampers."

Philothea hung on Philip's arm and fairly skipped across the meadow with him, leaving Catherine to walk quietly beside them, wearing the natural calm solemnity of her expression that showed nothing of the pain she was feeling. Was this what it meant to love—truly to love? This caring so much you thought you couldn't stand it? And then not being able to do anything about it?

She sat on the rug Durial indicated. She held her plate of food and slipped enough of it to Isaiah Smithson to make it appear she had eaten and then sent her greetings to his parents who were eating with the servants. And she listened to the countess holding forth: "England is darkened with clouds of ignorance and sin. If God spares us this night, I shall turn upon our country the light of divine truth. The church is slumbering at ease, benumbed by the poisonous influence of error. I shall arouse the careless sleepers and apply the gospel antidote. Throughout England, Wales, Scotland, and Ireland I shall repair the ancient altars and enkindle fresh fires. If we are spared the fires of judgment tonight . . ." But when Ned and her father began gathering the party together to sing hymns, it was more than Catherine could bear. She slipped away to sit in the carriage.

Across the meadow candles and lanterns flickered like overgrown fireflies, and the voices of the singers carried to her on the night air: "All hail the power of Jesus' name! / Let angels prostrate fall . . ."

They had begun the third song when Catherine heard a soft rap at the carriage door. At first it was so gentle she thought she was mistaken, but then she saw Philip's dear craggy profile in the moonlight.

"Catherine, may I come in? I must speak to you." The calmness of his voice sounded as forced as was her effort at sounding cheerful as she offered him the seat facing her.

It seemed he dreaded what he would say as much as Catherine dreaded the reply she must give. He regarded her in silence, a soft glow of moonlight falling through the carriage window. For a moment she who had learned to read him so well saw an opening, a readiness to speak, and then something snapped shut inside.

Now that they were together, they must speak. If only she could reach him, pry open that spring that always closed her out. Philip seemed to realize how near he had come to letting the barrier down. He put his hands over his face as if to rebuild the piece he'd let fall from the wall.

At last he took a breath so deep that Catherine felt as if the whole carriage shook. "I shouldn't have come. I don't know why I did. Catherine, I cannot speak. I long to, but I may not. Surely you know how l feel about you, how tenderly I regard you. I had hoped to have something to offer you. But I have nothing."

And the barrier was sealed again.

In the dimness of the night, from the dark of her own pain, Catherine reached out to him and took his hand. "Nothing to offer but your dear self, Philip."

The term of endearment seem to wound him. He pulled his hand away. "I had hoped to have something of substance—a place to offer you."

"And I had hoped to accept—"

"Catherine, I have refused Mr. Whitefield's offer. Now I have nothing. I tried to accept, but it was wrong. I was considering it for the wrong reasons—to make a home to offer you, not to serve God."

The relief was overwhelming. For long minutes Catherine could only swallow. At last the burning lump in her throat dissolved, and she could pray, *Thank You, my God, thank You.*

"Catherine, I cannot tell you."

With a sudden force that would make an observer think the earthquake had struck the Perronet carriage, Catherine moved across the seat and into Philip's arms. "Oh, Philip, that's the best news I've ever heard. Why didn't you tell me? I had come to the same conclusion. I was determined to go in order to be with you, but then I knew it was wrong. I thought you were going to ask me to go, and I should have to refuse you. Oh, Philip!"

And at last, after months of waiting, he kissed her—or she kissed him. It was impossible to tell. But as the choir in the meadow sang, "Love divine, all loves excelling, / Joy of heav'n to earth come down," the two in the carriage knew a bit of that divine love on earth.

Then Philip pulled away. "It's not possible. Life's not really that good—not mine."

"I intend to do my best to see that it is from here on."

"Catherine, in my whole life I've never loved anyone—nor anyone me. I'm afraid l don't know how to go about this."

She traced the hollow of his cheek with a gentle finger. "You're doing very well for a beginner."

But the tender mood broke as he firmly set her back on her own side of the carriage. "What was I thinking? Forgive me. Catherine, nothing has changed. The fact still remains that l am a foundling without place or prospect. Even if I were such a self-ish bounder as to ask you to sacrifice yourself to me, it must be clear to you that the honorable, respected, not to mention well-to-do Vincent Perronet would never give his daughter to one with such a background."

"Philip, what nonsense! My father believes we are all equal before God, all sons and heirs. There are no foundlings in God's family."

"Spiritually, I do not doubt that. But in the terms of this world I am a foundling who—"

"A foundling who has found grace in the sight of God and favor in the eyes of the woman who loves him."

This time he came to her across the carriage width, and at long last everything about him told her that he had come home. Philip had found a place of belonging as he had never belonged before.

Nothing was solved, but for the moment, having Philip love her and loving him in return was enough. And she had her firm faith that God would guide them, would open a door for them in time.

The singers in the meadow began another hymn. Catherine turned her head slightly from Philip's shoulder and looked out the small window. Across the meadow candles and lanterns flickered, and the women's pale muslin gowns ruffled in a gentle predawn breeze. The night appointed for terror and catastrophe was flooded with peace and beauty. She turned back to Philip and closed her eyes.

Perhaps they dozed, because streaks of red and gold were filling the eastern sky when a sharp rap on the carriage door brought its occupants back to the present world.

"Well, it appears the hand of the avenging angel has passed us by. But I must say, if I were the Almighty, I'd be hard pressed to find a reason to spare this lot." The Countess of Huntingdon held the door for them to step out. "I have ordered breakfast served, and I have an announcement for which you might wish to be present."

Everyone looked drowsy after the night's vigil but not the least bit chagrined that they had awaited a calamity that failed to occur. Joseph, Audrey, and Elmira Smithson were passing around cider and pork pie as the morning sun broke over the meadow. Standing in the center of the group, his arms held up to heaven, Vincent Perronet prayed, "For our deliverance, our Father, we thank Thee. Help the lives which Thou hast spared to be lived worthily unto Thee. Amen."

And the people who had sung through most of the night responded, "Glory be to the Father and to the Son, and to the Holy Ghost. As it was in the beginning, is now and ever shall be, world without end, amen."

Then Lady Huntingdon took center stage. "Since the world has not ended, it appears the Almighty intends that we should go on with our work. My chaplain, Mr. Whitefield, is soon to depart for America, and I shall be in need of a replacement for his services. Therefore, I appoint Mr. Philip Ferrar to fill his vacancy." She looked at Philip. "You, sir, are not to go to America. I have determined it will not suit."

Catherine gasped and turned to Philip. The look of astonishment on his face told her he had no idea this was coming.

"This position is, of course, only temporary." Her Ladyship paused. "I have determined to build a private chapel in Tunbridge Wells and install a permanent chaplain there. Mr. Ferrar, you shall have that position."

With the precision with which he did everything, Philip rose to his feet and bowed to the countess. "Yes, Your Ladyship."

Only Catherine saw the twinkle of amusement behind his smile of pleasure.

"And," the countess turned a half-circle to take in the entire company and then focused directly on Philip, "you are to marry this young lady."

The amusement and pleasure on Philip's face were eclipsed by the look of open love he turned on Catherine as he extended his hand to help her to her feet.

"Yes, Your Ladyship." They replied to the countess, but they looked only at each other.

All Hail the Power

EDWARD PERRONET
Alt. by John Rippon

OLIVER HOLDEN

1. All   Hail the pow'r of   Je-sus' name! Let an-gels pros-trate fall;
2. Ye   cho-sen seed of   Is-real's race, Ye ran-somed from the fall,
3. Let ev-'ry kin-dred, ev-'ry tribe, On this ter-res-trial ball,
4. O   that with yon-der sa-cred throng We at His feet may fall!

Bring forth the roy-al   di-a-dem, And crown Him Lord of   all;
Hail   Him who saves you by His grace And crown Him Lord of   all;
To   Him all maj-es-ty as-cribe, And crown Him Lord of   all;
We'll join the ev-e-last-ing song, And crown Him Lord of   all;

Bring forth the ro-yal di-a-dem And crown Him Lord   of   all;
Hail   Him who saves you by His grace, And crown Him Lord   of   all;
To   Him all maj-es-ty as-cribe, And crown Him Lord   of   all;
We'll join the ev-er-last-ing song, And crown Him Lord   of   all;

Historical Footnote

This book is a work of fiction with a great deal of history woven in. Especially when many of the characters are familiar to the reader, it can be important to separate fact from fiction. The accounts given of the Wesleys, the Foundery, the Methodist Society, the Countess of Huntingdon, George Whitefield, and William Law are accurate, taken from the journals and biographies listed in the bibliography.

The earthquakes and reactions to them are matters of historical record; the "earthquake theology" sermons were preached as quoted.

The story of the Perronets is as accurate as I could make it, but here the novelist's imagination was called into greater service, as the references to members of this large family in journals and historical accounts are tantalizingly brief. I have used all I could learn of Catherine. She was indeed on the eligibility list John Wesley presented to Charles, but of her later life nothing is known.

Philip Ferrar is entirely fictional, but he is in many ways a composite of the early Methodist preachers recorded in history. Most of his sermons were patterned on John Wesley's. None of the hardships encountered on the preaching tours are made up. All are taken from the journals of John and Charles Wesley and George Whitefield. As Betty Waller, who previewed the manuscript dedicated to her, said, "And to think, we sit Sunday after Sunday in our nice comfortable pews and don't have any idea what others went through for our faith."

Emmanuel College has made posthumous amends to William Law for the deprivation of his Fellowship. Only two

Emmanuel men have been honored by being pictured in the stained glass windows of its chapel—John Harvard and William Law. On April 28, 1961, the rector and people of King's Cliffe held a service to commemorate the two-hundredth anniversary of Law's death. A party of members of Emmanuel, including the master, several fellows, and the whole of the chapel choir, went up to King's Cliffe for the occasion.

In spite of Wesley's great desire that the people saved under Methodist preaching would become the "saving salt" for the Church of England, that was not to happen. In 1784 Wesley sat in an Anglican service and heard a tirade against Methodists. That night he sorrowfully recorded in his *Journal*, "All who preach thus will drive the Methodists from the church, in spite of all that I can do." That is what happened after Wesley died in 1791. Not all ties with the establishment were broken, however; for when Wesley's New Chapel, built in 1778, was reopened after complete restoration on All Saint's Day in 1978, H.R.H. Queen Elizabeth II attended. Her comment as she thanked the minister at the door was, "You Methodists do sing loudly."

The church of St. Peter and St. Paul at Shoreham continues to serve its parish under the guidance of the present vicar, Geoffrey Sedgwick Simpson, an American from Vermont. I visited Shoreham on a day filled with sunshine, flowers, and bird-song and suggested to the vicar that he had chosen to serve in Shoreham because he didn't want to wait until the afterlife for Heaven.

I wish to express my deep appreciation to John Charles Pollock who read my manuscript for solecisms and anachronisms; and to Cyril Skinner, managing curator, and Douglas A. Wollen, historian, who were so helpful during my research at Wesley's New Chapel.

DONNA FLETCHER CROW

BOOK TWO

THE CAMBRIDGE CHRONICLES

TREASURES
OF THE
HEART

To Jennie Crow Speicher
in memorium
*A gracious mother-in-law
is one of God's most precious gifts.*

The Tudway & Hill Families

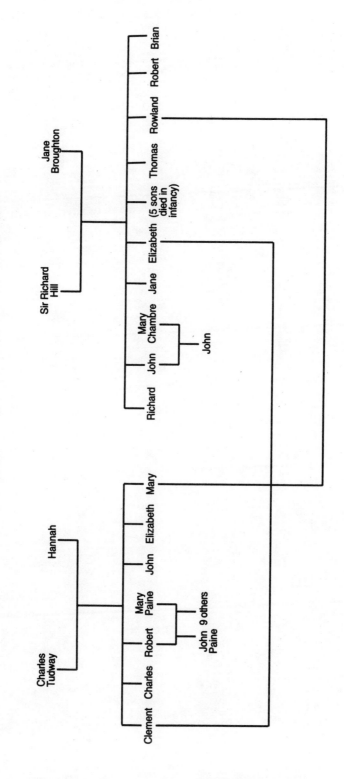

*R*owland, you simply must give up this insane enthusiasm! You are accomplishing nothing but trouble for yourself and embarrassment for your family." Mary Tudway snapped shut her painted silk fan for emphasis. "Including the more distant members of your family." She stamped her foot to show how firmly she held her ground.

"In other words, you find me an embarrassment." Rowland spoke slowly, almost in a drawl, his tall form relaxed and his brown eyes sparkling.

Mary's chin rose in fury and frustration. "You are an embarrassment and—and an irritant, sir!" She whirled and swept from the drawing room before she could soften under the gaze of his kind, laughing eyes.

But her triumphal exit was spoiled. She forgot that she was wearing her extra wide hoops, and she stuck in the doorway. Had Rowland laughed at her predicament, her temper would have forced her through the door even if it meant bending her hoops and tearing the chenille embroidery from her gown. But his soft entreaty, "Mary, please, let me speak," extinguished her anger as quickly as it had ignited.

After his long fingers disengaged her hoop from the carved

door jamb, he held out his hand to lead her back into the room. She placed the tips of her fingers in the palm of his hand and followed him to the damask-covered sofa.

Yet it was Mary who spoke first. "Rowland, you know I regret my hasty temper. But I do not apologize for my sentiments. No one suggests you should give up your desire to take holy orders. That is most admirable and praiseworthy. With your distinguished family background, you will rise quickly and be able to hold a high office in the church. It is just this ridiculous Methodist notion you have taken into your head—"

"Mary—"

"Your sister Elizabeth has spoken to me of it often. What if it were to be generally known in Wells, and the electorate refused to return my brother Clement to Parliament? Have you given no thought to the effect your actions will have on those near you?"

"Mary—"

"Look at you! When we met at Clement and Elizabeth's wedding, I thought you the most handsome man I'd ever seen— in your red velvet coat embroidered in silver. And you danced the cotillion quite to perfection. Now you tell me you have given all that up for some nonsensical religious ideas."

"Mary—"

"Elizabeth says you are quite alone in your views at Cambridge and that the authorities are seriously alarmed by your activities. And she also says your mother is prostrate with worry. If you care nothing for my opinion, you must care for hers."

"Mary—"

This time he was interrupted not by Mary, but by a bewigged and liveried footman announcing that dinner was served. Rowland bowed as Mary preceded him from the room, remembering to turn slightly sideways at the door. "Indeed, Mary, I thank you for granting me this interview. I do feel relieved at having been allowed to speak my mind." Again his eyes sparkled.

For all her outward poise, Mary felt strangely shaken inside.

It was nothing unusual for her to lose her temper, no matter how much she might wish it otherwise; nor was it unusual for her to speak the bold truth to any situation as she saw it, no matter how often her mama reminded her that tactful dissimulation would be more ladylike. But this confrontation with Rowland was different. Why had he undertaken this course of action that could lead to nothing but disaster?

She sighed. It seemed that even all her arguments could not make him change. Of course, she knew he had espoused a personal faith since he'd been a student at Eton. But visiting jails and hospitals was simply not done by people of consequence. Certainly not by a son of Richard Hill, Baronet of Hawkstone, who could trace his family lineage back to Edward I and who was descended from Richard Hill, the first Protestant Lord Mayor of London, a man knighted by King Henry VIII.

She entered the anteroom and crossed to her mother who was chatting with their guests newly arrived from London. "Ah, here you are, Mary, my dear. You have hidden yourself away from our guests, and Sarah is simply bursting to talk to you, I'm sure."

Mary's friend, Sarah Child, flew to her with a flutter of silk skirts, lace flounces, and giggles. "Mary, I haven't seen you for such ages. I have the most handsome new beau to tell you about—"

Mrs. Tudway interrupted Sarah by leading the guests into the dining room in strict order of rank, ladies first. A footman held the chair for her at the top of the table among all the women, with the most important female guests next to her. The master, Charles Tudway, sat among the men in order of rank at the bottom end of the table. The first course consisted mainly of meats—roasted, boiled, stewed, and fried—some with sauces. But the dish of which Charles Tudway was most proud was served by the butler from a large silver soup tureen on the sideboard.

"Finest turtle soup you'll ever taste. My estate manager sends the turtles over from Antigua—always marked CT on the tail so there won't be any likelihood of my turtles being substituted for smaller ones bound for some house in London."

Robert Child took a rather noisy sip of his soup. "Ahhh. Tastier and richer than any we have at Osterley Park."

"I'll have my manager send you a turtle," Tudway offered.

The men then fell to a discussion of the parliamentary session in London, kept lively with anecdotes from the two MPs seated at the table. Wells was represented in the House of Commons by Clement Tudway and his neighbor, Robert Chylde, a distant relative of the Robert Child of Osterley Park. Having two men with the same name at the table added confusion to the conversation.

At the other end of the table, Hannah Tudway turned to Mrs. Child. "My dear Sarah, your fine taste in decorating Osterley is quite famous. Perhaps you could just put a word in for me with Mr. Tudway. Don't you find this room somewhat lacking in ornamentation?"

Mrs. Child gazed around the elegant dining room with its rich paneling and ornate stuccoed ceiling. "The carved fireplace is one of the finest I've ever seen. It rivals anything we have at Osterley—" She hesitated, looking at the marble-encased flames chasing the chill from the January night.

"Ah, you see my point precisely. The west wall is so plain, is it not? I have tried for months to persuade Mr. Tudway that we should have our portraits done by that Mr. Gainsborough who has set up his studio in Bath. Now wouldn't that be just the thing to hang there?"

Mrs. Child agreed enthusiastically, and Mary smiled at the new strategy in her mother's campaign.

"This is famous," Mary said to Sarah seated next to her. "If Papa can be persuaded to go to Bath soon, we will be there while your mama is still taking the waters. I should like above all things to be in Bath with you."

Sarah returned her friend's smile. "We shall have ever so many beaux. Westmoreland has promised he will follow me to Bath. I can't fathom why Papa doesn't approve of him. He is prodigiously handsome, even if he does have a squint in one eye.

But as soon as Papa returns to London and his musty old bank, Mama won't refuse to let me dance with anyone the Master of Ceremonies presents."

Mary was three years older than her friend; but Sarah, raised in the social whirl of London society, was far more experienced in the ways of the world. The pampered only child of one of London's richest bankers, she had been denied nothing. Although Mary's embroidered cream satin gown was made by Wells's best dressmaker, she knew it lacked the French elegance of Sarah's brocaded white silk with undulating trails of flowers in shades of cream, green, and pink. And although Mary's brown hair was piled fashionably high on her head with a tiny lace frill perched on top and one long curl caressing the side of her neck, she knew that Sarah's hair, formed several inches higher over a wire frame, far outdid hers in style.

Mary shivered with excitement as she thought of the fashionable beaux she and Sarah might spend time dancing with in Bath. Then she looked down the table at Rowland. He threw his head back in laughter at a witticism of her father's, and the pose showed off his luxuriant brown hair, with the front brushed straight back and the back portion long and tied with a black ribbon which he brought round and tied in a bow over his fine lace cravat. Although she had berated him earlier for his lack of fashion, she had to admit he did look well in his cutaway coat and matching waistcoat of green poplin decorated with silk braid. If only he had instructed his tailor to add some gold embroidery and metallic lace. Ah, well, there would be plenty of handsome young men in fashionable coats to show her a good time in Bath.

Her father's voice came again to Mary's ears. "The last letter from my manager in Antigua brought distressing news. There has been a sudden fall in the price of sugar." Mr. Tudway shook his head, his bob-wig swaying.

"Confidence, that's all we need, more confidence. The markets will rise again. Oversupply at the moment, I'm sure," the banker reassured him. Child ladled a scoop of sugar over his macaroni mold.

But Squire Tudway was not so easily comforted. "But then there's the matter of my rum—a whole shipment aboard *The McHeale*. It seems to have slipped the captain's memory."

Child laughed and raised his wine glass with a flourish. "More like it strengthened the memory of the sailors. If the captain knew nothing of it being there, he certainly could have no care of it."

Tudway frowned. "That is precisely my worry. I have known sailors to drink more than one-third of a vessel's cargo in a voyage and fill the bottles up with water. But I hope this is not the case."

Now Mary was worried. Papa did not sound at all in a mood to remove to Bath for Mama's portrait scheme—still the topic of conversation among the women. "Everyone of importance has been painted by Gainsborough," Elizabeth was saying to Mary's mother. "If Father Tudway refuses to go to Bath, perhaps you could accompany Clement and me, Mother Tudway. I'm sure when he sees how handsome your portrait is, he'll agree to sitting for one of his own."

On Mary's other side, Child had returned to his favorite topic. ". . . but Child's Bank won't back such risky schemes as those. Yes, sir, my family's been doing business for over a hundred years in No. 1 Fleet Street at the sign of the Marygold, and I have no intention of weakening that position by backing a crackbrained scheme to settle New Zealand . . ."

Mary had heard the story often of Francis, the Child ancestor who had abandoned his trade of goldsmith in 1642 to devote himself to looking after other people's money—thereby becoming London's first banker and earning himself the title of "Father of Banking."

". . . and if I have anything to say about it, there will be a Child doing business at the sign of the Marygold for another hundred years," continued Sarah's father. Mary wondered how this was to be, since Sarah was an only child and would take her husband's name even if she inherited the business. Well, perhaps there was a cousin to carry on the Child name.

The circle of conversations had taken the diners through two courses, and now the servants entered bearing silver salvers with high pyramids of sweetmeats. The highest of the structures, a golden tower of candied apricots, was placed in the center of the table. Other three-sided pillars surrounded them in descending heights, offering confections of dried fruits and nuts, tiny tarts filled with fairy butter or jams, and marzipan formed into tiny flowers and birds.

Mary loved to take a variety of them on her plate and admire their cunning shapes and delicate colors. But she could never hold out for long against the sugared almond paste, and her plate was soon bare. In spite of Hannah Tudway's repeated warnings that Mary should grow quite stout if she continued to indulge, Mary's dressmaker assured her that her form was the most graceful she had the honor of dressing.

The servants left, and Mary noted that the men had turned to discussing politics again. She wondered at Rowland's unusual silence throughout the meal. He listened to the conversation with apparent interest and made appropriate comments, but without his usual liveliness. She hoped it wasn't due to her anger with him earlier. She had no desire to wound him, although it was flattering to think he might care that much for her opinion.

Had her sharp words gone deeper than he had shown? Or were his problems with his family and the Cambridge authorities weighing on him more than he would admit? Ostracism couldn't be easy to bear, even for one so constantly cheerful as Rowland.

Then a new thought struck her. How hard it must be for someone who enjoyed being surrounded with friends and who would have been one of the most popular men at Cambridge to be forced into virtual isolation. Suddenly she had a different picture of him. Her sympathetic nature, as quickly aroused as her temper, reached out to him.

She recalled their meeting at the wedding of her brother

Clement to Rowland's elegant sister Elizabeth. It had been one of the social events of the season. Mary was only a schoolgirl, but her mother had allowed her to dance three dances with family members. Rowland paid great attention to her and smiled at her so kindly, even when she tangled her feet in an intricate step and almost fell against him.

Since then when the families were together for Christmas, Rowland would give her the most thoughtful gifts. She especially treasured the vellum-bound volume of Milton, though she was now determined to read more fashionable poets.

"Indeed, we must make our plans soon." Elizabeth's voice interrupted Mary's thoughts. "Before all the fashionable people are driven from Bath by the Countess of Huntingdon and her enthusiastic preachers."

Mary noted the long look this drew from Rowland seated just down the table from Elizabeth, but he made no comment. To Mary's surprise, it was her mother who came to the countess's defense. "It may be that she goes too far, but I believe she did well to bring some moral fiber to the city against that libertine Beau Nash. I am told that it's not unusual for those who go to Bath to be cured of the gout to find themselves with a new case of the disease—a sure sign of overindulgence. I myself would not be adverse to visiting the countess's chapel while we're in Bath. I'm told Horace Walpole was most entertained there."

"Oh, no, not another church service," Sarah groaned. "Attending the Abbey every day after breakfast is surely quite enough care to take of one's soul."

"But I should hope you won't attend the countess during any regular services of the Abbey." Maria, John Tudway's shy wife spoke up for the first time that evening. "That would show the greatest disrespect to the established church. My dear papa feels such behavior can lead to grave errors. He has warned me repeatedly against entanglements with enthusiasts."

Mary thought Rowland looked a little uncomfortable at this speech from the woman seated next to him. It gave Mary great satisfaction when she was able to catch his eye with a telling look.

A few moments later, Maria requested her mother-in-law's permission to leave the table. With a look that clearly expressed her hopes that Maria's desire for rest would soon be followed by an interesting announcement from her second son and his wife, Mrs. Tudway nodded approval. This left no one sitting between Elizabeth and her brother. She turned to him and spoke in a low voice. "Rowly, I have had a letter from Mother. As I know you intend to depart early in the morning, I feel I simply must speak to you most plainly."

Mary could not help overhearing.

"Elizabeth, you know how dear Mother is to me. I would never choose to cause her distress." The candlelight shone on his long face with the square jaw, heavy eyebrows, and kind mouth.

"Then, Rowland, you must give up this course you are pursuing. Enthusiasm can only bring disgrace upon yourself and the entire family. Papa has received a letter from the Master of St. John's." Elizabeth paused for emphasis.

"Yes?" The tight voice with which the single word was spoken revealed Rowland's nervousness.

"If you continue to visit the prisons and hospitals and preach in the fields around Cambridge, you will force the authorities to take action. Rowland, you must give this up."

"But no one tells our brother Richard he must give up his faith. No one tells our sister Jane she has disgraced the family by espousing a personal religion."

"Your personal faith is just that—a personal matter. I do not speak of it. As indeed such matters should never be spoken of. It is your activities. Why can't you behave as other young men your age? All of England, except a few Jews, are Christian—why must you make public display of it?"

"'To him that knoweth to do good and doeth it not, it is sin.'" Rowland spoke quietly. Mary could see that this was one situation he did not find humorous.

"But does not the fact that you are the only one who believes so in your entire class of thirty-two gownsmen indicate that perhaps it is you who are wrong?"

"Nay, sister, it is you who are wrong." And Mary noted that the sparkle had come back into his eyes. "In the entire university there are three others who would be identified as Christians."

"My point precisely. A total of four gownsmen and no Master or dons?"

"I fear not. But the shoeblack at the gate always has a smile for me. Indeed, for the first year I was there, until I found my three friends, he was the only one in the university who would smile at me. But truly, our numbers have grown."

Knowing the real situation, Mary realized that his humor was self-deprecating. For a moment her heart went out to him. How difficult to be one of only four holding out against the entire university on a matter of faith.

Later when the other guests had departed, Rowland took his leave of Mary. Again he showed no sign of humor as he bowed over her hand. "Mary, I am to return to Cambridge for my final term. If all goes well, I should be ordained by summer. When that is accomplished, I wish to speak to you more to the point."

Even more than his words, the look in his brown eyes elated and confused Mary so that it was impossible for her to form a reply. Fortunately his rapid departure made speech on her part unnecessary. She stood in the hall with the warm memory of his lips just brushing her fingertips as lightly as if she had dreamed it. His words left no doubt of their meaning; yet what could he be thinking? Did he expect her to marry a Methodist?

Then she smiled with a brilliance born of new hope. If he cared for her as deeply as his words indicated, he surely would change his actions. On their next meeting she would persuade him. It was only a matter of time until Rowland Hill would be a sensible young man.

*I*t was to be some time, however, before Mary had her chance at persuasion. A few weeks later, Rowland sat studying the Greek New Testament with a newly enlarged group of gownsmen in his rooms at St. John's, Cambridge.

"I daresay," said Robinson, yawning as he ran a hand through his blond hair, "my brain has had all the Greek it cares for tonight, and I still need to read that passage of Locke before the lecture tomorrow."

Frampton, a newcomer to the circle, looked at Rowland and the three others who had started the group. "I'm afraid my brain has had quite a bit *more* than it cares for. Did you say you fellows have been swatting away at this for years—on your own?"

Rowland smiled. "Ah, now we are a veritable houseful—twelve of us, just like the early disciples. But for my first years here, Penty, Sims, Robinson, and I had to make do with one another's company *en toto.*"

"Which wouldn't have been so bad," Pentycross said grinning, "except that it meant putting up with Hill's little jokes."

"An unhealthy situation, you'll agree." Simpson waved at the air around him as if to clear away the harmful humors.

"Ah, yes." Rowland nodded. "I have always been most grateful to the letter *H*, for without it I should have been ill all my life."

The gownsmen's groans were interrupted by Rowland's somber gyp Bottisham bringing in a tray of coffee. But a short time later, over steaming cups of the milky liquid, the conversation turned serious again. "It does seem to me," observed the freshman Frampton, "that since St. John's is a richly gifted college in livings and so many of the gownsmen look forward to a clerical life, the college preparation of only a chapter or so of weekly Greek construing from the Gospels is hardly adequate."

"Which is why we read together on our own, no matter how the authorities frown on it," Robinson said. "Of course, we are also required to attend lectures, but not one word do we ever hear of the early church, of the fathers of the faith, or of the doctrines of Christianity. We have Locke and Aristophanes, but not one work of true religion."

"And so the young gentlemen obtain college prizes, proceed to ordination, and have livings bestowed upon them," Simpson complained angrily. "After which they grow obese, read the *Quarterly Review*, and die at last of fat rot. These, my friends, are England's clergymen."

Frampton set his cup down and drew back in his chair. "Surely you are a bit harsh."

Rowland shook his head. "Sims is harsh but not inaccurate. The clergy are not entirely to blame though. They receive no instruction in Christian doctrine. Every word of the mysteries of the faith is as strange to their minds as if they were Mohammedans or Buddhist monks."

"Little wonder our churches are mortuaries when our church leaders are dead." Simpson's frown darkened.

"Sick, very sick, but not quite dead, Sims," protested Rowland. "Some of the serious clergy have been brought to deep repentance and converted from a life of debauchery. Then for the first time they begin to read the Scriptures and find a true knowledge of God."

But Rowland's words had little effect on Simpson. "Indeed, I hope there are many. But you'll not find them at Cambridge. The university produces half the clergy of the kingdom. It is an ever-teeming fountain of bishops, priests, and deacons. The Masters of colleges are mostly dignitaries of the church, and two-thirds of all the fellows of the colleges are ministers. And yet religion at Cambridge is entirely theatrical; everything is done for show. All is pomp and ceremony—white linen and scarlet robes, wax candles, organs, anthems, and processions."

"But not just at Cambridge," Robinson reminded them. "The sermons in most pulpits are dull and the gospel unknown. Preachers talk about virtue and justification by good works, a little against enthusiasm, and a good deal about the duty of being an Englishman."

"And when our small number is gone, who shall be here to light the flame in all this darkness?" Pentycross asked.

Rowland Hill nodded. "I too have given that serious consideration. I am convinced that we must pray heartily for the next generation of Cambridge students, that they will have someone to lead them in the way."

After his companions departed, Rowland sat over his guttering candle. How he longed to change it all. If the divinity students filling Oxford and Cambridge could be taught the truth of the Scriptures, presented with honest faith, and meet Jesus Christ personally, the entire nation could be changed in a generation. But the pulpits and pews would have to be filled with people whose hearts burned with vital faith. The empty churches needed to be turned into centers of holy fire. Then England could blossom as the truly Christian nation it was meant to be.

Rowland slipped to his knees. For some time he interceded for God to bring this miracle of renewal to his land, to his fellow gownsmen, to those he preached to around Cambridge, and finally to his own family. At last he came to prayers for Mary. His last talk with her had been far from satisfactory, and her heated words stung his memory. He had cared deeply for her for many years. Would he have to choose between his love for her and his vision of reawakening England to a true knowledge of Christ?

He stayed long on his knees, the room growing cold as his mind struggled—visions of life with Mary playing tug of war with his visions of preaching the gospel. At last he rose and snuffed his almost-drowned candle flame. "Lord, I love You more even than I love her." As he pulled his blankets over his head, he knew his prayer was right, but he didn't find it cheering.

The next morning, Rowland found nothing to comfort him but his naturally buoyant nature and his faith in God's lordship over all. The morning's lecture on Locke was cold and sterile, but less numbing than the compulsory chapel service that followed it. Rowland couldn't help wondering if required chapel attendance wasn't actually an evil. At that moment he could conceive of nothing worse than forcing undergraduates to attend chapel and take the sacraments. The Scripture was clear that one should not partake unworthily, and yet the system forced troops of young profligates to receive the Lord's Supper.

"'... Therefore with angels and archangels, and with all the company of heaven, we laud and magnify Thy glorious name, evermore praising Thee, and saying, Holy, holy, holy, Lord God of hosts; heaven and earth are full of Thy glory; glory be to Thee, O Lord most high. Amen.'" The priest monotoned at such speed that, had Rowland not known the words by heart, he would have had no idea what was being said.

Their black academic robes and caps whipped by the spring wind that whistled through First Court, Rowland and Pentycross left the chapel, crossed into Second Court under the statue of the college founder, Lady Margaret Beaufort, and went up the staircase to Rowland's rooms.

Crossing the larger outer room where the group had met the night before, they went on to the inner sanctum, as Rowland called it. This was a smaller, cozier room with a well-worn green carpet and a case of his most cherished books. Pentycross was telling of the time he went out shooting with a local clergyman. "We were some two or three miles from Cambridge when he said to me, 'We must go on a little to the right to St. Mark's Church. I have promised to take a funeral there at three o'clock.' We reached it in time and stopped at the outer gate. 'Keep the dog and my gun,' quoth he. He leaned the gun by the gate, tucked up his trousers into breeches, went in, performed the funeral, came forth, took up his gun, patted doggie on the head, and we went on as before, shooting our way home. Now I ask you, Hill, would you like to be buried by such a priest?"

"Indeed, not." Rowland rang the bell for his gyp to bring their morning coffee. "I should not like to be buried by any priest just at the moment. There are a number of things I hope to accomplish first."

"Fah, Hill!"

Rowland held up his hand. "No, no. I quite take your point. A minister who truly cared for his flock would use such a time to offer the comfort of true faith in Christ—which this man couldn't do because he didn't know it himself."

Pentycross's reply was cut short by the entry of Rowland's servant.

"Nice to see you looking your usual cheerful self this morning, Bottisham." Rowland took his coffee and the morning post the college servant held out to him. "Ah, riches indeed. Three letters in the post." He started to set them aside, then noted that the top one was from John Berridge. Rector of the nearby village of Everton, Berridge was one of the small number of clergymen in the established church who preached a personal, saving faith in Jesus Christ. He served as mentor to the young band of

Cambridge Christians. "This one's from Berridge. Shall I read it out?" As Pentycross agreed, he began.

Dear Rowly,

My heart sends you some of its kindest love. How soft and sweet are those silken cords which the dear Redeemer ties about the hearts of His children!

I hope you will have leisure to call upon me soon at Everton. Until then may grace, mercy, and peace be with you. May heavenly truth beam into your soul and heavenly love inflame your heart.

Be faithful and diligent, and look up to your Master continually for direction and assistance. Remember His gracious promise, "Lo, I am with you alway, even unto the end of the world." He will supply you with wisdom, strength, and courage, for He sends none upon a warfare at their own cost.

Go out, therefore, and work whilst the day lasts; and may the Lord Jesus water your own soul and give ten thousand souls to your ministry. I am with great affection your

J. Berridge

Rowland looked puzzled. "I wonder what prompted that?"

Pentycross shrugged. "He has undoubtedly heard of the official objections over your preaching to those in prison and visiting the sick and orphans."

"Yes, I suppose that's all. Well, I must call on him soon."

Rowland smiled and sipped his coffee, but he was unusually quiet. A small frown creased his forehead.

"Do you preach at the Castle today?" Pentycross asked, as he set down his empty cup.

"Yes. In about an hour's time. Will you go with me?"

Pentycross nodded, agreed to meet him at the Magdalen Bridge, and then took his leave.

Rowland turned to his unopened post and broke the red seal on a missive in his father's unmistakable, powerful handwriting. He had read only a few lines when he knew he was glad he had read Berridge's words of encouragement first, because his father's were far from encouraging.

> ... and, therefore, I hope to hear you have renounced this irregular preaching. Your mother and I deeply regret this signal mark of indifference to the established church, which we fear might soon strengthen into defiance of its power and renunciation of its principles.
>
> Your activities are such as to represent you as a head-strong and heedless zealot. Such a hopeless branch many would cut off and leave to take root and flourish where it could or wither through want of stability and support. It is through the influence and intercession of your brother Richard, however, that I will not take such a drastic step. You must know though that if such activities continue on your part, I will be forced to reduce your allowance, at the very least.

Rowland put the letter down sadly. Why couldn't his family understand? They were such good people—the solid aristocracy upon which the strength of England rested. There was nothing they wouldn't do for their family, their country, or their church. But there was nothing they could do for God because they did not know Him, although they called themselves Christian and attended church regularly.

And Rowland respected all the traditions they stood for. He would never willingly do anything to hurt or embarrass his family. He was proud of his pedigree and hoped his family could be proud of him. But his allegiance to his Heavenly Father demanded first place. If only he could make them understand.

He turned with relief to the third letter, this also from his family seat, Hawkstone, but in his brother Richard's hand. Here he would find support and encouragement from one who understood his heart and shared his faith.

But Richard wrote to inform him of storm clouds gathering at Oxford over the heads of a small band of Christians very like his own society at Cambridge. Rowland had kept up a lively correspondence with the Oxford group and had encouraged them much. But it had been several weeks since he had heard from them, and now he knew why. Their activities had come to the attention of the college authorities.

> ... In spite of repeated warnings from the dons, our friends think it cowardly to desist, even though they are threatened with loss of character, degrees, orders, and even expulsion itself.
>
> Our friend Mr. Hallward assures me that they are unmoved by these things and that for his part he "considers it a happiness and privilege to be counted worthy to suffer reproach for Jesus' sake with the little flock."
>
> Dear Rowly, you must proceed cautiously that you not bring similar recriminations upon your own head. In Oxford the lion has roared, though I think he has had but little real cause. Beware you give him not cause in Cambridge.
>
> I am your ever faithful bro,
> Richard

Rowland dropped the letter on the table. First Mary, then Elizabeth, then their father, and now Richard, who had always been his strongest encourager, who most truly understood his urgency to preach. That Richard should ask him to pull back in his effort...

He wasn't even aware of the knock on his door until Pearce, his tutor, stood before him. Rowland's heart sank even further at the look on Pearce's face. "Hill, you must take me seriously."

"I always take you seriously."

The tutor sat stiffly upright in a straight wooden chair. "I have come from the Master with the gravest news."

Rowland looked at him levelly, awaiting the blow.

"He is determined to expel you unless you cease your preaching outside the established church. That is final."

Rowland looked at his tall, broad-shouldered tutor with dark hair tied back in a neat queue. This was indeed serious news but hardly unexpected. Rowland could give only one reply. "My irregular meetings may not be sanctioned by man, but they are sanctioned by a Higher Power. Which would you have me obey, Pearce?"

Suddenly he smiled. This blow, coming after what he had thought to be the final stroke, instead of making him crumple, fueled his determination. "Do not look so dismal, Pearce. I know you are on my side and want only the best. And I know how it is with the authorities. Much good has been done lately in the town and in the university, so they naturally suppose me to be at the bottom of it. Well, I may be at the bottom of it, but I'm not at the top. The Lord is King."

Pearce was not mollified. "Hill, it is because I am as much your friend as ever that I want you to continue in college. At first I thought the Master agreed to my plea. But then he seemed sorry for what he had granted. He does not accuse you of any fresh disobedience. It is yet again the old score—if you are to stay in college, he insists upon your promising never to make any more converts in the university or to go into any house in the town to offer relief. And you must give all your alms into the hands of others to dispense for you."

Rowland rose to his full height and took several quick strides around the room on his long legs. At last he came to a stop in front of his tutor. "These terms are utterly against my conscience. I never could consent to them. My activities are by no means against any law of God or of man. I would sooner leave the university than stay on such terms."

There was absolute silence in the room. Then with a small nod of his head, Pearce rose. "I will go again to the Master." He gave Rowland a firm handclasp before he left the room.

"Well, at least he didn't forbid preaching in the prison," Rowland said to the closed door. He shrugged into his wool coat and tugged the inch-wide frills of his linen shirt out from the narrow coat sleeves. He picked up his tricorn hat, walking stick, and well-worn Bible and prayer book. He closed the door firmly as if shutting all controversy and opposition into the room behind him.

The afternoon was as blustery as the morning had been, and Rowland shivered as he went out the main gate. He paused beneath the statue of St. John bearing the arms of the college founder and a bunch of marguerites for her name, Lady Margaret. Rowland took a vague comfort from the fact that for centuries this ground had been hallowed by service to needy people and to the glory of God—first occupied by a hospital and then by the college which became a center of Renaissance scholarship.

"Good day," Rowland greeted his faithful friend the shoe-black at his place of business just outside the gate.

The man's weathered, wrinkled face broke into a smile made brilliant by his white teeth and round eyes. "Good day, Mr. Hill. The good Lord bless you. You want me to black your shoes today? Free for you, as always."

"Thank you, Cobbleton. I appreciate the offer, but they'll need it a lot worse when I come back down the hill."

"You goin' to preach to the captive souls, eh?" He smiled at his own joke. "Well, God give you freedom."

Another gownsman approached with shoes clearly in need of Cobbleton's services, and Rowland turned toward the river. At the bridge he met Pentycross, and the two continued up the slight incline of Magdalen Street. Only a mound remained to mark what had been Cambridge Castle in medieval times. The castle had been little used since the fifteenth century and had fallen into ruins. All that now remained was the gatehouse, which was used as a prison.

Rowland was a familiar figure to warders and prisoners alike and had no trouble gaining admission. After all the opposition he had faced recently, the prison seemed almost friendly; but he was still grateful for the companionship of Pentycross. The turnkey showed them into the largest of the common cells. Unlike the rowdy, egg-throwing townies and sneering, supercilious gownsmen Rowland encountered when he preached in the marketplace, the prisoners were grateful for any break in the boredom of their days. Whether they listened for spiritual counsel or merely for entertainment, at least they listened.

"Ah, 'tis Parson 'ill. Climbed the 'ill to bring us a word, 'ave ye?" The words whistled through the spaces in the old man's teeth.

"That's right, Nettle. Didn't think I'd forget you, did you?"

"Ye might as well. All else of 'um 'ast."

"No, my friend, not quite all. The Lord hasn't forgotten you."

"Nor 'as ta grim reaper. Old Jones died o' the grippe three days past. Death an' disease don't forget no one."

Rowland looked around the filthy cell to include everyone in his reply to Nettle. "May God bring you to the only remedy against that most direful of diseases—sin. This poor sinner who speaks to you found the remedy at the foot of the cross.

"In this dark place we need to let the light shine—the light of God's love. We cannot shine with rays of our own, but we can shine if shone upon."

As Rowland spoke, a deep quiet descended on the rough, untutored worshipers, as if the old stones of the Castle gatehouse were hallowed ground. The sense of reverence touched Rowland's own rapidly beating heart as he looked from face to face; a few stood out clearly—the grizzled Nettle who always greeted him with the latest news of their small community, imprisoned for debts that probably would never be paid; the sneering but attentive Jakeman, proud of his escapades as a thief and likely to return to them unless God changed his heart; Gastard, the youngest of the prisoners.

At the end of the service Rowland prayed. Then he and Penty retraced their steps back down Castle Hill. Pentycross chatted about the service and college affairs, but Rowland hardly listened, simply nodding when his friend paused.

"You all right, Hill?" Pentycross asked when they reached St. John's gate. "Never knew you to keep quiet so long altogether."

Rowland smiled at his friend. "Yes, I believe I'm all right.

Thank you for accompanying me. Must hurry now; not good form to be late for Hall."

Back in his rooms, putting on the satin knee breeches and heavily embroidered coat required for college dining, Rowland was able to define the feeling that had been growing on him since the service at the Castle. It was the most wonderful sense of release. Whatever the outcome with the college authorities, he had done right.

"Some hot water, please, Bottisham." He sent his gyp out of the room so he could exult in the experience alone. When the door closed, he flung out his arms as if to embrace all of God's world and threw his head back and laughed—a deep, rich laughter that came from his heart and winged upward to Heaven like a prayer.

He might have continued laughing until Bottisham returned had he not caught sight of the hastily discarded letters on his table and been reminded again of his family's disapproval. Rowland could be sure in his own mind and heart that he was doing right, but how would he convince those dearest to him?

$Nothing$ was further from Mary's mind than preaching in a prison. At high noon the Tudway coach-and-four rolled past the fashionable shops lining the Pulteney Bridge and made a triumphal entry into Bath. Squire Tudway had not come on the trip himself but made no objection to his wife and daughter accompanying Elizabeth and Clement. And so, after days of hurried packing and last-minute calls to the dressmaker, Mary was making her first visit to the fashionable spa.

The city of graceful spires and ringing bells, of golden buildings—each as beautiful as an artist's sculpture—of glorious flowers against a hillside of emerald greenness, of the greatest elegance the aristocracy of England could produce entranced Mary. The bells decreed by Beau Nash to ring welcome to important new arrivals pealed and echoed against the blue March sky. She had never been happier. Cloistered in the quiet cathedral city of Wells, she had longed for this gaiety. Beaux and courtesans, macaronies and the cream of society—this marvelously brilliant company she would now enter.

When the coach turned into Broad Street, Mary's head felt like a shuttlecock as she turned from side to side, trying to take in the shops and the parade of fashion. Elegant ladies with coiffures almost a foot high swept up the street followed by maids and pages carrying colorful band boxes; ornate gilt and tapestry sedan chairs bearing ladies of even greater importance were carried on poles by liveried chairmen. And then Mary, who thought she was prepared for any sight, cried in astonishment, "Oh, pray tell, Elizabeth, are those macaronies?"

Elizabeth bent her head carefully so as not to hit her headdress on the panels of the coach and looked out. "Indeed they are," she laughed. "But perhaps rather restrained ones."

The two young swells walked slowly so that all might admire. The one closer to the Tudway carriage wore a towering white wig. On top of it perched a tiny tricorn hat. At that moment a lady of his acquaintance approached, and he had to use his gold-knobbed, tasseled cane to raise his hat to her, since the hat was well beyond the reach of his arm.

His companion, clad in a form-fitting suit in startling shades of scarlet and cerise, flicked open a jeweled snuffbox before making the lady an elegant bow, and then tottered on up the street on his three-inch red high heels.

Mary now turned around in her seat watching the amazing sight through the rear window. "Restrained?" she gasped.

Elizabeth smiled. "Well, not *too* restrained. But since the supreme goal in life to all members of the Macaroni Club is to be different, you may meet some more alarming specimens yet."

"Elizabeth," Mrs. Tudway said sharply, "I hope you use the term 'meet' loosely. My daughter may *see* such oddities, but I do not want any such ridiculous fops presented to her."

Elizabeth was immediately as serious as her mother-in-law. "Certainly, Mother Tudway. That would be most unsuitable. I shall watch carefully that none but the most proper young men are introduced to Mary."

Mary gritted her teeth. What was the good of coming to a fashionable spa if one could meet only suitable people? There were plenty such people in Wells—canons, deacons, worthy squires like her father and brothers. As she drank in the heady atmosphere, she realized more clearly than ever just how circumscribed her life had been. Since her come-out two years before, she had attended all the city of Wells offered—fetes at the Bishop's Palace, picnics in the summer, dinner parties with the local gentry. It had been just enough to whet her appetite for more fun and fashion. And before that there had been yearly trips to London, with extended stays when Papa was in Parliament; but she had been a schoolgirl then, never out from under the careful eye of her governess, Miss Fossbenner. Mary had quickly learned that pianoforte, embroidery, French, and watercolor lessons were quite as dull in London as in Wells, even when relieved by a carefully supervised outing to a museum or park. There was certainly never a glimpse of such amusements as the elegant Vauxhall Gardens she had read and dreamed of, with its grand promenades, fireworks displays, and even masquerade parties.

Mary's active imagination had fed richly on such scenes, and letters from her father's estate manager in Antigua telling of life in that faraway island with strange people and exotic customs fired her daydreams. Well, she wasn't in Antigua or in London, but Bath would do very well for the moment. She hadn't even brought any of her needlework with her.

The coach swept around the Circus, a magnificent circle of homes designed in the classical style with a green park in the center. "Oh, Clement, how grand. I wish we could have taken rooms here," Mary cried.

"Just wait, little sister. I have done better for you. The Circus is very fashionable, but offers no view except of one's neighbor. I find the Royal Crescent much more to my liking."

The coach rattled to the end of Brook Street, and Mary gasped at the sight of a vast green lawn sweeping up the steep hillside to a crescent of buildings even more beautiful than the Circus. "It is considered to be the finest crescent in Europe," Clement said. "I would not dispute that, but it is the view clear down to the River Avon that made it my choice. Also the fact that the Childs are staying here. I thought Mother would be more comfortable with neighbors she already knows."

Mrs. Tudway beamed her approval. "Excellent, Clement, very well done."

When the coach stopped before number 6, Clement ushered the ladies into the entrance hall hung with paper skillfully marbled to resemble a golden Italian terrazzo. He held open the door of the drawing room. Mary admired its green silk damask wall hangings, melon-colored Chippendale sofa, and amber Axminster carpet.

"I'll tell Benson to send in a dish of bohea while the luggage is being attended to." Clement turned to direct the servants he had sent ahead from their home in Wells.

But Mary could not sit still and drink tea. She wandered around the room, gazing at the marble fireplace, the pianoforte, the chandelier of Bristol glass, wondering how long she could contain her impatience to explore more of the city. She wasn't required to wait long. Benson quickly returned to announce Mrs. Child and Miss Child.

"Sarah!" This time it was Mary who flew to her friend. "We have come! Isn't it famous! Just as we planned!"

The girls sat on small velvet chairs, their heads bent together as Sarah chattered on about the city. "Everyone rises at six for a soak at the hot baths. The doctor says Mama must bathe every day, and I often accompany her. Then we go to the Pump Room. The water is unspeakably foul, but you won't be obliged to drink it. Mr. King, the Master of Ceremonies—everyone says he's quite as good at it as that autocratic Beau Nash who set all his fusty rules—every morning picks out the finest beau in the room to present to me. Mama is very careful that he not introduce any fortune hunters; but after all, that is why one relies on a Master of Ceremonies, to keep off the undesirables. There must be enough of them in a place like this.

"After the Pump Room everyone takes breakfast. Now that the weather is warmer, perhaps we may get up a party to Spring

Gardens across the river. Then there's holy service at the Abbey. Really, one must go—it's quite *de rigeur* to be seen there—and, of course, only the quality attend, so one can always hope to meet a beau to escort one to the bookstore or the shops afterward."

After Sarah's excited buildup, it was with anticipation simmering almost to the boiling point that Mary entered the Pump Room the next morning. "If you will stay here just a moment, I will secure a table." Clement bowed before leaving his mother, wife, and sister. And Mary was indeed happy just to stand and survey the great room. Around the walls Corinthian columns rose white and gold. At the far end of the room in a galleried alcove, a trio of musicians played a lively Haydn air for those promenading around the room in elegant dishabille after their morning baths. Along the wall to her left was a smaller alcove backed by tall French doors where pumpers behind a counter served glasses of Bath's famous mineral water. And indeed the invalids leaning on sticks or being pushed around the room in wicker chairs, their heavily bandaged, gouty feet elevated for comfort, indicated the popularity of the remedy.

"We are in luck." Clement returned in triumph. "There are no tables available, but Mrs. Child has invited us to join her party." Clement led the way to the center of the room where mahogany Sheraton chairs clustered around small tables.

Clement then left to get the mineral water. Everyone was expected to down three glasses of the health-giving liquid. Even before he returned, the Master of Ceremonies was begging Mrs. Child to present the new members of her company. Mr. King carried a cream-colored three-cornered hat to match the gold-frogged, lace-edged coat he wore over an embroidered waistcoat and ruffled shirt—as close a replica as possible of the deceased Beau Nash whose shoes he attempted to fill. He chatted for a few moments with Mrs. Tudway and Elizabeth and then bowed his leave-taking. But in a very few minutes he returned with two young gentlemen.

Mary's heart leaped at the sight of the shorter and more handsome one. His powdered hair was arranged with just the right amount of curl and elevation to accent his classic aquiline nose and fine cheekbones, just as the particular shade of blue-green ribbed silk from which his coat and breeches were cut emphasized the color of his eyes. The exquisite chenille embroidery and silver sequin ornamentation of his waistcoat revealed that he was a gentleman of the finest taste.

"Miss Tudway, may I have the great honor of presenting Roger Twysden, nephew of the Bishop of Raphoe," Mr. King said. The nephew of a bishop. Even her careful father couldn't fault such a family—even if the bishopric was in Ireland. Mary smiled radiantly as Mr. Twysden bowed over her hand.

A sharp jab in her ribs from Sarah brought Mary back to attention, and she realized the Master of Ceremonies had left them each with a beau, just as Sarah had foretold. But the suppressed excitement on Sarah's face told her something special was afoot.

"Mary, you were quite lost when Mr. King made his introductions. Now I must do it all over again. May I present John Fane, the Earl of Westmoreland. You will hear his friends call him Rapid, I believe."

Mary acknowledged the introduction as it had been given, as if this were the first meeting between Sarah and His Lordship; but she was certain this was the beau Sarah had told her of in excited whispers at The Cedars—the one her father disapproved of, but who had sworn to follow her to Bath. Mrs. Child, deep in gossip with Elizabeth and Hannah Tudway, showed no disapproval, however; and as Mr. Child was in faraway London toiling at his sign of the Marygold, there seemed to be no threat to Sarah's happiness.

A short time later, when Mrs. Child accepted Westmoreland's invitation for the company to join him at a concert breakfast,

Mary's suspicion was confirmed. Either Mrs. Child didn't know of or didn't share her husband's disapproval.

At that moment, there was a stir in the crowd. A small, severe-looking woman in a dark green gown and full white headdress that gave the effect of a prioress entered through the French doors. An assortment of followers trailed behind at a respectful distance, but Mary's attention was caught by the sweet-looking young woman a few paces behind the "prioress." The girl, in a gown of heavy ivory satin over a pale blue petticoat, was older than Mary by perhaps six years.

"Egad." Roger flipped the lace handkerchief he carried. "It's Her Holiness, the Countess of Huntingdon, honoring us with her presence. Probably come to lead in prayers or bless the water or something."

The Master of Ceremonies rushed forward to greet Her Ladyship and escort her party to a hastily prepared table near the musicians' gallery. Mr. King himself brought glasses of water to the countess's table.

Mary turned to gain a clearer view of the celebrated lady. "And who is the young woman with her—the pretty one?"

Sarah leaned closer. "That's Lady Selina, the countess's daughter. She's really perfectly amiable, for all she embraces her mama's fusty theology."

"I hope I shall have opportunity to meet her."

The words were no more than out of Mary's mouth when Elizabeth spoke up. "I believe I should pay my respects to Her Ladyship. The countess is a great encourager of my brother; and before his death, her chaplain, Mr. Whitefield, wrote Rowland numerous letters boosting his faith."

For a moment Mary was stunned. In the excitement of Bath she had all but forgotten the young man who so recently had caused her such emotional stir. This great lady had taken notice of Rowland? And he had come under the tutelage of the famous George Whitefield? What had her friend done to catch the attention of such noted people?

But Mary's questions went unanswered as Clement hurried off to secure Mr. King's services to present their party to the countess and to secure additional chairs.

"Ah, yes. The sister of our dear Rowly," Lady Huntingdon said to Elizabeth a few minutes later, casting a sharp eye at Elizabeth's fashionably low-cut neckline. "Well, make certain you stay away from the card rooms. Society here is nothing but one vast casino. I would not have our dear Rowly's sister drawn into the evils of this place. I daresay you have come for the waters and will find them quite invigorating, but the rest is an unending pursuit of pleasure occupying the whole day, to the exclusion of anything useful or sensible."

Some gave unintelligible murmurs as the countess paused for a sip of water. Then she continued, "All here is a tedious circle of meaningless hurry, anxiety, fatigue, and fancied enjoyments the entire day. In short," she said directly addressing Mary and Sarah, "nothing can be more trifling than the life of a lady nor," turning to Roger and Westmoreland, "more insipid than that of a gentleman at Bath. The one is a constant series of flirting and gadding about, the other of sauntering from place to place without any scheme or pursuit. Scandal and fashions engross the entire of conversations." Now she looked at Mrs. Tudway. "You and your party will, of course, choose a higher way of life, but you must be on your guard. The evil is insidious."

Mrs. Tudway offered a reassuring answer for the company.

Lady Selina smiled pleasantly at Mary. "Would you care to take a turn around the room? Colonel Hastings will escort us."

Mary agreed, and the handsome uniformed man sitting on Selina's left instantly rose, held their chairs, and offered each one an arm. The rest of the company was engrossed in conversation—or more particularly in listening to the countess who dismissed the three with a brief nod—as Selina and Mary left.

"Have you been in Bath long?" Lady Selina asked.

"We arrived only yesterday."

"And are you enjoying it?"

After the countess's blunt words, Mary wasn't sure what to say. She didn't want Lady Selina to think her lost to all sense of propriety. "It is very beautiful."

"Indeed it is. And do not let Mama frighten you. You will find many delightful pastimes, though what she says about the vices is quite true. You must attend a service in our chapel when you have time. Mama is preparing a great celebration for the seventh anniversary of its opening. Rowland Hill—he would be your brother-in-law, would he not?—has preached there several times for Mama."

Mary was stunned. "Rowly? But he isn't ordained yet."

"No, and, of course, he doesn't celebrate Communion. But Mama has a seminary in Wales, and she often offers opportunities for students to bring addresses in her chapel. Rowland Hill is the best I've ever heard. I believe he will be as great a preacher as Mr. Whitefield. There are even those who say Whitefield's mantle has fallen on him."

Again all Mary could say was, "Rowly?"

They continued around the room, and Mary was glad to see that the tête-a-tête at the countess's table was concluding when they arrived. She had not adjusted to Bath hours and at home would have breakfasted long ago.

Since the concert breakfasts were considered polite entertainment, the countess joined Westmoreland's party. The entire company took to their carriages to travel back up the hill to the Upper Rooms on Bennett Street off the Circus. The Upper Assembly Rooms, opened just the year before, had been designed by John Wood the Younger at the staggering sum of twenty thousand pounds. These rooms now served as the center of the city's social life.

Breakfast was set in the main ballroom, the tables and chairs dwarfed beneath the magnificent high ceiling. The pale blue room with its white plaster ornamentation and row of crystal chandeliers seemingly suspended in midair seemed to Mary the most beautiful she'd ever seen. From the musicians' gallery, the orchestra filled the room with baroque music as ornamented as the architecture itself.

With the abundance of fashionable company, beautiful music, and delectable food, it was easy to understand why these events were so popular. The menu was an elaborate affair of three courses of boiled and roasted meats, savory pies, and the famed Bath buns chock full of currants and with sticky icing that required licking of the fingers after eating.

But the countess did not approve of the menu. "I never cease to be amazed by the folly of men. They realize that without health life is a burden and that this blessing can only be obtained by exercise and abstinence; yet even after the heyday of youth is passed, they will go on loading their bodies with distemper, pain, and sorrow till life is not worth accepting. Then they repair to Bath where they drink three pints of the waters, and then sit down to a meal of hot spongy rolls rendered high by burnt butter. Such a meal few young men in full health can get over without feeling much inconvenience, and I have known it to produce almost instantaneous death to valetudinarians."

Roger, who was enjoying his third such roll "high with burnt butter," tried to mollify Her Ladyship, or at least to change the topic. "May I have the honor of escorting those who wish to go to the Abbey for matins? My uncle is to read the service. Dreadful bore, I fear, but one must do one's duty."

The countess and her party had had morning prayers hours before in her private chapel, and Mrs. Tudway declined as she was to have her first meeting with Mr. Gainsborough that day. But Elizabeth agreed to go, and Mrs. Child felt she would be sufficient chaperone for Sarah. So the smaller party arranged themselves in Westmoreland's elegant town coach and journeyed back down the hill.

Mary caught her breath as she entered the majestic nave with its lacelike vaulting of pale gold stone arches and the brilliant stained-glass window glowing from the midday sun.

"Pray, hurry along, Mary. We want to get the best seats," Sarah urged.

On Roger Twysden's arm, Mary walked the full length of the nave to the front seats reserved for members of the bishop's family. To the left of the altar sat the visiting bishop on his throne, splendid in a surplice of finest lawn and lace mantle. The light from the jeweled window fell across his mitered head and added a glow to the look of benediction on his face.

Glancing around her, Mary saw that the Abbey was almost filled. And the worshipers nearly rivaled the gorgeous east window for richness of color and design. Everyone was clad in silk or satin ornamented with gold or silver lace, metallic embroidery, and silk flounces. The towering headdresses of the women and powdered wigs of the men seemed to be reaching toward the Gothic arches above them. But the coiffures were the only part of the audience that reached heavenward. The elderly settled into comfortable sleep with their hands folded across their laps, and the young people flirted, the girls behind fluttering fans.

At first Mary was shocked at such behavior in church. Then Roger winked at her in a way that made his blue-green eyes dance, and she responded by fluttering her own fan. She decided this was all quite natural. Surely God wanted people to be happy in church.

The organ prelude came to an end, and the bishop rose and walked to the reading stand. In somber, melodious tones rivaling those of the organ, he read from the prayer book.

Mary slipped to her knees with the rest of the congregation for the general confession, the rich solemnity of the bishop's voice making her think seriously of her own shortcomings and her need to seek forgiveness. "Almighty and most merciful Father, we have erred and strayed from Thy ways like lost sheep . . ." Mary was repeating the words as her own prayer when she felt a nudging from Roger behind her. She opened her eyes and saw that he was holding out a note to her. In some surprise she took the folded square of paper and opened it while the bishop was reading the absolution.

To Mary

Your eyes are as blue as the sky of Bath,
Your voice as sweet as the bells in their spire,
We met but this morn, and already you have
Captured my heart; you my rapture inspire.

Confusion reigned in Mary's mind. Should she be flattered by Roger's attentions or outraged by their impropriety? Was he so overcome by passion for her that he couldn't restrain himself, or had he no sense of what was appropriate during a holy service? And then she became aware of the company around her. She had focused on the beauty of the service and had truly worshiped, as she always did in church. But even as the bishop was reading, she heard giggles, sighs, and whispers all around her. Out of the corner of her eye she saw other notes being passed, even across the wide aisle.

So Roger was merely trifling with her, writing some flattering words—in bad verse—to lessen the boredom of listening to his uncle. Her temper flared. Taking the prayer book from the rack in front of her, she brought it down with a sharp crack across his knuckles. She was only sorry that she couldn't bring it down on his head.

But, as always, her temper died as quickly as it flared and left her horrified at what she had done. Everyone must be staring. Her mother would hear of it, and she would be borne back to Wells in disgrace. Roger would be humiliated and never speak to her again. The first poem she received in Bath would be her last.

Then she looked up and saw Roger grinning at her saucily. No one else was looking at her. All were intent on their own flirtations. Even Sarah and Westmoreland beside her had not noticed. And then she heard a similar sharp crack behind her and knew that another girl had rapped her suitor's knuckles with a fan. She suddenly realized that the girl behind her was teasing, and Roger thought she was also.

Still confused by the topsy-turvy values of this society, Mary returned Roger's smile. But after the service, she declined his invitation to escort her to the bookseller's. This was no coquettish device. She really wanted to be alone for a while to think.

The beauty and order of the house in the Royal Crescent welcomed her; and her room, serene with its green and white striped wallpaper, gold-draped white French bed, and silk-skirted dressing table, was the perfect place to try to order her thoughts. Even in one day she could see that Bath offered the amusement she sought, but how did she reconcile this to the values of her home in Wells?

If she must choose among the stolid boredom of a country life, the charming but superficial pleasures of the fashionable world, or the long-faced religion of an enthusiast like the Countess of Huntingdon, it all seemed a rather hopeless lot. But her frown turned to a smile as she thought of the humorous moments of the day, and she wished that Rowland could have been there to share her amusement. At the same time, she was glad he wasn't. What would he think of the company she had chosen?

In the days that followed, Mary had little time for reflection. With Roger as her constant companion, she became well acquainted with his uncle, the bishop, who was a close friend of Mrs. Child's. Any time a doubt prickled her mind about the attitudes of the bright company Sarah Child gathered around herself, Mary could readily salve her conscience with the thought that, after all, a bishop was among them.

The only real cloud to her happiness appeared the following week when she and Elizabeth returned from making the rounds of shops in Milsom Street with two footmen carrying parcels of the finest of spangle-embroidered fans, kid gloves, silk mesh mittens, and satin ribbons.

"Oh!" Elizabeth picked up the post Benson had placed on the hall table. "A letter from Jane! I haven't heard news of Hawkstone for ages. Come to my room, Mary, and let me share it with you. Send up a tea tray, Benson."

But as soon as Elizabeth opened her letter, her face fell. "Mary, I fear the news is not good. Jane has received a letter from our Rowland. He has been much in the furnace these past weeks."

Mary instantly felt a pang of shame for the mindless gaiety of her last few days while her friend had been suffering.

"Jane has copied out part of Rowland's letter. Shall I read it to you?"

Mary nodded, her eyes wide.

> The Master said I might stay in university provided I would not disturb the town by public conventicles; and would also give him a promise not to teach in the university any doctrine contrary to the Thirty-Nine Articles. To the former, I answered I had no intention of doing so, as I had told him before; and though I could safely give him a promise to the latter in the absolute, if he really meant that I should not talk about religion to the gownsmen, as I supposed he did, I could make no such promise.

Elizabeth paused for a sip of tea. "I cannot bear to think what it will mean if he is forced to leave the university just two months before degrees are awarded. It would be a disaster for Rowland, but it would kill our parents. Such a thing is unthinkable."

She picked up the letter, read a bit in silence, and then put it down again with a sigh. "More bad news. The authorities at Oxford have expelled six undergraduates who believe as Rowland does, but did not so much as preach publicly. What will Cambridge do to one so outspoken as our brother? I tried to warn him when I saw him at Wells. He must give this up! Enthusiasm in religion is social suicide."

Mary nodded unhappily. She had spoken to Bishop Twysden on the subject only that morning—in veiled terms, of course, so he could not guess her reason. The bishop had been outraged. "Mad men, the lot of them. Believe we are all sinners, and God will punish us. Such ideas won't hold today. Much too enlightened for that. Of course, it's in the prayer book, but that's just tradition; nobody really listens to it."

Mary took a long sip of tea. Who was right? Rowland was prepared to put his entire career and future success on the line for his faith. The countess had devoted her life and private fortune to promote personal religion. Yet who should be a better guide in spiritual matters than a bishop? Sarah was perfectly happy without any notions of a personal God. Roger was a delightful companion of the first fashion, and as the nephew of a bishop, he surely had proper instructions in all matters of the church.

And what difference did it all make anyway? She had been baptized as an infant, confirmed when she was twelve, and had attended services regularly with more devotion than most. Surely that was sufficient. If poor Rowland was determined to be stubborn, she would simply have to consign him to his chosen fate. Other than listening to Elizabeth's worries, it needn't affect her. What did it matter to her what Elizabeth's brother chose to do?

At Cambridge, still awaiting the fateful decision of the Master of his college, Rowland struggled over a letter to his sister Jane. But before he started putting his thoughts into words, he pulled a small packet of letters from his desk—letters of encouragement he had received from George Whitefield. He was glad he had kept the letters. The great preacher had died in America two years earlier. Rowland missed him sorely.

The first letter was written several years before when the conflict began, but it was as if Whitefield had foreseen the very situation Rowland faced now.

> About thirty-four years ago, the Master of Pembroke College, where I was educated, took me to task for visiting the sick and going to the prisons. In my haste I said, "Sir, if it displeaseth you, I will go no more;" my heart smote me immediately—I repented and went again. He heard of it, threatened, but for fear he should be looked upon as a persecutor, let me alone. The hearts of all are in the Redeemer's hands. I would not have you give way, no, not for a moment. The storm is too great to hold long. Visiting the sick and imprisoned and instructing the ignorant are the very vitals of true and undefiled religion. If threatened, denied degree, or expelled for *this*, it will be the best degree you can take. A glorious preparation

for, and a blessed presage of, future usefulness. Now is your time to prove the strength of Jesus yours.

Blind as he is, Satan sees some great good coming on. We never prospered so much at Oxford as when we were hissed at and reproached as we walked along the street. It is a poor building that a little stinking breath of Satan's vassals can throw down. Your house I trust is better founded—is it not built upon a rock? Is not that rock the blessed Jesus? The gates of Hell, therefore, shall not be able to prevail against it. Go on, therefore, my dear man, go on. You are honored in sharing Christ's reproach and name.

God bless and direct and support you—He will, He will. Good Lady Huntingdon is in town—you will not lack her prayers.

Yours, in an all-conquering Jesus,
G. W.

Yes, Whitefield was right. But how could he make his family see this? How explain to his mother and father that it would be a *good* thing to be expelled for conscience' sake? And Mary—would she ever speak to him again if he presented himself to her sans degree, sans ordination? He had been so sure when last he talked with her at The Cedars and hinted so broadly of what was in his heart. What would his great stand for conscience' sake mean to her?

He turned to his second letter from Whitefield.

I have had a profitable conference with your brother Richard. He tells me your brother Brian may soon be gained for the Kingdom. What grace is this! Who knows but the root as well as the branches may be taken by and by: Abba, Father, all things are possible with Thee. Steadiness and perseverance in the children will be one of the best means, under God, of convincing the parents. Their present opposition I think cannot last very long; if it does, to obey God rather than man, when forbidden to do what is undoubted duty, is the invariable rule.

Satan sees he is only a mastiff chained. Continue to

inform me how he barks and how far he is permitted to go in your parts, and God's people shall be more and more stirred up to pray for you all.

Yours, in our all-conquering Emmanuel,
G. W.

If only Whitefield's prophecy might come true, that his parents would see the light. But so far there was no sign of it.

A knock came on his outer door. Rowland put the letters away and rose. Why did he always feel a sense of dread these days when an unexpected caller came by? If this kept up much longer, he would soon be as long-faced as Bottisham. But he relaxed when he saw his old friends Pentycross, Simpson, and Robinson.

"Come to escort you to the Greek Testament lecture, old man. You look as though you could use some help," Pentycross greeted him.

"Egad, is it six o'clock already?" Rowland hurried back to his inner room to throw on his black robe and grab the soft black cap required for lectures. "Been looking over Whitefield's letters."

"Oh, yes," Pentycross said. "I remember the verse he sent me when my exhibition was withdrawn for visiting the sick and such.

'Satan thwarts and men object;
Yet the thing they thwart, effect.'"

"And so it is with you, eh, Penty?" Simpson said.

"Yes, I have continued quite well without their grant of thirty pounds a year. And Frampton told me later it was hearing the story of my steadfastness that brought him into our society. Would that I had thirty thousand to give up for Jesus' sake."

This lecture, which the vice-provost conducted at a sacrifice of his day of rest, was the college's great concession to the idea that young ordinands should be given some background in the Holy Scriptures. It purported to be a critical and exegetical analysis of the Gospels. The students were asked to construe a passage from St. Matthew or St. John, and occasionally the vice-provost would read from some commentator, offering an explanation of the text.

Rowland would have infinitely preferred quiet reading in his own rooms or a study time with his friends. He felt the lecture did more harm than good, for a wine-gathering always followed Hall on Sundays. A great deal of wine was consumed in a very short time on the plea, "We've no time to lose, so pass the wine." Rowland had accepted an invitation to only one such party, but it showed him why scarcely any of the gownsmen were clear-headed enough to understand the lecture.

The week wore on with similarly unprofitable lectures. Rowland chafed at the enforced curtailment of his activities, but he was grateful for the loopholes that allowed him to visit the sick beyond Cambridge and to preach at the Castle. Of course, if the authorities had thought of those things, they would have forbidden them also, but for the moment he could continue. At times he wished for the final blow. If the decision came on the side of expelling him, then he would be released from all bounds by the college, and he could preach wherever anyone would listen to him.

But when Pearce appeared at Rowland's door, it was merely to inquire into his charge's studies. He had no news of his own to deliver.

"Pearce, you're a good fellow to carry this brief for me. But I am wearied with the waiting. I believe I should beard the Master in his den myself. I feel such a coward hiding behind my tutor's skirts."

"It's nothing of the kind, Hill. The Master has chosen to operate in this fashion, and we must be content. If you were to go to him yourself, he would merely see it as another infraction of the rules."

And so Rowland waited. The one bright spot of those weary days was a letter from the Countess of Huntingdon inviting him to attend the celebration of the seventh anniversary of the opening of her chapel in Bath.

Our dear Charles Wesley will lead the music, and our old friends Romaine and Fletcher have promised their attendance. I have hopes of Berridge. If only Whitefield were here to preach again as he did at the opening. But we must carry on apace. I shall expect you.

Well, if he were not allowed to remain in Cambridge, his time would be his own. But even if he did complete his degree, there would be time for a visit to Bath at Easter. And if the Master's decision was negative, he would not likely be welcome at Hawkstone; so all around the countess's invitation was a cheering prospect. Except that in her last letter, Elizabeth informed him that Mary and Mrs. Tudway had accompanied her to Bath. If Mary were still in the city at Easter, it could mean only a renewal of the argument started at The Cedars. He had so hoped that when he saw Mary again, he would come to her complete with his degree and ordination—solid credentials which would put an end to her pleas that he give up his irregular preaching. When fully ordained, he would not need to hold irregular services. "Lord, speed the day," was his heartfelt prayer, as he thought of all that ordination meant to his future. But he must have his degree first.

The last Saturday in March was mild and sunny with clumps of daffodils and crocuses blooming on the Backs of the colleges along the river and a soft spring-green frosting the fields, fens, and hedgerows beyond Cambridge. This would be a perfect day to call on his old mentor, John Berridge.

The ride to Everton did much to restore Rowland's humor. He even found himself singing the last few miles.

Just outside the village, however, he stopped singing to observe an interesting sight. A butcher, proclaimed so by his heavy, blood-stained apron and the square cap on his head, was marching straight for his shop with a trail of five fine cows following him. There was no driver with a whip behind the cows, and the butcher didn't even look behind to make sure they were following. Rowland reined in his horse and sat a moment, observing. What secret did this pied piper possess that the cows would follow him to slaughter so docilely of their own free will? At last he spotted a clue and, laughing, spurred his horse.

At the old stone vicarage, he tossed his reins over the post and bounded forward. Berridge, who had seen him coming, threw open the door and stood with arms outspread, a broad smile wreathing his round face.

"My dear Rowly, my very dear Rowly, what a joyous surprise! I see by your demeanor that you bring me good news."

Rowland clasped his friend's hands. "Indeed, I bring you excellent news. I have just discovered a new illustration for a sermon."

"Well, come in, come in, and tell me." The white-haired man led the way into his book-lined study.

"As I was coming along, I saw a butcher followed by a number of cattle. I couldn't at first make out how he got them to follow him. But presently I saw that he dropped some beans as he went along, and the animals picked them up and ate them. Thus he got them into the slaughterhouse and closed the door." Rowland thumped on Berridge's desk as if on a pulpit. "This, I say, is just what the devil does. He drops worldly pleasures and concerns in the path to lead sinners to the slaughterhouse. We must warn them before the door is slammed."

Berridge threw back his head and laughed. "My dear Rowly, a most excellent example indeed. But have you come to tell me that you have been permitted to preach?"

The pleasant ride, the joy of singing his favorite childhood songs, and the unexpected delight in finding new sermon material had put Rowland's troubles completely out of his mind. But now they were back. He sank into a chair. "Alas, no, sir, I have not. There is no news. The Master delays, and Pearce tells me there is nothing more I can do but to behave with circumspection and attend lectures. It is frustrating."

Berridge nodded, his face serious, except for the perennial twinkle in his eyes. "Yes, it chafes. When I was a fellow at Clare

Hall, Cambridge, I was surrounded with witty and amusing companions such as you well know the university abounds in. But when I 'turned Methodist,' I too found that the jeers and rejection indeed chafed. And I can see by the glow your little anecdote brought over you that preaching is your great love."

Berridge rang a small bell on the table by his chair. When his housekeeper appeared, he requested a tea tray—a hearty one to refresh his young friend. Then he turned back to Rowland. "Luther used to say that when the Lord had fresh work for him, a strong trial was sent beforehand to prepare him for it by humiliation. So take these present slings and arrows as precursors of God's blessings."

Rowland started to speak, but Mrs. Stoke entered with a tray of cold meat, cheese, bread, and jellies. Rowland found he was indeed hungry—the hungriest he had been for days.

"Eat up, my dear Rowly. And listen well. What better bargain can you find than to fill your stomach and your mind at the same time?" Berridge took a sip of tea laced with milk and sugar and then continued. "Study not to be a fine preacher. Jerichos are blown down with rams' horns. Look simply to Jesus for preaching material, and what is wanted will be given; and what is given will be blessed, whether it be a barley or a wheaten loaf, a crust or a crumb."

He paused to push Mrs. Stoke's basket of buns closer to Rowland. "Your mouth will be a flowing stream or a fountain sealed, according as your heart is. Avoid all controversy in preaching, talking, or writing. Preach nothing down but the devil and nothing up but Jesus Christ."

Rowland shook his head with a rueful smile. "Avoid all controversy! You cannot know how I should like to follow your advice. But controversy follows me as the tail follows the dog. It seems the only way I can avoid controversy is by avoiding preaching. And if I am to do that, I may as well quit breathing."

"No, no, you must not do that. Breathe deeply. But breathe of His Spirit. I think your chief work for a season will be to break up fallow ground. This suits the accents of your voice at present. God will give you other use of your tongue when it is needed; but now He sends you out to thrash the mountains, and a glorious thrashing it is. Go forth, my dear Rowly, whenever you are invited into the devil's territories; carry the Redeemer's standard along with you and blow the gospel trumpet boldly, fearing nothing but yourself. If you meet with success, as I trust you will, expect clamor and threats from the world and a little venom now and then from its children. These bitter herbs make good sauce for a young recruiting sergeant, whose heart would be lifted up with pride if it were not kept down by these pressures."

Berridge refilled his guest's cup. "The more success you meet with, the more opposition you will find; but Jesus sits above the floods and remains King forever. His eye is ever upon you, and His heavenly guards surround you. Therefore, fear not; go on humbly, go on boldly, trusting only in Jesus, and all opposition shall fall before you. Make the Scriptures your only study and be much in prayer. The apostles gave themselves to the Word of God and to prayer. Do thou likewise."

Rowland had been listening with pleasure to the words of his spiritual guide, drinking them in, savoring them, and showing his agreement with a slight nod of his head. But suddenly Berridge took a new tack. "Now is your time to work for Jesus; you have health and youth on your side and no church or wife on your back."

Rowland could not keep the frown from his face, and his cup clattered in its saucer. "Ah, I see that I have touched a sore spot." Berridge laughed. "You are thinking that now I have ceased preaching and gone to meddling."

"As things now stand, it appears unlikely that I shall ever, as you say, 'have a wife on my back.' But I do not view that as a happy state of affairs. Preaching is *first* in my heart, but it is not quite *all*."

Berridge was serious now. "Indeed, I am sorry to hear it. Very sorry. Grieved even. Have you not read St. Paul's advice on the subject? I am unalterably opposed to the marriage of our young Methodist clergy. Those who will try it have been punished for their folly. Charles Wesley was spoiled for his work by his happy marriage. John Wesley and George Whitefield were only saved from making shipwreck of the cause by God's sending them a pair of ferrets for wives."

"It is your advice then that if I must marry, I should take a shrew for a wife?"

"How many a minister we have seen who in early life was active, zealous, and useful, who, when settled as pastor and united in wedlock to an amiable and agreeable woman, became—if not entirely negligent—at least comparatively indifferent and useless to the work. The attractions of domestic life are powerful; the spirit of the world creeps in, the strength of personal piety lessens, and he becomes—alas, for himself and others—at ease in Zion."

The conversation turned to happier subjects while Rowland finished Mrs. Stoke's repast. He then took his leave, for he had a long ride before him. And much to think about. Was Berridge right? Even if he could persuade Mary to become his bride, would it spell disaster for his ministry? Perhaps his lack of success in wooing her was God's answer for the pattern his life was to take. If this were so, he should rejoice in her indifference to him. But he could not do so.

Later in the week, when his long-awaited answer came from the Master's lodge, he found that it further complicated the matter of his love for Mary.

The warmth and scent of spring filled the air, and Rowland had no desire to return to his room or visit the library after lecture, so he continued on across tiny Third Court squeezed between Second Court and the river and walked across Kitchen Bridge. The Backs were landscaped with walks, a bowling green, carefully trimmed hedges, and a wilderness bounded by a yew hedge. Rowland was strolling along one of the gravel paths, considering following it to the fields beyond, when he heard Pearce's voice calling.

"Hill, I say, Hill. I have word at last."

Rowland started toward Pearce. He could read nothing in either his tutor's voice or stance. Had he come as executioner or pardoner? It suddenly seemed to Rowland that he had been holding his breath for months waiting for this moment, waiting for the blow to fall.

Pearce didn't even wait for Rowland to voice his questions. "I have purchased for you a peg tower. I have assurance all will be amicably settled. You will receive your degree."

"And what are the terms fixed upon?" Rowland was careful not to claim victory before he knew the terms of surrender, or indeed which side had surrendered.

"In the end, the Master was exceedingly vague. Never a word was mentioned of your visiting the sick and imprisoned, dispensing Methodist books, or of frequenting houses suspected of Methodism."

"In short, I am free to do just what I please!" Now Rowland would permit himself to rejoice. "I perceive that the Master only wanted to draw his head out of the halter as handsomely as he could. Blessed be God!" He grabbed Pearce's hand and pumped it up and down vigorously, but Pearce was too much the dutiful tutor to give himself over entirely to celebration. He could not consider his commission complete without a sturdy word of warning. "And now that this matter is successfully concluded that you may remain for your degree, may I suggest that you put all other matters out of your mind but the successful completion of your work. We have but one term left now to prepare for exams and orders!"

"Indeed, Pearce." Rowland was still shaking his hand. "Indeed. I shall be entirely at your command—after vacation. I go to Bath next week. Then my brain shall be all yours for the term to cram as much learning into it as your heart desires."

At last Pearce extracted his hand from Rowland's large grip and turned toward the library. To his surprise, Rowland accompanied him. "I had thought my news might send you off on one of your famous swims or out to gather a crowd to preach to."

Rowland looked longingly at the river sparkling in the afternoon sun. "Alas, there are those whose concern over this matter has been greater than my own. I must write to my sister Jane."

But the task was more difficult than he had anticipated. Such happy news should have come tumbling out on the paper before him; but as Rowland sat in St. John's library with dark wooden shelves of books running up to the ceiling on three sides of him, the narrow space filled with birdsong from the open window and the splash and plod of barge horses pulling their loads up the Cam just beyond the window, he found it hard to discipline his thoughts into words. He dipped his pen and tried again.

> My very dear sister,
>
> I am ashamed that I have been so long in writing, but I thought you would like to hear from me when all things were settled. I have met with delivery from the Master's clutches. He commissioned my tutor to meet with me and to tell me that *I might stay.*
>
> The town and university are entirely surrendered to my episcopal visitation *a prelate*. My only grief is that for the present I am in a great measure an unpreaching prelate. However, this unmixed mercy will soon be remedied. My remarkably kind tutor tells me he has not the least doubt but that I may be ordained next May. How wonderfully this is ordered! 'Tis well the government is upon Jesus' shoulders, though my rebellious heart thought very hard of so many seemingly reverse providences in the past. I must learn by experience that glorious song, "Worthy Is the Lamb."
>
> I prepare now to go to Bath for our good Lady Huntingdon's celebration. For this reason excuse the haste of this from your poor unworthy bro.
>
> > Ro Hill

But the last line to Jane brought directly over his head the small dark cloud that had been following him for days. For a moment he could have thought the sound of splashing water from the river was rain on his spirits.

He had won his hard-fought battle. He had stood strong on matters of conscience, and authority had capitulated. There now appeared no barrier to achieving all he most fervently desired—degree, ordination, Mary.

He should have been full of joy at the thought that he would see Mary next week, especially now that he had good news to bring her. But Berridge's solemn exhortation was heavy on his mind.

He had always assumed that his longstanding fondness for Mary, coming about so naturally through family connections and fired by her personal charms, had been of God's directing. But if Berridge was right, far from being a bounteous blessing, his tender feeling for Mary must be regarded as a temptation, an ensnaring trap to be avoided at the peril of his soul.

$\mathcal{B}$ut why should I go to the baths when I am not ill?" Mary frowned and tossed her head as she and Sarah strolled across the courtyard linking the Abbey, the Pump Room, and the King's Bath at the heart of town. The two women and their escorts, the ever-present Roger and Westmoreland, paused to look over the stone wall surrounding the largest and most popular of the city's five public baths. Several of their fellow promenaders had like-wise paused to observe the bathers bobbing in the steamy air of the mineral water pool. Bath had been a popular resort since the Roman legions had used the hot waters as a substitute for the balmy Mediterranean.

Mary looked up at the arched windows of the Pump Room and observed a number of the promenaders there likewise watching the bathers. "If I am to bathe, I should prefer a less public place."

"Certainly. You must attend the Cross Bath just at the end of Bath Street. It is much more genteel," Roger said.

Sarah laughed. "Fah, sir. Is such a description intended to tempt her? You make it sound a dreadful bore. Never fear, Mary. You will find it quite invigorating and much more a social event or a sport than a mere physician's prescription."

So the next morning Mary and Mrs. Tudway arrived at the Cross Bath with Sarah and Mrs. Child shortly after the popular hour of six. Since they were driven there in a closed carriage, they wore the regulation gowns of yellow canvaslike material.

"This scratches." Mary tugged at the square-cut neckline of her bathing garment.

"Never mind. It will feel more comfortable in the water. And it's quite necessary. It would be most unfortunate to go into the water in a garment that clung to one's form when wet."

Mary shuddered at the idea and tucked a linen handkerchief into her chipstraw bonnet. She had been warned that she would need it to wipe the perspiration from her face. A woman attendant came forward to lead them down the stairs into the water and presented each of them with a little floating dish containing confections, a handkerchief, and a vial of perfume. The attendant stayed with the older women, but Sarah and Mary chose to cross the bath by themselves, pushing along their black lacquered trays.

The great billowing sleeves and skirts of their garments filled with water. Mary giggled. "Oh, I shall be bobbing like a cork in a moment. Pray, hold my hand, Sarah, so that I won't float away."

"Will my hand do?" A familiar masculine voice made her start.

Mary splashed the water in her surprise, making Roger cry out in protest. "Egad, if you wish me to take my leave, just say so. No need to drown me."

"But I thought . . . that is, I had heard—" Mary was confused by this unexpected turn. "I had supposed men and women bathed separately here," she finished.

"Yes, I believe there was some fusty notion of that." Roger laughed and presented her with a nosegay of fragrant violets and lily of the valley. "But no one pays it any heed. No more so than any other of the Beau's Rules of the Bath."

"Indeed." Westmoreland joined them. "But this one is honored in the breach, while the others are simply no longer necessary as matters of enforcement."

"Such as?" Sarah sniffed prettily at her nosegay from Westmoreland and then set it afloat, its pink and violet ribbons drifting in the water.

"Such as that no man or woman should go into any bath by day or night without a decent covering on their bodies, under the penalty of three shillings and fourpence. Or that no person shall presume to cast or throw any dog or other live beast into any of the said baths, under the like penalty of three shillings and fourpence. And that no person shall thrust, cast, or throw another into any of the said baths with his or her clothes on, under a penalty of six shillings and eightpence."

Laughing at Rapid Westmoreland's account, they made their way to the far end of the pool, past the bath's namesake—a large stone cross in the center of the water which stood as a memorial to the consort of James II, who had been cured by the waters.

"Indeed," Mary said, "I'm most grateful to Mr. Nash. I shouldn't find it at all pleasant to bathe with dogs or other beasts." And she thought it quite all right that the prohibition against mixed bathing had gone unenforced. The men looked most handsome clad in breeches and waistcoats from the familiar yellow canvas with their tricorn hats on their powdered hair. But that observation made her think of her own appearance, and she dabbed lightly at her glowing face with the handkerchief from her bowl.

From the stone-arched gallery along the side of the bath, an orchestra began playing, and the idle visitors who had gathered to watch the bathers applauded. Mary would have been more comfortable without the gallery viewers, but the bath was as invigorating as Sarah had promised.

Roger, noting her uneasy glance at the gallery, leaned close to her ear. "The bath is most becoming to you, my dear. You can be assured that no man who has seen you here would part with you for the best mermaid in Christendom."

Mary felt flattered. Any misgivings she might have had at his meaning were forgotten as Westmoreland began theatrically to quote a popular couplet:

275

"And today many persons of rank and condition
Were boiled by command of an able physician."

Everyone laughed.

Not to be outdone, Roger sprang to the side of the pool and struck an antic posture, balancing on one foot like a statue. Then pretending to lose his balance, he teetered dangerously on the edge and plunged into the water, showering the ladies with drops of silver. He bobbed to the surface, floating on his back, and gazed up into Mary's face. "Ah, what rapture! It is Neptune's lady love I see! Ah, Fair Damsel, take me, take me!" He held out his arms to embrace the elements and sank in rapture beneath the surface to the accompaniment of laughter.

How long such acrobatics might have continued they were not to know, for Mrs. Child sent an attendant to inform them that she was ready to leave the bath.

That afternoon, as had become their habit, the gentlemen escorted Sarah and Mary to the shops. On the way up Milsom Street toward the book room, they passed by a coffeehouse designated for ladies; gentlemen read the papers in another establishment across the way. Sarah looked longingly at the women of fashion entering their meeting place. "Alas, I should like to attend there someday. But my mama says young girls are not admitted, insomuch as the conversation turns upon politics, scandal, philosophy, and other subjects above our capacity. I think it sounds far more interesting than the fusty old bookseller I was obliged to subscribe to for a crown and a quarter."

"In truth, Miss Child." Westmoreland tapped his walking stick on the cobbled walk. "I can warrant that you miss nothing in passing by the forbidden fruit. In your Office of Intelligence all the reports of the day and all the private transactions of the Bath are discussed as fully as in any other room."

The men stood aside at the door to allow the women to enter first. Mary could not help but feel flattered by the warmth of Roger's admiring glances as she folded her parasol and walked before him.

She knew she looked her best in her cream silk polonaise gown and its overskirt in a Chinese pattern with pink and green. But as she went up the stairs, she could not help blushing as she felt his gaze upon her ankle, made visible by the shorter French style.

As they entered, the Abbey bells pealed forth, announcing the arrival of someone of importance—probably a member of the aristocracy, from the length of the ring. Sarah led the way directly to a table already occupied by a set of her acquaintances who were deep in gossip.

"They say Lady Lechmere lost above £700 in one sitting at the gaming tables."

"Wait until Lord Lechmere hears of this—"

One of the gentlemen took a pinch of snuff.

"It will be a wonder if all the sweetness the waters can put into Lord Lechmere's blood can make him endure it!"

"Then Miss Nunsworthy danced three times with Mr. Runstrete. When her guardian hears word of *that*, I shouldn't care to be responsible for the outcome."

The conversation continued, punctuated with giggles and the flutter of fans; but Mary soon wearied of the veiled innuendos and shredding of reputations. She rose and walked around the room, spending more time looking at the books on the tables than at the fashionable people pretending to read them. In spite of her desire for a gayer life, Mary was by nature a quiet, peaceable person, not a meddler or a gossip.

"May I help you select a volume to your taste?" The ever-attentive Roger was by her side. "Do you prefer to read novels, plays, pamphlets, or newspapers?"

"Is there no poetry, sir?"

"Ah, indeed, Milady." After making an excellent bow, he selected a small volume of Cavalier poetry and began reading to her as they strolled around the room.

> "Gather ye rosebuds while ye may,
> Old Time is still a-flying! . . ."

He read the verse in a charming manner, but Mary was troubled by the words. "It seems, sir, that if time is short, the poet should urge people to make the most of it to accomplish something of value, not to fritter it away gathering rosebuds."

"Where did you come by such a gray-beard notion? I find the poem excellent advice myself. One sees enough of the broken-down, superannuated in the Pump Room to serve as a warning. Now is the time to live for pleasure; another opportunity is unlikely to come." To add emphasis to his argument, he turned from Robert Herrick to the poetry of Thomas Carew.

> "Then, Mary, let us reap our joys
> Ere time such goodly fruit destroys."

She blushed at his insertion of her name in the poem and quickly changed the subject for fear he might pursue the innuendos. "I confess to preferring more thoughtful work—such as *Paradise Lost*. But I have of late begun reading novels. Mama says it is quite acceptable now that I am out. Mr. Fielding's books make me blush, but *The Castle of Oranto* gives me the chills."

"Ah, indeed. You fancy Walpole's apparitions, do you—the giant in armor, a skeleton perambulating in a hermit's cowl, a statue that drips blood?"

Mary laughed. "Perhaps it is the chills that I enjoy more than the phantoms themselves."

"Allow me to select a novel for you." Roger paused before a bookcase on the wall. "Ah, I fancy you will find this to your liking. Smollett's *Humphrey Clinker*, written only last year and set largely right here in Bath. It is rumored he borrowed freely from Anstey's *New Bath Guide;* but be that as it may, it is quite a diverting work." He handed the bookseller two shillings for the volume and presented it to Mary.

Sarah and Westmoreland were still deep in gossip, so Roger offered to escort Miss Tudway back to the Royal Crescent.

Benson opened the door at their approach. "Mrs. Tudway—Mrs. Clement Tudway, that is—has a guest just arrived, miss. She asked me to show you into the drawing room as soon as you returned."

"Oh?" Mary undid the ribbons on her round straw hat. "I didn't think Elizabeth would be back from her portrait sitting yet. A new arrival? How exciting. I heard the bells ring—were they for Elizabeth's guest?"

Mary was looking down, pulling off her white lute-string gloves as she entered the room, so she was fully in front of the visitor before she saw who it was. "Rowland! What a first-rate surprise! I had not thought to see you for months yet."

As he rose, she noted his handsome stature in his finely cut cinnamon coat, but something was amiss. The sparkle with which he always greeted her was gone. She took a step backward. "Oh, Rowly, do not tell me. You have been sent down! Oh, this is dreadful." Although she had warned him of the likelihood and could now have the pleasure of saying, "I told you so," she had not thought she would find the event so wounding.

Rowland bowed stiffly over her hand. "On the contrary, Mary, I appreciate your concern, if not your confidence, but I have just been informing my sister that the Master has consented that I may take my degree."

Before Mary could reply, Roger, who had remained in the entrance hall to give Benson his hat, gloves, and walking stick, entered.

Mary introduced the two men, and they acknowledged each other coolly. In an attempt to bridge the distance between them, she offered, "Mr. Twysden's uncle is a bishop. Undoubtedly you know of him, Rowland."

His reply was indistinct.

After paying his respects to Elizabeth, Roger told Mary he hoped to see her at the Assembly Rooms that evening and took his leave.

Mary turned to sit on the sofa beside Elizabeth, and Rowland went back to the Sheraton chair. She started to speak, but Rowland was first. "Is that fellow a proper person for you to know, Mary?"

Rowland's high-handed attitude made Mary's temper flare. "La, sir, are you to superintend me now that Miss Fossbenner has been dispensed with? I *told* you he is the nephew of a bishop. And what have you to say to it if my mama approves?"

"You are quite right. Forgive me."

"Faith, sir, that is much better." Mary smiled at him; her point won, her temper cooled. "Now, tell me you have agreed to refrain from your irregular preaching."

"No. The authorities made no such demands. Had they required me to act contrary to my conscience, I should have accepted expulsion rather than submit."

"Oh, lud! If you aren't the most starched-up person I have ever known. Why must you be so obdurate, so intractable, and—and so mule-headed?"

"Is that what I am? Indeed, I must apologize for my character. I had thought a stand upon principle admirable, but I see I mistook. I shall attempt to amend my ways. Perhaps a dose of the waters here would make me more wishy-washy." The sparkle had returned to his eyes.

And his amusement lighted her own. "How unhandsome of you to roast me, sir, when I was merely giving you valuable advice."

"And how unjust of you to accuse me of grilling you when all I did was to agree with you."

As usual Mary found that she couldn't maintain her irritation with Rowland for more than five minutes in his company, so she relaxed with the laughter she felt bubbling inside her and noted that his initial coldness toward her had thawed considerably.

To her surprise, Rowland rose a few minutes later to take his leave. "But aren't you staying here? I am certain Clement would wish you to," Elizabeth protested.

"No. I thank you, but I have accepted Lady Huntingdon's invitation. Since it is her celebration that brings me to Bath, it will be most convenient."

"Oh, indeed. The chapel is attached to her house so you can pray ever so much more often." Mary could have bitten her tongue as soon as the words left her mouth. And her desire to recall them increased when she saw that the ice had returned to Rowland's countenance.

Elizabeth smoothed the situation. "Clement and I are getting up a party to attend the gala at Sydney Gardens tonight. Won't you join us, Rowly? I sent a card to Lady Selina and Colonel Hastings, so you could come in their carriage."

Rowland accepted his sister's invitation before bowing his farewell to the ladies.

Elizabeth turned to Mary. "And what of you, my dear? Will you join our party tonight?"

For a moment Mary was tempted. Then she stiffened in her resolve. Rowland must not think her softened to his nonconformist ideas. "Thank you, Elizabeth, but I have engaged to join the Childs' party to the cotillion ball in the Upper Rooms." When Mary and Sarah formed the plan, an evening at the ball had seemed the height of bliss. But now as Elizabeth left Mary to see to the arrangements for the evening, Mary felt strangely depressed.

When she returned at eleven o'clock with Roger's meaningful stares and sometimes ribald witticisms fresh in her mind, she was even more depressed. Especially when Elizabeth came in to inquire how she was and went into raptures over the gardens with their shady groves, grottoes, labyrinths, and waterfalls. "And the illuminations, my dear. It's quite marvelous how they contrive to light the trees and borders. It all gives the effect of giant fireflies or of stars having come down to rest in the branches.

"And we had excellent company. Lady Selina was ever so charming in her quiet way. Have you noticed how remarkable she is? She always thinks of others first, and yet she never makes one uneasy with it. Most people merely call attention to themselves."

Elizabeth paused to kiss her sister-in-law good night. "I'm pleased you had a pleasant evening, dear."

Mary nodded in reply.

"We breakfast at Spring Gardens in the morning. Will you go with us?"

Mary's peevishness almost made her refuse, but just in time her common sense prevailed, and she accepted.

The next morning, clad in her most charming straw bonnet decorated with cherry ribbons and bobbin lace and wearing a *levette*, a simple loose gown with a sash cut from silk of shaded pink and crimson stripes on a ground of pale cream, Mary rode in the carriage with her mother, Elizabeth, and Clement to the dock. A ferry would take them to the gardens across the Avon River.

In spite of her confused feelings about Rowland, she was determined that her smile should match the brightness of the morning. When they first met those from the countess's party, Mary felt the barrier of Rowland's new coldness. But then the countess, who had surprised everyone by accepting Elizabeth's invitation, prodded him between the shoulders with her walking stick. "Rowly, offer Miss Tudway your arm." And Mary could see his irrepressible humor conquer his reluctance.

"At your service, Miss Tudway." He extended his hand, Mary placed hers atop his, and they stepped onto the gently rocking ferry boat behind Lady Selina, likewise holding Colonel Hastings's hand for support.

As Selina and her colonel took seats in front of Mary and Rowland in the ferry, Mary considered the pair and the happy future in store for them. According to Elizabeth's report, Colonel George Hastings, two years Lady Selina's senior, had been brought up with her elder brother under the Earl of Huntingdon's care at Donnington Park, their family seat, so that their present friendship was based on a lifetime of companionship.

As Francis, Earl of Huntingdon, had shown little inclination to marry, and as Colonel Hastings's elder brother was childless, it was possible that Colonel Hastings would succeed to the earldom of Huntingdon, and there would be a second Selina, Countess of Huntingdon.

But what meant even more to Mary was the adoring gleam

in the military man's eyes when he looked at Lady Selina and the charming, almost shy manner in which she returned his regard. It seemed a glow of gentle happiness surrounded Selina. The blissful ending Mary supposed in store for the couple made her smile and reflect that it couldn't befall two nicer people.

As soon as they were midway across the river, they could hear the strains of French horns and clarinets playing in the gardens. Spring Garden had been laid out as a charming retreat for visitors to Bath, with acres of walks and ponds and ornamental beds of flowers bordering the blue Avon.

The party made their way along the sweetly scented hyacinth-bordered path to the long room where breakfast was served. The invigorating atmosphere of fresh air, sparkling scenery, and pleasant companions encouraged Mary to approach the cakes and rolls and pots of chocolate with abandon. As they began to eat, they overheard laughter and gossip from the party at the next table. ". . . and then Miss Braddock, enamored of such a complete rogue, spent £6,000 in paying his debts and lost both money and lover."

Lady Huntingdon's voice cut sharply across their story, undoubtedly reaching tables beyond her own. "And they think it a matter for levity. Rogues, charlatans, mountebanks, and strumpets—that's who are behind the pomp and elegant facade of this city. Just like that folly of Mr. Allen's—Sham Castle, indeed! A great castle on a hill that's nothing but a front to look at. Fah! That's all these fribbles of society are—just outward show with no thought for their eternal souls.

"All about, one sees the vice, intrigue, and corruption of a society which values pleasure and luxury and nothing else—a jostling crowd of highborn and lowborn all engaged in a frantic round of pleasure and diversion. They should look to the healing of their souls rather than their bodies."

Elizabeth looked distinctly uncomfortable at this breakfast-table homily. In her unobtrusive way, Lady Selina signaled a footman to offer one of the plainer buns to her mother. The diversion was successful for only a few moments, however, as Lady Huntingdon's determined chin rose, and her snapping eyes and sharp words compelled the company to her attention. "But judgment will not always be stayed, as in the case of the young man who dropped dead after dancing thirty-three *couples* in the Assembly Rooms. His partner fainted, but was at it again after being revived by spirit of hartshorn and tincture of tiddlen. She had another chance; but his soul was required of him that very night, as it someday will be of us all."

Having unburdened her soul, Her Ladyship at last turned her attention to her plate.

"Would you prefer tea, Mama? I'm persuaded your chocolate must be quite cold." Selina gave her mother a sweet smile and again signaled the footman.

"You are my support and stay, Selina," the countess said in an uncharacteristically soft voice. Then she turned to Elizabeth. "She is the only one I can rely on since my husband died and the young earl moved to London." With a look of tenderness which Mary would not have guessed had she not seen it herself, the countess's eyes filled with tears. Lady Selina again smiled at her mother, and the conversation around the table became general.

By now Mary was aware of a slight tightness of her sash. She set her last cake aside unfinished, even though it contained her favorite almond paste filling.

Lady Selina leaned toward her. "Would you care to take a turn through the parterre?"

"Indeed. I find formal gardens most charming," Mary quickly agreed.

Colonel Hastings hurried to assist them with their chairs and was fumbling to hand them their parasols when the countess's voice rang sharply down the table, "Rowly!"

His slow grin lighted his eyes, and he stepped to her chair. "You would care for a stroll, Milady?"

"I would not. For the son of a baronet, you are very slack in your duty to the young ladies."

Rowland bowed. "I thank Your Ladyship for reminding me of my duty." He extended his hand, palm downward, to Mary.

She took it in silence, but when they were out of hearing of the rest of the party, following several paces behind Selina and the colonel, Mary said, "Rowly, why have you been avoiding me?"

"Ah, I would not like to damage your social position by having it voiced abroad in this gossip-ridden town that you have taken up with an enthusiast."

"Don't be absurd. I have heard that Mr. Wesley's sermons are very popular in town."

"Quite so. Above five thousand attended his first sermon here. But whether that is an indication of spiritual hunger or merely a desire for entertainment is uncertain. Wesley thought it unlikely the gospel could have a place where Satan's throne is."

"Satan's throne?" Mary recalled the countess's words at the breakfast table. "Surely that is an exaggeration."

"Perhaps. Wesley once said the people of Bath are all children of wrath, and their natural tempers are corrupt and abominable. The sheriff asked him on his next visit not to preach; but then the local authorities realized the effect of his work on the morals and the peace of the place, and a member of the city corporation presented him with a roasted ox."

"And do you expect your own irregular preaching to have such a happy outcome?"

But Rowland would not be drawn to discussing his personal affairs. "Pray, what should I want with a roasted ox? But truth to tell, not all of Wesley's confrontations went that well. Have you heard of his encounter with Beau Nash?"

"Indeed I have not." Mary leaned closer to Rowland as if to hear a delicious tidbit of gossip.

"It seems that at the time when nothing occurred in Bath without the authority of the Master of Ceremonies, Beau Nash asked Wesley by what authority he was preaching. Wesley replied, 'By that of Jesus Christ, conveyed to me by the present Archbishop of Canterbury, when he laid his hands upon me and said, "Take thou authority to preach the Gospel!"' Nash, however, protested that it was contrary to law, adding, 'Besides, your preaching frightens people out of their wits.' 'Sir, did you ever hear me preach?' Wesley asked. The Beau replied that he had not. 'How then can you judge of what you have never heard?' 'By common report.' 'Sir, is not your name Nash? I dare not judge of the things I hear of you by common report!'"

Mary looked up at Rowland, her brown eyes wide with interest. "Pray tell, what was the outcome?"

"Nash accepted the challenge to hear Mr. Wesley and later commented that it was easy for the Methodists to preach extempore since they had a certain string of words and expressions that they consistently used on every subject. 'It is such a string as must draw you to Heaven,' Wesley replied, 'if ever you intend to go there.' 'I thank you,' said Nash, 'but I don't choose to go to Heaven on a string.'"

Rowland told the story with a lightness, but the fact that this one-time uncrowned king of Bath had now gone to his eternal reward added an unspoken gravity. The Beau was no longer ruling the aristocracy, but reaping the consequence of his choices. Mary walked quietly for some time, apparently admiring the bright spring flowers around the ponds; but she was really considering the story Rowland had told and the earlier words of the countess, in contrast to the life she had been leading, and more immediately disturbing—Rowland's reticence to discuss his personal affairs. This was the same Rowland who had been her laughing companion on family occasions since childhood. Yet he accompanied her now only at the direct order of the countess and with the formality of a newly introduced stranger. She had seen flickers of amusement warm his eyes briefly in the last two days, but not once had his affectionate smile rested on her. He had come yesterday specifically to report that his troubles at the university were settled, but it was obvious that he was worried about something.

Their rambling walk had taken them in a circular pattern,

and they now were again approaching the long room when two familiar male figures appeared on the path in front of them. Roger and Westmoreland made sweeping bows, and Westmoreland, who possessed an alarming memory for poetry, greeted them with another snippet from the *New Bath Guide:*

> ". . . and there all went,
> On purpose to honor this great entertainment;
> The company made a most brilliant appearance,
> And ate bread and butter with great perseverance;
> All the chocolate too that my lord set before 'em,
> The ladies despatch'd with the utmost decorum."

"I trust you've had a pleasant breakfast, Miss Tudway." Roger again swept an arch with his pale blue tricorn. "But it grieves me to find one of such tender sensibilities as you in the company of a noted irreligious." He fixed Rowland with a challenging stare.

Rowland remained expressionless at the taunt in the guise of a witticism, but Mary flew to his defense. "Irreligious! I beg your pardon, sir. Mr. Hill is exceeding religious! He's fanatic in it."

"Ah, exactly so." Roger smiled. "A regular fanatic—or is that irregular?"

Mary drew herself up taller. "Not so! His preaching may be irregular, but—"

At this point Rowland, his lip quivering with amusement, intervened. "Pray, Mary, cease defending me while I still have a shred of reputation left."

Again Roger bowed. "Forsooth, forgive me if I have offended. I had thought to compliment, but now I have quite lost track of the conversation."

"If you meant to say I am religious, I indeed take it as a compliment." Rowland's voice was mild.

"As would your friend, Lady Huntingdon, I believe. My uncle informs me there is to be a celebration at the pope's—er, I mean, Her Ladyship's chapel. I think I shall attend; it would be great fun to sit in the Nicodemus chamber with Uncle."

Westmoreland called again on his ready store of poetry:

"Hearken, Lady Betty, hearken,
to the dismal news I tell;
How your friends are all embarking
for the fiery gulph of Hell:
Cards and dances ev'ry day,
Jenny laughs at Tabernacle—"

Roger interrupted his friend with a stricken pose. "But I forget myself. Is there indeed to be a celebration? There is a rumor here in everybody's mouth that the countess is confined or has run in debt and squandered away a great deal more than her annuity upon vagabond preachers and places for them to preach in. I cannot learn with any certainty what the case really is, but there is something or another at the bottom of this rumor which will soon be better known."

Westmoreland picked up his story. "We are told that her son has taken out a statute of lunacy against her, that madness is incident to the family, and that she is sister to that lord who was hanged at Tyburn not long since for willfully killing his man. And worse yet, a nephew of hers, Walter Shirley, has published a volume of Methodist sermons."

"No! Now, I say, Westmoreland, if you are to recount tales stricken in years, I much prefer the one of Beau Nash's vintage. After he had attended one of her drawing rooms in suitably somber attire, verses appeared pinned to the pillars of the Pump Room stating that the countess, attended by a saintly sister, was to preach in that room the next morning and that Mr. Nash, to be known henceforth as the Rev. Richard Nash, was expected to preach in the evening in the Assembly Rooms. It was hoped that the audience would be numerous, as a collection was intended for the Master of Ceremonies, retiring from office."

Mary, who would ordinarily have been amused, recalled

the touch of genuine emotion on Her Ladyship's face and felt a quick, rising anger that such a lady, no matter how medievally autocratic, should be the butt of unkind jokes. "The Countess of Huntingdon is a fine and upright lady who serves God according to her own conscience, and I will thank you not to make light of her in my presence." She snapped her fan for emphasis and turned so sharply that she almost slammed into Rowland. To her own amazement, hot, angry tears stung her eyes.

Mary and Rowland rejoined their party. All the way back to the Royal Crescent, Mary didn't say a word. She couldn't understand what was wrong with her. Bath had proved to be everything she had dreamed of and more; she had attended more balls, more concerts, and more parties in a month here than she had thought to enjoy in a lifetime; and she had a beau of the first fashion who was, if anything, overattentive.

What more did she want? And why was she worried about Rowland? He would take his degree, and then it was but a short step to the ordination he had his heart set on. And his cool attitude toward her seemed to make it clear that she needn't worry any longer about his making her a troublesome offer. So why didn't that cheer her?

The carriage rolled to a stop before number 6 at The Royal Crescent. Mary placed her hand in the one extended by the liveried footman to descend, but she didn't turn into their own doorway with Elizabeth. "I believe I'll have a chat with Sarah," she announced. And she hurried off.

Settled comfortably in Sarah's blue and white bedroom, Mary let out a depressed sigh. "Sarah, do you ever feel empty?" Sarah looked puzzled. "That is, do you ever get tired of the routine?"

Sarah's infectious laugher filled the room. "Mary, what nonsense you do talk! Tired of having fun, of being admired by beaux, of buying pretty fripperies? Are you chaffing me? That's not possible. You don't mean to say *you* are weary of it, do you?"

Mary sighed again.

"Goodness, you are moped! You need a rest, that's all. You

aren't tired of having fun; you're just plain tired. Go home now for a nice lie-down, and then we'll find a new diversion—or at least a new bonnet to purchase."

Sarah had made it clear. Whatever was bothering Mary, the problem was with herself; her feelings were unnatural. Mary decided to let the matter drop.

But Sarah persevered. "And what of this Mr. Hill, Mary? I think too much time in his company has turned you melancholy, probably from boredom. I'll grant he is a baronet's son and exceedingly handsome with excellent manners, but surely you wouldn't consider forming an attachment to a Methodist? Westmoreland assures me Roger is perfectly taken with you— and he is his uncle's heir. Now *there's* a catch worth setting your cap at."

"Sarah! What a vulgar expression. I haven't 'set my cap' at anyone and have no intention of doing so. I simply find myself a bit fatigued, as you say. At any rate, a baronet's son becoming a Methodist may be an oddity, but he's certainly not a bore."

"And Roger is?" Sarah asked in shocked tones.

"Well, he's very amusing, but that's all. There seems to be no real depth to him. I don't believe he ever really thinks about anything of importance."

Sarah could not believe her ears. "Importance! He knows all the latest fashions and has an endless flow of entertaining gossip, and I heard him reading some charming poetry to you the other day. What more could you want?"

Mary didn't know. But as she walked slowly back to number 6, attended by Sarah's abigail, she thought over her own words. Rowland Hill could be irritating, maddening, and worrisome, but he was never boring. She laughed quite as much in his company as she did in Roger's; but Rowland's companionship had the added quality of making her think, even if the thoughts weren't always comfortable.

*B*ack at The Vineyards, the Countess of Huntingdon's house in Harlequin Row, Rowland searched his soul about his intentions toward Mary. Had it not been for Berridge's warning, he would be the happiest of men, feeling assured of his future and basking in the company of the woman he adored. Or if the Master of John's had refused him, he could have taken comfort from Berridge in that he could not ask a woman to share the life of a lay itinerant, even though he was the son of a baronet.

But as matters stood, to be with Mary when he felt he must resist her and believed he had no right to challenge Roger's attentions for a place in her heart brought despair, despite his normally cheerful outlook.

Perhaps he had misunderstood his old mentor's advice. He felt a sudden longing to talk more with the venerable man. Rowland went in search of Her Ladyship, hoping she might have received word that Berridge was to attend the anniversary. He found her in her upstairs parlor, glowering out one of the Gothic windows that lined the front of the building.

"I can't think what they were about, making those Paragon Buildings seven stories high. One would think they set out to scrape the sky. It's a wonder God didn't strike them down as at the Tower of Babel. Formerly we had a quite perfect view from these windows." She turned to look at Rowland. "And what may I do for you, sir?"

"I have come to inquire if you have received word from Berridge, Your Ladyship. Will he attend the anniversary?"

"I have, and he will not." She crossed the room with quick, measured steps, picked up a letter from her desk and read:

> As for myself, I am now determined not to quit my charge. Never do I leave my bees though for a short space only, but at my return I find them either casting a colony or fighting and robbing each other; not gathering honey from every flower in God's garden, but filling the air with their buzzing, and darting out the venom of their little hearts in their fiery stings. Nay, so inflamed they often are, and a mighty little thing disturbs them, that three months' tinkering afterwards with a warming pan will scarce hive them at last and make them settle to work again.

Rowland, whose smile had grown throughout the reading, chuckled at the closing remark.

"I suppose you find this amusing, do you? You and Berridge share the same besetting sin. Humor, sir, is most inappropriate and unbecoming in a man of God. You must work to expunge it from your nature."

Rowland considered inquiring why she thought God had given him a sense of humor if He had no use for it, but not feeling equal to a lecture on original sin at the moment, he merely bowed.

The anniversary service celebrating the seventh year of the opening of the Countess of Huntingdon's Bath chapel was to be held at six o'clock in the evening on the Sunday following Easter. Mrs. Child had declined the invitation, but the entire Tudway party was to attend. Mary chose a small but lavishly trimmed hat and set it at a sharp angle on her elaborately dressed hair, highly pleased with the new style Bath's most fashionable hairdresser had created for her. She picked up a wide, black silk scarf edged with frills and allowed Elizabeth's dresser to drape it carefully around her shoulders just before Mrs. Tudway knocked at her door. "Are you ready, my dear?"

"Coming, Mother." Mary turned toward the door. "Oh, I almost forgot my ticket." She moved the numerous pots and jars around on her dressing table until she uncovered the small strip of cardboard. "Other foundation can no man lay, than that is laid, which is Jesus Christ. 1 Corinthians 3:11." She read the text to her mother.

"Yes, my dear, but no matter what it says, I do believe Her Ladyship has laid quite a few foundation stones. I understand she has built something like fifteen chapels and staffed them with chaplains at her own expense—at Brighton, Tunbridge Wells, over in Wales and Derbyshire. It makes one quite tired to think of such energy." Mrs. Tudway led the way to their carriage.

Mary was mildly surprised to meet Roger just outside the door to the chapel, but she was completely amazed that Bishop Twysden should be there too. She presented her family to the important guest and then remained with Roger as the others went in. "How gracious of you to attend the countess's celebration, Bishop Twysden," Mary said. "I'm sure Her Ladyship will be sensible of the honor you do her."

The bishop laughed and held out his ringed hand for Mary to curtsey over, his lawn sleeves billowing over his wrist. "I doubt she will feel honored; more likely invigorated by the opportunity to convert me."

"Convert you?" Mary was astounded.

"Oh, yes. Her Ladyship is convinced of the sinfulness of all men, no matter of what station."

"But that's impossible—a bishop. Surely you were baptized—"

"In my infancy at Westminster Abbey, with a bishop presiding, and later I was confirmed. But what is good enough for the church isn't necessarily good enough for the countess." Rather than leading the way through the main door, the bishop walked farther toward the back of the building to a small door. "The countess was most thoughtful in her accommodations, however. Realizing that higher members of the church might feel—ah—uncomfortable among her more enthusiastic worshipers, she has provided us with a private chamber. Would you care to see?"

The bishop opened the door on a small room to the right of the pulpit, curtained from the general view. The cubicle contained a comfortable padded chair, a tiny fireplace, and a special niche where the bishop could set his claret. Here he could see the service only imperfectly through a tiny window, but he could hear clearly, without the disgrace of being seen in such a place.

"Perfectly cozy, is it not? I understand even the Archbishop of Dublin has occupied this eccentric bishop's seat." Bishop Twysden arranged his robes carefully in the chair, poured out a glass of claret, and set it at hand in the niche. "Yes, I believe this will do quite well to view what Horace Walpole termed 'Mr. Wesley's opera.'" He took a long sip of claret and then waved his hand. "Run along now, children. This should prove most amusing."

Mary and Roger found seats near her family; but unlike the comforts provided for the bishop, they sat upon forms—long, backless benches. Even the galleries behind and on both sides of them were full. It was clear that Lady Huntingdon's celebration was to be one of the events of the season.

"Most appropriate that this should have been built in Harlequin Row," Roger observed. "We shall no doubt be treated to comic entertainment. What do you suppose those eagles signify?" He waved a scented, lace-edged handkerchief in the direction of three large, white, spread-winged eagles that stood behind the ornamental iron altar rail.

"They are very handsome, aren't they?" Mary replied.

"Perhaps they are from the Huntingdon family crest. At any rate, they make most unusual reading desks."

The preacher's eagle was in the center of a platform, elevated three steps higher than the others with a heavy, dark oak pulpit behind it. Behind the other eagles were scarlet damask chairs. But Mary was most taken with the elaborate candelabra. On each side of the pulpit were eight branches with five candles in each branch, and so on around the room, until there must have been upwards of a hundred candles lighting the chapel.

Roger, who had also been looking around, tugged at the lace frill on his sleeve. "Faith, I am glad to see that luxury is creeping upon them before persecution."

Mary was spared making an answer to this as the organ pealed an anthem from the gallery behind them, signaling the start of the service. The countess and her entourage of fine ladies with a few male escorts took their places in chairs down front, and the officiating clergymen walked to the scarlet seats behind the eagles. Mary caught her breath when she saw that Rowland was in the reader's seat on her left. She had no idea that among the many notable visitors, he would be chosen for so important a post.

She had a vague feeling she should recognize the fine-featured man with the luminous brown eyes and finely curled white hair in the preacher's seat. He stood to lead the congregation in singing "Jesus, Lover of My Soul."

Mary then recognized him as the composer of the hymn, Charles Wesley. She leaned forward to get a better view. So here was the famed singer, preacher, and leader, with his brother John, of the Methodist Society. But she was even more intrigued when a woman, introduced as his wife, joined him, and together they sang "Love Divine, All Loves Excelling." It was obvious as they sang about the love of God that they had experienced this love personally. But it also seemed to Mary that when the song spoke of "Joy of heav'n to earth come down," their expressions took on a double meaning, as if they had also experienced an earthly love with each other for which they praised their God.

Sally Wesley had a fine figure in a modestly cut gown of a heavy blue fabric. The white lawn fichu filling in the square-cut neckline highlighted her bright eyes and sweet smile, but Mary was shocked at the heavily pockmarked skin which quite spoiled her looks. *She must have been beautiful before she was stricken with the smallpox,* Mary thought. *What a pity!*

Whatever the illness had done to the woman's appearance, it could not mar the beauty of her voice. "Finish then Thy new creation, / Pure and spotless let us be; / Let us see Thy great salvation / Perfectly restored in Thee: / Changed from glory into glory, / Till in heav'n we take our place, / Till we cast our crowns before Thee, / Lost in wonder, love and praise!"

And at the end of the song, Sally Wesley's smile was first for her husband and then for the congregation.

Rowland stood to read the lesson for the day from 1 John 5: "'Whatsoever is born of God overcometh the world: and this is the victory that overcometh the world, even our faith.'" Mary, who was perfectly acquainted with his conversational voice, had never heard Rowland address an audience. The extraordinary clarity and sweetness of his words as he read the passage held her spellbound. And she was amazed at the elegance of his appearance as he stood behind the large white eagle in a plain black suit. Not yet ordained, he was not wearing clerical garments as the other clergymen on the platform. She would never have guessed that a man could look so handsome in drab black with no lace, embroidery, or metallic trim.

"'And this is the record, that God hath given to us eternal life; and this life is in his Son. He that hath the Son hath life; and he that hath not the Son of God hath not life.'"

Mary felt bereft when he quit reading—she could have listened to him for hours. But the lesson was followed by a choir of boys and girls who sang hymns to Scottish ballad tunes. When they began their third melody, Roger leaned close to her and commented too loudly, "They have charming voices, but they sing so long one would think they were already in eternity and knew how much time they had before them."

Mary gave him a disapproving look that silenced his cynical humor. At last the children finished their songs. The clergyman sitting behind the eagle on the right, whose outstanding features were his gentle smile and long, lank hair, rose and led the congregation in prayer. He began by reading, "Almighty Father, who hast given thine only Son to die for our sins and to rise again for our justification . . ." But then the preacher continued on *in his own words* at the end of the printed prayer, his soft Swiss dialect giving the words a special emphasis. Mary had never heard anyone do that and was shocked into lifting her head and looking around her. She found that many of the fashionably dressed worshipers had a similar reaction, and an undertone of astonished whispers accompanied the prayer.

The whispers ceased, however, when Charles Wesley mounted the steps to the center eagle and read his text. "'There was a man of the Pharisees, named Nicodemus, a ruler of the Jews. The same came to Jesus by night.'" As the reading continued, Mary smiled, wondering what the bishop, tucked away in his Nicodemus chamber, thought of the text. "'Verily, verily I say unto thee, Except a man be born again, he cannot see the kingdom of God.'"

The preacher paused, surveyed his audience, and then spoke with a level voice that reached to the farthest corners of the galleries. "The greatest sham of our age is the same as in Nicodemus's age—the profession of religion without knowing its power. The hypocrisy which hides the hideous deformity of a Christless character by the cloak of a plausible profession is one of the most odious of which a man is capable."

Wesley smiled at Lady Huntingdon sitting before him. "We are gathered here today to celebrate a great occasion in the work of the Kingdom—the opening of this chapel in one of the most wicked cities of our nation. . . . Matters of salvation are of infinite importance. The glory of bringing souls to Christ is the greatest honor God can confer upon us. The salvation of one soul is of more worth than a thousand worlds. My dearest brothers and sisters, may God fill us with like ardent desires to those which warmed the apostle's heart, when he was constrained to declare to his Galatian hearers that he travailed in birth till Christ was formed in them.

"And in this mighty congregation, if there are those here—and I am persuaded there are—who do not know this divine power and assurance in their own life, let me proclaim to you that this divine happiness and peace is unto all men and women."

The preacher's words caught at Mary's heart. Could the dissatisfaction she had been feeling indicate a spiritual need? She cast back in her mind to her discontent in Wells, which she had attributed to the need for more social excitement. Had she looked for her solution in entirely the wrong place?

But how could her need be spiritual? She was baptized. As she groped for assurance, she turned the pages of her prayer book to the "Baptism of Infants." "Dearly beloved, forasmuch as all men are conceived and born in sin; and that our Saviour Christ saith, 'None can enter into the kingdom of God, except he be regenerate and born anew of water and of the Holy Ghost' . . . ye have brought this child here to be baptized, ye have prayed that our Lord Jesus Christ would vouchsafe to receive him, to release him of his sins, to sanctify him with the Holy Ghost, to give him the kingdom of heaven, and everlasting life. . . . Our Lord Jesus Christ has promised in His gospel to grant all these things that ye have prayed for. . . . This infant must promise by you that are his sureties *until he come of age to take it upon himself* that he will renounce the devil and all his works and constantly believe God's holy word and obediently keep His commandments."

Well, she supposed she had taken the promise upon herself. She attended divine service regularly and fully believed all the creeds. Certainly she shared none of Rowland's enthusiasm which could lead one into socially unacceptable extremes, but she was not a heathen. She did believe. She could see no solution for her problem in seeking spiritual fervor, but she determined to talk to Rowland about the matter.

The service concluded with another extempore prayer by the kind-looking minister with the lank hair, who was identified as John Fletcher. Then Mary's thoughts were lost in a bustle of gathering her parasol, prayer book, and scarf. "I must confess the lessons were read very well and the hymns sung very sweetly," Roger announced. "Had there been no preaching, which was in the highest attitude of rhapsody and rant, nor extempore prayer, the whole would have been much to my satisfaction. I found the old praying parson to be a perfect specimen—he has true Methodistical hair."

Elizabeth made her way to Mary through the press. "We are to attend a private reception in the countess's rooms. Will you come with us?"

Mary glanced uncertainly at Roger. "Egad! Such stamina. I beg I may be excused. I feel quite surfeited with holiness." And then in a voice which only Mary could hear, "And I have no doubt my poor uncle will be entirely overcome. If the first improvised prayer didn't knock him up completely, I'm persuaded the second one may have finished the poor fellow off. He will be in want of my support to see him home to something stronger than claret." Making a sweeping bow, Roger left.

Mary was happy to join her family in the elegant drawing room next to the chapel. Having the countess's living quarters attached to the chapel meant that it was constituted by law a private chapel and that Her Ladyship had complete authority over its services and ministers.

Mary would have liked to congratulate Rowland upon his fine reading, but he was surrounded by a group of important-looking clergymen and ladies of the countess's private party. So she went instead to the long table bearing an elegant buffet. She took a generous portion of orange souffle and was helping herself to the celerata cream when Lady Selina joined her. "Don't miss the ratafia biscuits; they're my favorite." She pointed to a footed plate just beyond the pastry basket. "Did you enjoy the service? I thought the children's choir charming."

Mary agreed. "And the Wesleys were—" She groped for the right word. She had meant to say *enchanting*, but that seemed too frivolous for music so profound.

"Quite sublime, are they not?" Selina finished for her. "Would you like me to present you to Sally? She's one of the people I most admire in the entire world—an opinion shared by all who know her, but especially by her husband."

"Yes, I could tell, just seeing them together. I was most taken by the radiance of it. She is so beautiful in spite of—"

"The smallpox? Yes, they had been married just five years when Sally's sister Becky, who was living with them, was inoculated. She brought the illness home with her. Their tiny son, Jacky, died of it, and for weeks Charles despaired of saving Sally. But when the fever was spent and she was left as you see her now, Charles declared he loved her more than ever. This disease removed the one barrier to the perfection of their union. You see, Sally is twenty years younger than her husband, but now they look the same age. And she thanked God she had chosen not to be inoculated."

Mary shook her head in silent awe of a love that could be so self-sacrificing, so unhindered by outward appearance. Just then Colonel Hastings joined them, tall and handsome in his regimentals. When Mary saw the smile that passed between him and Selina, she felt sure that another such match was in the making. "Yes, I should be most honored to be presented to Mrs. Wesley," Mary said.

Sally Wesley was as gracious in person as she had appeared on the platform. She welcomed Mary to their circle, and then went on telling the countess of their two musically gifted sons—

whom Charles felt would far outshine their father in the world of composing and performing—and of their six-year-old daughter, Selina, named for the Countess of Huntingdon.

Also noting the special bond between Charles Wesley and his wife, Rowland had separated the preacher from the others to question him about Berridge's advice.

Charles Wesley spoke thoughtfully. "Certainly, if Berridge feels it would be wrong for him to marry, then it would be. God leads us each according to His holy will. I can speak only for myself. God gave Sally to me to love. And she has been of inestimable value to my work."

"To your work?"

"Indeed. My brother John for a time shared Berridge's views and was opposed to our attachment on that grounds. But he came about and finally married us himself."

"And there was truly no cause for his concern? I beg your forgiveness if I seem to pry, but I have wrestled much with this lately."

"A valid question for any young man. Certainly, marriage changed the nature of my work. I have undoubtedly done more hymn-writing with Sally's fine musicianship to help me, and my ministry has been in a more settled area around Bristol. Not many family men can put in thousands of miles of circuit-riding in a year. But who is to say one is of more value to the Kingdom than the other? And the slack left by one man is always taken up by another." He looked over at the other man who had shared the pulpit that evening. "Our dear Fletcher is a case in point." He gave the name its Swiss pronunciation, *Flechaire*. "His beloved wife was taken from him at an early age, but she worked with him heart and soul during the short time their union lasted. She was of enormous service to his presidency of Lady Huntingdon's College at Trevecca and made their vicarage at Madeley a haven for all who came to them weary and heavy-laden, sick and sorrowful."

Others joined them, and the conversation became general; but Rowland could not rid his mind of Wesley's phrase as he looked across the room at his adored wife, "God gave her to me to love."

The next day was an exciting one for the Tudway family. Mary's father was to arrive about noon, and the family would go together to Thomas Gainsborough's house at the Royal Circus to see the finished portraits. Now that the work was completed, Mrs. Tudway was filled with anxiety. What if her husband was displeased with the outcome? What if he still refused to have his portrait painted, and her picture would hang alone in the dining room? Had she been wrong to wear her emerald green gown for the sitting? Perhaps the amber would have been more becoming. Was it a mistake to pose in her white lace calash? Perhaps a smaller cap with lappets would have been more flattering.

Rowland joined the family to see his sister's portrait. As it was a fine day, the entire party chose to walk the short distance down Brock Street to the studio.

The painter met them at the door of his home, clad in teal velvet coat and breeches, with a red waistcoat, his rich brown hair tied at the nape of his neck. His clear eyes shone with pleasure as he led the way to his studio. "I am so happy you could join us today, Mr. Tudway. I believe you will be most pleased with your wife's portrait—and those of your son and daughter-in-law as well." His arm swept an arc around the room, as if he were presenting the company to the portraits, rather than the other way around.

Mary was the first to speak. "Oh, Mama, you look perfectly lovely! Exactly the sensible, competent creature you are. And how clever of you to choose your green gown; it just sets off your eyes." Hannah visibly relaxed under her daughter's approval.

"And your choice of cap," Rowland added. "It shines like a halo against the dark background."

When her husband agreed, Mrs. Tudway could have been no closer to Heaven. "Fine work he made of you too, Clement." Squire Tudway stood before the head-and-shoulders portrait of his son wearing a red coat with brass buttons, his powdered hair curled just above his ears. "Very fine, just the right dignity for a Member of Parliament."

He continued on around the room to the easel bearing the waist-length portrait of Elizabeth. "Well, Hill, did you know your sister to be such a beauty? Very fine, very fine." He turned to the artist. "I congratulate you, sir."

"Oh, Elizabeth, it's perfect," Mary said. "You couldn't have chosen a lovelier ornament than the pearls in your hair and at your neck and at the yoke of your dress."

Elizabeth laughed. "I'm glad you approve, Mary, but it was Mr. Gainsborough who selected the pearls. The rose dress was my selection."

Gainsborough rang for refreshments, and soon his house-keeper was handing around wine and biscuits while the family continued to discuss the details of the portraits. "Papa, you must be painted full-length like Mama," Mary said abruptly, and with that note of decision in her voice that her family knew all too well. "Perhaps outdoors," she continued. "As Mama is sitting by an open window, it would be a charming idea to think that you are in her view."

Charles Tudway considered for a moment while Hannah held her breath. "In my brown frock coat, do you think, daughter?" His smile spoke his consent.

The rest of the family was to return to the Crescent to dine, but Mary had hoped to do some shopping that afternoon. Her sister-in-law Maria had informed them that, indeed, the wonderful event Mrs. Tudway had hoped for would occur in the summer, and Mary thought this an excellent excuse to visit the toymaker's shop in Milsom Street. "May I accompany you?" Rowland asked. "Or would you prefer your maid to go with you?"

Mary returned his smile. "Indeed, sir, as you are much stronger than Minson, you will do much better as a package-bearer." Mary was surprised by the warmth that had returned to Rowland's attitude toward her. She was still mystified as to the cause of his earlier aloofness, but was glad it had passed.

The toymaker presented a delightful assortment of cleverly carved toys and beautifully dressed dolls, tiny china tea sets, and bags of shiny marbles. After careful consideration, she chose a small carved bear with jointed legs on a stick. Mary and Rowland laughed together as she made the brightly painted bear dance on the end of his stick.

That errand completed, Mary and Rowland both seemed hesitant whether to turn their steps back to the Crescent or continue on downhill toward town. "Would you care to stop at Mr. Gill's for a jelly tart or a basin of vermicelli?" Rowland suggested, as the pastry shop was only two doors down from them.

Mary considered. "I would like something, but perhaps not vermicelli right now. Are you acquainted with any tea-rooms?" They were quite near a coffeehouse, but that den of masculine gossip and politics was not a place to which a gentleman could escort a lady.

"Why, yes. Just on the other side of Abbey Green is Sally Lunn's House."

They proceeded at a leisurely pace, admiring the goods arranged in the various windows to tempt the casual shopper. At a jeweler's they halted to take a closer look at his merchandise. Jeweled fans, hair ornaments, and gold snuffboxes took their places among the necklaces, brooches, and earrings. But one item caught Mary's eye. "Oh, Rowly, look at those silver filigree shoe buckles! Have you ever seen finer workmanship? They have been made by a true artist." The delicate openwork buckles were ornamented with silver-petaled roses with a setting of pink jade in the center of each flower. Mary gazed at them for a full minute and then turned away.

"Let us go on. I am getting hungry," she said.

They had taken no more than six steps, however, when the door of the milliner's shop they were passing flew open, and Sarah dashed out. "Mary, just the person I most wanted to see! You must come in at once. Mama and I are having a dreadful row over the suitability of this most charming hat with blue lace bows and lavender ostrich feathers. Do tell her it's not at all too old for me."

Mary was drawn into the shop by her friend, but Rowland asked to be excused, saying he would rejoin them in a moment. Mary looked at the hat in question and then pointed out another hat lavishly trimmed with pink silk roses. "This one is beautiful."

"Oh, thank you, Mary. I knew I could rely on you. Look, Mama, the roses just match the embroidery on my new silk petticoat, do they not?" Sarah turned this way and that so all could admire the hat perched atop her coiffure.

At that moment Rowland returned, and he and Mary resumed their walk. As they neared the Abbey, a small dog ran out into the street in front of them and then sat in the gutter looking forlorn. "Oh, poor creature," Mary cried. "Do you suppose it's a spit dog?"

The back alleys of Bath abounded with scraggly dogs that spent most of their lives running in metal wheels attached to geared machinery turning the spits roasting sides of beef in the huge fireplaces of the kitchens serving Bath's well-fed patrons.

"Indeed, I expect it is."

"Can't we do something for it, Rowly?"

"Shall I see if he'll come to me? We could at least treat him to a meaty bone that he didn't have to cook himself." Unconcerned about his coattails, Rowland knelt down on the cobbles and held out his hand. "Here, fella; come on, boy."

At the sound of a kind voice, the mutt perked up his ears. "Come on, this lady wants to be your friend." The dog took a step closer. "Atta boy." Rowland scratched the little brown-and-white ears and then scooped the dog into his arms. "What shall we call him?"

Mary considered for a moment. "Spit. What else?"

Rowland laughed and scratched the dog again. "Spit it is."

Then Mary took the small bundle of matted hair into her arms. "What a horrid practice, putting such sweet animals in wheels!"

"It is. But it's much worse making small boys sit by the fire and turn the crank for hours on end."

"Is there no alternative?"

Rowland considered for a moment. "Perhaps a system of weights attached to a wheel, something like a hall clock."

"Excellent! If I am ever mistress of a large kitchen, I shall require such a contrivance for the roasting."

Spit snuggled comfortably in Mary's arms and went to sleep. Just a step down off North Parade brought them to the Abbey Green and a small house with a bow-fronted window. The hostess at the door frowned at the blissfully dreaming Spit.

"The lady's particular pet," Rowland explained, as he removed his tricorn. The hostess showed them to a table in the window. No one would question the right of a lady of quality to take her lapdog with her wherever she chose, even if it was a scruffy specimen.

Rowland requested the waitress to bring coffee and a Sally Lunn apiece. A moment later, Mary gasped at the size of the bun placed before her. "That's not a bun—it's an entire loaf!"

"Don't worry," her companion assured her. "It's all cloud."

One bite proved it to be the lightest bread one could imagine. They began making jokes about the difficulty of baking buns that insisted on rising and floating about the oven.

It seemed to Mary that she had never known time to pass so swiftly or so pleasantly. But then the happy haze dissolved as reality intruded. "So now that the portraits are finished, you'll be leaving Bath?" Rowland asked.

Mary nodded, not willing to admit how little she looked forward to the departure—especially now that Rowland had come.

"Has it been a profitable time for you, Mary?"

Not for the world would she admit that the revels she so longed for had been the least bit of a letdown. "It has been exceedingly diverting," she said with forced enthusiasm.

Rowland regarded her levelly. "Mary, you needn't pretend with me. I don't know what's wrong. But I do know something has happened to put you in a pother, which you are trying very hard to bottle up."

"Oh, dear. Is it so obvious?"

"To me, yes, though I doubt anyone else would have noticed. I wish you would tell me what has destroyed your tranquillity." He paused. "But if you don't choose to, I won't press you."

She stroked the soft head of Spit curled drowsily in her lap. "I have become a bit wearied with all the gaiety. Sarah says I need a rest, and I expect she's right. But the thought of returning home to an endless round of neighborhood calls and *needlework*—" she gave a small shudder, "is not invigorating."

His long solemn look made her catch her breath. It was as if his eyes spoke words his mouth would not—words he was not ready to say nor she to hear. If the moment had held and gone no further, it would have been perfect. But Rowland had a way of looking beyond her mind and heart to her very soul. And when his gaze seemed to touch a sore spot, her defenses came up.

"And have you no deeper need you wish to speak of, Mary? I am your friend. I would do anything in my power to help you."

"La, and what 'deeper need' could that be, sir?" She unfolded her fan and fluttered it at him.

"I was thinking of spiritual matters, Mary." His voice was so soft that for an instant she thought she had imagined the words.

Then her temper flared. Was he accusing her of being an infidel? "Pray, and do you imagine yourself a priest that I should confess to you? I was baptized as an infant and have attended church all my life. My soul is quite the property of myself and the church—not of an enthusiastic divinity student, I thank you, sir." She snapped her fan shut.

"No, Mary. One's soul is not the property of any person or institution—even of the church. It belongs to God, just as one's commitment must be to God. The church's rituals are merely dead formality and will lead to death of the soul if relied upon for salvation."

"La, tell that to the mobs you preach to in the fields, sir. Sally Lunn's House is not the place for your irregular preaching. When I want advice for my soul, I'll ask a bishop, not your female pope."

Rowland's smile only fed her anger. "Ah, yes, the countess is often called Her Holiness behind her back; but for all her dogmatic ways you'd do better to listen to her than to your Bishop of Raphoe."

"Rowland! How dare you abuse a bishop? Have your Methodistical manners made you lost to all sense of propriety? The bishop is a fine gentleman of elegance and learning and fashion and—"

"And refinement," Rowland finished for her. "May I never be the retailer of a whipt-syllabub divinity. Better to keep a cook-shop to satisfy the craving appetite than a confectioner's shop to regain the depraved appetite of the dainty. Good brown-bread preaching is best after all."

"A whipt-syllabub religion! Sir, is that what you would call the established church? Why, I—"

In her agitation she leaned forward and knocked Spit's head against the table, causing him to give a sharp yap, which rang through the small room.

Mary instantly leaned back in her chair and took refuge behind her fan until the murmur of voices in the room resumed. But the moment was all that was needed to cool the argument.

"Mary, I am to leave day after tomorrow. Tomorrow, if your

mother permits, will you accompany me to Wotton-under-edge? I am to preach there, and you may see and judge for yourself that which you argue against."

Mary agreed to the plan, and Mrs. Tudway gave her permission. So the next day Rowland and Mary drove northward out of Bath almost to the border of Wales. As it was to be a long drive, they left early and made such good time that they arrived ahead of the appointed hour for the service. Rowland drove on through the town and turned toward the Severn River. "Let me show you what I believe to be the most paradisiacal spot I have ever seen. I would that someday I might live here—or that Heaven might be like this."

He stopped the carriage opposite a hillside that formed a perfect amphitheater—three sides clothed with a wood, the other side open to a richly fertile dale. Rowland offered his hand, and they walked to the top of the hill. Mary caught her breath at the landscape before her. As she turned slowly in all directions, the panorama changed from the Welsh mountains, the Malvern Hills, the rich vale of Berkley, to the broad course of the silvery and majestic Severn River. And in the foreground, grassy knolls and hanging woods blended in a scene of unspeakably lovely harmony. Before them a rocky path wound through a sloping wood of beech. They followed it to an orchard where branches of bursting buds promised frostings of pink and white flowers, to be followed by succulent fruit.

Rowland looked at the trees for a moment. "I love to see the flowers and fruit which God makes the earth bring forth to please us, and then I think, oh, that I could bear more of the fruit of righteousness to please Him."

Mary was impressed by the solemnity of his thoughts, but displeased that in this romantic spot his words should be so pious. "Oh, Rowly, is that all you think of—pleasing God?"

Rowland turned sharply to her and took her hand. "No, my dear Mary, there is another I would please too. If only it pleased her to be pleased by me."

"In faith, sir, I can't follow all your pleases. But I'm sure it was a very pretty speech."

Mary found her heart was beating rapidly, and she would have liked to continue that dialogue. But there was not time, for on the road below them they could see people coming up from the dales around, walking toward town to attend the preaching service. When Mary and Rowland arrived at the marketplace, a great crowd had gathered. Rowland stood on a wagon in the center of the square and read his text: "'Awake, thou that sleepest...'"

Mary overheard two women talking.

"Ann, that's the baronet's son who goes about preaching."

"Are you sure it's the baronet's son himself?"

"Yes, that I am, for I saw his brother, Mr. Richard Hill, not long ago, and he is so like him. I am sure he is of the same family."

The women settled down to listen, but a man near Mary seized a stone and pulled back his arm, taking careful aim at the preacher. Mary had a fleeting thought of flinging herself in front of the man when a burly arm reached from behind him, grasped the arm holding the rock, and said in broad Gloucestershire dialect, "If thee dost touch him, I'll knock thy head off." The assailant dropped the stone. The audience became quiet, awed by the solemnity of the subject and the earnestness of the preacher. Mary listened with particular closeness, hoping to find answers for some of the questions plaguing her.

"Think particularly," the preacher urged his listeners, "whether you're choosing for time only or for eternity. For, of course, a sensible person will wish to choose that which will be best in the long run. It is just as much part of the consideration of what will be best for me between my thousandth and two-thousandth year as between my twentieth and thirtieth. It is curious how our estimate of time is altered by its being removed to a distance.

"And so, my friends, be certain that the choices you make will last for eternity—choose to spend your life on those things that will count for as much two thousand years from now as twenty years from now or twenty days from now."

Mary was thoughtful on the long drive back to Bath. There had been a power and a logic to Rowland's words that she couldn't deny; and yet she did not want to discuss them, for fear that bringing her thoughts into the open would force upon her a choice she was not yet ready to make.

"You are weary, Mary?" Rowland asked as they neared Bath. "You have not told me what you thought of the service."

"In faith, I'm not sure what I thought. I should have been outraged at such unseemly worship. And yet there was a truth to the preacher's words." And that was as far as she would say.

When they reached the Royal Crescent, Rowland reached under the carriage seat and produced a small white package tied with red ribbons. "I leave Bath tomorrow, as you do. Think of me kindly as I prepare to take my degree and apply for ordination." He held the package to her.

She fumbled with the ribbons eagerly. How amazing that he should have thought to bring her a farewell gift. The paper fell away, and Mary gasped with delight. The silver filigree shoe buckles ornamented with delicately wrought roses lay in the folds of paper.

Mary smiled into the brown eyes beside her. "Indeed, I shall think of you, sir." Then her chin tilted, and her lips curled in a saucy smile. "But I shall leave it to your imagination to decide what is in my thoughts."

$\mathcal{R}$owland's final term at Cambridge was a steady grind of studying, relieved occasionally by the stimulation of preaching to one of his congregations. On the night of May 18 he wrote in his journal that he had preached in his first barn—and he hoped it might not be his last. A sudden rain shower had prompted the farmer to invite all those standing in his field into his barn where, he remarked, their singing might prove soothing to his animals.

The country people warmly welcomed Rowland. "Been away a long time, young fella. Ain't 'eard no real preachin' since you been gone." A burly farmer engulfed Rowland's hand in his mighty grasp.

"Sakes alive, it's Mr. 'ill a-come to preach to us." An old grandmother gave him a toothless grin. Then her eyes filled with tears. "I thought not to 'ear ye again."

And Rowland saw with amazement many damp eyes in the hay-scented barn. He knew he had missed his people, but he had not known *they* had missed *him* so much. "The Lord keep you," he replied. "I always find more comfort in speaking to my own people than anywhere else." Whenever Rowland faced discouragement, he always looked for refreshment in the responses of those he preached to. And the greatest discouragement came on those occasions when his preaching provided him with little comfort.

But that was not to be the case this evening, as the barn continued to fill. Rowland talked directly to the people, his examples drawn from things he had seen in the fields or villages. Only one segment of the audience did not respond with favor to such homespun wisdom. A group of gownsmen had interrupted their country ride to join the service that evening.

"Egad! It's Pierrot Hill practicing for his entertainment at Midsummer Faire."

"There is much humor in his performance, but I find his costume somewhat dull."

"Zounds! You've hit upon it! He must be fitted for cap and bells."

Rowland paused and gritted his teeth at the ridicule. His first impulse was to give the gownsmen a good trimming. But instead, he prayed silently for grace to act with forbearance. "If I must be a fool, I would choose to be God's fool," he said quietly, and allowed the words time to sink in before he continued with his preaching. The gownsmen moved on.

But the students were not content to let the matter rest. Fortified by a supply of port and recruits to their cause—both collected at a public house where they stopped on their way back to the university—they marched to Rowland's rooms. "All right, Hill, we'll show you who's the fool!"

Heavy blows fell on Rowland's outer door. He rarely bothered to close this extra door meant to provide added privacy and protection. But tonight, weary as he was, he had closed the barricade. Now, though, he doubted even this defense would withstand the pounding.

"What, are you coward as well as heretic?"

"Brave enough words in the barn where your friends have pitchforks, but now you hide."

The shouts and bangs showed no indication of stopping. Rowland knew the mob was perfectly capable of keeping up such a row much of the night, and the university authorities, accustomed to turning deaf ears to the frequent riots between town and gown, were unlikely to intervene. It seemed best to face his assailants before their frenzy grew. Maybe they would listen to him.

He unbarred the door. "My fellows, I—"

The first blow sent him staggering backward. Before he could gain his balance, he was knocked to the floor.

Rowland struggled to get up, but at least ten pairs of feet trampled over him as the inflamed, drunken gownsmen rushed into his rooms and began ripping papers from his writing table and pulling books from his shelves.

"No, not my letters!" he cried as the leader of the mob flung open a box and began ripping his letters from Wesley and Whitefield. Rowland lunged for the man but had to duck a volume of sermons hurled at his head. On his right a large, black-haired fellow picked up a flint and tried to strike a spark to a pile of Rowland's sermon notes. Rowland started to fling himself toward the arsonist when suddenly the rioters fell back.

Rowland looked toward the door in amazement. His normally placid gyp had entered the fray swinging a weighty poker, his cliff-faced visage made awful by the fire in his eyes.

"He's an avenging angel—or demon, more like."

"I'm sped!"

They departed as abruptly as they had entered, leaving a wreckage of scattered papers and dumped books behind them.

"Thank you, Bottisham. Most timely."

The gyp presented him the sturdy metal instrument with an equally poker face. "Might I suggest you lay this in as a weapon of defense, sir?"

The next day Rowland headed for his lecture a bit hesitantly, wondering if the gang might be lying in wait for further vengeance. Much to his surprise, he was greeted cheerfully by classmates who had barely deigned to nod to him the previous term. Persecution had secured him instant popularity—a status Rowland never thought to achieve at Cambridge.

A student he knew only by sight approached him in New Court. "Sorry to hear you were rioted last night, Hill. Shameless bunch of fellows."

And just outside the lecture hall, Pentycross saluted him. "Hill, I've just heard the news. You all right? Need any help setting your room to rights?"

Rowland assured him that all was well, and that he and Bottisham had everything back in order.

Pentycross grasped his hand once more before hurrying into the lecture. "Can't have any harm come to our best-loved homilist."

Inside the classroom others smiled at him or raised a hand in greeting. Rowland was completely overcome. How strange that the ostracism he had suffered should suddenly be wiped away, not by any great mark of success on his part, but by one of the most humiliating things that could occur to a gownsman. It was certainly true that God worked in a way mysterious to man.

But as the press of studies bore in, Rowland had little time to "assert eternal Providence and justify the ways of God to men." As the line from Milton flitted through his mind, he thought of one who had been a most devoted reader of the Puritan poet before her mind had turned to more worldly things. Closing his volume of Locke for an instant, he prayed for Mary.

Pearce, who was tutoring him closely for his degree exams, noticed the waver in Rowland's concentration and brought him back to the second *Treatise on Government.* "State the contract theory of government, sir."

Rowland rubbed his forehead in an attempt to focus his thoughts on the matter at hand. "The authority of the people is supreme, founded as it is in natural rights. These rights include life, liberty, and property. The people have the right, through their representatives, to judge whether rulers have violated the contract and whether changing times have made a change in government necessary."

"Well done, Hill. You will have no trouble with the examiners." But in spite of his encouraging words, Pearce insisted they continue at the books for an hour longer.

Rowland had no argument with Locke's theories nor with the requirement to study him; but it never ceased to seem strange to him that in a school of theology, as St. John's purported to be, besides the study of Locke, courses in physics and mathematics bulked the largest. At St. John's even the classics had fallen into great contempt, and honors were based entirely on mathematical ability. What that had to do with preparation for ministry one could only guess.

A week later, when the study and exams came to a close, Rowland risked tarnishing his new popularity by declining an invitation to a wine party and went instead to his rooms to write a long overdue letter to his sister Jane.

Camb. Tuesday Eve

My very dear sister,

I ask my dear sister a thousand pardons for not answering her kind letter long before this. All last week almost every moment of my time was taken up in preparing for my degree, which being now over, I'm more at leisure to write.

I was examined by my tutor, then by the senior dean, and then by the junior dean, and then by the Master, who all made me but construe a verse or two apiece in the Greek Testament; except the Master, who asked me both in that and in Plautus and Horace too. I must conclude that my time at Cambridge has not been an intensely intellectual life.

Earnest effort seems to have gone out of the life of the college, as if the loss of religious passions of an earlier generation resulted also in the loss of serious academic endeavors. A college in need of a measure of reform, I should characterize it.

And now but one step remains—ordination. All things continue to give me the safest assurance of an entrance into the ministry by next summer. My heart trembles at the thought of my admission into such an important office. I see myself nothing but ignorance and blindness, utterly unqualified for so great an employment.

If ever I should make an able minister of the New Testament, I see that I must be first wholly given up. I see it requires much grace simply to follow the Lamb wherever He goeth, to forget self, love of ease, and look up to the glory of God.

I fear much lest my treacherous heart lead me to dissemble. I know that a faithless minister cannot but be a curse instead of a blessing to the church of Christ. Pray for me that Jesus' love may ever constrain me to be faithful unto death.

Therefore, my dear sister, I must subscribe myself,

Yr. poorest tho' affect Br.
Ro Hill

He scattered sand on the ink to dry it, then folded and sealed the document with a blob of blue wax, and addressed it.

He sat long looking at it, thinking of what he had said. He did fear his heart. He knew the awesome responsibility of his calling—to speak for the mighty God of the universe, creator of heaven and earth; to call sinners to repentance that they might spend eternity in the Heaven God had created for them. And yet he knew his weakness, his fears.

He was only a man. And next to his longing to serve God, he longed for the companionship of one he had loved for years. In spite of the fact that Charles Wesley's words and example had laid to rest his worst anxieties over Berridge's warnings, he was deeply concerned for Mary. What if she refused him? Or—and a deeper ache caught at his heart—what if she remained in the spiritual confusion she exhibited at Bath? He knew that her religious upbringing had been sound, if rigidly formal, and that her words in their last times together had been spoken in the heat of argument; but he must pray that Mary find her way out of this spiritual wilderness for her own dear sake even if she was never to be his wife.

Then one final worry nagged at him. What if he should fail the ordination examination? The degree exam had been painless enough, but what if Bishop Sparke should require a depth of learning he had not acquired? He turned again to study his notes from the Sunday afternoon Greek Testament lectures.

Three days later Rowland assembled with fourteen other men of St. John's and other colleges to travel to Ely for examination and admission to holy orders. As Rowland looked at those around him, it was obvious that the church attracted every sort of man. Some, as one would expect, were sons of clergymen. Others were sizars who had worked their way through college as servants to more privileged students—the attainment of a benefice from the university being the most obvious way for a poor man's son to rise in the world. But more than half of the group were, like Rowland, gentlemen's sons.

The group was ushered into a large room in the Bishop's Palace where the bishop's chaplain, serving as proctor, distributed a separate text to each ordinand with the instructions that he was to write a Latin theme sermonette on the topic. The entire morning passed without a sound in the room except the scratching of fifteen quills across paper. Only two small events provided a break in the protracted concentration. A son of the chaplain came in to talk to his father. And shortly after noon, one of the examinees blurted out, "Egad! I've blotted my page!" crumpled up his paper, threw it to the floor, and began again.

By the time the proctor collected the papers, Rowland's hand ached, but he felt satisfied that he had expressed exactly the right balance of scholarship and practical application in his sermonette. If the rest of the examination went as well, he should soon be a deacon.

At three o'clock the chaplain began ushering the ordinands singly from the room, and a housekeeper served around dishes of tea and slices of spice cake to those still waiting. Hill was the fifth to be called. He followed his guide down a long, polished hallway through double, Gothic-arched doors, and into the Presence.

Bishop Sparke sat behind a large, carved desk, lavender and gold streaks of light from the stained-glass window behind him falling across his face and on the white sleeves of his robe. A slight nod of the eminent head told Rowland which straight-backed chair to sit on. The bishop picked up his sermonette and read it out aloud. He went straight through without expression or pause. Not another word was spoken.

Rowland bowed and left the room.

When all had been interviewed, they returned to the inn, where relief at having the ordeal over led them to consume vast quantities of roast joint, pudding, and ale. When Rowland finally went up to his room, it was to the sound of his fellow ordinands singing songs that would not be heard in any of the churches they hoped to shepherd.

Rowland slept fitfully. Tomorrow would not be the culmination of all he had dreamed of and worked toward for years—it would be the beginning. He wondered what living would be assigned to him. He didn't care about status; he wanted to serve wherever God could best use him. And the income was of no great concern, for he had a competent allowance from his father; now that he was to be ordained, he needn't fear the patriarchal threat of being cut off. But he did hope the vicarage would be a comfortable one, for Mary's sake. No matter how his rational mind worried him with questions over whether Mary would become his wife, the fact was that he never pictured the future without her.

At last he heard the stirrings of breakfast being prepared below. He rose and dressed for the day that was to launch his career.

The candidates assembled in the anteroom to the bishop's private chapel where the ordination service was to take place. The chaplain entered, followed by his son bearing the deacons' mantles which the bishop would place on their shoulders. The chaplain began calling names. As each name rang through the hall, the candidate stepped forward, draped his mantle over his arm, and passed into the chapel. Fourteen names were called. Rowland Hill was not one of them.

The chaplain turned and followed the others into the chapel. His son paused at the door and turned to level a haughty stare at Rowland. "Bishop Sparke is ordaining Anglican deacons, not Methodist enthusiasts."

Rowland had been refused ordination. He stood frozen in the empty chamber as sounds of the beginning service came through the door to the chapel.

He felt amazed that the bishop had even known. But then he recalled the slightly sneering tone of voice in which the bishop had pronounced certain words and phrases in his ser- monette—*regeneration, inspiration, drawing nigh unto God.* He had thought that the bishop's normal voice, but now he knew. He should have taken warning.

He thought of his six friends who had been expelled from Oxford. Someone had remarked, "If these were expelled for hav- ing too much religion, it would be very proper to inquire into the conduct of some who had too little." If he was refused for believ- ing too much, what would become of the ministry of those who were ordained because they believed too little?

Stunned, he rode back to Cambridge alone. His mind would not even let him think of what this would mean to his chances with Mary. And he must consider a specter that loomed even larger at the moment—returning to Hawkstone and facing his family. The baronet had all along insisted that his son's ruinous fanaticism would have consequences.

It was night when he reached his rooms, which were bless- edly empty as Bottisham didn't expect his return until the next day. A sleepless night brought him no closer to finding an answer for his future. The question he must settle first in his mind was his own assurance that he had done right. What about his view of a personal God who forgave men their sins individu- ally and filled their hearts with assurance of salvation? A God who listened to impromptu prayers from any sincere heart, no matter how unlearned, and who answered those prayers per- sonally? Was this an accurate understanding of God?

Or were such men as Bishop Sparke and Bishop Twysden right? Did God only require a formal assent to the doctrines of the church and take no interest in how people lived their daily lives?

After all his struggles, must he acknowledge that the school authorities and his parents and Mary were right? Should he follow in established paths, seek prestigious livings, and rise in the church hierarchy? Was this doing the will of God?

By morning he was no nearer an answer. He needed to go to someone for counsel. The week before he had received a note from John Berridge, saying that he would be preaching in Grantchester while staying at the home of a friend. Berridge hoped Rowland could call on him there. Putting on his waistcoat and jacket, sadly rumpled from having been tossed carelessly aside the night before, Rowland suddenly felt better.

As he crossed the Kitchen Bridge, he became aware of the beauty of the morning, a feeling he would have thought impossible a few hours earlier. The early summer sun sparkled on the waters of the Cam, and the gardens of the Backs shone in green and floral radiance. When the turmoil in his own mind quieted sufficiently for him to listen to the birdsong from elms and willows, he knew that he must believe in a personal God. One who would create so beautiful a world for His creatures' earthly pilgrimage must also care for their eternal souls.

"Hill! Hadn't thought to see you until later today." Simpson and Pentycross crossed the Mathematical Bridge behind Queen's College to join him.

"Forgive me, I should say Deacon Hill." Pentycross sketched a bow.

Rowland shook his head. This was the part he hated most—having to tell people. "I was refused."

His friends' faces registered shock. They insisted on bearing him company to call on Berridge. But as they passed the mill and walked on up the shady bank, it seemed that there was no more to say. The silence became heavy, and as the midday sun warmed the air, it became uncomfortably muggy. At last Rowland stopped and without a word pulled off his coat, shoes, and hat, and turned to the river.

Pentycross yelled and made a grab for him when he saw what Rowland was about. "Hill, don't! It's not that final! I say—" But it was too late. Rowland's leg just brushed his friend's hand as he plunged into the river.

"Hill! Hill!" Simpson's voice rose in panic as the water closed over Rowland's head.

The two stood on the bank transfixed in the awfulness of the moment. Then several yards up the river they heard a splashing and a laughing voice calling their names, "Penty! Sims! Bring my clothes. I'll swim to Grantchester."

Rowland turned over on his stomach and struck out with long, sure strokes, with which his friends on dry land had no hope of keeping pace.

"Can he do it?" Simpson asked.

Penty nodded. "Oh, yes. I should have realized when I saw him plunge in—strongest swimmer I've ever known—his favorite recreation. But what a crackbrained thing to do at a time like this." Pentycross picked up Rowland's shoes and hat and handed his coat to Simpson.

Rowland emerged dripping and refreshed, if somewhat tired, from the two-mile swim. And Berridge, who greeted him at the door of William Matthews's home at Grantchester Mill, hardly noticed the unorthodox attire of his young friend, although his housekeeper insisted he have a thorough rubbing with an entire stack of towels before he sat on any of the furniture. By the time Rowland had used the third length of linen, Berridge interrupted the athlete's efforts. "I've a much better idea, my boy; we'll sit in the garden and let God's sunshine finish the work. Why must man toil and labor when his Maker has provided for all his needs, if he will only look around him?"

When they were settled in the garden, Rowland's companions joined them, looking hot and dusty and much in need of the lemonade the housekeeper was handing around. "Our friend has been telling me of his fellowship with Bishop Sparke," Berridge said.

"In short, he took to me like poison," Rowland concluded.

Berridge smiled but shook his head. "Bishops' powers are very strong indeed—specially in being possessed of the absolute right of conferring orders on whom they choose, without any established regulations.

"When they are once determined no longer to lay their sacred hands on the wicked heads of those whose motives for ordination are the most sacrilegious and impure, and in direct defiance of their most solemn oaths before God, many of those presumptuous intruders into sacred office would seek for their support in some other line, less inconsistent and dishonorable to themselves and less destructive to the souls of men. Certainly, such a conduct, according to the present corrupted state of things, would procure for their lordships many frowns from the great—but better that than to sustain the eternal frown of God."

All in the circle nodded in somewhat glum agreement at Berridge's summation of the state of things. "But about your present situation, my young friend, you must simply stand still and not hurry. When the cloud seems to move toward any place, prepare to follow it and pray to be kept from the delusions of your own spirit and from the wrong counsel of others." Rowland's open look told Berridge much that had not been put into words. "Yes, I see that you have been wrestling with questions of great import since this befell you. Do not let your faith be overset. God is the same yesterday, today, and tomorrow. He will not fail."

Berridge accepted a refill from the housekeeper's pitcher. "Be not anxious about orders. They will come as soon as needed. Nor be anxious about anything but to know the Lord's will and to do His work. One of our Master's titles is Counselor, and a wonderful Counselor He is. Therefore, take no counsel but of the Lord; so shall you walk more evenly than if you had the whole congregation of gospel divines at your elbow every moment to advise you."

He smiled as Rowland rubbed at a streak of mud on his breeches. "Your swimming expedition seems a providential prelude for a field preacher this summer."

"Yes!" Rowland brightened visibly. "That is the answer, of course! I must become that which the world despises—a lay itinerant." The words did not seem like cheerful ones, but the twinkle was back in Rowland's eyes. For a few hours he had lost his vision, his sense of God-given mission. But now he knew where the pillar of cloud was leading, and he would gladly follow, convinced of his Lord's blessing. Bees buzzing in the flowering border recalled the allusion Berridge had used in his letter to the countess. "My desire is to win souls, not livings. If I can secure the bees, I care not who gets the hives."

It was a tedious four-day journey by mail coach from Cambridge to Shrewsbury, each day increasing Rowland's discomfort because he was nearer to facing his father. He had intended to hire a horse at Shrewsbury to carry him the remaining way to Hawkstone, but as the coach rattled up to the inn, he caught a glimpse of his brother Richard going in to take his afternoon meal.

"Richard! Well met!" In the instant joy of seeing Richard, Rowland forgot the bad news he bore with him like a dark cloud. Berridge's words and his own sense of calling had cheered him, but he knew they would mean little to the rest of his family, even to those who supported him and had great faith in his future.

Richard clasped Rowland's hand warmly, then picked up two of his brother's valises, and led the way into the coaching house.

"Why didn't you write that you were coming? Jane will be beside herself with delight. She's been having a bad time of it; Mother's not well, and all the nursing falls on her." Richard interrupted himself to direct the landlord to send their meals to the private parlor he always used when in Shrewsbury. They settled themselves in comfortable chairs on either side of the table.

"You're unaccountably quiet, Rowly. So what living were

you given? The bishop send you to Northumberland until you learn some manners, did he?"

"The bishop sent me to Jericho."

Richard was stunned. "What? You were refused? What will you do?"

The question hung in the air as the serving girl entered with a hearty pork pie and platters of rabbit stew. Rowland, whose troubles seldom dulled his appetite, took a wide wedge of pie and did justice to several bites, followed by a long drink of cider before he answered.

"I shall preach."

Richard shook his head. "I admire you. I must tell you that I have bent to our father's persuasion and am no longer preaching. As the heir, I let myself be convinced to exhibit my Christianity in other ways."

Rowland frowned. "Were you directly forbidden?"

"Not quite, but I could see it would soon come to it. And with Mother's health so poor, it seemed best."

Rowland nodded. "Perhaps for a time. But I could no more stop preaching than I could stop breathing. I'm sure if I were to do the one, it would lead to the other. If ever you hear I have ceased sermonizing, send a note round to the coffin maker." Rowland ate the tender white meat off a bone before he continued. "I have been thinking much of the letters you wrote me at Eton. Do you recall them?"

Richard shrugged. "I remember writing them certainly and encouraging your fledgling faith. I hope they may have done some good. It would be a shame if the amount of ink and paper expended, to say nothing of the candle wax, should come to nothing. But I don't recall any of my words exactly."

"I have the advantage of you, Richard. I have kept them all and reread them from time to time. Their language is worthy of a preacher. 'Consider, my dear brother, how that when you as a poor helpless sheep were gone astray, this dear Shepherd sought you and brought you back. Remember how, when wandering further and further from His fold, He made you hear His voice and follow Him, carrying you as a lamb in His bosom and gently leading you whilst you were yet young.' That is an image that I have dwelt on often in time of trial."

"I wrote that, did I? Yes, it does have a nice turn of phrase, and the doctrine is sound. Do you recall more?"

"A bit. 'Think of this love which passeth knowledge, and may it fill your heart with praise and your tongue with thanksgiving. Let it constrain you to live to Him who died for you and to grow daily more and more in conformity to His blessed image that so you may adorn the doctrine of God our Saviour in all things, and by well doing put to silence the ignorance of foolish men, who would falsely accuse your good conversation in Christ.' That is what I have endeavored to do, Richard."

Richard was thoughtful for some time. "With such fortification you shall succeed. But convincing our parents of the rightness of the matter will be quite another affair."

A few hours later, Richard's carriage rolled through the large tract of rocks and woods at the entrance to Hawkstone. Unlike the gently wooded, rolling green estates found over much of England, the Hill lands contained steep rocky outcroppings interspersed with woods, patches of undergrowth and bushes, and crannies of stone where oaks of huge size seemed to grow from the rocks themselves.

Rowland, who had always thought the landscape most appropriate for their family name, could only hope that it was not symbolic of the reception he would receive. Then as they trotted around the final sweep, Hawkstone House came into view. The pale stone mansion set on the side of a hill glowed like Roman marble in the dusk, its many columns, arches, and classical proportions giving support to the allusion. From the center of the house, Palladian wings curved forward on either side, a one-story portico connecting higher sections and then coming to a graceful conclusion by rooms of lower elevation again. The roof of the central mansion and the lower connecting sections was adorned with rows of classical stone urns, at the moment tinted red by the dying rays of sunlight.

"Welcome back to the noble pile." Richard handed Rowland's bags to the groom who came out to meet them. "But don't expect a fatted calf. Not that Jane wouldn't have put one on if she'd known you were coming."

But Jane had seen from an upstairs window and now came running with open arms.

"Dear Jane, it's so good to see you, but you look fatigued. Richard said you've been nursing Mother much of late." He returned her embrace and fond greetings, then held his sister at arm's length and surveyed her. "Can't someone help you? Have you written to Elizabeth?"

"Oh, yes. I have done so. But caring for our mother is not the wearying thing." Jane paused with a sigh. "We are a house divided against itself. When will it ever end, Rowland? It is inexpressibly painful that our dear parents, so worthy of honor in every other way except in that having to do with our Christian obligations, should be so desperately misled."

"What? Jane, has our father become despotic? I never found him so."

Jane, who as the at-home elder daughter of the thirteen Hill children, oversaw the housekeeping duties, led Rowland to his room. "No, no. He is never unjust. Oh, there are occasional explosions of his wrath, to be sure, but I am not kept from practicing my faith. It is just that the years of internal warfare with those whom I love and desire to please is sometimes unutterably wearing."

"Dear Jane." Rowland took his sister in his arms. "You have always stood a second mother to me, from the time you taught me my letters. I wish I could help you, but I fear I have only come to add to your burden."

"No, Rowland. How is that possible?"

Rowland looked her straight in the eyes. "I must tell you that I have been refused ordination."

Far from the shock and disbelief the news had produced in

others, Jane's reaction showed calm common sense. "Then you must apply elsewhere. The Bishop of Ely is not the be-all and end-all of ordination powers."

Rowland smiled. "Jane, Jane. What a tonic you are. It's no wonder we all look to you to hold the family together. I shall take your advice and apply to the next bishop I encounter."

Alfred, Sir Richard's first footman who always acted as Mr. Rowland's man when he was home, unpacked for him. After a brief look-in on his mother to let her know he had arrived and to wish her a speedy recovery, Rowland faced the duty that could no longer be delayed.

The study was in a far corner of Hawkstone House, so Rowland had plenty of time to dread his father's reaction as he made his way through the marble-floored halls with their ornately plastered walls. Sir Richard's library occupied a spacious room with high arched windows, fine marble fireplace, and floor-to-ceiling books that could be reached by a wheeled stepladder. Rowland's father sat at his desk going over some papers, but at his son's entrance, he came forward.

"Ah, Rowland, welcome home. I had word of your arrival, but I knew you would call on your mother first. How do you find her this evening?"

Rowland's eyes were sad. "Fearfully reduced, sir. What does Dr. Fansham say?"

"Nothing much to the purpose. But tell me of yourself, son. You have taken your degree?"

"Yes, sir, but—"

"Come, come. Let us not stand upon ceremony but sit in comfort." Sir Richard sat back down at his desk, and Rowland sat in an upholstered chair nearby.

His father was silent, so Rowland forged ahead. "I was denied orders, sir."

The silence hung heavy in the room. Sir Richard's features were immobile. Then he clapped his hands together so sharply Rowland jumped. "Well, that's fine. Sparke did quite right. Now that you've seen the error of your ways, you can renounce your enthusiasm and receive ordination from Bishop Exley. I'll have a word with him about it—just a hint that youthful follies are to be readily forgiven. Your mother and I shall be very proud of you; you'll rise high in the church once your foot is set on the right course. Shouldn't be surprised to see you a bishop yourself someday."

Rowland looked at the floor. This reaction was far worse than if his father had burst out in anger. Slowly raising his head, he looked his father in the eyes. "No, Father, I do not renounce my belief in a personal God nor my determination to preach this gospel."

Now the anger Rowland had expected from the first came. "What! You mean to continue in this disastrous way? Have you no common sense? Are you all stubbornness? How bitter it is to have an ungrateful son—more bitter far than the sting of an adder."

"Please, Father, I am not ungrateful for all you have done for me. You've always been most generous. But neither can I be ungrateful for what God has done for me. Even with all you have provided, His mercy has been greater. I cannot refuse what He would have me do. 'How can we escape if we refuse so great a salvation?'"

Again Sir Richard was silent. Then he said, "I do not comprehend this—that my son should be openly counted among the publicans and sinners, one of the curiosities of the day. It is hard enough to have Richard and your sister Jane share this Methodistical bias, but they do so quietly, whereas you are making a public figure of yourself and leading others into your way."

"I hope so, Father. To lead others is my calling." Rowland spoke the words quietly so as to give no hint of disrespect.

"Leave me now. I shall speak further to you on this matter at a later date. Try not to upset your mother."

Rowland bowed and took his leave.

The next day after breakfast, the summer sun shining on Shropshire's green rugged hills drew Rowland to take a walk around Hawkstone's fields and call on their tenants. He had gone only so far as the bottom of the field, however, when he realized word of his arrival had run ahead of him. A large number of his father's tenants, as well as people from the village, had come to greet him.

To Rowland a crowd in a field meant just one thing—a congregation to be preached to. So after a few minutes of chatting with folk he had known since childhood and inquiring after their various ills and numerous family members, he jumped up on a large boulder in a corner of the pasture.

"Friends, if you will it, I shall preach to you."

A cheer went up from the crowd—a rare experience for a field preacher who was more likely to be egged or pelted with mud clods. "You allus told me yer stories when ye were a wee lad," called an old shepherd bent over his stick. "And right fine stories they allus were. Tell us another now, lad."

The crowd agreed, and Rowland, who never read his sermons anyway, now found himself without even a Bible in his hands. He looked around for inspiration. Seeing the path across the sheep-dotted hillside which he had thought to follow for his morning ramble, he began, "Some of you may think I am preaching a rambling sermon, but if I should be able to reach the heart of a poor rambling sinner, I'm sure you'll forgive me. My friends, you may ramble from Christ, but He will ramble after you and try to bring you back into His fold."

His hearers laughed at the homely allusion and called hearty encouragement to the speaker.

But back in the study at Hawkstone House, the unusual sound met the ears of Sir Richard, who hastily dispatched a footman to bring young Richard to him. His heir arrived in a matter of minutes during which time more disturbing sounds reached the study, led by one clear male voice with exceptional carrying quality.

"Richard, I wish you would tell me—whose voice is that assaulting my ears?"

Richard was quiet and listened for a moment. "Why, sir, that is Rowland preaching to the people in the neighborhood."

Sir Richard was not surprised. Nor was he pleased. "Go tell him to come to me." Richard started to turn for the door. "Immediately!"

Richard was no more than halfway across the wide green lawn when he could hear Rowland's words distinctly. "I cannot fathom with my puny understanding the mystery of the divine decrees. I can only say with St. Paul, 'O the depth of His riches!' We know nothing—can any man tell me *why* grass is green?" Rowland drew a wide arc with his arm, encompassing all the emerald hillside. As his hand swept across the path, he saw his brother approaching. He knew instantly why Richard was coming, but he continued the thought he was developing. "Then let us leave all *explanations* and simply believe what God has revealed.

"My friends, think on these matters for a moment, search your hearts, and we will speak more on the matter." He turned to Richard who now stood at the foot of the rock.

"Our father bids you come to him—immediately."

"What shall I do with the congregation?" Rowland directed Richard's gaze to the crowd who now numbered close to fifty. "I cannot go unless you come up and finish my discourse."

Rowland jumped down from his granite pulpit, and Richard, with an amused grin at his brother, climbed up. Rowland walked quickly along the path, hearing Richard's quieter voice urging the farm laborers to follow the Good Shepherd.

Sir Richard was ready for his erring son. "You pray without the *Book of Common Prayer*, hold what are termed evangelical sentiments, and preach to a mixed multitude of people in unconsecrated places. Bishop Exley will never ordain you. I shouldn't even ask him." He broke off his colloquium as a new sound came through the open windows. "I hear some other person preaching. Who is that?"

"I suppose it is Richard finishing my sermon, sir."

Sir Richard banged a fist on his desk. "Go immediately and

tell him I command him to come at once to me." Rowland took
an obedient step toward the door. "And you come with him."

By the time Rowland reached the bottom of the field, however, Richard had finished and dismissed the congregation.
When both brothers returned to their father, he continued the
reprimand with doubled vigor. "You are degrading yourselves by
preaching in the open air without so much as a proper pulpit."

Sir Richard paused for breath, and Richard dared a quick
allusion. "But surely, Father, trained in the law as you are, you
can see the precedent. Our sermon was on a mount, just as our
Lord's example of field preaching."

Sir Richard's mouth was open to continue his lecture, but
his son's shot was so apropos that no words came out.

Rowland was quick to take up the advantage. "And, Father,
our words were much appreciated. Old Molly from the dairy told
me it was the finest preaching she had ever heard. I would have
been much complimented if I didn't know Molly has been stone-
deaf these twenty years." Sir Richard's gape turned to the merest
shadow of a smile. "And Crooker's wife listened the whole time
with a young lamb in her arms. It was impossible to tell which
had the broader smile, she or the lamb."

Richard took up the story. "And as the lamb hasn't yet
grown any teeth and Mrs. Crooker has lost all of hers, they made
a fine twin set."

Sir Richard relaxed into a smile. "Well, I am pleased that the
people on my estate should be kept in good humor."

The sons, knowing when they had pressed their advantage
far enough, bowed and retired.

It was late that evening when the sound of carriage wheels
on the gravel drive brought Rowland, Richard, and Jane to the
front steps of Hawkstone House. Rowland was the first to recognize Clement's coach-and-four. "Here's support for you, Jane.
Our sister Elizabeth has arrived."

With a glad cry, Jane rushed forward to greet her sister.
Elizabeth hugged all her family members roundly before

Rowland realized that the footman was handing another woman out of the carriage.

Mary Tudway emerged, shaking the wrinkles from her blue traveling dress with one hand and holding a well-brushed Spit in the other. As Rowland stepped forward to welcome Mary, Spit saw his rescuer from the gutters of Bath and with a glad, shrill yap leaped from Mary's arm straight to Rowland's. Fortunately, Rowland was nimble in the catching, but the unexpectedness of it caused him to step backwards onto the hem of Elizabeth's full skirt, adding a sharp tearing sound to the rest of the noisy greeting.

"Sir, if you were not my brother, I should rap you severely for such an affront."

"I beg your pardon, sister, but it was your back."

It was not until after dinner, which the baronet always ordered served in midafternoon, that Rowland had opportunity to talk to Mary alone. "I am so pleased you have borne my sister company—both for her sake and my own. I had not hoped to see you for some time yet."

As he spoke, the words brought home to him more sharply than anything yet had done the unenviable position he was in. He had looked forward to this as the time to make Mary an offer. Here she was, unexpectedly, delightfully, at Hawkstone, holding his arm as he led her on a walk around the grounds, and he could speak of nothing but the landscape.

It seemed now that he would be forever debarred from speaking what was in his heart. "Would you prefer to sit in the summer house or to visit the grotto?"

"Oh, I should far prefer the grotto. And Elizabeth told me you have a hermit cave and a castle ruin. What a perfect setting for the *Castle of Oranto!*"

Rowland laughed. "Yes, and the eminent Dr. Johnson would agree with you. After his visit here, he wrote to our father that he found Hawkstone quite marvelous. 'It excels in the extent of its prospects, the awfulness of its shades, the horrors of its precipices, the verdure of its hollows, and the loftiness of its rocks. The ideas which it forces upon the mind are the sublime, the dreadful, and the vast. Above is inaccessible attitude, below is horrible profundity. He that mounts the precipices at Hawkstone wonders how he came thither and doubts how he shall return. His walk is an adventure, and his departure an escape.'"

"Oh, sir, you have stimulated my appetite for adventure beyond all bounds. Lead the way, I pray."

They started with the grotto, a large oval cavern hewn in the rocky hillside behind the house. It had been cut far into the rock, and pillars chiseled in imitation of stalagmites and stalactites supported its winding recesses.

"Can we go in?" Mary stood on a boulder on the downhill side of the stream issuing from the grotto and peered into the stone chamber.

"If you are very careful. I did it often as a child. But I fear for your skirts."

"Oh, fah. What consequence are they when such an adventure offers?"

Rowland leaped across the stream and extended his hand to Mary to steady her jump to the stone ledge forming the floor of the grotto. Her jump was strong, but she was not prepared for the slickness of the damp stone. As her feet slipped from under her, she gave a small cry and reached out to Rowland. His strong arms scooped her up and set her firmly on the solid rock. She clung to him. Nor did he release his hold on her but drew her closer. There was no resistance as his adored Mary settled in his arms. He dropped his head to hers, his lips in her hair, bared by the hat that had fallen to the rocks in the mishap. She smelled of lavender. "Mary—" He dropped his lips to her cheek, with every intention of going further to find her lips. But the sound of his own voice echoing in the rocky cave brought an awareness of the enormous impropriety of what he was about. And worse, the fact that he would likely never have the right to hold her so.

"Mary." He pushed her away from him, retaining hold only on one arm to steady her. "Forgive me. I have in the past indicated to you my feelings, but I did not mean to—I would never—forgive me for—"

Mary laughed. "La, sir. What a fuss you make. Forgive you for rescuing your sister-in-law from a nasty fall on the rocks? What gentleman would beg forgiveness for such an act? Should I have preferred you to allow me to dash myself on the stones?"

Rowland smiled his appreciation of her easing the situation, and they left the grotto and continued their tour on toward the Red Castle ruin. Only one tower and three walls of the keep remained of what had once been a mighty medieval fortress. Ivy grew over most of the fallen stones. Rowland cleared a space on a seat in what had once been the Great Hall and spread his linen handkerchief for Mary to sit on.

But that activity accomplished, he could not bring himself to tell her what he must. So instead he asked, "And how are your family in Wells?"

"All are well in Wells, sir," she answered with a straight face, and Rowland laughed appreciatively.

"And events?"

"If I said as dull as ditch water, you would accuse me of deplorable humor, so I shall desist. The answer, however, would be quite accurate. For lack of anything else, I have returned to the activity I hate most in this world—making embroidered seat covers."

"Do you not read?"

"Ah, yes, I have read and reread *Humphrey Clinker*. Its delightful descriptions of Bath only sink me deeper by making me miss the pleasures I once knew." She turned aside and looked out over the evening-shadowed expanse.

Rowland wondered if she were also missing Roger, but he only asked, "And is that truly the life you would choose, Mary?"

A sigh escaped her. "I don't know. I think so when I recall the pleasures. But at the time, I found it palled a bit. One must have *something* to do, however, and if I am required to accomplish any more needlework, I shall needs be clapped into Bedlam.

Elizabeth has invited me to accompany her to London when they remove there, but it is months until Parliament opens."

"And in London you will seek more pleasures?"

"What else is there? The opera, the theater, Ranelagh, and Vauxhall."

If Rowland had been depressed when he began this conversation, every word Mary spoke made his prospects look more dismal. "But, Mary, you could find occupation of more lasting importance."

She gave a brittle laugh. "La, what do you suggest, sir? That I take up field preaching?"

A new idea struck him. "Mary, next week I go to preach to congregations near Welshampton and Ellesmere. Would you accompany me?"

"If I don't have to take my embroidery with me."

Her light answer would have been a happy conclusion to the conversation if there were not one more matter yet to discuss. "I shall be particularly glad of your company, Mary. You see, I may be obliged to spend a rather long time engaged in field preaching."

"Nonsense, Rowland. You have taken your degree. Won't you pass on to orders soon? I had thought you might already have done so. Maria, whose father is a canon, told me it is often done immediately upon taking degrees. What—"

Rowland interrupted, "Yes, for all but one of our number it was so."

Rowland was becoming accustomed to the shocked silence that always followed this intelligence.

After a moment Mary clasped her hands firmly together and said in a decided voice, "Then, sir, you must abandon your irregularities. I did warn you it would be so. Now you must see—"

Rowland's voice was equally firm. "I did not expect that of you, Mary. It is the advice of a coward. When we are afraid and begin to shrink back, the devil knows he is gaining ground. I cannot bear flying away and turning my back—there is no armor given for the back."

"Are all who are not fanatics cowards? I don't ask you to give up your religion or your preaching, just your enthusiasm."

Always fond of making his point by telling a story, Rowland's eyes twinkled for the first time since the conversation had turned serious. "Because I am in earnest, men call me an enthusiast. But I am not a zealot; mine are the words of truth and soberness. Three summers ago I was walking on yonder hill." He pointed to the west where a rocky hill rose in the distance. "I saw a gravel pit fall in and bury three human beings alive. I lifted up my voice for help so loud that I was heard in the town below at a distance of a half-mile. Help came and rescued two of the poor sufferers. No one called me an enthusiast then. And when I see eternal destruction ready to fall upon poor sinners and about to entomb them irrecoverably in eternal woe and call aloud on them to escape, shall I be called an enthusiast now?"

Mary gave no reply, but the furrow to her brow showed that she was considering his words.

"When you come with me next week, you shall see and may judge the matter for yourself." He extended his hand to escort her back.

Mary was quiet on the return walk, like the thoughtful girl Rowland had known her to be before the frivolities of Bath and Sarah Child's example had turned her head to more worldly things. Rowland ached for the meditative companion she had once been to him. He knew that whatever turn her mind took, he would always love Mary Tudway, and he prayed that God might direct her mind and heart in ways he was incapable of doing.

Later in her room, Mary knew a similar conflict. Rowland's words made sense, and yet she could not accept them, could not think that his way was right. She wrestled with the matter until her head ached. Then determined to find lighter amusement, she picked up *Humphrey Clinker.* She smiled at the servant girl's letter to her friend back home.

> Oh, Molly! You that live in the country have no deception of our doing at Bath. Here is such dressing, and fiddling, and dancing, and gadding, and courting, and plotting—gracious! If God had not given me a good stock of discretion, what a power of things might not I reveal.

The amusing pictures those words called to mind made Mary relax, and her head ceased to ache. She read on through a few more letters of the novel until she came to one from an Oxford student.

> London itself can hardly exhibit one species of diversion to which we have not something analogous at Bath . . . and daily opportunities of seeing the most remarkable characters of the community. One sees them in their natural attitudes and true colors, descended from their pedestals and divested of their formal draperies, undisguised by art and affectation . . . There is always a great show of the clergy at Bath, waddling like so many crows along the North Parade. None of your thin, puny, yellow, hectic figures, exhausted with abstinence and hard study, but great, overgrown dignitaries and rectors with rubicund noses and gouty ankles—the emblems of sloth and indigestion.

For a moment Mary could see nothing but Bishop Twysden in his gorgeous robes, sipping claret in the countess's Nicodemus chamber.

Was this truly what she wanted for Rowland? Should he abandon his passion for God and the souls of men for the sake of money and honor? And yet what if no bishop could be found to ordain him? Would he spend his life in a field? A baronet's son?

And if he obtained ordination and a living and spoke the words to her he had so long hinted at, what would her answer be? There was no doubting her pleasure in his company, but would she be a worthy wife for a man of such serious calling?

Shouldn't he take a more serious wife to whom doing good came naturally—such as Lady Selina? But such musings did nothing to answer her question to herself—would *she* make a fit wife for Rowland Hill?

If he were to be anything but a clergyman, she knew that she wouldn't hesitate. Every occasion with him taught her heart more clearly what was truly in it. But having a good time was very important to her. She couldn't live as pious Lady Huntingdon did. If that was how she'd have to be . . . She shuddered. But if she were to refuse him, if life were to hold no more pleasant times with Rowland . . . Her throat closed, and her eyes filled with tears at the thought.

And then Rowland's twinkling eyes filled her mind. He wasn't a long-faced ascetic, and she doubted he would want her to be one either.

Still in the mood of serious reflection, she turned to her old favorite, Milton. But she didn't find his sonnet on the brevity of youth to be of much comfort.

> How soon hath Time, the subtle thief of youth,
> Stol'n on his wing my three-and-twentieth year! . . .
> Yet be it less or more, or soon or slow,
> It shall be still in strictest measure even
> To that same lot, however mean or high,
> Tow'rd which time leads me, and the will of heaven;
> All is, if I have grace to use it so,
> As ever in my great task-master's eye.

If only she could have Milton's confidence that after her twenty years of accomplishing little more than three embroidered seat cushions, she could do something truly splendid.

$\mathcal{T}$he following week not even the drizzling August rain could dampen Mary's sense of adventure as she set out in Sir Richard's closed carriage with coronets on the door. Surely no one had ever been more elegantly conducted to a field service. Elizabeth's maid Minson sat on the seat facing her, holding Spit on a cushion on her lap. The little dog, usually a sleepy creature, today sat alert, his ears perked, watching everything outside the carriage window. Raindrops on the window pane dimmed Mary's view of the Shropshire fields, some more green than ever in the rain, some the soft gold of ripening wheat.

She had argued without success that it was quite ridiculous for Rowland to ride in the rain when he could just as well sit dry and comfortable in his father's carriage. But he merely laughed and replied that he shouldn't shrink from a little wetting—and it might not be such a bad thing if he did. And besides, the experience would be useful if he chose to preach a sermon on Noah.

Although female members of Methodist societies often took such jaunts, Mrs. Tudway would have been unlikely to grant permission for her daughter to accompany a field preacher. But as Elizabeth had some sympathy for her brother's activity and was far too occupied in nursing her mother to give

343

the matter much attention, there was no one to forbid the excursion.

As they drove northwestward toward the Welsh border, the scenery became more mountainous and more intensely green. After traveling some miles in a narrow cultivated valley between wooded mountains, Mary could see the descent into the vale in which they would meet the first congregation. Through a succession of gentle hills carefully cultivated by Marcher farmers wound the Afton Dyfrdwy, a tiny blue line. On the declivity of a mountain about a mile away stood a castle.

Mary felt there could be no more beautiful country in the world. She wanted to drive on and on, deeper into this land she had never seen before. She had heard of the majesty and ruggedness of the mountains in Wales—and this was only a foretaste. She leaned forward on the carriage seat and pressed her face against the window. Rowland saluted her with a wave and a smile. Mary suddenly realized that the country could be quite as exciting as the city.

After a night passed pleasantly at a rustic but comfortable inn, the party rose at five o'clock and drove a few miles northward toward Wrexham where Rowland planned to address his first congregation. He told Mary he had chosen to begin there because he had preached in that area before and knew the people to be friendly and receptive. As soon as Mary saw the sun rise over the mountains, she felt sure this would be a happy day. It was impossible to think of anything going amiss in this world.

As the carriage slowed to a stop at the spot where Rowland knew people from nearby villages would be passing on their way to market, Mary saw another delightful scene. It appeared that giant spiders had been busily spinning through the night. An entire field was covered with fine white thread glowing silver in the morning light. "That field!" Mary pointed as Rowland helped her descend from the carriage.

"A tenterfield," Rowland said. "The women of the villages use it to dry their yarn. Be sure Spit doesn't try to run in it.

Neither he nor the women would be happy with the job of untangling him."

Rowland walked to the edge of the field and spoke to the women guarding it, inviting them to attend his service. They unlatched the gate to the field and followed him back to the stile he would use as a platform. Soon several laborers from neighboring fields, a group of dairymaids, and some families on their way to market had gathered around the preacher. It seemed to Mary almost magic that as soon as Rowland began preaching, his crowd of twenty listeners multiplied to forty and upwards. She thought fleetingly of the miracle of the loaves and fishes and smiled. She couldn't wait to tell Rowland. He always liked commonplace illustrations, and she had found one for him.

Three lads driving a pack of pigs stopped at the back of the crowd and let their charges root in the grass while the boys leaned on their staves and listened.

"Often when I have been preaching, I have thought a whole village to be dead in trespasses and sins. But then success for the work of God came from a few quiet ones whom I left like a nest of eggs." He pointed to a girl's basket of eggs, carried on her arm, and she blushed with pleasure. "When I visited the people again, the numbers had increased, so that the little nest of eggs became a healthy brood.

"Now I ask you to look into your own hearts. How many of you—"

The most dreadful squalling Mary had ever heard suddenly drowned out the preacher's words. Squeaking, grunting, and snorting were followed by sharp, frantic female screams. Spit, secure in Mary's arms, added his yapping to the din. The entire congregation moved toward the sound of the disturbance. When Mary reached the fence, chaos met her gaze, but she couldn't help laughing.

The pigs, left to their own devices by their drivers, had wandered into the tenterfield, which the women in their hurry to attend the meeting had left unbarred. Five fat pink and black porkers had gotten their snout rings entangled in the yarn. The more they shook their heads to free themselves, the more they became imprisoned.

It was impossible to say which made more noise—the women bemoaning the calamity to their yarn, the drivers shouting at their pigs, the congregation who had found a better entertainment than the preacher, or the frightened and enraged pigs. But it was the women who took the matter in hand. Each one grasped a hog by a back leg and, throwing her weight against the broadside of the pig, turned it on its back. Then straddling the animal to keep it capsized, each began to disentangle the muddy head from the twine—to the accompaniment of cheers and clapping from the crowd.

Rowland took Mary's arm and turned her toward the carriage. "I know when I've been outdone. There'll be no more preaching here today."

Mary worried that he would be terribly disappointed. When he had tethered his horse to the back of the carriage and joined her and Minson inside, however, he exploded into laughter so hearty that the carriage rocked on its springs. "I had to get away before I disgraced myself by laughing," he explained after regaining control.

"Why should you, who are noted for your humor, not laugh?"

Rowland shook his head and dabbed his eyes. "It's one thing to make people laugh. It's another to do it yourself. I wouldn't want to become characterized as a laughing parson, even though I do hope to counteract the current notion that wit is wicked and humor sinful. Or that dullness is holy and solemn stupidity is full of grace." He reached up and rapped sharply on the roof of the carriage as a signal to the coachman to drive on. "If dullness were a divine power, the world would have been converted by now."

After a few miles Rowland signaled the driver to stop. He would continue the journey as outrider. "We should have a large meeting across the border at Garth. I have preached there many times, and they have put up notices of my coming. I want to think how I can liken our pigs in the tenterfield to the story of the Gadarene demoniac."

That evening it seemed that, indeed, the entire town of Garth had learned of Hill's coming. When Mary saw the size of the congregation, she was delighted. But he had no more than mounted the haywain, his platform, when a terrible din began. People banged on pans, shovels, buckets—anything of tin or iron that would make a noise. Others blew horns and rang bells.

For a moment Mary hoped the din might be some sort of welcoming band, but when she saw Rowland pelted with eggs and mud, she knew the truth. And she knew too the truth of her feelings. She wanted to leap on the wagon and fling herself in front of him to protect him from the degrading missiles. She wanted to tell that ragtag mob just what she thought of them. She wanted . . . Spit began yapping shrilly and struggling in her arms so that she became aware of her own voice. With red-faced alarm, she realized that the things she wanted to do she had actually done in a burst of temper.

"Rowland Hill has come here at considerable discomfort to himself so you can hear the Word of God. And this is the way you treat him! He'd be far better off preaching to a flock of sheep or a field of stones. They'd be more polite, and they'd get just as much out of it!"

Spit caught her fervor and barked an emphatic punctuation to each sentence. Whether it was her outraged action or Spit's fine performance that carried the day, she couldn't tell, but the crowd suddenly grew quiet.

Rowland stepped to her side, wiping a blob of egg off his cheek. "Thank you, Mary. Stay with me," he said in her ear. Then he turned to the audience. "I see we are a band of music lovers gathered here tonight."

The crowd roared with laughter. "Now it's exceedingly fine to love music—but it's important to understand the difference between music and noise. If you will, I'll show you how we can work together and turn this hubbub into harmony."

Not a murmur sounded in the field as they waited to hear what the preacher had to say. "This fine lady, Miss Tudway, has come all the way from Wells." The fact that few in the crowd knew where Wells was made the announcement more impressive. "And she is going to help me lead in singing Charles Wesley's hymn, 'Blessed Be the Name.' Now here's what I want you to do. Those of you with, er, drums will mark the rhythm. Those with bells will ring them on the phrase, 'Blessed be the name of the Lord!' and those with horns will blow them at the end of each phrase. Now let's try it!"

Mary sang her heart out, trying to add a bit of real melody to what was only a slightly more organized version of the earlier din. The thumping and banging accompanied, "O for a Thousand Tongues to Sing" followed by an ear-splitting blast from the horns; then "Blessed be the name of the Lord!" could just be heard above a jangle of bells.

The results left Mary, who had a strong but untrained voice, wishing heartily she had not begged to be allowed to discontinue her music lessons. But the mob loved it, and Rowland good-naturedly led them on through succeeding verses. They sang, "Jesus, the name that charms our fears," with a blare of trumpets and ended with a final, triumphant, "Blessed be the name of the Lord!" that left everyone panting for breath.

"And I'm sure the angels are applauding you right now!" Rowland congratulated his audience as he handed Mary down off the makeshift platform. "Now my audiences almost always stand while listening to me, but as you've worked so hard, I'd like to invite you to sit right down in God's green grass while I tell you a story."

After they were settled, Rowland told of their morning encounter with the pigs. He went on to recount the story from Mark 5 of Jesus casting out a legion of demons from the possessed man and then granting their request that He not send them out of the country but allow them to enter a herd of swine. "Now I'm not suggesting that those pigs this morning were demon-possessed, though you might have thought so to hear the ruckus they set up. What I want you to notice from this story is that Jesus did this because those demons asked Him to. Now if Jesus would grant the request of demons, just think how much more readily He will grant the prayers of His children."

The anger and antagonism of an hour before was completely gone, and a sense of relaxed warmth pervaded the meadow. The setting sun painted the western sky pink and gold, more elegant than any stained-glass window. Mary, who could never before have imagined worshiping without a prayer book in her hand and a prayer rail at which to kneel, looked around her. She noted the richness of Rowland's voice, the ease with which his words came, and the good sense they spoke to her heart. She saw how much Rowland's preaching meant to him and how right he was for the task, even if no bishop could be convinced of that.

That night over a late supper at the inn, Mary tried to convey some of her feelings to Rowland. "I understand much better now what you've tried to tell me. I won't say I've been wrong to urge you to seek a less irregular path, but I do have a better idea of the force of your preaching."

He looked at her in the fire-lit room. "And, Mary, if circumstances arrange themselves so that our paths become—ah, closer, can you be content to see me despised and rejected in my Master's service?"

She dropped her head. That was the crucial question. And she didn't know the answer. A day ago she would have thought an affirmative impossible. But after her quick, protective action that evening where for a moment she had entered as wholly as he into the service . . . She finished her meal in silence.

"Go have Minson tuck you in bed." Rowland smiled at her. "We have just one service tomorrow, and then I must return you to my sister."

As they drove toward Oswestry the next day, Mary couldn't help wishing that the meeting might be sparsely attended. The fact that the rain seemed to be getting heavier gave rise to her hopes. Surely a smaller crowd would be more orderly, and only those who truly wished to hear the preacher would come out in the wet. But as they neared the town, the road became increasingly filled with traffic. Mary had the disturbing feeling that they all had the same destination.

The crowd that met them at the appointed field told Mary she was right. Rowland was just helping her from the carriage when a rough-looking man approached with a determined look in his eye. Mary blanched and pulled back into the carriage. Then, angered at her own cowardice, she stepped forward to take her place at Rowland's side. But the man had not come to mill Rowland down, rather to whisper a warning in his ear. He said something Mary couldn't hear and pointed toward the front of the crowd, to a man standing head and shoulders above everyone else. Rowland nodded, thanked the man, and shook hands with him heartily. Then he turned to Mary. "Our friend tells me that the local publican has engaged a prizefighter to disturb the meeting."

"The mountain?" Mary nodded her head at the enormous fellow. "What are you to do? I have heard of bulls being let loose on field preachers, but he looks far more fearsome."

Rowland just smiled and walked toward the man. "Ah, my good Goliath!"

The fighter turned to him with a surly look and flexed his muscles. A murmur went through the nearby observers.

"Excuse me, sir." Rowland spoke just to his Goliath but in a voice that others could hear. "I have come a great distance to preach to this congregation, and you can see from their carriages and other conveyances that the people have traveled a long way to hear me. I am therefore anxious to have an orderly service. Now if anything should occur, you are just the man to put matters straight. Can I rely upon your honor to do so?"

Goliath raised his huge, hairy fist and shook it in the air, causing those around him to take a step backwards. He glared into the crowd, then turned back to Rowland, and spoke in a booming voice. "If anybody meddles with you, he will have to take the consequences."

That afternoon Rowland preached on the Scripture verse, "Ye must be born again." There was not a single interruption to the entire service. Before the hour was out, the rain ceased and upwards of a hundred souls sought the salvation Rowland Hill preached to them. "How can we escape if we refuse so great a salvation?" The theme ran over and over in Mary's head. But the question she longed to have answered was, how did one *know?* Perhaps Rowland was right that there was more to salvation than obeying the rules of the church. But if so, how did she find the answer? Certainly, she must seek forgiveness of sin—the Bible and the catechism said so. Certainly, God offered salvation—but if baptism and confirmation and taking Communion weren't enough, what else was there?

She thought she might speak to Rowland about it over dinner. But he invited Goliath to dine with them, and Rowland encouraged their guest to spend most of the meal talking about his pugilistic tactics and his many victories in the ring.

"I had told Elizabeth she might expect us tonight. Do you object to traveling late?" Rowland asked as he handed Mary into the carriage once again. It was already midafternoon, and they had many miles to go.

The roads were not crowded in this part of the country, so one had less to worry about when meeting another vehicle on a narrow, curving road. But the sparse traffic also put the lonely traveler more at the mercy of highwaymen.

However, getting back to her comfortable room at Hawkstone offered an irresistible prospect to Mary. Besides, she felt perfectly secure with Rowland riding guard.

"No objection at all." She leaned back against the squabs, thinking she might sleep for a time.

It was nearly dark when she awoke. "Minson! How long have I slept?" She reached out and took Spit from the maid's lap.

"Indeed, I couldn't say, miss. I've been a-nodding too."

Mary could see from her window that they were traveling through a sparsely populated, hilly country. A glimmer of water in the distance suggested they might be near the mere, and a growl that came from her stomach told her it was past supper time.

A light mist was rising, adding its grayness to the dusk, and large, dark boulders seemed to loom up suddenly on the mountainside. Mary shivered and hugged Spit tighter. She looked out the window but couldn't see Rowland. He must be riding ahead of or behind the carriage because of the narrowness of the road at this point. Mary shivered again, wishing there were more rugs in the chaise. The cold and damp of the fog seemed to permeate the carriage.

She looked again for Rowland, peering as far in every direction as she could, but saw only grayness with dark shapes in it. She wished she hadn't looked. She was just considering knocking on the roof to signal the coachman to stop when the carriage lurched so sharply she would have been thrown to the floor had not Minson caught her.

The coach rolled to a stop amid gruff commands from Coachman John, a creaking of wheels and springs, and the stamping and whinnying of horses. There was a harsh sound Mary could not identify. And then she knew.

"Out of the carriage, me pretties!" a rude voice ordered.

Spit set up a wild yapping, and Minson went into hysterics. Mary was more disconcerted by her maid than by the robbers. She turned from her half-opened door to calm Minson.

Suddenly the air reverberated with the most bloodcurdling shrieks, shouts, and howls she had ever heard. The alarm rang from the hillside and seemed to echo from every rock. It was as if the elements themselves had taken up battle and the very stones were crying out. Then out of the fog rode a fearsome figure with full greatcoat billowing behind him like giant wings.

"Fecks! We've stopped the devil by mistake!" The highwaymen took to their heels. But just before they disappeared into the gloom, Spit leaped from the coach with an angry growl and chased the bandits up the road.

Mary collapsed on her seat in laughter. Minson, now limply quiet after her hysteria, sat in the far corner, and Rowland climbed aboard the bench facing Mary.

"Rowland!" She gasped for air. "Whatever possessed you? It was the finest performance I've ever seen, but you could have been shot. We could have all been shot."

"It didn't seem likely an attempted shot would be very accurate in this gloom—specially if I could make them quake a bit. As I wasn't armed, all I could see to do was to fly at them with all the noise I could make."

"Quake a bit! They'll never stop shaking. You've affected them permanently with the palsy, I'm sure." She giggled. "They'll have to give up highway robbery and look for honest work now."

"Then I have done a good night's work. Perhaps I should take up reforming highwaymen as a calling."

"That would certainly be a unique form of field preaching—and, goodness knows, there are enough of them about."

The thickening fog and their unsettling adventure made the travelers decide to stop at an inn for the night, so it was mid-morning the next day before they arrived back at Hawkstone.

Elizabeth came to greet them before they had crossed the entrance foyer. "I am so glad you are returned. A messenger came from The Cedars yesterday. Maria has been taken to bed with child."

"Has the babe come? Do I have a niece or a nephew?" Mary clapped her hands.

"It's likely she has been delivered by this time. I most heartily hope so for her sake. But the event had not occurred when the messenger was dispatched. As our mother is some improved, I should like to leave as soon as possible. I know you've just had a long journey, Mary, but could you be ready to set out again in the morning?"

Mary choked back brief thoughts of the rambles over the

Shropshire hills she would like to have taken with Rowland, but she smiled at her sister-in-law. "Dear Elizabeth, you must needs take up nursing as a profession. Whatever should we do without your skills? And you too, Jane," she added as the elder sister entered the room. "I am pleased to hear that Mrs. Hill is stronger. And you look much less fatigued than when we arrived."

"I am refreshed," Jane said, "and shall be able to carry on very well now. I do thank you for your help, Elizabeth."

Mary left the sisters and went on up to her room to repack her belongings for the return journey.

Rowland, after calling on his mother, went on to seek his father in his study. He gave him a brief account of his itinerancy and a rather full account of the highwayman episode, knowing it would put his father in a good humor.

But the baronet's amusement was short-lived. "I have a matter of an extremely serious nature to discuss with you, Rowland."

The son nodded.

"Somewhat against my inclinations, I have spoken to Bishop Exley of Lichfield. He said there were no favors he would willingly deny our family. But granting ordination to a Methodist was so far beyond his scruples that, should he do such a thing, he would then be obliged to resign his office for conscience' sake.

"He said he was sorry his young friend should so openly countenance dissent from the established church, and he was alarmed lest your eccentric spirit should lead you to a departure from its doctrines as well as its discipline."

Sir Richard paused for his words to make an impression. "I thanked him sincerely for his attention and assured him I bore him no ill will for acting on his conscience. On the contrary, I admire his principles."

Rowland nodded. He would ask no man to act against his own conscience—no matter how mistaken he thought the person.

"And now, son, I must ask if you mean to continue the path you have chosen?"

"I can do nothing else, Father. It is not my choice but God's."

The baronet gave a sigh of irritation, but he did not argue with what he obviously thought to be gross wrongheadedness. "Very well, I too must act according to my conscience. I have firmly resisted using any force upon you in this matter."

Rowland nodded. "Indeed, Father. You have been most kind and forbearing."

"I believe I have. But now to continue so would constitute negligence on my part. Were I to keep supporting you financially in an activity I believe to be wrong, I should become a party to your malfeasance."

"I would not want you to act against your conscience, Father."

"Nor do I intend to do so. I will not disinherit you as, you will allow, most fathers in my position would do."

Rowland agreed. It was absolutely true. At the first sign of disobedience, most offending offspring would be stricken from the will.

"Nor will I entirely discontinue your allowance." Here was leniency, indeed. Rowland's eyebrows raised. "You are still my son, and I will not have a Hill starving. But from today your allowance is reduced to that which will be sufficient only to buy your bread. Beyond that all pecuniary supplies are to be discontinued. My man of business shall be informed forthwith."

"You are very good, Father. I understand fully. As soon as possible, I shall begin a circuit ride, and I shall not be ungrateful for any pennies you give me. My friend Cornelius Winter has offered me the use of his little pony, so there will be no need to request a horse from your stable."

There seemed to be little left to say, so Rowland withdrew to make his plans. As well as drawing a route for his preaching, he planned a call at every cathedral to request the bishop to sign his orders. Gloucester, Hereford, and Worcester were all easily within reach. As to his preaching itinerary—preaching twenty sermons a week would not strain his powers. He would preach in fields, in streets, and on quays. And he must go to London. He had been invited frequently before to preach in Whitefield's old chapel in Tottenham Court Road and in the Tabernacle. And, of course, the countess would open her drawing room in Park Lane to him as she did for all preachers she supported. No, there would be no shortage of opportunity to preach the Word.

And so early the next week, after Jane had received word that Mary and Elizabeth were safely arrived in Wells and Maria had been delivered of a fine son, Rowland prepared to set out on his little gray pony. His long legs barely cleared the ground.

"Like Don Quixote on Rosinante," Richard said as he slapped the animal's dappled rump.

"No, Richard. It is not windmills I mean to joust with but the devil himself." Rowland smiled. "But I think I should prefer to be compared to the apostles who went forth without purse or scrip."

"Rowland—" Richard's concern showed in his face and voice. "Do you need—"

"No, no. I thank you heartily for the offer, but I have enough for the bare necessities, and the Lord will supply the rest. Besides, when our father reduced my aid, I believe he meant for it to apply to all our connections. I would not want you to distress him further than I have already done. Oh, except for one small matter."

Richard looked at him quizzically.

"When I concluded my sermon to the congregation in the village last night, I announced that next week the message would be preached at the same time by my brother, Richard Hill, Esquire."

And so it was that Rowland left Hawkstone on a warm late August day to the accompaniment of groans and laughter.

*L*ook, he reached for the rattle!" Mary cried in delight as four-month-old John Paine held out a chubby hand to the noisy enticement his aunt offered him. "What a prodigy you have produced, Maria!"

Maria gave the seraphic smile so often on her face since the arrival of her son. "I can think of no greater delight than to have so fine a baby. I should like to have ten of them."

Mary gasped.

"Well, not all at once, of course," Maria laughed.

As they were talking, Elizabeth entered the nursery. She paused to chuck her nephew under the chin and receive one of his coveted toothless grins. Then she turned to Mary. "Your mother said I should find you here. The postman has brought a letter from Jane which I think might be of interest to you."

Maria was fully engaged with her son in his cradle, so Mary and Elizabeth moved to the window seat at the far end of the room, looking out over the bare branches of trees and bushes in the winter garden below. "She copied out portions from a letter she received from Rowly. Really, it is most vexing!" Elizabeth unfolded the letter she carried and read, "'On return to Bristol, I paid passage across the Severn for myself and pony, but had not sufficient left in my purse to procure a night's lodging, so was obliged to go on hungry and exhausted.'" She laid the letter in her lap. "I think you know, Mary, that our father reduced his annual allowance in hopes of diverting him from his erratic career and inducing obedience to order and regularity. But it seems the opposition of family, friend, and foe only serve to fire his heroism." She shook her head and then picked up the letter again. "'I was refused orders by the Bishops of Hereford and Gloucester on grounds of my enthusiasm. The Scripture admonishes us to patience, and I find that virtue to be like a stout Welsh pony—it bears a great deal and trots a great way. But it will tire at the long run. I pray for strength not to tire before my task is completed. I shall next apply to the Bishop of Worcester.'"

Elizabeth stood up, crumpling the letter in agitation. "This situation is intolerably wrongheaded on both sides. His condition in life, his youth, the sprightliness of his imagination, the earnestness of his address—all produce amazing attention and effect in his hearers. He could be one of the great preachers of our day. And yet he is refused ordination over a theological squabble. And he, who could easily mend matters by mending his manners, will not give in. I do not know what is to be done."

"Is there more in the letter, Elizabeth?"

Elizabeth looked at the letter. "Oh, I had not meant to rumple it." She sat down and smoothed the letter on her skirt. "Jane also quoted from a letter she received from Lady Huntingdon. 'I, who have known your brother from his first setting out, can testify that no man ever engaged with more heartfelt earnestness in bringing captives from the strongholds of Satan into the glorious liberty of the gospel of our Emmanuel; and it will require all the energies of his zealous and enterprising spirit to erect the standard of the cross in parts of London where ignorance and depravity prevail to such an awful degree.' I take that to mean that my brother means to preach in such places as Whitefield's Tabernacle and in Tottenham Court Road when he completes his tour of the West Country." She stood up again, shaking her head in exasperation.

"If only he could be prevailed upon to use caution," Mary said quietly.

Both women were silent for a few moments, dwelling on the difficult—seemingly impossible—situation. Then Elizabeth spoke. "But I have not come merely to trouble you with worries over my errant brother. Clement says we shall remove to London immediately after Christmas. Do you mean to go with us?"

Mary jumped to her feet and hugged Elizabeth. "Do I mean to go with you? It is doubtful anything less than a direct command from Papa could prevent it—and even then I'm not sure." She laughed. "Do you realize, Elizabeth, it has been seven years since last I was in London, and then never out of the sight of Miss Fossbenner?"

"Well, that is one matter we must consider. Miss Fossbenner would hardly answer, but we will need to engage an abigail for you. Minson will be far too busy seeing to my needs in London to attend both of us. Should you prefer to engage one in Wells or wait until we get to London?"

Mary considered for a moment. "I think it would be best to wait. It would be best to have an abigail acquainted with London ways."

Elizabeth agreed, and they fell to making plans regarding wardrobe needs and packing arrangements.

If Mary had found the sights in Bath surprising, London was completely astounding to her after a seven-year absence. "Oh, but is not the Irish saying true, 'London is now gone out of town!' Clement, were not those open fields producing hay and corn when last I was here?"

Her brother agreed that this section of streets, squares, shops, and churches was all newly built. "And I am informed that eleven thousand new houses have been built in one-quarter of Westminster in less than ten years."

But the innumerable streets, squares, rows, lanes, alleys, palaces, and public buildings were not so striking as the crowds of people swarming about. It was enough to make the Bath population seem sparse and Wells entirely desolate. The streets were choked with an infinity of bright equipages, coaches, chariots, chaises, and other carriages, continually rolling and shifting before her eyes until her head felt quite giddy.

When Clement's carriage rolled down Marylebone Road, Mary caught sight of a spire rising ahead. "Oh, Elizabeth, there is St. Marylebone Church. How well I recall your wedding there. It is the most beautiful church!"

Elizabeth smiled. "Yes, indeed. Ten years ago that was."

For a moment Mary thought her sister-in-law's eyes misted. Was she regretting that in that time she had not borne a child—an heir for Clement? It was indeed unfortunate, but John Paine's arrival had secured the Tudway line. And if Maria were to be granted the brood she desired, there would be plenty of Tudways to carry on at The Cedars and in Antigua.

The carriage stopped in front of No. 1 Devonshire Place, and two footmen and the butler came forward to welcome them. "Miss Child has sent messages around for the past three days, miss," the butler said to Mary. "You will find them on the hall table. Each requested a reply. I answered merely that you were not arrived yet."

"Thank you, Knebworth." Mary hurried up the steps to see what her friend had written that required such an immediate reply.

"Elizabeth, Mrs. Child is giving a grand ball at Osterley Park to open the season. It is in only three days' time, and Sarah is in a pelter that I reply. We will attend, will we not? The invitation is for you and Clement too." She held the card out to Elizabeth. "Well, actually, the invitation is to you and Clement, and I am included. But Sarah's note is to me."

"Pray, my dear, go calmly. Allow me to remove my traveling clothes before I open my social calendar." Elizabeth laughed. But a short time later a note was dispatched to Osterley Park that Mr. and Mrs. Clement Tudway, MP, and Miss Mary Tudway would be honored to accept Mrs. Child's invitation.

"What shall I wear, Elizabeth? Will my coral silk do? I have no notion of what is worn to a grand ball in London, but the lace is all Mechlin, and the silver embroidery on the skirt will be just the thing with the silver shoe buckles Rowland gave me. Perhaps we can fashion roses from silver tissue for my hair. Oh, my hair! I must have an appointment with a London hairdresser." Mary looked in the gilt oval mirror in her room and determined that her West Country coiffure would never do for London.

Elizabeth laughed. "We shall see to it all. I shall instruct Knebworth to begin interviewing abigails tomorrow morning. I can see that we shall require one that can serve as dresser also."

Two days later Elizabeth presented Mary with her new maid. Brickett had smooth pale hair, intelligent eyes, and a ready smile. She had lived in London for all of her thirty-five years and had served Lady Towton for twenty years before the lady's death in childbirth. "So I believe you may rely on her advice. I questioned her carefully, and she seems to be up on all the London ways." Spit jumped off his cushion and began sniffing at the newcomer. "Oh, and she likes dogs," Elizabeth added.

Not the least among the excellent Brickett's talents was a gift for hairdressing. On the afternoon of the ball she spent three hours arranging Mary's long brown tresses over masses of black wadding, pomading them, and then powdering the entire confection like the frosting on a cake. "There now, miss. I'll stake my reputation that you'll be the belle of the ball." Brickett surveyed her work.

"Thank you. You've done very well. And now I trust you to take good care of Spit in my absence."

"To be sure, miss." Brickett dropped a curtsey.

Hampstead Heath, which lay between London and the

palatial home of Robert Child, looked drab and desolate in its winter slumber. As the carriage rolled across the miles, Clement entertained the ladies with information on the sights they were to see. "The place belonged to Sir Thomas Gresham in the 1500s, but the present house is modern. Sir Thomas is said to have feasted Queen Elizabeth there and to have pulled down a wall in the night which she found fault with. The next morning when she saw that it was gone, she was highly pleased with a subject so anxious to please his sovereign."

"Have you been here before, Clement?" Mary asked.

"Yes, to a levee in honor of some foreign dignitary last year. I believe you were ill then, Elizabeth."

"Yes, and I was desolate at missing the grand sights. Osterley is all the talk of the great world."

"And you won't be disappointed, my dear," Clement assured her. "Every attempt has been made to recreate the classical age. Every decorative motif, statue, or wall painting was chosen to carry out a theme in Greek and Roman architecture or literature."

"But how was that achieved? Surely Mr. Child makes no pretense to classical scholarship."

"I believe Adam followed Robert Wood's *Ruins of Palmyra* most carefully. And he must have done well because Walpole declared the double-porticoed entrance to be as noble as the entrance gateway to the Acropolis at Athens."

Mary found herself sitting forward in her seat, as if to speed the carriage onward to this amazing sight.

"Osterley was conceived as a pantheon of the arts and sciences, and you will find each room decorated in praise of its own god or goddess—Bacchus for the dining room, Cupid and Venus for the state bedchamber, and so forth."

Mary tried to picture it all in her mind, but only achieved a muddle of images in which white marble statues and the paintings of Rubens floated amid rows of marble columns. The carriage swept through meadows hinting at their lush greenness to come, crossed a Roman bridge spanning a lake, and pulled up in front of the red brick mansion with its neoclassical temple portico. A double row of liveried footmen lined the broad entrance steps up to the portico, which was flanked by stone-carved statues of eagles with adders in their beaks—the Child family crest. They made Mary think briefly of the eagles in the countess's chapel. Nothing else in this ostentatious setting, however, reminded her of an austere religion, but rather, as Clement foretold, of the feasts and revels of Olympus.

They had just crossed the courtyard and were about to enter the hall when Sarah came skipping across the stone and slate floor to greet Mary. Sarah's high, powdered hair and lightly applied face paint were done to perfection, but she wore only a robe thrown on in haste over her petticoats. "Forgive my dishabille—I am so pleased you could arrive early. I haven't seen you for such ages, and I have three new London beaux. They shall all be here tonight! And Roger is arrived with his uncle and is most impatient to see you again—" Sarah interrupted her flow of chatter to remember her duty as a hostess. "Forgive me, Mr. Tudway, Mrs. Tudway. Welcome to Osterley House. My mama directed me to bid you welcome and suggest that you might like to refresh yourselves after your journey. A light collation has been set out for early arrivals. It is such a nuisance living so great a distance that one must drive upwards of two hours from London with the whole of that horrible heath between us. But Papa will not take a house in Grosvenor Square, no matter how much I beg. Stifford," she said to the butler standing by the door, "show Mr. and Mrs. Tudway to the eating room." She clasped Mary's hand and pulled her forward. "Come, we can have a gossip while Padlett dresses me. You have no notion how elegant my new gown is. I instructed Madame Egaltine it was to be the talk of the season."

"Wait!" Mary protested, breathless from just listening to her friend. "I want to look at the room."

"Oh, I forgot you haven't been to Osterley before. But let's not waste time in this tomb." She waved her arm at the magnificent hall, its gray walls ornately stuccoed with classical medallions, with statues and urns of flowers decorating the spaces between the narrow benches lining the walls. "I don't care a fig if it is supposed to be a Roman vestibulum like the Emperor Diocletian had in his palace—I think it's cold and drab."

In spite of the fires burning in fireplaces in alcoves at both ends of the hall, Sarah was quite right—the room was cold. "Come, I'll show you my favorite room. The bishop is staying there—he always does. Insists on a bedchamber on the ground floor so he can look out over the park, but I can show you the antechamber. We call it the tapestry room." She turned left out of the entrance hall and led Mary across a passage, turned left again, and then stopped.

"Ooh!" Mary gasped and stood silent for several moments. At last she ventured, "It's the most gorgeous—most elegant—most ornamented—" Again words failed her. The glowing red-and-gold Gobelin tapestries covering the walls were woven with garlands and urns of flowers so rich that Mary felt she must touch them to assure herself the room was not actually wreathed with living flowers. And in the center of each tapestry were woven medallions of Boucher paintings copied from those commissioned by Madame de Pompadour depicting the loves of the gods. Not only the wall hangings, but the overmantel, the fire screen, the carpet, and the upholstery of the gilt furniture were all woven in the same sumptuous pattern of flowers, birds, and love scenes. Mary felt she could stand there for hours, just drinking in the rich beauty.

"Pretty, isn't it?" Sarah asked. "But come, I must dress." She led Mary back across the entrance hall to the great staircase on the opposite side of the house. The stairs were set behind a screen of Corinthian columns with oil lanterns suspended between the tall white pillars, but Mary barely had time to glimpse them or the Grecian stucco work on the Wedgwood green walls as Sarah sped up the stairs, her gown billowing behind her.

"Sarah, is that you, my love?" Mrs. Child called from her dressing room, as the girls reached the top of the stairs.

"Yes, Mama." Sarah paused in her flight to step into her mother's chamber, Mary following close behind. While mother and daughter deliberated—should Mrs. Child wear the pearls and silk roses in her hair or the blue ribbons and feathers?—Mary surveyed the sapphire blue room with its lustring festoon window curtains and gilt wood cabinet displaying Mrs. Child's remarkable collection of gold filigree and Chinese black lacquer chests. But the centerpiece of the room was the scrollwork chimney piece and mantel mirror, which incorporated in its graceful design a delightful crayon portrait of Sarah made about seven years before when she was ten. The little girl's skin glowed petal-soft, and her large, brown eyes were lustrous. It was a charming picture; but more than that, Mary felt the prominence given to it in the room spoke clearly of how much the parents adored their only child.

Sarah, with Mary in tow, hurried down the hall to her room where Padlett waited to help her into the dress that was to make history that season. The gown was of white satin, embroidered with chenille twined with gold threads in the patterns of urns. The flowers filling the urns, however, were not of mere embroidery, but actual artificial flowers fashioned of pink silk and gold tissue. The dress indeed lived up to Sarah's report, but Mary already felt she had seen so much ornamented elegance her mind could take in no more.

By the time Padlett declared Miss Sarah to be "quite finished," Mary could hear the musicians tuning their instruments in the gallery stretching across the entire west front of the house. A steady crunch of carriage wheels on the gravel drive told her the ball was about to begin.

"Shall we go down?" Sarah pulled on long white kid gloves that covered her arms from fingertip to above the elbows and picked up her hand-painted Chinese fan. All the way back down the grand staircase, she talked of her suitors. "Lord Blandford—the son of the Duchess of Marlborough, you know—is frightfully handsome and an excellent sportsman. He's been terribly attentive ever since we returned from Bath. The Marquess of Graham perhaps cuts a better figure—I'm sure he makes a much finer leg in the drawing room—and I do believe he means to offer for me. Of course, Westmoreland is still about. I simply can't make up my mind which one to accept. I don't believe Papa approves of any of them, but I can't fathom why. They are all men of family, wealth, and position.

"Ah, here is Roger come to claim you before the dancing has even begun. Mary, I must warn you what a naughty fellow this is. A few nights ago he came in quite bagged after an evening of good company. It was most fortunate I sent for his man before his uncle caught sight of the matter. But I dealt with him most properly—gave him a sharp rap across the knuckles and upbraided him for being a wicked fellow and a sad wretch. Did I not do right, Mary?"

Mary smiled at Sarah and then at Roger, but she did not know what answer to give. She felt there was so much of the polite world she didn't understand, and at times she wasn't sure she wanted to.

Sarah rapped Roger's knuckles again with her fan. "La, sir, and here you are to be an improper fellow again and press your advantage of prior acquaintance upon Mary. I have invited men from all of London to dance with my friend. You must not monopolize her."

Smiling at Sarah's banter, Roger made a leg to the ladies, extending his right foot and bowing deeply to each one of them. "Indeed, I do claim the right of prior acquaintance. Miss Tudway, may I have the honor?" He extended his hand, and Mary took it to pass on to the door of the gallery where Stifford stood to announce each guest.

Mary danced the first cotillion with Roger and then sat on

one of the gold brocade sofas against the wall while Roger secured a glass of punch for her. Nearby Bishop Twysden was holding court with a number of dowagers.

"But charming—charming. I protest, my dear Mary, make an old man happy and sit with me." The bishop presented her to his company. "You must know that my nephew has eagerly awaited your arrival, Miss Tudway, as have we all. Do you find Osterley to your liking?"

"I find it breathtaking. The entire mansion looks like— like—" She surveyed the room of gorgeously attired people whirling in the intricate pattern of the dance. "It looks like a cotillion."

"Ah, an apt description, my child. I take it this is your first visit?"

"Yes, it is. Are you a frequent guest here?"

The bishop laughed and took a sip of claret from the long-stemmed glass. "You might say frequent, although I believe constant would be more accurate. I find the beauty offered here fills a deep spiritual need, and Mr. Child is a most gracious host." He spoke of his spiritual fulfillment in deep tones of ecclesiastical unction.

The ladies on the bishop's left required his attention, and Mary was happy simply to sit and observe. The Bath gatherings seemed restrained in comparison to the show of fashion here. And certainly there was no mingling of the classes here as the spa had allowed. *Surely*, she thought, *this is life at its best.* How right she had been to try to persuade Rowland to quit his gloomy pursuits. If only he could be here with her, he could see for himself and understand. Not that there was any need for him to abandon his calling to the church. Certainly no member of the company seemed to be enjoying himself more than the bishop. Mary watched as he accepted another glass of claret from a passing footman and continued flirting with the lady in a daring décolletage gown. Then Mary was jolted by her own thought. Surely she had been wrong to call the bishop's actions flirting.

No, he was merely entertaining the lady in a lively manner as became those in the great world.

Finally, a somewhat red-faced Roger appeared before her with a glass of negus. "Forgive my long absence, Miss Tudway. Rather than setting up a long banqueting table in the hall, Mrs. Child seems to have taken the eccentric notion of serving in the drawing room, the eating room, and in the breakfast room. Of course, the punch bowl was in the last room I tried."

Mary laughed. "Like a runner bearing a cup from Mount Olympus, you have returned victorious."

"Does that mean you will honor me with another dance?"

Mary would have preferred to sit and observe, but it did seem that Roger had earned his dance. This was a minuet, and Mary delighted in the slow graceful steps as she moved in rhythm to the music in three-quarter time, forward balancing, bowing, and pointing her toe, which exhibited her silver shoe buckles to perfection. At the conclusion of the number, however, she firmly insisted on the impropriety of granting Roger another and asked that he take her to Elizabeth. They found her in the gold damask-draped drawing room with its gilt plasterwork sunburst ceiling copied from the Temple of the Sun in Palmyra. "Come sit by me, my love." Elizabeth adjusted her skirt to make room for Mary on the gold brocade sofa. "My Lady Anstine was just explaining to me that the designs on the marquetry tables symbolize sacred and profane love."

Elizabeth presented Mary to her acquaintance, and the conversation continued. "On this medallion we see Diana, the chaste huntress, who could give herself only for true love. On the other table is Venus, goddess of a more—er, voluptuous love life." Lady Anstine continued her lecture, but a few minutes later Mary was borne away again, this time by a fluttering Sarah.

"Mary, you must come with me. I've never been in such a pother. Lord Graham has offered for me—I knew he was about to, but I had no idea it would create such a stir in me."

"Well, what did you answer him?"

"Why, naturally, I told him he must ask Papa. What other answer could I make? That is what has me so astir. I told him Papa might be found in his library; he doesn't care much for balls, and he always retreats for a cigar by this time of the evening." Sarah grasped Mary's hand and began pulling her down the passage past the great staircase. "Hurry, we may be too late to hear! My fate may be already sealed, and I know nothing of it!"

"But, Sarah, have you nothing to say to the matter? Do you love Lord Graham?"

Sarah stopped in her rush to stare at Mary. "Love! What has that to say to it? Mama says that will come much later—if it does at all. One must look to figure and fortune for a proper mate."

The flight continued until the sight of a retreating Lord Graham leaving the library with slumped shoulders told the girls they were too late. Mary was relieved. She had no taste for crouching in passages, listening at keyholes. Sarah flew right on into her father's room; but Mary, feeling an intruder on a family matter, stayed outside the door. As Sarah had left it wide open, however, there was no question of stooping to a keyhole to hear.

"Of course, I sent him packing, Sarah. You don't think I'd consent to your marrying a titled lord, do ye, miss?"

"But, of course, Father. Then I should become titled too. Wouldn't that be a fine thing? I thought you would be happy. Miss Marford's papa won't let her marry poor Mr. Winston, and they are quite desperately fond of one another. But Mr. Marford says that as she is not obliged to marry for money, she must marry for a title—it seems perfect sense to me."

"Of course, it is perfect sense for her. But think, daughter. Marford has six sons—each will marry and produce heirs to carry on the Marford name. You, my pretty, are my only chicken. I will not have the name of Child die out. Do you think I've built this house and our family fortune and our business at the Marygold for an heir to be named *Graham?*"

"But, Papa, what am I to do?"

"I will not have you becoming attached to a title, daughter! You will marry a plain man who will take my name and become my heir. Anyone encumbered with a title will have his own line to worry about. I'll have none of it."

Sarah opened her mouth to argue, but Mr. Child raised his hand. "Enough! And I'll just drop a hint to that starched-up Duchess of Marlborough that she might as well call off that puppy of hers. She'll have to rebuild her family fortune with some other heiress."

Mary didn't know Sarah was capable of walking so slowly. As they returned to the passage, Sarah negotiated each step by dragging the toe of her silk embroidered shoe, her chin dropped to her chest.

"Come, come." Mary felt far older than her three years seniority to Sarah. "You can't feel it so deeply. You said you didn't love Graham."

Sarah shrugged. "Graham doesn't matter. But I must marry someone. And I don't know anyone at all suitable who doesn't possess a title." She started back toward the music of the gallery and then stopped. "I can't face our guests, and it is so stuffy in here. Mary, let's just slip out to the temple for a moment. I need to collect myself."

From the window of Sarah's room, Mary had glimpsed the Doric garden temple in the west lawn just below the orangerie. Now lanterns among the trees and bushes made it appear indeed inviting. But Mary reminded her friend that the chill of the January night air was not at all inviting. "I can't face Padlett. She'll fuss on forever. Mary, you run up and tell her I want both of my fur-lined cloaks. Then we shall be as warm as grigs. I shall just dash on down to the temple very quickly. Meet me there."

"Sarah, you'll be taken with the ague if you get a chill."

Sarah laughed as she scampered across the lawn. "I'm very hearty. But hurry."

Mary did her friend's bidding. A few minutes later she descended the staircase wearing one fur cape and carrying

370

another. She dashed across the smooth lawn, hoping the damp grass wouldn't stain her kid shoes or the filigree silver buckles. She slowed her pace as she neared the little building with its four Doric columns across the front. She heard voices coming from inside and thought Sarah must be talking to herself—until a strong male voice rose in argument. Mary was unsure what to do. Should she creep away and leave her friend to shiver in the cold or risk intruding where she wasn't wanted?

As she paused, Sarah decided the matter for her. A trill of laughter rang out. "Oh, la, Westmoreland, I cannot possibly decide such a weighty matter when I am freezing to death. No gentleman would hold a lady at such a disadvantage."

"But if you would permit me to hold you in my arms—"

Mary stepped into the temple, Sarah's cape outstretched to her. Sarah snuggled into it gratefully. "Ah, sir, you are outdone. This is much warmer than your arms could be. You may leave us now. I thank you for bearing me company until my companion arrived."

Westmoreland took his congé in good grace, making a leg to each lady before he departed.

"Sarah, you were here *alone* with a man?"

Sarah giggled. "Well, you mustn't sound so fusty. You could hardly expect him to propose in front of the entire company, could you?"

"You mean Westmoreland just made you an offer?"

"Yes, he declared he had been hoping to get me alone all evening, and when he saw me leave by the side door, he followed me."

"And you told him to speak to your papa?"

"Indeed not. There's no good to come of that. I told him how the matter stood."

"And so you refused him?"

"Well, not precisely. I explained Papa's eccentricity, and Westmoreland begged me to elope with him. Wasn't that romantic of him?"

"Sarah! You didn't agree to such a thing?"

"Certainly not. I simply said I wouldn't elope without my father's permission."

Mary almost choked on a gurgle of surprise and amusement. "What kind of elopement is done with permission?"

"That's what Westmoreland demanded to know too. I told him I didn't know, but I love and respect my father. As much as I'm willing to forsake all others for Westmoreland, I won't wound or deceive my papa to do it."

When they returned to the gallery, Roger approached Mary to request another dance. She couldn't help noticing a certain unsteadiness as he made his leg. He had apparently been partaking too freely of Mr. Child's claret. She had no desire to dance with a half-flown partner and was relieved to be rescued by Elizabeth. "There you are, my dear. Clement is anxious we should be off. He has been told that there is a highwayman operating in the vicinity, and he doesn't wish to cross the heath in the wee hours of the morning."

Mary snuggled into a corner of the comfortable chaise with rugs tucked securely around her feet and legs to keep out any chill. She let the images of the evening dance through her head—the beauty, the elegance, the exhilaration; the flirting, the drunkenness, the shallowness. The excitement of her friend receiving two offers in one evening and the sadness that Mr. Child would never consent to either man.

Yet with all that, she couldn't help asking herself if the evening hadn't been the least bit flat, like a ship with no wind in its sail. Again she thought over the opulence and gaiety and wondered what was missing. And then she knew—Rowland was missing. How delightful it would have been if he had been there with her. His witty comments on the events and his warm eyes and twinkling smile were all it would have taken to make her evening complete.

But that could never be. Rowland would not approve of such an affair, and so she must choose between them.

She was jolted out of her reverie by the coach rolling to a stop. "What is it, Wheeler?" Clement opened the carriage door and called to his driver.

"Tree across the road, Mr. Tudway, sir."

"Well, clear it quickly! I don't fancy being stopped in the middle of the heath in the dark."

Wheeler had no more than climbed down off the box, however, when a dark-cloaked figure with a scarf over his face galloped up out of the darkness, a long-barreled pistol pointed at the passengers. "Stand and deliver!" he shouted. His voice was muffled by the scarf, but the words and his determination were clear enough. Clement stepped out of the coach. "And the ladies!" Elizabeth and Mary emerged also.

This time there was no delivering battle cry from a rescuer. The outlaw commanded Elizabeth to lay her necklace and diamond hair ornament in the bag he held out. Clement followed with his gold ring and the contents of his purse. By the steadiness with which this bandit held his pistol and the evident strength of his spirited horse, Mary thought it just as well there would be no rescue attempt this time. It was doubtful that such tactics would have scared off this iron-nerved robber. "And now, miss," he shouted.

"I'm not wearing any jewels," Mary replied, pulling back her cloak to demonstrate the fact. But as she did so, her skirt was also pulled back, and the moonlight shone on her silver buckles.

"Those will do well enough." The highwayman pointed his firearm at Mary's feet.

Not until that moment had she realized how much Rowland's gift meant to her. Her fingers trembled as she knelt in the dirt to slip the buckles off her shoes and place them beside Elizabeth's diamonds. Her last afternoon in Bath with Rowland came back to her, the fun of his companionship, the concern he showed for her, his kind friendship, and the joyous surprise of his gift.

She stepped forward, shaking a fist at the highwayman

who still kept his gun steadied on her. "How dare you! You should be ashamed! Those were a gift from a very dear friend. They won't mean a thing to you—you'll just melt them down into a little lump of silver and sell it for a few pennies. I would cherish them for the rest of my life. You're just a lazy bully preying on helpless people instead of earning an honest living. But don't worry, you'll get yours. Someday your soul will be required of you. God will—"

Two sharp shots split the air, and Mary cried out. Elizabeth screamed. Clement dragged both ladies into the carriage with a shout to Wheeler to drive on. The highwayman gave a triumphant, mocking shout of laughter as he clutched the valuables and spun his horse around to gallop across the heath.

"Mary, Mary, where are you hurt?" Elizabeth clasped her hand. "Mary, can you speak?"

Mary gave a shout of angry frustration. "Of course, I can speak! He only shot the ground beside me. But to think that I gave in to him like that. I'm so mortified! If only Spit had been with me, he should have shown that ruffian what for."

In the following days, Mary told the incident over and over again as she and Elizabeth made the endless round of social calls that filled their calendars. And every time she told the story, Mary was aware that she missed the cherished shoe ornaments far less than she missed the one who had given them to her.

*R*owland had progressed in his field preaching all the way down the country to the English Channel. In the port town of Exmouth, he rode his trusty little pony, whom he had christened Barnabas, to the dock area. He wanted to preach to the sailors who lounged around the quay resting up before their next sailing or waiting for casual labor. They were a weather-beaten lot, with eyes that had seen the sights offered by the seven seas and stomachs that had tasted the rum of every port. And they were not inclined to spend their afternoon being preached to.

Rowland stayed mounted on Barnabas and kept the seawall to his back, which protected his posterior from flying missiles and projected his voice forward above the surly catcalls. But at length he could see that nothing was to be gained by shouting them down. He held his hands in the air, a gesture which caused some of the more raucous to lower their voices. "My lads, I have no right over you. If you do not choose to hear me, I have no authority to force your attention; but I have traveled some miles for the sake of doing or receiving good. I have, therefore, a proposal to make to you. I always did admire British sailors, and I see here some able-bodied seamen. Some of you have no doubt seen a great deal of service and been in many a storm and perhaps in dangerous shipwrecks."

"Tha's right, matey."

"So ah 'ave!"

"Now, as I am very fond of hearing the adventures of seamen, my proposal is that some of you stand up and tell us what you have seen and suffered and what dangers you have escaped. I will sit and hear you out upon the condition that you agree to hear me afterward."

Coarse laughter filled the air and bounced against the seawall. "Do you stand up and give a lecture, Skegness."

Another called out, "Tha's a ticket, 'arry. Give 'im a sermon!"

The sailors laughed and Rowland laughed. Sitting patiently on Barnabas, his reins looped at ease, Rowland asked, "Will none of you fine adventurers take up my proposal?"

For the first time since his arrival, the quayside was quiet.

Rowland cleared his throat. "Well, I'll tell you then—you think me naught but a havey-cavey field preacher, one like as not to pitch a strange doctrine; but I came not long since from the University of Cambridge. If you had taken my proposal and heard me, I should have told you nothing but what is in the Bible or prayer book, even though I don't preach in a cathedral. I will tell you what I intended to say to you if you had heard me quietly, for I too have a story of seafaring adventure to recount to you."

And he went on to tell with robust detail of St. Paul's distresses. "Three times he suffered shipwreck. Once he spent a day and a night in the deep before rescue came. If you had chosen to listen to me preach, I should have told you the message this intrepid sailor bore." And to his spellbound crowd Rowland Hill began with a declaration of the grace and compassion of Christ in dying to save all penitent sinners. Then he led them to consider the thief on the cross, and then to the character and circumstances of the prodigal son and the compassion of his father.

His description of what he *meant* to have said riveted the attention of all, and more and more gathered around to hear. As he spoke, his hearers gradually drew nearer and nearer, hanging upon each other's shoulders as if they were on shipboard. In this position they listened with almost deathlike silence till he finished telling them what he should have said, if they had been willing to hear him.

He then took off his hat and made them a bow. "My fine men, I thank you for your courteous civility to me in allowing me to tell you what I should have liked to tell you."

An appreciative laugh reverberated against the wall, a far different tone than echoed earlier. "I say we give 'im three cheers!" an old salt near the front of the group yelled.

" 'ip 'urrah!"

" 'ip 'urrah!"

" 'ip 'urrah!"

On the final cheer the men threw their hats in the air and then scattered to retrieve them. But some remained to talk. "Never 'eard no preachin' like that."

"When will you come again, sir?" a surprisingly well-spoken midshipman asked.

Before Rowland could answer, a burly sailor stepped forward. "If you will come again, I say no one shall 'urt a 'air on you 'ead if I am on shore."

"I must ride on to Exeter tonight," Rowland replied. "But should I be able to come this way again, I would consider it an honor to have you serve as bodyguard."

"Oh, going to Exeter, is it? Goin' to take a dish o' tea with 'is Lordship, the bishop?"

Rowland laughed at the fellow's witticism and waved farewell, but inside he felt the tension of drawing near to Exeter. The wit had not been far from wrong. The Bishop of Exeter would be the sixth to receive an application for holy orders from Rowland Hill, A. M. of Cambridge University. He recalled

Berridge's words that when the time was right, ordination would come.

Well, he had gone out, following his pillar of cloud and fire, preaching wherever he could find hearers. And that had not been difficult through the late summer and harvest months. He had joined the harvesters in the field and preached to them at their horkey, attended harvest home festivals in village churches and preached in the new-mown fields afterwards. And through Advent and Christmas he preached wherever the village waits sang. He spoke of Christ's coming to earth as a babe and to the hearts of men as a Savior. But now the winter months drew on. His reduced allowance was not enough to cover lodging every night, and it was too cold to sleep in the fields where he preached. At one service the Methodist band had proposed to take an offering for the young itinerant. "I hope everyone will give at least a little," the gentleman taking the offering said.

"I hope everyone will give a great deal," Rowland said. They laughed as they turned out their pockets, and he lodged for a week on the generosity of that night.

Opposition and threats served as spurs to him, but as always, the moments of greatest discouragement for Rowland came from small attendance or lack of response at his meetings. Now the cold weather made attendance and response ever thinner. "Lord, what an unprofitable servant!" he prayed after many a sparse meeting. "Oh, that I might do better for the future."

If only he could receive ordination. Then he could preach in churches, he could return to his family, and he could speak to Mary—the three things he most wanted in this life, apart from the privilege of serving Christ.

As Barnabas plodded the eleven miles to the cathedral city, Rowland's thoughts were all of Mary. He knew there was much lacking in her spiritual commitment. He knew she sensed it vaguely, even if she would not admit it to him or to God. And he knew that God could take care of that lack. To the clop-clop of his pony's feet, he prayed for Mary. "If You made her for me, as I believe You did, make her also the woman for my calling, I pray. Visit her with Your grace. Enable her to open her heart to Your calling." His heart contracted as he thought of Mary because he knew that even if he received ordination, even if she seemed disposed to accept him, he could not take a wife who would oppose God's call for him. That thought followed him like a small black cloud all the way into Exeter.

Exeter Cathedral had been the seat of the bishop who held jurisdiction over Devon and Cornwall since the year 1050; for a hundred years before that, the site had been home to a monastic church. As he rode through the black and white Tudor close, Rowland prayed that in this place of great tradition of service to God and man he might at last come into harbor. He spent his last shillings on food and lodging at the inn and sent the boot boy round to the Bishop's Palace with a note requesting that he might call on Bishop Fullerton to be examined for ordination the following morning.

The reply was affirmative, so the next morning Rowland dressed with meticulous care in a coat newly pressed by the innkeeper's wife. Carrying his Bible, prayer book, and Cambridge papers, he walked round to the Palace.

He was shown into the bishop's study and welcomed with a degree of courtesy he had grown unaccustomed to meeting in the past months. But after the initial pleasantries and Bishop Fullerton's cursory perusal of Rowland's credentials, the interrogation began. "I am pleased to see that you took your university degree with some *eclat*. We need more clergymen with solid scholarship. But what of the report I have heard that in London you preached at the Tabernacle and at Tottenham Court Road Chapel?"

"That is true, sir. I have occasionally done so. I had the honor to be invited by Mr. George Whitefield to fill both those pulpits while I was a student."

The bishop shook his head slowly. "Does not the catechism teach us that our duty towards our neighbor is to submit to the king and to all that are put in authority under him—governors, teachers, spiritual pastors, and masters? To order ourselves lowly and reverently to all our betters? Have you not violated this in choosing to preach in places unconsecrated by the Church of England?"

"I hope not, sir. I love the Church of England. I am unalterably attached to her articles and liturgy."

"And you are not troubled with conscientious scruples in subscribing to them, as are many Methodists?"

"None, sir. I believe no person could ever exceed my admiration of the spirituality and beauty of the *Book of Common Prayer*." Rowland reverently rested his hand on that book as he spoke.

"And yet I have heard many reports of your preaching in fields and praying extempore. This is not showing submission to your spiritual masters."

"If it seems so, sir, it is because I put my duty to God first," Rowland spoke quietly.

"And what is your duty toward God?" the bishop catechized him.

Rowland answered in the words of the prayer book in a voice that told they were indeed the words of his heart also. "My duty toward God is to believe in Him, to hear Him, and to love Him with all my heart, with all my mind, with all my soul, and with all my strength; to worship Him, to give Him thanks, to put my whole trust in Him, to call upon Him, to honor His holy name and His Word, and to serve Him truly all the days of my life." As the bishop was silent, Rowland continued. "I believe I can best fulfill this duty and serve Him most truly by preaching. I long to be ordained that it might be within the church; but if that is not to be, I must do as my conscience tells me and preach without."

The bishop continued to sit in silence for long moments, the tips of his fingers pressed tightly together before his face. At last he spoke. "It grieves me to have to refuse so qualified and intent a young man, Mr. Hill. But I detect in you what I can only name as a spirit of rebellion to authority, which I believe to be of grave danger to yourself and to the church; and, therefore, I cannot sign your papers."

The bits of snow and frozen rain that flew at him were nothing compared to the icicles those words stabbed into Rowland's heart. As he made the torturously slow two-hundred-mile ride to London, he saw places where he might have held field services, villages where he knew farmers likely to loan their barns for his use, but he hadn't the spirit. For once his passion to preach was quenched. Without the heart to proclaim the Word of God, he had no heart for anything else. It was as if Barnabas carried him along the London road by his own volition.

And once there? Rowland had no desire to stay with Elizabeth and Clement, for he knew Mary was with them, and he could not face her in his hour of defeat. He considered going to the countess, but felt he would rather remain free of her authority. Perhaps the rooms maintained for itinerant preachers at the Tabernacle House in Moorfields? Able to think of no better plan, that was where he went.

The spacious edifice stood on the ground of the small shed Whitefield had erected thirty years before to assault the "vanity faire," as he called it, of holidayers who assembled in Moorfields for entertainment at booths and sideshows on fete days. There Whitefield recorded, "Three hundred fifty awakened souls were received into the Society in one day—numbers that formerly seemed to have been bred for the hangman were plucked as brands from the burning." As Rowland approached the large white building, he could only hope that he would find shelter for his weary soul as well as for his exhausted body.

And comfort was waiting there for him, in the form of a letter from his old friend Berridge. He flung his saddlebags across the single chair his room provided and sat on the hard bed, feeling warmed just by holding the letter and looking at its familiar hand. And the words brought more comfort.

My dear Rowly,

With desire that this may soon find its way into your reading, I shall address this to you at the Tabernacle, where I am sure you will receive it when your path takes you to London. I have heard of your many hardships. I look upon your present trials as a happy omen of future service. If you continue waiting and praying, a door will open by and by. Be not solicitous about orders. When the time is right, they will drop into your lap. I would observe, concerning your present situation, that it may possibly grow more dark before it clears up. The darkest moment in the whole *nucthemeron* is just before break of day.

Many souls here remember with joy and gratitude the happy times they enjoyed under your ministry. Further, I have received word from my friend in Bristol who reports that "from the Sabbath on which I had the pleasure to introduce Hill in the chapel pulpit, religion has been reviving through his instrumentality, and the flame has burned strong ever since. Other instruments may have helped, but it began with him."

It is without doubt, my dear Rowly, that the Lord has blessed the truth you have delivered to hundreds, nay, to thousands. I earnestly entreat you to continue in your work, as multitudes everywhere long for the time when they should hear you again. Many I have visited on their sickbeds bless God for the time they heard you, and I know of whole families stirred up to seek the Lord by your ministry.

I continue,

Yr friend in the faith,
J. Berridge

Rowland read the letter three times. Each time the smile on his face grew wider. He would have read it again, but the bells announcing time for service began to peal. Rowland Hill was to preach tonight, and he must wash the dust of the road off his hands and face first.

It was the bells of St. Marylebone that Mary heard a few days later, as the Tudway carriage bore Elizabeth and her sister-in-law to Lady Anstine's home in Portman Square. As soon as the callers had been served dishes of bohea in Milady's best china, their hostess questioned them excitedly about the young preacher who was causing such a stir. "Lady Huntingdon is demanding all her friends accompany her to hear him. I haven't done so yet, but I doubt I can hold out against Her Ladyship any longer. But I simply *must* know, my dear Elizabeth—can he be a relative of yours? I know you are the daughter of Sir Richard Hill, and all the world says that the preacher is the son of a baronet. Can there be more than one Hill so titled?"

Elizabeth shook her carefully coiffured head. "I believe not, Lady Anstine. Rowland Hill is indeed my brother. But that he should be in London and causing a stir with his preaching astounds me. I have heard nothing of it."

Lady Anstine was clearly pleased that she should serve as informant on the person leading the gossip sheets of London society. "Well, I pride myself on staying abreast of the news." She refilled her callers' delicate handleless tea dishes. "But you must be most anxious to hear him. Shall I send a note to Her Ladyship that you will make up her party tonight? I believe the preaching is to be in Tottenham Court Road Chapel." She crossed to the fireplace and looked through several cards set there. "Ah, yes, here is Her Ladyship's card. Yes, at the chapel. I believe that is the place Dr. Johnson called 'Mr. Whitefield's soul trap.'"

As Elizabeth had no other engagements for that night, the matter was settled. Mary approached the evening with trepidation. She longed, yet feared, to see Rowland. If her heart had been in a turmoil the past weeks with him off in another part of the country, what would it be like now to come suddenly face to face with him after so many months apart? She was at times able to put him out of her mind for quite a whole day at a stretch, but to be with him again and to hear him preach once more would end the tenuous peace she had achieved.

The turmoil she dreaded began even before she saw Rowland, for the countess could talk of nothing else. "The popularity of Mr. Hill and the crowds that follow him wherever he preaches overwhelm me with astonishment and gratitude to the God of all grace, who has endowed him with such gifts."

Mary looked around at the large chapel chock-full of those who had come to hear the preacher. The countess's words were true. Adding much to Mary's amazement, the congregation drew from all classes of society. The poor who lived in the alleys of Tottenham Court Road sat on the back benches and under the galleries; actors from nearby theaters and music halls, their bright clothing and face paint proclaiming their profession, filled the galleries; and those of the quality, as in Lady Huntingdon's party, occupied the front pews.

"I am so pleased you have come to town," Lady Selina said to Mary in her soft voice. "I shall see that Mama sends you a card for her next drawing room. It is to be a very special one." From the smile she gave Colonel Hastings sitting beside her, Mary had little doubt as to the purpose of that occasion. She assured Selina she would be delighted to receive the invitation.

Then the countess's voice claimed Mary's attention again. "Rowland boldly proclaims the doctrines of the cross, and the Word of the Lord is glorified in the conversion of multitudes. Dear Captain Joss told me above a hundred awakened souls—the fruits of his preaching—have been received into the Tabernacle Society—so eminently does the benediction of our dear and precious Emmanuel rest on the labors of His servant. Excepting my beloved and lamented Mr. Whitefield, I never witnessed any person's preaching wherein there was such display of the divine power and glory as in Mr. Hill's. I believe him to be a second Whitefield."

Mary paid scant attention to the singing of the hymn, so anxious was she to hear Rowland. When the music ended, he took his place in the pulpit. The fact that he wore a froth of white lace at his neck, rather than the severe Geneva bands of the clergy, proclaimed him to be yet unordained. Mary was shocked that the fact should strike her so deeply. Wasn't this what she had wanted—that he should be refused on grounds of his enthusiasm, until he came to see he must join the established church? But now as she saw him standing tall and dignified before her, she was glad he had not denied his belief, and she shared what she knew must be his hurt at being denied orders.

"Matches! Matches! Matches!" This startling cry began Rowland's sermon. He had everyone's attention.

"You may wonder at my text. This morning while I was engaged in my study, the devil whispered to me, 'Rowland, your zeal is indeed noble, and how indefatigably you labor for the salvation of souls.' At that very moment a man passed under my window crying, 'Matches! Matches!' And conscience said to me, 'Rowland, you never labored to save souls with half the zeal this man does to sell matches.'"

He then went immediately to the heart of his sermon. "How happy is the man that can assume this character to himself—a sinner saved! Stop and consider—is it you? Oh, then, what miracles of mercies have been revealed to your heart! The world by nature knows nothing of our Emmanuel; but the convinced sinner knows that he is lost without Him. He sees that he cannot be more completely fallen or more certain of destruction than he is in himself. This strikes at the root of all his self-righteous pride and compels him to cry out as with the prophet of old, 'Woe is me, for I am undone!'"

This strikes at the root of all self-righteous pride. Mary shifted in her seat, hoping that the stab those words brought to her heart was mere coincidence. Pride was not her problem, and she was not a sinner. Why should she feel uneasy?

"The sinner now trembles at justice and prays for mercy," Rowland continued. "His hopes from a covenant of works now fall to the ground. Then it is that the Spirit divinely convinces of the work of Jesus; the sinner sees it and is enabled, as his faith increases, to rest satisfied with the fullness of the work of Christ;

he rejoices in the dignity of it and is happy in its security. This teaches him boldly to renounce all his *homespun righteousness;* he dares not bring it as a condition at first or as a wretched adjunct to complete the whole at last. No. He renounces it *wholesale* and is enabled to rest only upon Jesus as his everlasting all."

Homespun righteousness? How dare he so characterize her faith built on all the teachings and rituals of the church! Temper pushed away Mary's tender feelings. Were it not for the throng around her, she would have told Mr. Rowland Hill just what she thought of *his* homespun religion lacking any stained glass or incense or embroidered vestments.

But the preacher continued. "So does this new man renounce the law? Yes. As a covenant of works unto salvation, he renounces it altogether. For he is under the law of Christ, and love to Christ makes him return obedience as his privilege. Besides, Christ has given him an obedient heart. How blessed are they then who believe in Jesus; they have all things, the best of things, and all too for nothing—the free gift of God."

And thus, after an invitation to those who wished to seek Christ to come forward for prayer, the service closed. At least, Mary thought, she had avoided the confusion she feared the preaching might arouse in her. She was more solidly convinced of her position than ever before. And she would so inform Mr. Hill at her earliest opportunity.

That opportunity came sooner than she thought. Rowland, who had seen the countess's guests from the pulpit, came to them directly after the service. After he greeted Her Ladyship and his sister, he turned to Mary. "I am happy to see you here tonight, Mary. I trust you enjoyed the service."

"Enjoyed it? Sir, I have never been so insulted—that you should accuse me of being proud and homespun. The bishops were right to refuse you."

"And because you refuse *me,* Mary, will you also refuse

Christ?" His voice was soft, and his intense brown eyes glowed with a warmth Mary found disconcerting.

"Certainly not! I don't refuse Christ or His church—it is you who do that."

Rowland moved as if he would take her hand and then stopped abruptly. "No, Mary. I will never do that. If the church refuses me to the end of my days, I will never refuse it. To acknowledge a higher Master is not to refuse His earthly instruments. But we must keep them in perspective. The rubric of the church is not our highest authority."

With a shake of her head Mary shifted the subject. "La, you should hear the countess sing your praises. Do you turn your back on preaching to the aristocracy? Do you mean to spend the rest of your life in Tottenham Court Road?"

It was as if she had asked a question he had longed to answer. "Mary, let me show you where I hope to minister. May I call for you tomorrow morning?"

"Yes, of course."

The next morning Mary insisted that Brickett arrange her hair as carefully as for any ball, and she chose her most elegant morning gown and most richly adorned hat. She was determined to show Mr. Rowland Hill what she thought of his Methodist ways. But the choice of a cloak brought her into conflict with her dresser. "Brickett, I'll have none of that heavy fur-lined cloak. What's the good of wearing my blue silk gown if I'm to cover all its lace and embroidery with black wool and beaver?"

"But, miss, the wind is exceedingly sharp today, and it looks as if it might rain."

"I shan't get wet in a closed carriage, Brickett. I shall wear my blue velvet shoulder cape."

But when Rowland called for her a few minutes later, it was not in an enclosed chaise as she had imagined, but in an open carriage. He apologized for his inability to provide a more elegant conveyance, but explained that he had been traveling on horseback, and this vehicle was the only one available from the Tabernacle stables.

Mary felt it a point of pride not to squabble over a mere detail. "The carriage will do quite well. And you can put the calash up if the weather turns nasty."

They drove through the heart of London, passed St. James Park, and crossed the Thames by Westminster Bridge. On the south side of the river the buildings immediately became shabbier, the children playing in the street dirtier, and lanes leading off the main road muddier. It seemed that a gin shop stood on every corner. "This is where you would choose to minister? Before we crossed the bridge, I had hoped you were taking me to Westminster Abbey." It wasn't just the chill in the air that caused Mary to pull her cape closer around her shoulders.

At the corner of Westminster Bridge Road and Blackfriars Road, Rowland pulled the carriage to a stop. Mary looked at the shabby neighborhood in dismay. "Here?" she asked in a small, choked voice.

"Here. With the Lord's help I would erect a standard for the gospel in the very middle of the devil's dominion. This is one of the worst spots in London. What fine soil for plowing and sowing!"

Mary could only shake her head.

"The Scripture says that those who are well have no need of a physician, but those who are sick do. Can you imagine a place more truly answering that purpose?"

Mary again shook her head, her eyes wide with horror at the poverty and depravity around her.

"I would go into the very stronghold of the devil's territory." Rowland pointed to two men in a drunken stupor on a doorstep, a jug of gin between them. "And I would build the chapel in circular form so the devil should not have a corner in it."

For the first time since the service the day before, Mary

laughed. "I am satisfied that if he entered, you could chase him out. And what else would you do?"

Three urchins, two boys and a smaller girl, walked by, staring at the elegant carriage. Mary opened her purse and tossed them each a halfpenny. They grabbed the coins with whoops of delight and darted off down the alley. "Start a ragged school," Rowland answered her question. "We should get at the children as soon as we can. The devil begins soon enough. If possible, let us steal a march on him."

Again Mary laughed. This was not at all what she had wanted to see, not what she wished for Rowland's future—whether she was to be part of it or not. And yet when she was with him, heard his excitement, she couldn't help but catch a bit of his vision. "And have you a name for this mighty work you would build?"

"I would call it Surrey Chapel, as belonging to all in the county." Then his voice became quietly serious. "I would pray that the worship of God in Surrey Chapel might prove the beginning of happy days to thousands who are already born of God and the cause of future joy to tens of thousands who are yet dead in sin."

Mary laughed at his solemnity. "In faith, Rowly, no one could ever accuse you of too small a vision."

They were halfway across the bridge when the rain began. Rowland couldn't stop on the bridge to put up the hood, and they were thoroughly soaked by the time they found a place to pull over in the traffic around Westminster Palace.

One result of Mary's outing with Rowland was that later that week when she again made the journey across Hampstead Heath to attend Mrs. Child's dinner party, she had a sniffle that threatened an unbecoming redness to her nose.

But the other result caused her more concern. She was more convinced than ever that Rowland's course was wrong and that if he bullheadedly insisted on following it, she should have none of him. And yet when she thought of the passion of his words in the pulpit, of the challenge of his plans for the future, of the pleasure she always felt in being with him . . . but no, that would not do. She must harden her heart to such thoughts.

It was Roger, favorite of the Child family and heir of Bishop Twysden, who could offer her the lifestyle she had determined on. And tonight she would put herself out to be all he could wish for in a companion.

*U*nder Mrs. Child's creative guidance, Osterley House had been transformed for the evening's festivities. A veritable wall of flowers and trees from the orangerie screened the hall from the eyes of arriving guests, who were escorted by elegantly clad footmen to the drawing room and invited to promenade in the long gallery where a harpist played for their entertainment.

Mary began her stroll down the length of the gallery on her brother's arm. They had paused to admire Van Dyke's equestrian portrait of Charles I on the south wall when Roger, in an elegant robin's-egg-blue coat and matching breeches lavishly trimmed with silver frogs and metallic lace, made an excessively fine leg to Mary, accompanied by three flourishes of his lace-trimmed handkerchief. "Miss Tudway, may I have the honor of escorting you to the other end of the room to view Rubens's portrait of the Duke of Buckingham? I find it a far more interesting work than this."

Clement placed Mary's hand on Roger's outstretched wrist and bowed them on their way. In keeping with her new determination, Mary smiled at Roger. "I believe we are quite well enough acquainted that you might call me Mary, sir." She gave a flutter of her painted silk fan like a practiced coquette, but she did not feel entirely comfortable in the role.

Mary smiled and nodded to all of Roger's witty comments as they sauntered the length of the room. All the while she wondered why she couldn't relax and flirt and laugh like Sarah, who was at the center of a group of male admirers on the other side of the room. Why must she be different? Why must snatches of sermons and visions of urchins joyfully clutching her halfpennies invade her thoughts at a time like this? Why must she think of Rowland Hill when she was trying to think only of Roger Twysden and his elegant manners?

"Ah, Uncle, I have brought Mary to view the same painting I see you admiring."

Mary dropped a curtsey to the bishop as Roger continued. "You will note I am making progress in my siege upon her heart. She has granted me the favor of calling her by her Christian name."

"In faith, it is a pretty girl, Nephew." Bishop Twysden held his hand out for Mary to bow over. "May I hope we might soon address you in nearer terms yet?"

Mary laughed and fluttered her fan, but the unmistakable meaning of those words alarmed her. It was the plan she too had fixed on, but she was not prepared to plunge so far so quickly. Fortunately, she was rescued by the butler announcing that dinner was served. Mrs. Child, on the arm of the guest of honor, led the way into the gray and white hall, which tonight not even the meanest could characterize as cold or dull. Long banqueting tables set in a U-shape were so heavily laden with flowers, candelabra, epergnes of fruit and sweetmeats, gold cutlery, and crystal that Mary marveled there was room for the guests to dine.

But the jewels of the guests far out-glittered even the cut crystal and gold and silver plates. Mary was sure she had never seen so fine a display, not even when Miss Fossbenner had taken her to see the crown jewels in the Tower of London years ago. Her hand went unconsciously to the single strand of Elizabeth's pearls she had borrowed for the evening, and she hoped she might not encounter the highwayman of Hampstead Heath. Certainly with such rich enticement as this, however, it was no wonder the villain was tempted to work that lonely road.

But then the footmen presented the first course of stuffed partridges, Scotch salmon, rice pilau, and pickled mangoes. Mary enjoyed the foreign delicacies, although the turtle steaks that followed were not half so fine as those they had regularly at The Cedars.

Roger, seated to her right, kept up a pleasant flow of social chatter, to which she replied evenly until he paused and considered her. "Mary, is something troubling you? You seem distracted. Is there any way I might be of service?"

She gave a bright but slightly forced laugh. "La, sir. I beg your forgiveness if it is making me a poor companion, but I will admit to a bit of unease at the thought of our return journey across the heath. Did you know we were accosted by that villainous highwayman last month?"

Roger blanched in his quick concern for her. "No, Mary. I had not heard. Were you hurt?"

Mary shook her head.

"But, my dear, it must have been exceedingly alarming for you! Did you lose much to the vile fellow?"

"Clement and Elizabeth were relieved of some gold and jewels. I lost only my silver shoe buckles. They were not of excessive value, but I had a great sentimental attachment to them as they had been the gift of—er, a dear friend."

"Oh, this is infamous that such rapscallions should be allowed to live! May I add my person to your escort tonight? I fancy I'm a fair shot, and I'd like a chance at the scoundrel."

"Indeed, you are most kind, Roger. I thank you, but Clement has provided himself and his coachman with extra arms and hired two postillions, so I fancy we'll be quite safe." She paused for a bite of macaroni Parmesan brought in from Italy, and then continued with a sigh, "But I fear all the precautions in the world can't restore my buckles."

The footmen brought in the second course, and it was now time for the ladies to turn and converse with the person on the other side. A young captain in His Majesty's Light Dragoons was seated on Mary's left. He had recently returned from service in the American colonies.

"My regiment was quartered in Boston with orders to watch out for smuggling, as the colonials take a very dim view of the import duties passed by Parliament."

"Were you treated badly?"

"Not on the whole. There are many loyal Tories in Boston who entertained us very well. But Sam Adams and his so-called Sons of Liberty were quite another matter. Always stirring up feeling against King George. We had one bit of excitement when a crowd of jeering ruffians began throwing snowballs at a group of our men. When the snowballs turned to stones and the rabble's taunts went beyond endurance, the men used their guns."

Mary's eyes grew wide with alarm. "But, sir, was anyone hurt?"

The soldier recalled himself. "Forgive me, miss. I fear I was carried away with my soldier's tales. This is not a fit topic for a lady's ears."

"Fa, Captain, you've begun the story; you must finish it."

The captain answered quietly, "Five were killed. I should not have spoken of it. Politics are not for polite company, but I have been so long away I forgot myself."

But Mr. Child, who had caught the drift of the conversation from the top of the table and was bothered neither by rules of conversing with the proper partner nor of keeping to proper topics, took up the subject of business which was never far from his mind. "Captain Felsham, are they such rabble, those colonists? What will come of my investment in the East India Company's tea business? It was hoped Lord North's plan to ship tea directly to America without paying duty at other British ports would keep the colonists happily buying our cheaper tea and drinking the company out of financial difficulty. But so far we've not had the returns we hoped for."

Captain Felsham shook his head. "I set sail several months ago, sir. But I believe the general feeling in the colonies at the time was that the move was an attempt to bribe them into accepting the principle of Parliamentary taxation."

"But why would they refuse to buy cheaper tea?" Mary asked. "Was not the quality as good?"

"The finest Darjeeling and Ceylon, miss. But they are an independent lot over there. They say they will not pay one penny of tax they have not voted for."

Several of the ladies were showing their displeasure that such unseemly topics should be discussed in their hearing, so the conversation returned to polite topics. Mary found herself unable to finish her servings of veal escalope with lemon and fish baked in pastry. During the last course her tendency to sniffle had been growing more and more severe, and now a headache was beginning at the back of her eyes. She had no intention of missing the final course where her favorite almond sweetmeats were sure to be served, but she felt she must get away for a moment and thoroughly blow her nose.

As Roger had left the table several minutes before, she signaled a footman. They were stationed every few feet around the room for the purpose of helping guests with their chairs should they wish to leave the table during the long evening of dining and drinking. Mary slipped quickly into the south passage nearest her end of the table and then stood wondering where she should go. She had first thought of Sarah's bedroom, but that was away on the other side of the house and up the great staircase. Then she thought of the Etruscan dressing room off the state bedchamber which she had glimpsed briefly on Sarah's whirlwind tour on her first visit. The footman who took their wraps had told Clement the gentlemen's cloaks and greatcoats were being put there, so it should be unoccupied now.

She slipped quietly down the passage and paused in the doorway to admire the decoration of terra cotta and black arabesque trellis work against a pale blue background, which gave the room the effect of an open Roman loggia. Then a sharp click from a window alcove told her she was not alone. She looked in the direction of the sound, and her startled expression relaxed into a smile. "Roger, what are you doing in here?" But then her eyes grew alarmed again as she saw that he held a long-barreled pistol. "Roger—"

He laid the firearm beside an Etruscan vase on the mantelpiece and came toward her, smiling. "Our conversation about the highwayman concerned me, my dear Mary. As most of the gentlemen carry their firearms inside their cloaks, I thought it would be best to be certain they were all loaded."

"But why didn't you just tell them to check their own?"

"And alarm everyone needlessly? I thought it much better to see to it quietly myself."

By this time Mary was quite desperate to use her handkerchief, so she merely nodded. "Yes. I shall join you in the hall soon, Roger."

Taking that for his dismissal, Roger left her alone. A few minutes later when she returned to the banquet, the courses had been changed. A silver platter arranged with a high pyramid of almond sweetmeats was being handed round. Mary savored a castle-shaped marzipan and turned toward the head of the table where Rapid Westmoreland was entertaining the ladies by engaging their host in bantering conversation.

"But, Child, it isn't always that easy. What if you were in love with a girl, and her father denied you permission to marry her? What would you do?"

Always the man of strong action, Child answered readily, "Why, I'd run off with her, to be sure!"

With an amused glitter in his eye, Westmoreland raised his glass to Mr. Child while the ladies applauded his answer and giggled behind their fans.

Shortly after that, Mrs. Child withdrew and led the ladies up to her dressing room where they might repair their face paint and coiffures and refresh themselves with tea until the gentlemen finished their brandy and any further political discussion. Mary, whose headache had increased, sat quietly by Elizabeth in spite of Sarah's attempts to draw her into conversation. Mary was not displeased when their coach was one of the first to be called for. And she was further relieved when neither Roger nor his uncle appeared to bid her farewell and hand her into the coach. She was quite content just to sink against the cushions and sleep all the way back across Hampstead Heath without giving a second thought to highwaymen or other alarms.

The next afternoon, after downing three doses of a nasty elixir mixed by Brickett and spending the morning tucked up comfortably by the fire, she felt well enough to accompany Elizabeth on a call to Lady Anstine.

Lady Anstine, who had attended a ball at court instead of the Osterley banquet, was all aflutter to hear every detail of the event; but Elizabeth had barely begun when their hostess interrupted, "Oh, but did you hear of the highwayman last night?"

Elizabeth and Mary both shook their heads. "It's shocking. Three coaches of guests from Osterley were robbed of their jewels on their return journey. One carriage was escorted by an intrepid Dragoon captain. He fired on the thief, but his gun misfired. Lady Houseton called here earlier. She said her husband attempted to fire on the rascal too, but his charges had been drawn."

"But Roger—" Mary paused in confusion.

"Yes, my dear, what did you say?" Elizabeth encouraged her.

"Oh, what a pity I interrupted him. Roger Twysden said he feared just such a thing might happen, and he checked on the gentlemen's firearms. If I hadn't interrupted his work, we might have had an end of the highwayman last night."

Elizabeth continued with her description of the evening, and then the conversation shifted to the next event on the social calendar—the Countess of Huntingdon's drawing room. "I believe this one is to be a purely social affair. I do hope so," Lady Anstine sighed. "I went quite unaware one time when George Whitefield preached. He was indeed a fine, entertaining preacher, but imagine my surprise when I had intended to spend the afternoon with light gossip and a little music. I'm better acquainted with Her Ladyship's ways now, however," she said with a laugh.

The following week early crocuses were in bloom in Hyde Park along Park Lane, which fronted the Countess of Huntingdon's London home. Mary arrived for the levee in the midst of a throng of fashionable carriages. As soon as she was inside, she did not need the direction of the footman to send her up the curving marble staircase, for the brilliant tones of a harpsichord drew her up to the green and rose damask drawing room. An elegant woman wearing a lapis-blue gown trimmed in French lace with a small lace cap on her dark curls was entertaining a group gathered near the harpsichord in the north end of the room. Lady Selina, looking radiant in a delicately embroidered rose silk gown, greeted Mary and then nodded toward the musician. "Isn't she marvelous? Have you met her? Catherine Ferrar. Her husband is the tall clergyman standing by the window smiling at her. He's Mama's chaplain at Tunbridge Wells. She's a daughter of old Vincent Peronnet whom they call the Archbishop of Methodism." The harpsichord switched from the Haydn air to a familiar majestic melody, but Mary couldn't place the tune. "'All Hail the Power of Jesus' Name,'" Selina said. "Her brother wrote it."

Mary smiled and nodded in recognition, and the two stepped closer to the group around the musician. At the end of the number, the listeners applauded. Mary was so intent on watching the tall clergyman approach Catherine at the harpsichord and thinking what a striking couple they made that she failed to notice the gentleman approaching her and Lady Selina, until Rowland made his presence known with a bow. "No ill effects from your wetting, I hope?" he inquired after the initial round of greetings.

His smile never failed to draw one from Mary, no matter how determined she might be to show displeasure.

"I'll admit to nothing more than a mild case of the sniffles. And may that be the worst I ever receive in your company, sir."

She meant it as a set-down, but his laugh and hearty agreement spoiled her effect.

Then the countess stood at the front of the room and cleared her throat sharply for attention. "My friends, I thank you for joining me here today on this happy occasion. I and my son, Francis the Earl of Huntingdon, do announce the engagement and forthcoming marriage of my daughter, Lady Selina, to Colonel George Hastings." A murmur of approval, delighted exclamations, and a scattering of applause met the announcement, as well as a hearty "Hear! Hear!" from some of Colonel Hastings's fellow officers. But the countess had more serious ideas for this occasion than cheering. As Lady Selina and her colonel stepped forward, both radiant with smiles, Her Ladyship held up her hands as if pronouncing a blessing and prayed, "God the Father, God the Son, God the Holy Ghost bless, preserve, and keep you; the Lord mercifully with His favor look upon you and so fill you with all spiritual benediction and grace that you may so live together in this life that in the world to come you may have life everlasting. Amen."

Many of the guests repeated the amen. Then they lifted the long-stemmed glasses of punch the footmen were handing around and toasted the happy couple with repeated wishes for prosperity and long life.

Rowland drew Mary from the center of the activity to introduce her to Catherine and Philip Ferrar.

"Your music is exquisite. I hope you'll play more for us." Mary smiled at Catherine.

Catherine responded warmly, and soon the women were deep in conversation about Catherine's life in London and

Tunbridge Wells and her active brood of six children. "They are a great delight, although I'd rather not rival my mother who had twelve children," Catherine laughed.

But the men's conversation was more serious. Rowland began telling Philip, who often preached at John Wesley's Foundery for the Methodist Society, of his repeated refusals for ordination. He described that last, most cutting blow of being refused for his having preached in the Tabernacle and at Tottenham Court Road Chapel. "I suppose they would not let St. Paul, if he were to come upon earth now, preach in his own cathedral," he concluded. Philip laughed.

"But do not cease trying." Philip returned to his former gravity. "I do not say that lightly. Although I had no trouble over ordination, I was removed from my first curacy for my Methodist ways, and for several years I was refused living after living until I despaired of ever having a place of my own to minister."

"And I despaired of ever having a husband." Catherine joined the conversation. "He would not ask for my hand without a living, and yet with each living that was denied, I seemed to grow fonder of him. It was a most unhappy coil. But I am sure it will all come right for you if you don't give up."

"Perhaps someday there will be a bishop who believes in a personal God as we do, but until that day we must do the best work we can with what we have," Philip said.

Rowland shook his head. "I do hope I won't have to wait for a far-off miracle before I can receive orders."

Mary was thoughtful for a moment. "Why have you not applied to the Bishop of Wells?"

"No particular reason. They are all alike. He has simply not crossed my itinerary," Rowland replied.

But that night Mary determined that Bishop Willes of the dioceses of Bath and Wells should be on Rowland Hill's itinerary. Never mind what she thought of Rowland's theological enthusiasm—the situation was intolerable, and she had no patience with what she saw to be a grave injustice. She wrote to her papa before she even allowed Brickett to get her ready for bed that night.

Dearest Papa,

To such a deplorable apostasy is the world come that young men who are steadfastly attached to the church and live exemplary lives can hardly get their testimonials signed for orders.

I doubt not but that you can set this situation to rights, at least in the matter of our brother-in-law, Rowland Hill. You know him to be a young man of zeal, untiring labors, and excellent family. You also know the expansive benevolence of his heart. He is an extraordinary person—far too good to be left standing in a field.

Will not you speak to Bishop Willes on his behalf? Surely the bishop can be made to see sense in the matter and forgive what others have termed youthful enthusiasms.

We continue well at Devonshire Place. Clement is much taken up with Parliamentary matters and I am

Yr loving and obedient daughter,
Mary Tudway

She went off in search of Clement for a frank for her letter, feeling exceedingly self-satisfied.

It was only when she thought over the fine things she had said about Rowland and her own determination to refuse him that her smugness wavered. Catherine Ferrar appeared to be a woman of accomplishment and fashion, yet she was not unhappy with her Methodist husband. And Mary knew that by forcing the issue of Rowland's ordination, she was also forcing the issue of her own commitment. He had more than once told her that when he was ordained, he would speak his heart.

The thought of hurting him with her refusal stabbed her heart with a physical pain.

*T*he conflict within Mary lasted several days. Then a note came from Sarah begging her to visit Osterley. "Mama is to give a musical evening *en masquerade*, so be sure to pack a domino and mask. Please do not delay—I have something most particular to tell you."

The delight of returning to Osterley, of being with Sarah, and of preparing for a masquerade drove all shadow of the doldrums from Mary's mind. Elizabeth consented to the plan, although she was less than pleased with part of the scheme. "Mary, I must tell you that I am not entirely happy with sending you to a masquerade. I can't think what your mother might say to it. I expect it will be perfectly respectable under Mrs. Child's supervision, but you must know that many seize upon such occasions to behave in a way they would not if they were recognizable."

"La, Elizabeth, you are talking like Lady Huntingdon. I promise not to flirt with any married men. And Spit shall be with me—he can warn off anyone who attempts to make too free."

Such a shocking thought, delivered even in jest, silenced Elizabeth.

Clement's coach carried Mary, Brickett, and Spit to Osterley early on the morning of the rout, complete with portmanteau bearing a long peach satin domino full enough to cover the widest hoop and a white satin half-mask on a stick in the shape of a butterfly trimmed with brilliants.

Sarah flew to meet her friend and dragged Mary directly to her own room with orders to Stifford to send Miss Tudway's luggage on to the yellow taffeta bedroom. As soon as the door was closed, Sarah flung her arms around Mary and cried, "You'll never guess! It's so excessively famous—the most romantic adventure you can imagine!"

Mary looked at her friend in bewilderment.

"I'm to elope!" Sarah cried. She clapped her hands over her mouth to muffle her squeals of delight.

Mary could only stare.

"Isn't it all too marvelous! My dear Westmoreland has convinced me it's the only thing for us. And Papa gave his permission—in a manner of speaking."

"But, Sarah." Mary sank into a chair. "The scandal—it's not at all proper!"

Sarah gave a gurgle of laughter. "Mary, if I'd thought you so starchy, I wouldn't have told you. But you know Papa will never give his consent to my marrying a title, and Westmoreland is quite desperately in love with me. I could not hope to do better than an earl. And Papa *did* say it's what he would do in the same circumstance."

Mary had to agree that she had heard Mr. Child say those very words at the banquet table. "But, Sarah, it will never do. You must be married in a church, not in some hole-in-the-corner. And think—you will be obliged to travel three nights alone before you can reach Gretna Green. Sarah, your reputation—"

"La, what fustian you do talk, Mary. The Countess of Westmoreland will have no need to fear for her reputation. Besides, we shall be accompanied by Westmoreland's man."

"That will hardly lend you countenance. At least take your maid."

Again Sarah laughed. "Next you'll tell me to take Mama. Padlett will be needed here to avert suspicion so we may get a safe start."

Mary could see that Sarah was firm in her plan, and nothing she could say would shake her. She watched as Sarah filled a valise with necessities for the journey and then hid it under her bed. Padlett would carry it down the servants' stairs as soon as the evening's guests began arriving. Then Sarah's concerns took second place in Mary's thoughts when a footman arrived with a message that Roger Twysden desired to speak to her in the drawing room at her convenience.

"Does he *live* here?" Mary asked as soon as the footman had departed.

"Only during the season. He and his uncle attend all our parties. They're excellent company, and Mama says having a bishop on one's list is better than having the Prime Minister."

"But is he a real bishop? He never seems to do anything religious. Where is Raphoe? Does he never visit his dioceses?"

Sarah laughed. "Silly, of course, he's a real bishop. He read the service in Bath—that was religious. I think Raphoe is in Ireland, so, of course, no one would expect him to *live* there. Now go see Roger before he expires of love for you. It shouldn't surprise me if you received an offer tonight. But don't breathe a word of our plans. You and Padlett are the only ones to know."

Scooping Spit up in her arms, Mary walked to the drawing room. Roger was waiting for her in a green suit and gold brocade waistcoat that matched the wall hangings of the room. He carried a small package. Much to Mary's relief, he did not throw himself upon his knees and beg for her hand and heart, as Sarah's words had made her fear. Instead, he chatted politely about the early spring weather and the delightful program their hostess had planned for the evening.

Mary smiled and chatted and agreed with his comments, but she was finding it more and more difficult to be charming in his company. For all his excellent fashion and ready supply of gossip, she could no longer deny that his shallowness was becoming boring.

She did not find his next topic the least bit boring, however. "And so, my dear, after you told me the distressing story of losing your cherished shoe buckles to the highwayman, I wasted not a moment, but set my man and uncle's also to comb every pawnshop in the alleys of London. Diligence was rewarded." He held out the package. "I have the great honor to restore your buckles to you."

Mary was overwhelmed with his thoughtfulness. "Roger— I don't have words to thank you properly."

"Words are not necessary, dear Mary." He moved a step closer to her. "Might I make so bold as to suggest an appropriate action?" He leaned forward as if to kiss her.

As a reflex Mary pulled back. Roger's arms came around her. What could she do? To fight off one who had done her so great a service seemed churlish; to shout for a servant, unthinkable. But she did not want to submit to these improper advances. "Pray, sir—what if a servant should enter?"

Her protest was muffled by his lips closing over hers. There was a sharp tang of liquor on his breath. She gave an involuntary cry of protest. Then came a much louder cry from Roger and a snarling and barking from Spit.

Roger began hopping around the room on one foot, holding his ankle in his hand. "That beast bit me! If he's put a hole in my stockings, I'll—" Spit held his ground firmly in the middle of the floor with continued yaps and snarls. Roger glared at him. "I'll teach you some manners, you mongrel!" Forgetting that he was holding his injured foot, Roger attempted to kick Spit. He fell hard on his backside, making a bull's-eye landing in the center of the sunburst pattern of the carpet.

In spite of her concern for her friend and her pet, Mary couldn't help laughing. And Spit added to Roger's discomfort by running up with wagging tail and licking him on the face. "Mary, call this brute off!" Roger scrambled to his feet and began shaking out his ruffled coattails. In an attempt to regain his dignity, he made a stiff bow. "I shall see you at the musicale this evening, Miss Tudway."

Just as the door closed on his departure Mary cried, "Wait, Roger, I haven't thanked you for restoring my buckles!" But he was gone, and Mary was free to hug Spit in her arms and collapse into the nearest armchair to laugh until her sides ached.

The Childs and their house guests dined *en famille* in the rose and aqua eating room reigned over by pictures of the god Bacchus. Then all departed for their rooms to don their disguising dominos and masks. Sarah's flowing hooded cape was of the brightest scarlet, trimmed with gold lace and a gold feathered mask. Mary wondered at her friend's choice of so remarkable a disguise when she hoped to slip off unnoticed. And Westmoreland was no less conspicuous with his great height swathed in lime-green silk.

Upon entering the long gallery, Mary had a brief conversation with Bishop Twysden and admired his royal purple domino and matching silk stockings shot with silver thread. He told her he had them woven especially for the occasion. Then she fell under the spell of the Chamber Orchestra de Milano performing at the north end of the room. All worries over Sarah and Westmoreland's plans fled from her mind. She found an empty chair next to a woman in an emerald domino, who turned out to be Lady Anstine. So the evening passed quickly as she gathered tidbits of court gossip in one ear and strains of Vivaldi in the other.

During a break in the musical program, Mary accompanied Lord and Lady Anstine to the buffet set in the hall. They had progressed less than halfway down the table lavishly set in three tiers when Lord Anstine's groom came to him. "Beggin' your pardon for the interruption, My Lord, but I thought you should know. After I 'ad everything settled all right and tight in the stables, I thought I oughter make sure of your pistol—things being as they are on the 'eath these days. Beggin' yer pardon for mentionin' the matter, ladies." He bowed to Lady Anstine and Mary.

"Yes, yes, get on with it." Lord Anstine looked at the delicate slice of roasted peacock cooling on his plate while his man prattled on. "What is it?"

"Well, like I said, I checked your firearm. Your charges 'as been drawn, sir."

"My gun unloaded?" Lord Anstine frowned. "Impossible. I made certain it was cleaned and reloaded just before we left."

"Bare as a garden in winter it is now, sir."

"Well, see to it, man. You know what to do. Borrow some shot from Mr. Child's head groom if you need to. Gillam, I think his name is."

"Yes, My Lord, I'll see to it. I thought you oughter know." The servant backed his way out of the room, bowing.

"Sorry for the interruption, my dears." Lord Anstine turned to the ladies and escorted them the remaining length of the table.

When they returned to the gallery, the Italian musicians were playing a highly ornamented suite by their countryman Luigi Boccherini. Mary looked around her, hoping to find Sarah. Ah, yes, there by the door was the scarlet and gold domino. Perhaps she had had second thoughts about her mad scheme. It was no wonder his friends called the earl Rapid. Mary twisted the stick in her hand, making her mask wave in greeting to her friend, and Sarah signaled back. Relieved of that worry, Mary relaxed in her chair.

After the next number Mary began to feel restless and told Lady Anstine she thought she'd take a stroll around the room. Lord Anstine and many of the men had by that time withdrawn to the eating room where card tables were set up. Mary could not see Westmoreland's tall form, nor had Roger made himself known to her the entire evening. She supposed he was too chagrined to show his face.

She approached Sarah. "Would you care to get a glass of ratafia with me?"

The gold-feathered mask tilted, and Mary gasped. It wasn't Sarah's lustrous brown eyes behind the mask, but Padlett's pale blue ones. Mary grasped the maid's arm and pulled her around the corner into the passage. "Where is your mistress?"

"Gone, miss." Padlett curtsied.

"With His Lordship?"

The maid nodded.

Mary didn't know what to do. By rights she should inform Mr. and Mrs. Child, even though they were occupied with their guests. But she hated to betray her friend, no matter how improper she believed her behavior to be.

Mary was spared having to make a decision, as at that moment Mrs. Child came into the passage. "Sarah, my dear—" She paused and frowned. "Stand up straight, Sarah. You know I cannot abide slouching! Now, Sarah, have you seen your papa? I must speak to him. I have been told our guests' firearms have been tampered with." She started to move on and then stopped. "Sarah, why are you so silent?" She pulled away her daughter's mask and gave a small shriek. "Padlett! What are you doing in your mistress's disguise?"

A footman was dispatched to fetch Mr. Child from his library, and in a few moments a sobbing Padlett had confessed all to her master.

"Faith and troth! Is this the way my daughter obeys my orders? We'll make short work of this scheme!" He strode off to the stables to order his horses put to. But as several of his guests were in various stages of departure, the stable yard was choked with horses, carriages, and servants. It was some time before the Child carriage could be readied to leave.

Mrs. Child bade farewell to her departing guests, including Lord and Lady Anstine. Then she turned to Mary. "You must go with us, my dear. You have such excellent sense, and perhaps

Sarah may be persuaded to listen to you, as she has already demonstrated she won't be guided by her father or me."

Mary did not want to tell Mrs. Child she had already failed to influence her headstrong daughter, so she hurried upstairs to change her domino for a traveling cloak. She was back in the passage again when a ball of brown and white fur came bounding after her. "All right, Spit, you can go too. It may be a long night, and I shall be glad of your company."

Mr. Child and the carriage were waiting just beyond the courtyard. "I sent Gillam ahead. He can make far better time on horseback. He'll know how to delay 'em!"

But it was the Child carriage that met delay. When the coach began to slacken its pace, Mr. Child opened the window and yelled out, "What are you thinking of, man? Faster! Let's not be stopping here in the middle of the heath. The horses have hardly worked up a lather yet."

"Carriage stopped in the middle of the road ahead of us, sir," the coachman answered.

Mary looked out her window. "Oh, it's Lord Anstine's coach. Do you suppose they've had trouble?" As the Child coach rolled to a stop, Mary opened her door and jumped out to run to her friend.

Then she stood stock-still as she saw the reason for the delay. The highwayman of Hampstead Heath held Lord and Lady Anstine at gunpoint. And now his gun was pointed at Mary too. She gave a cry of alarm. Then her cry increased as, with a growl and a sharp bark, Spit sprang from her arms and leaped at the mounted highwayman's leg.

The confusion was all Lord Anstine needed to get off a shot. The robber gave a shout of pain, spun sideways in the saddle, and clutched his shoulder. Then he galloped off across the heath.

Trembling, Mary picked up Spit and allowed a postillion to hand her back into the coach. "Oh, my dear! You could have been shot!" Mrs. Child grasped her hand. "Whatever next? An elopement and a highwayman in one night! It's too much."

Mary quite agreed, but she felt too weak to say anything as the coach rushed on into the dark.

"But what's that?" Mrs. Child leaned forward and looked at Spit. "Blood on your poor doggie's mouth?"

Mary looked down in alarm and then smiled. The dark streak running from Spit's mouth was not blood but a piece of fabric. "Good boy, Spit. You gave that highwayman what-for, didn't you? My valiant spit dog, what an adventurous life you lead!" She tucked the scrap into her reticule.

Streaks of morning light filled the sky by the time they neared Luton, north of London. "We'll change horses at the postinghouse here," Mr. Child said. "And I'll inquire for word of our miscreants. Gillam should have passed here hours ago; he'll have left a message."

Ostler and stable boys had fresh horses harnessed to the carriage before Mr. Child returned with his information. "They were here, all right. Gillam's about an hour ahead of us. Good road now. We should catch up. And when we do, I'll disinherit her, that's what I'll do. Cut her off without a penny. If that's what she thinks of my name and my fortune, she shall have neither. Confounded ungrateful—"

"Now, Robert, don't upset yourself. It'll bring on your gout again."

But Mr. Child's prophecy met with frustration a few miles outside Northampton. Here a detachment of King's Dragoon Guards were exercising on the road. No matter how violently Child raged and swore, the King's own would not be hurried or moved in their maneuvers.

"Egad, I'd tear the fence down and go around them if the bank weren't so steep," Child blustered.

There was nothing to do but to pull to the side of the road and wait until the company had finished its drill. While they were waiting, one of the officers rode by. Mary was surprised to recognize him. "Captain Felsham!" she called through her open window.

He rode up to the carriage and saluted the ladies without the least sign of surprise at seeing them there.

"Forsooth, Felsham, is it necessary to exercise these fellows on the public highways?" Child bellowed.

"Not *precisely* necessary, sir. But sometimes it can be—er, expedient."

Mary caught the gleam in his eyes. "Captain, do you mean to say you've thrown up this roadblock on purpose?"

"Let us just say that Rapid Westmoreland is an old friend of mine." The captain saluted and spun his horse about to return to his men.

"That blackguard! That rapscallion! That—I'll write to His Majesty, that's what I'll do!" It wasn't clear whether Child was raging at Westmoreland or the captain, but as the road cleared and allowed them to continue at that moment, he subsided. After a bit of silence he added, almost under his breath, "But it was quick-witted of him."

It was nearing noon, and Mary had begun to wonder if Mr. Child intended to drive clear to Scotland without stopping for a meal. The farther they went, the more rutted the North Road became and the more slowly they traveled. "Only consolation is that it'll slow down those young scamps just as much," Child said.

Finally he ordered the coachman to stop at an inn. But inside they discovered that Westmoreland had not been the only one slowed by the road. "Gillam! What the—what are you doing here? I sent you out to chase down that good-for-nothing who made off with my daughter, not to loaf around coaching houses!"

"Sorry, sir. 'Unter threw a shoe. I'm just a waitin' for the farrier to finish 'is work."

"Why the devil didn't you change horses, man? You could be five miles down the road by now."

"Beggin' your pardon, sir, but 'ave you seen the cattle they 'ave to offer 'ere?"

Mary fell gratefully to the slab of thick bread and cheese the innkeeper's wife served them. She slipped bits of her crusts under the table to Spit, who likewise hadn't eaten for hours. She had barely finished eating when Child bustled them back in the coach again.

"One thing about it, my Sarah won't travel on an empty stomach. I'll wager she's wheedled her beau into feeding her at every inn. Bet old Rapid didn't plan on that." Child sounded smug as he banged on the carriage roof for the driver to carry on. "And spring 'em!" he hollered out the window.

Mary was beginning to wonder how much more of the harsh jolting in the swaying carriage she could endure when Gillam rode up to Mr. Child's window. "Carriage up a'ead, sir. Coronets on the door. Can't make 'em out though."

Child gave a shout of triumph. "Aha! Caught 'em, we have. Now we'll see who that lass will obey. Overtake 'em, Gillam!" At the same time he pounded his signal for the driver to lay on his whip.

The top was down on Westmoreland's carriage. Mary could see Sarah's dark curls tossing in the wind under her bonnet as Westmoreland whipped the horses. Then, more alarming, she saw Westmoreland draw a pistol and wave it at Gillam. Surely he wasn't so desperate that he'd shoot Child's groom. Mary leaned toward her open window. She heard the pounding of the horses' hooves, the crack of Westmoreland's whip, and above all, she heard Sarah shout gaily, "Shoot, My Lord! Shoot!"

Westmoreland shot.

The next moment one of Mr. Child's favorite hunters lay dead beneath his groom. Mrs. Child took one look at the flow of blood from the animal's chest and fell across Mary in a swoon. With slumped shoulders, Mr. Child got out of his carriage and helped Gillam to his feet while the runaways sped off, Sarah waving in farewell.

The chase was abandoned. By the time they made their way back to Osterley with frequent stops for food and rest, there was no doubt that Sarah was now the Countess of Westmoreland. "Married in some alehouse in Gretna Green," Mrs. Child wailed. "After all the plans I had for my daughter." She thought that perhaps the bishop could comfort her, but Stifford informed his mistress that Bishop Twysden had returned to his London house the night of the musicale. Mr. Roger had come for his bags the next day.

Bereft of its company and of the daughter of the house, Osterley seemed barren. Mary suggested that she should return to London also, but Mrs. Child begged her to remain and keep them company. Mary hadn't the heart to argue, and Mr. Child dispatched a groom to London with a note to Elizabeth.

The following week the newlyweds returned, flushed and pleased with themselves and not at all penitent, as Mr. Child wished. "My dear, why were you so fast when I had much better parties in view for you?" Mrs. Child asked her daughter.

"Mama, a bird in the hand is worth two in the bush," Sarah replied, pulling a long curl over her shoulder.

"That's as may be, young lady," her father said with a degree of severity that cut the preening short, "but I'll tell you right now, I've already seen my man of business. My estate is to go to your *second* child. I'll not have Westmoreland's heir getting my property."

Sarah wrapped her arms around her papa's neck. "Now, Daddy, don't be cross. After all, we were only taking your advice. And it has been a fine adventure."

While Mr. Child sputtered, Mrs. Child drew Sarah and Mary aside to discuss the lavish wedding she was now determined her daughter should have. "It's the only way to put a good face on things and quiet the gossips. I'm determined you shall be married by a bishop, my dear." She paused and looked at her daughter. "Shall I have to call you 'Your Ladyship' now that you're a countess? My, it feels quite grand to have such a title in the family, no matter what your papa says."

"Shall we have Bishop Twysden for the ceremony?" Sarah asked.

"That's a splendid idea! There's nothing like an old family friend at a time like this. We haven't seen him since he removed to London. We'll call on him tomorrow and make all the arrangements, and we must order you a new wardrobe, my love."

Mary saw the excursion to London as an opportunity to return to Devonshire Place, but she accompanied her friends to the bishop's home in St. James Square first.

As they waited in the fine anteroom, Mary couldn't help musing on her friend's attitude to marriage—a new wardrobe, a fine adventure, a bird in the hand. Sarah seemed to be happy, but there had to be more to marriage than that.

Her reverie was interrupted as the servant came to lead them to Bishop Twysden. He was in his study, but his desk did not look as if he had been doing any work. He did not rise from his sofa at their entrance, but instead merely offered two fingers on his left hand for them to clasp. "I beg your pardon, but I have suffered a slight accident on my right shoulder." Even under his robes Mary could see the bulky bandage. "Most stupid of me—I was careless cleaning my fowling piece. Now, how may I serve you, madam?" he asked Mrs. Child.

Without mentioning the awkward fact of the elopement, she merely told him that Sarah and Westmoreland were to be married, and they wished him to perform the service. They talked of publishing banns and setting of dates, but Sarah set all such delay on end when she announced, "Fah, what a lot of nonsense. We shall not wait upon all that. We are to be married next week by special license."

Mrs. Child started to argue and then apparently remembered that her daughter was now a countess and that such pronouncements were quite within her rights. "As you wish it, my dear," she said meekly.

Bishop Twysden waved a scented handkerchief with his left hand. "Egad, it's an impatient lass. I fear my physician will not hear of my performing any such arduous episcopal duties for many weeks yet."

Sarah rose regally. "Then we shall find another bishop. I'm sorry we have troubled you, sir. I wish you a speedy recovery."

Thinking their interview would last longer, Mrs. Child had sent their coachman to Oxford Street on an errand. Now they had to wait again in the anteroom for his return. Mrs. Child turned to her daughter. "Don't give it a thought, Sarah. We shall have the Archbishop of Canterbury. I can't imagine why I didn't think of him in the first place—he's much higher. And I was thinking, instead of some commonplace London church, why not be married at Westmoreland's seat? Apethorpe is such a magnificent establishment."

The wedding talk continued, but Mary sat frozen as events of the past weeks made a pattern in her mind. It was unthinkable, yet the pieces fit too tightly. *He always demands a room on the ground floor,* Sarah had said. Was the bishop more interested in free passage in and out his window than in the scenery? *I wanted to be sure the guns were all loaded,* Roger had said, but Lord Houseton had found his charges drawn when he tried to shoot the highwayman. Had Roger been unloading the firearms? She looked at the silver shoe buckles peeping from under her petticoats. *I set my man to search for them.* Had Roger asked his uncle for them in his cut of the booty? In her mind's eye, she saw the highwayman grab his wounded shoulder and knew it to be precisely the same location as Bishop Twysden's bandages. And yet it was all circumstantial. Surely she was wrong. A strange coincidence. A bishop was a holy man of God, set apart for the work of the church. He could not be a highwayman.

She opened her reticule and drew out the scrap Spit had bitten off the highwayman's stocking. Purple striped with silver thread. *I had them woven especially for the occasion.* Here was evidence she could not argue with.

416

She sat staring at the scrap in her hand, too angry and amazed for words. When she thought of all Roger's flowery speeches to her, when she considered his audacity in returning her stolen goods as a love token, when she recalled his broad hints that he would ask her to marry him—and all the time he was no better than a common thief! The very idea! Her temper surged.

Suddenly Roger entered and made a deep bow. "Ladies, I have just this moment been informed of your honoring us with your presence. If I had known sooner—"

"If you had come in sooner, sir, you might have prevented my solving the puzzle." Mary held out the purple and silver scrap. "Would you be so good as to inform your uncle of my possession of this bit of evidence and convey my advice that he spend more time reading his prayer book than taking exercise upon the heath."

Before the open-mouthed Roger could respond, a footman announced the arrival of Mrs. Child's carriage. Mary swept from the room without giving Roger another look. But another carriage was in first position before the bishop's doorstep. Lady Anstine emerged in a spring bonnet lavishly adorned with yellow and lavender flowers and feathers. "My dears, have you heard the news? It's too alarming for words. They are saying that the highwayman is—well, I simply couldn't credit it, so I had to call on dear Bishop Twysden myself to make certain—because, of course, it wouldn't do to spread a rumor that isn't strictly true."

Mary nodded. "It's quite true, Lady Anstine." And she passed on into the carriage. The polite world would see to Bishop Twysden's punishment. Highwaymen were romantic creatures in books, but one would not tolerate a criminal in one's drawing room. The bishop's penance would be far harsher than any the law could require.

As the carriage rolled across London to the Tudway home, Mary couldn't help recalling the first time she saw Bishop Twysden in Bath Abbey, with the light from the stained-glass window falling across his vestments. And she recalled the words he had read, "The Scripture moveth us in sundry places to acknowledge and confess our manifold sins and wickedness; and that we should not dissemble nor cloak them before the face of Almighty God our Heavenly Father; but confess them with an humble, lowly, penitent, and obedient heart."

How was it possible for a man who professed belief in God and in His Word to live such a life? Could one really become so hardened to all God required that his only thoughts were for riches and position? Would the bishop and his nephew ever be able to humble themselves to confess their sins before God with lowly, penitent, and obedient hearts?

With a jolt she recalled that for a space of time she had been determined that she would accept Roger. The thought of what she had been spared left her weak—weak and longing for Rowland. For his comfort, for his rocklike values that one could anchor to, for his twinkling brown eyes that could make one relax and forget one's troubles.

When they reached Devonshire Place, the sight of the rather shabby Tabernacle carriage outside made her heart leap. Rowland was here.

But when he came down the steps to meet her, his eyes were not twinkling, and the drawn lines of his face told her all was not right.

$\mathcal{L}$ady Selina is ill. I have come to take you to Park Lane."
Rowland's clipped sentences told Mary more clearly than anything else how desperate the situation was.

She didn't even go into the house, but bade Sarah and Mrs.
Child good-bye and wished Sarah happiness with her
Westmoreland. Then she directed Knebworth to take her bags
up and inform Elizabeth of her whereabouts.

"Has she been ill long?" Events had rushed in upon her so
of late that Mary struggled even to recall what day it was.

"She was stricken with the fever Sunday night. She and
Colonel Hastings attended service at the Tabernacle that morning, and she looked as happy as at the drawing room."

Mary nodded. She knew how quickly fevers could strike
and carry their victims off—but surely not Selina. Such a good,
kind creature, her mother's support, Colonel Hastings's whole
delight—and two months before her wedding. Surely that was
not to be!

When the carriage arrived at Park Lane, Mary thought how
impregnable the great house looked, as if death couldn't possibly enter. But death had entered the countess's life many times;
it had borne off her husband the earl, a daughter Elizabeth, three

sons—George, Fernando, and Henry. Now was it to strike again and take her most beloved child?

They entered the quiet, dim hallway and were shown up the grand staircase, past the drawing room where the happy couple had announced their engagement only short weeks before. In a small sitting room outside Selina's bedchamber, they found the countess, supported by her old friend Berridge. "How good of you to come, Rowly, Mary. The physician is with her now. We may go in soon."

Rowland went to Hastings standing in stiff silence in the far corner and grasped his hand. "My dear friend—"

Hastings continued to hold onto Rowland. "Only a few days ago she said, 'Certainly I am the happiest woman in the world. I have not a wish ungratified—surely this is too much to last.'" There was a crack in his voice, but his countenance betrayed nothing.

Berridge spoke. "How striking it is to see a tender-spirited young woman looking the last great enemy in the face, with as much calm resolution as was ever shown by any military hero in the field—with far more, indeed, for surely more is required where all around tends to soften the mind, than when the drums and trumpets and artillery and the bustle of war have excited all the passions." He then turned to the countess. "Your daughter has long been Your Ladyship's consolation and earthly support. But the day will, I doubt not, arrive when the mother shall see that her daughter was selected as the honored instrument of obtaining still more excellent blessings. Oh, my dear friend, the day is coming when it will be delightful to follow out all these now-mysterious lines of Providence from the dark cloud in which they are presently wrapped into the full brightness of celestial glory."

The countess nodded, her sharp features tensely drawn after days of watching by her daughter's bedside. "We have every reason to be thankful for the state of our dear one's mind. A holy calm and humble reliance on her Savior enables her to enter the dark valley with Christian hope, leaning as it were, on her Redeemer's arm, and supported and cheered by the blessed promises of His gospel. We are in the hands of our Heavenly Father. And I am sure no one has hitherto had more reason than myself to say that goodness and mercy have followed me all my days."

The physician came out and closed the door of the sick room quietly behind him. Her Ladyship rose and faced him. "Well? Speak plainly, I pray you. This is no time for dissimulation."

"I have done all I can do."

The doctor left them, and the small party went quietly into the darkened chamber. The countess leaned over her daughter's bed.

"Do you know me?"

Lady Selina's eyes were startlingly dark in her thin face. Only two bright spots of red on her cheeks separated the whiteness of her skin from the pillows. "My dearest mother," she replied, her voice barely above a whisper.

"Is your heart happy?"

Lady Selina raised her head from the pillow. "I am happy, very happy."

Her mother bent her head, and Selina kissed her. When Selina's head returned to her pillows, she ceased to breathe.

Berridge made the sign of the cross over the still form and prayed, "Support us all the day long until the shadows lengthen and the evening comes and the busy world is hushed, until the fever of life is over and our work is done. Then in Thy mercy grant us a safe lodging, and a holy rest, and peace at last. Amen."

"And may light perpetual shine upon her soul," the countess added.

Mary walked to the window and drew back the curtain a few inches. Outside, the sun was setting. Inside, all was silent with the quiet grief in every heart. Lady Selina had taken her departure with the same simplicity and sweetness that had marked all the actions of her life.

Colonel Hastings knelt for a few moments by her bed; then,

visibly shaken by his terrible desolation, he opened the door and went down the hall to his own room.

Mary slipped out to the sitting room and dropped into a chair with her head in her hands. Very soon the house and all in it would become involved with the bustle that attended hard on the silent detachment of death, but for these few short moments she could grieve the loss of her friend.

And look to her own soul. The events of the past days had taught her how selfish and shallow she had been. She saw now the false values she must turn away from for true holiness, which was the only way to happiness. And she realized that could be accomplished only with God's help. Now she knew that it was the shallowness of her own commitment that had made her resent the depth of Rowland's.

But the realization of how close she had played to the brink of destruction gripped her with a paralyzing fear. She might have sat there for hours, frozen with her misgivings, had not Rowland come to her.

Her face clearly showed the spiritual struggle he had long known was in her heart. He sat beside her and took her icy hands in his. "Mary, Mary. You are too much looking into yourself. All you find there is misery."

She nodded her bowed head.

"Oh my dear, look but to Jesus. There is salvation in abundance. It is a glorious thing to know our sins and to hate them. But when this is known, we fly to the gospel for a remedy. Remember, Mary Tudway is as bad as she can be—she is utterly undone." The bowed head before him sank even lower. "Now where is she to look? Only to Jesus. Her heart can never withstand the power of His grace. Has she millions of sins that threaten her destruction?"

She nodded.

"Then be glad, my Mary. The Lord has received double for them all. In Jesus Mary is complete—the Lord will give her poor trembling heart faith to believe this." He paused to smile. "And then as she is soon to change one of her names, so she will soon lose another—that ugly *Much-afraid* you will entirely disown."

Mary's head jerked up. "Change my name?"

"There has been no time to tell you, Mary. But at last I am free to speak. You can have no doubt of the love I've carried in my heart for you. But I finally have a right to speak it. Bishop Willes will ordain me. I received a letter yesterday. Oh, but my dear Mary, I gallop ahead. Our friend lies dead in the next room. I came to counsel you for the sake of your soul, and I end speaking of my own happiness. Forgive me. I must return you to your brother's home."

Mary wanted to protest that she was quite prepared to hear what he would say, and yet she knew she wasn't. She was fatigued beyond bearing, her heart was full of grief for the loss of Lady Selina, and she had much she must say to God before she could answer Rowland.

He left her in the entry hall at Devonshire Place. "I'll call tomorrow, my dear Mary. Rest you well tonight."

At first, though, she thought she would not sleep at all, as once more grief washed over her. Lady Selina was gone. Mary had known her for only a year, and yet she ached for the young woman whose quiet smile and gentle encouragement had gladdened all who knew her—she whose quiet, devout life pointed the way to God for many who needed a signpost; she whose loving heart had found its mate and joyously planned their future . . .

Lady Selina was gone, and to what purpose? Her smile, her beauty, her love—all were stilled in the grave. What could now give meaning to that life and death?

And with a sudden light in her heart as brilliant as if someone had lit a candle in her dark room, Mary knew that she could give a meaning. Following the truth Lady Selina had lived for, walking the path God had shown her, would give meaning not only to Selina's life but also to her own. Lady Selina was gone, but Mary Tudway was here, and she would live for those things of lasting value that her friend had chosen.

Even that cheering determination, however, did not immediately bring quietness to Mary. At first her sleep was full of visions as if in a nightmare. She was in a cold, dank church, alone, desolate. Then she walked outside, but the garden was barren, a withered brown without leaf or flower. She existed in a world without comfort, without solace, without beauty.

And then Rowland came to her. She was back inside the church, this time surrounded by a mighty congregation singing praises to God. The scene shifted. She was in a green garden gathering roses to the accompaniment of birdsong. With Rowland beside her she was rejoicing in a world of beauty, of joy, of love.

It seemed the hours would not move fast enough the next morning until Rowland called. Surely she had not misunderstood him—he did say he would call, did he not?

Rowland's call came at an hour so early that the family was still at breakfast. Clement was the first to greet their visitor. "I understand I am to congratulate you. I have received a letter from our father, and he tells me Bishop Willes has consented to your ordination. It should have come long ago."

Rowland thanked him. "It seems the bishop is not to be put off by my preaching at the Tabernacle. In short, he did not impose any conditions whatever. He said in his letter to me that as the Tabernacle is licensed, he 'thought it not improper and that I might consider my opportunities to preach in irregular places as providential calls from Him, who on earth taught all who were willing to hear—whether on a mount, in a ship, or by the seaside; and who, at His ascension, commanded His ministers by His apostles to be instant in season and out of season.'"

He looked at Mary. "But I hear I have more to thank for this happy turn of events than merely the reputation of my preaching."

Mary lowered her head, but her eyes sparkled. "I knew you would not wish to rely on influence, sir. But may a dutiful daughter not write what is in her heart to her father?"

Rowland laughed. "Perhaps we should consider that you have been an instrument of God's using."

Clement and Elizabeth soon left the room. Rowland looked at Mary. "Mary—" He paused with uncharacteristic uncertainty. He looked as though he did not know whether to hope or to despair. The imminence of the certainty made his heart pound. "Mary, is all clear in your heart?"

"Oh, yes, Rowland! I see it all so clearly now—the need for a personal commitment rather than just a formal faith. You tried to tell me so many times. How could I have missed it?" She looked up at him with a shy smile. "And how could you have been so patient with me when I seemed so hopeless and added to your troubles with my nagging?" Then suddenly she knew the answer. "Rowland, it's just like God's grace, isn't it? He waits for us in patient love to accept Him."

"Yes, my dear. And I am fully persuaded of the truest work of grace upon your soul. Though I know your sincerity sometimes made you doubt, yet your very doubts were to me the strongest evidence of the sincerity of your heart." He came to stand before her. "Thus, Mary, as a man and as a Christian, with your leave I would be glad to make choice of you as my partner through life."

He held out his hand to her. She readily put both of hers into it, to be covered by his left. "Oh, yes, yes, yes. I have grown up, Rowland, and I thank you for waiting for me. But still I must apologize for my unsteadiness, for making you wait so long."

"No, Mary, not a word of it. Because your heart was harder won, I shall cherish it even more. And never fear, my dear, you shall be a better minister's wife for all your struggles. Having seen the world, you will understand what I am preaching against. You have had your time of preparation just as I have had mine. And now we can get on with our work."

"Yes, I should like that—working together for something of value."

"Indeed. For life's greatest treasure and Heaven's."

Epilogue

*T*hree months later, Mary, now Mrs. Rowland Hill, walked through the nave of Wells Cathedral, her footsteps making a faint echo in the stillness, her spirit rejoicing with the lift of the Gothic arches. With a smile she took her seat beside the other members of her family gathered for this occasion.

The silence suddenly filled with chords from the great organ, which vibrated the stones beneath their feet. The processional of officiating clergymen and choir, followed by those to be ordained by Bishop Willes, came down the nave and took their places before the high altar. Mary watched through a mist of joy as the archdeacon approached the bishop sitting in his chair. "Reverend Father in God, I present unto you these persons present to be admitted deacons."

The bishop turned to the congregation. "Brethren, if there be any of you who know any impediment in any of these persons presented to be deacons, let him come forth in the name of God."

Mary held her breath. Surely, after all the struggle, there could be no objection now. There wasn't. The service continued with a sung liturgy, the Lord's Prayer, and Holy Communion.

Then the bishop, still in his chair, administered the oath. Mary heard Rowland's firm, resonant voice above the others. "I, Rowland Hill, do sincerely promise and swear that I will be faithful and bear true allegiance to His Majesty, King George the Third. So help me, God."

The bishop asked, "Do you trust that you are inwardly moved by the Holy Ghost to take upon you this office and ministration, to serve God for the promoting of His glory and the edifying of His people?"

As the ordinands answered, "I trust so," Mary made the same answer in her heart, vowing to support Rowland.

The bishop continued, "Do you think that you are truly called according to the will of our Lord Jesus Christ and the due Order of this Realm to the ministry of the Church?

"I think so," was the reply.

"Do you unfeignedly believe all the canonical Scriptures of the Old and New Testament?"

"I do believe them."

As Mary continued to answer the examination in her own heart with her husband, she felt the next question had special application to her. "Will you apply all your diligence to frame and fashion your own lives and the lives of your families according to the doctrine of Christ, and to make both yourselves and them, as much as in you lies, wholesome examples of the flock of Christ?"

"I will so do, the Lord being my helper."

Mary knew that none of those receiving ordination could take deeper joy than Rowland at the bishop's next words. "Take then authority to execute the office of a deacon in the Church of God committed to you, in the name of the Father, and of the Son, and of the Holy Ghost."

Holding the Bible, he continued, "Take authority to read the Gospel in the Church of God and to preach the same."

The bishop then rose and prayed, "Almighty God, who has given you this will to do all these things, grant also unto you strength and power to perform the same; that He may accomplish His work which He has begun in you, through Jesus Christ our Lord. Amen."

The bishop then laid hands on each ordinand. "Receive the Holy Ghost for the office and work of a deacon in the Church of God, in the name of the Father, and of the Son, and of the Holy Ghost."

Mary thought her heart would burst with trying to express her praise to God, who had brought them to this moment, who had answered all their prayers, and who, she knew, would continue to lead them in His service all their lives.

Historical Note

*I*n telling this story, I have blended four true accounts from the late 1700s. As fanciful as it may seem, Bishop Twysden's story is true, as, unfortunately, is the account of the death of Lady Selina.

The Earl of Westmoreland became Viceroy of Ireland, and Lady Westmoreland, the Vicereine. True to the terms of Robert Child's will, Osterley passed to Sarah Sophia Fane, Lady Westmoreland's second child, who married George Villiers. He took the name Child-Villiers and became the fifth Earl of Jersey. Readers of Regency romances will recognize her as "Queen Sarah," Countess of Jersey, member of the famous committee that ruled on rights of admission to Almack's.

Rowland Hill and Mary Tudway were married in June of 1773 at the Church of St. Marylebone in London. He was ordained deacon that same month by Dr. Willes, Bishop of Bath and Wells. At the insistence of the Archbishop of York, however, he was never granted priest's orders and so was, he said, "required to go through life with only one shoe on." His parish was on the green banks of the Severn at Wotton-under-edge in Gloucestershire, and he built Surrey Chapel "round so the devil should not have a corner in it." Attached to the chapel were thirteen Sunday schools with over three thousand children on their rolls. Later in life he described himself as "rector of Surrey Chapel, vicar of Wotton-under-edge, and curate of all the fields, commons, and pastures throughout England and Wales."

I wish to express my special appreciation to Mr. David Tudway Quilter who sent me his excellent book on his family's history; to the librarians at the Huntingdon Centre at The Countess of Huntingdon's Chapel, especially Andrew Ballinger and Ayeli Barett; and at Wesley's Chapel, Mr. Cyril Skinner, Managing Curator, and Rev. Douglas A. Wollen, Historian.

DONNA FLETCHER CROW

Time Line
THE CAMBRIDGE CHRONICLES

UNITED STATES		ENGLAND
George Whitefield begins preaching	1738	John Wesley's Aldersgate experience
French and Indian War	1756	
	1760	George III crowned
	1760	Lady Huntingdon opens chapel in Bath
	1766	Stamp Act passed
Boston Tea Party	1773	Rowland Hill ordained
The Revolutionary War	1776	The American War
	1787	Wilberforce begins antislavery campaign
Constitution ratified	1788	
George Washington elected President	1789	
	1799	Church Missionary Society founded
	1805	Lord Nelson wins Battle of Trafalgar
	1807	Parliament bans slave trade
War of 1812	1812	Charles Simeon begins Conversation Parties
	1815	Waterloo
Missouri Compromise	1820	George IV crowned
John Quincy Adams elected President	1825	
	1830	William IV crowned
Temperance Union founded	1833	William Wilberforce dies
Texas Independence	1836	Charles Simeon dies
	1837	Queen Victoria crowned
Susan B. Anthony Campaigns	1848	
California Gold Rush	1849	
	1851	Crystal Palace opens
Uncle Tom's Cabin published	1852	
	1854	Florence Nightingale goes to Crimean War
Abraham Lincoln elected President	1860	
Emancipation Proclamation	1863	
	1865	Hudson Taylor founds China Inland Mission
Transcontinental Railroad completed	1869	
	1877	D. L. Moody and Ira Sankey London revivals
Thomas Edison invents light bulb	1879	
	1885	Cambridge Seven join China Inland Mission

Word List

Abecedarian - an ABC book that also taught prayers and the rudiments of the Christian religion

Adam - Robert Adam, 1728-1792, leading English architect

Bagged - drunk

Bagnio - brothel

Beard the master in his den - to confront with boldness. As in "To beard the lion in his den." (Sir Walter Scott, *Marmion*)

Beau Nash - Master of Ceremonies of Bath, called its "uncrowned king"

Bohea - black tea

Butter pond pudding - steamed pudding served in a pond of melted butter

Calash - folding top of a small, light-wheeled carriage; a style of woman's cap resembling the carriage top

Cassock - long, closed garment worn by clergy

Chaise - a light carriage or pleasure vehicle

Chalybeate - spring water containing salts of iron

Collation - a light meal

Collop - a small slice of meat, such as a rasher of bacon

Commination - a recital of God's anger and judgment against sinners

Congé - dismissal

Conventicling - preaching in an unconsecrated place

Couple - a musical episode, as a rondo

Curate - an assistant to an Anglican vicar

Dishabille - casual clothing

Domino - long, loose hooded cloak worn as a masquerade costume

Don - a head, tutor, or fellow in a college at Oxford or Cambridge

Epergne - ornamental stand with separate dishes or trays

Exhibition - a grant drawn from the funds of a school to help maintain a student

Farthing - smallest coin of English currency, valued at ¼ penny

Fichu - a kerchief of fine white fabric draped over the shoulders and fastened in front to fill in a low neckline

Foundery - abandoned ironworks John Wesley bought in 1739 near Moorfields and converted into chapels, school, medical clinic, living quarters, etc., for the Methodist Society

François Boucher - French painter, 1703-1770

Frank - free postage granted to a Member of Parliament or peer of the realm

Gownsman - student at the university

Grig - lighthearted child

Havey-cavey - unsteady, helter-skelter

Hectic fever - a fluctuating but persistent fever, such as accompanying tuberculosis

Honored in the breach - alludes to "But to my mind—though I am native here,/And to the manner born—it is a custom/More honour'd in the breach than the observance." (William Shakespeare, Hamlet)

Horkey - harvest dinner

Jugged pigeons - pigeons stewed in an earthenware jug

Lappets - lace streamers falling from cap to shoulders

Lawn - a sheer, plain-woven cotton or linen fabric, as used in the sleeves of an Anglican bishop's robes

Macaroni - member of a class of young Englishmen that affected foreign ways; dandy

Marcher - an inhabitant of the border between Wales and England

Mechlin - delicate bobbin lace made in Mechlin, Belgium

Mere - lake

Methodist Society - a religious society open to all people, designed to enrich and purify all churches. Societies promoted preaching, fellowship meetings, Sunday schools, day schools, orphanages, and numerous other services for members' faith, education, health and well-being

Nicodemus chamber - "closet" in the countess's chapel for bishops who did not wish to be seen at the service

Nonconformist (dissenter) - member of a religious body separated from the Church of England

Nonjuror - Anglican clergyman who refused to take the oath of allegiance to William and Mary and their descendants

Nucthemeron - a calendar of hours

Oast house - a conical-shaped kiln used for drying hops or malt

Open gown - dress with skirt open in front below waist to reveal an ornate petticoat

Ordinary - a clergyman appointed to give spiritual counsel to condemned criminals; an official position comparable to chaplain

Pannier - hooped petticoat that supported a skirt

Parterre - ornamental garden

Pease porridge - split pea soup

Peg tower - a statement used as a support or reason

Postillion - one who rides as a guide to a coach

Publican - innkeeper, keeper of a public house

Quid - slang for one pound sterling

Rector or vicar - clergyman of the Church of England who has charge of a parish

Riding pillion - to sit behind the saddle on a small pad

Round gown - dress with skirt closed in front, not showing petticoat

Shilling - British coin equivalent to the U.S. nickel

Sizar - Cambridge student who receives college expenses in return for acting as servant to other students

Squab - cushion

St. Dunstan - religious reformer who served as Archbishop of Canterbury from 959 to 988

Syllabarium - a section of a primer that began with two-letter syllables and gradually increased in length until six-syllable words were taught

Tabernacle - a chapel established in 1741 for the preaching of George Whitefield and others in Moorfields, London, near Wesley's Foundery

Tenterfield - field used for drying or stretching cloth

To make a leg - to bow with the leg extended in front

Tottenham Court Chapel - erected by George Whitefield in the west end of London in 1756

Turnkey - one who has charge of a prison's keys

Tutball - an early form of cricket

Verger - an official in church who serves as caretaker and attendant

Waits - carolers

Whipt syllabub - a frothy, sweet dessert made of cream and liquor

Bibliography

Babington, Anthony. *The English Bastille*. New York: St. Martin's Press, 1971.

Barker, Esther T. *Lady Huntingdon, Whitefield, and the Wesleys*. Private printing, 1984.

Book of Common Prayer. Oxford: T. Wright and W. Gill, 1773.

Boyle, P. *The Fashionable Court Guide, or Town Visiting Directory for the Year 1792*. London.

Brailsford, Mabel Richmond. *A Tale of Two Brothers, John and Charles Wesley*. New York: Oxford University Press, 1954.

Charlesworth, V. J. *Rowland Hill, His Life, Anecdotes, & Pulpit Sayings*. London: Hodder & Stoughton, 1877.

Connely, Willard. *Beau Nash, Monarch of Bath and Tunbridge Wells*. London: Werner Laurie, 1955.

Earl of Jersey. *Osterley Park Isleworth*, a guide for visitors. London: G. White, n. d.

Hardy, John and Maurice Tomlin. *Osterley Park House*. London: The Victoria and Albert Museum, 1985.

Hill, Rowland. "Glorious Displays of Gospel Grace," in *Missionary Sermons*. London: T. Chapman, 1796.

_____. *Recommendatory Preface to Refuge for the Prisoner of Hope*. London: M. Lewiss, 1772.

_____. *The Sale of Curates by Public Auction*. London: M. Jones, 1803.

_____. Unpublished letters to his sister, by permission of the Masters and Fellows of St. John's College.

Jones, William. *Memoirs of the Life, Ministry, and Writings of the Rev. Rowland Hill, M. A., Late Minister of Surrey Chapel*. London: John Bennett, 1834.

Kendrick, T. D. *The London Earthquake*. London: Methuen & Co., Ltd., 1956.

Kirby, Gilbert W. *The Elect Lady. Trustees of the Countess of Huntingdon's Connexion*, 1972.

Knight, Helen C. *Lady Huntington [sic] and Her Friends: The Revival of the Work of God*. New York: American Tract Society, 1853.

Law, William. *A Serious Call to a Devout and Holy Life*. London: J. M. Dent & Sons Ltd., 1906.

"Law's Serious Call." *The Emmanuel College Magazine* 31 (1937-38).

Lord Sheffield, John. *Miscellaneous Works of Edward Gibbon, Esq.* Vol. 1. London: 1796.

McClure, Ruth. *Coram's Children, the London Foundling Hospital in the Eighteenth Century.* New Haven: Yale University Press, 1981.

Melville, Lewis. *Bath Under Beau Nash.* London: Eveleigh Nash, 1907.

Member of the Houses of Shirley and Hastings. *The Life and Times of Selena, Countess of Huntingdon,* Vols. 1, 2. London: William Edward Painter, 1833.

Member of the Houses of Shirley and Hastings. *The Life and Times of Selina Countess of Huntingdon.* London: William Edward Painter, Strand, 1844.

Memoirs of the Rev. Rowland Hill, A. M. London: Thomas Ward & Co., 1835.

Miller, Edward. *Portrait of a College: A History of the College of Saint John the Evangelist in Cambridge.* Cambridge University Press, 1961.

Mitchell, T. Crichton. *The Wesley Century.* Vol. 2. Kansas City: Beacon Hill Press, 1984.

Moreton, G. *Memorials of the Birthplace and Residence of the Rev. Wm. Law M. S. at King's Cliffe in Northhamptonshire.* London: The London Printing Works, 1895.

Neale, R. S. *Bath, a Social History 1680-1850 or A Valley of Pleasure, yet a Sink of Iniquity.* London: Routledge & Kegan Paul, 1981.

Penrose, John, Bridgette Mitchell, and Hubert Penrose, eds. *Letters from Bath 1766-1767.* Gloucester: Alan Sutton, 1983.

Pollock, John. *George Whitefield and the Great Awakening.* New York: Doubleday & Co., 1972.

Quilter, David Tudway. "The Cedars and the Tudways," *in Wells Cathedral School.* Wells: Clare Son and Co., Ltd.

Rodenhurst, T. *A Description of Hawkstone, the Seat of Sir John Hill, Bart.* London: John Stockdale, 1811.

Senior, Benjamin. *A Hundred Years at Surrey Chapel.* London: Passmore & Alabaster, 1892.

Sidney, Edwin. *The Life of the Rev. Rowland Hill, A. M.* London: Baldwin & Cradock, 1834.

Smith, Nila Banton. *American Reading Instruction.* Newark: International Reading Association, 1974.

Smith, R. A. L. *Bath.* London: B. T. Batsford, Ltd., 1944.

Tighe, Richard. *A Short Account of the Life and Writings of the Late Rev. William Law, A. M.* London: J. Hatchard, 1813.

Told, Silas. "An Account of Mr. Silas Told" (reprinted from *Life and Adventures of Silas Told*). *The Arminian Magazine* 11 (1788).

Tyerman, L. *The Life and Times of John Wesley.* Vol. 3. London: Hodder & Stoughton, 1880.

Tytler, Sarah. *The Countess of Huntingdon and Her Circle*. London: Sir Isaac Pitman & Sons, Ltd., 1907.

Ward-Jackson, Peter. *Guide to Osterley Park*. London: Her Majesty's Stationery Office, 1954.

Wesley, Charles. *The Journal of Charles Wesley*. 1849 ed. Ed. Thomas Jackson. Grand Rapids: Baker Book House.

Wesley, John. *Journal*. Standard ed. 8 vols. Ed. Nehemiah Curnock. 1909-1916.

"William Law: A Bicentenary" (including the text of Professor Chadwick's sermon reprinted from *The Anglican World*). *The Emmanuel College Magazine* 43 (1960-61).